A HEART BEATING HARD

T0341830

A HEART BEATING HARD

Lauren Foss Goodman

University of Michigan Press
Ann Arbor

Published in the United States of America by the
University of Michigan Press

Printed and bound by CPI Group (UK) Ltd, Croydon, CR0 4YY

2018   2017   2016   2015   4   3   2   1

DOI: http://dx.doi.org/10.3998/tfcp.13240726.0001.001

ISBN 978-0-472-03616-5 (paper : alk. paper)

ISBN 978-0-472-12097-0 (e-book)

For Mom and Dad

1. MARJORIE

Ma?

2. MARGIE

Margie started as a suggestion. A frustration. A night out. A drink. A lot of drinks. A thin-lipped smile and some small talk about the Sox. A beer-cold hand on the inside of a soft warm thigh. A laugh, a nod. A locked bathroom stall and a skirt hiked up high. A hand pulling hair. A space, filled. A need. A cry. A release. A disappointment.

Margie started there in that small empty place and there single-celled Margie started to divide and divide and divide. Unseen, unknown Margie, what was Margie before she was Margie, burrowed and billowed and became. Swimming in the warm dark waters where we all live before we live, growing skin to contain, lungs to breathe, a heart to beat.

Margie, started, sprouting legs to kick and eyes to see and a mouth to speak.

Margie, at the start, small and secret and shaping into the shape we all take. Growing and pushing inside that space that becomes smaller and smaller with every new bone and ear and eyelash. Turning and floating and kicking inside all of that inside fluid. Fish-like, flapping, fat forming, warming. Filling with the blood that would be her blood, building the brain that would be her brain, finding the lines of the body that would be her body.

Margie, started inside, hiding.

Margie, from the start, her body made secret.

Margie, from the start, the same.

Margie, from the start, different from the rest of us.

Margie, starting, eyes opening, light let in, waiting for what would come.

3. MARJORIE

Tomorrow is coming. Or here, almost. Tomorrow is almost today and still Marjorie is not sure if she should call Steve at the Store and say that today she will take her vacation day.

Marjorie, in her soft purple pajamas, sits sunk down into the deep shape of Ma left behind in this bed. Marjorie, in Ma's bed, sits still as she can in the quiet, quiet bedroom, in the weak blue light at the beginning of morning. Shoulders down low, the hard of the headboard making pains in her back. Marjorie sits, has been sitting for a long time, listens to Gram roll and snore and sigh in the next room. Looks at the dark turned-off shape of the no-sound television. Listens to her self, her wind, to her own breath breathing the last of Ma in and out. Marjorie sits and smells the smell of Ma, the late-night secret cigarettes, the sting of salt-and-vinegar potato chips, the sour of a shut-door room and a body gone long unwashed. She squeezes her hands shut tight, holds, lets them go and feels how they tingle. Marjorie, sitting, breathing, listening, watching, waiting. Sleeping here, now, in Ma's bed. Living, here, now, right now, alive, awake, up high off the ground on Ma's soft sheets, Ma in the smell all around her. Marjorie, here, now, grown, feeling, free, alone, and here there are no Ma sounds and here there is no Ma, anymore.

Marjorie is not thinking about Ma.

Marjorie is thinking about the People who will come and how to tell Steve that today she cannot do her job.

She is looking at the light blue light coming in through the gaps in the window blinds. This is the light she likes most, the underwater light at the end of night. Marjorie is rocking just a little from this side to this side, feeling the deep strong spring of the springs inside this mattress, the shape of Ma that holds the body of Marjorie. Inside, she feels her pains, the hurt behind her knees and up and down her back.

Marjorie is thinking about the big and the soft of this bed. How different and good it might feel to sleep in a bed that is just a bed, that is wide and thick and does not need to be pulled out from the sofa at night and pushed back in the morning.

Not that Marjorie minded where she was before. Ma coughing, living, sleeping in Ma's room and Gram, with her Stories, away, in Gram's room. Marjorie coming back late from the Store, from the Club, to the small quiet of the living room, to the squeak of the sofa's metal inside, the thin hold of the sofa bed. Marjorie did not mind. Marjorie had her place. Her place that was shaped like her, that was good and wide and soft enough, for her.

For years and years, from when Ma had stopped working and they all had to leave the tall windows and big rooms of Apartment #2 at the end of dead-end Summer Street, Marjorie has slept fine in her space on the sofa bed. All of them, together, fine in the place let out cheap to Gram by the Department of Apartments. Crowded, but fine, together. Better since He went away.

But the sofa bed. That sofa bed was Marjorie's space and she knows the touch of those springs, knows not to roll too far to the right, knows how to measure exactly where her body is in that place and how to move around in it. Marjorie knows the living room, the sofa bed, the shape of that space and how to fit her self inside.

But change. People here and People gone. Marjorie blinks her eyes and looks at the blue light slowly turning white in the spaces between the blinds. Gram sleeping her loud sleep behind the shut door across the hall. Him gone, left, taken away. Ma done, gone, given up. Ma's room, free, left behind and Marjorie the only one still here to sleep in the wide high soft of this bed. Ma's bed.

And Lucy. Almost here Lucy. Gone, gone, the big long gone of Lucy.

No. Marjorie is not thinking about Lucy. Marjorie is tired. Marjorie is sitting, still sitting, just sitting, not sleeping, not thinking, is here now in her self, in her new place. A headboard. This too-soft bed with a long wooden part and for what? A hard place for putting her head. Marjorie breathes her breath, follows her wind out of her mind, away from the departments where she does not want to go, far from the aisles of things she does not want to think about.

Marjorie, doing what Dr. Goodwin tells her to do.

Breathing, feeling, seeing.

Marjorie looks at the blue-wallpapered walls and sees them mostly as shadows, closes her eyes and sits with all that dark, looks at the wall and sees a little more of what is here, closes her eyes and sees nothing.

Open your eyes, Marjorie. Open your eyes. Here is today.

Marjorie is very good company for her self. Always alone and never alone, always together with her mind, her body, big, beating, her wind blowing through her and all the things stacked neatly on shelves built in the space of her inside. This whole long night Marjorie has felt good and quiet and safe sitting up in this bed, squeezing her hands together in the dark to remember that she is, was, will be here now in this place where Ma is not. In the dark she looked straight ahead at the dark and now in the getting-stronger light Marjorie looks right at that blue wallpaper and she knows that she is here, that she is here in the room that is for her now. She knows the sofa is just a sofa with a bed hidden inside it and that the sofa bed, the place that for so long has helped shape the shape of her, might never be pulled out again.

Gone, the sofa bed. Still there, inside, but gone, pushed down, in, away.

Sitting here, in the slow blue-to-white-to-orange sunrise walking up the walls of what was or is or was Ma's room, Marjorie feels her self feel almost bad. Something like bad. Like empty, or upside-down, or blown open for all the People to see.

But no. No. No, a sofa is not something to feel bad about.

Marjorie thinks this is a good thought. Some good words to tell Dr. Goodwin. Something true and real and right.

In the deep soft orange light of the almost-here morning, Marjorie says it out loud, quiet, so that she can hear how the sounds sound outside her self.

A sofa is nothing to feel bad about.

4

No, no sorry.

A sofa is not a thing to feel sorry for.

Marjorie whispers because it is early, because this night in here has been so long and unmoved, because she is not yet sure what her voice will sound like in the shape of this space that so suddenly stopped being for Ma.

No need for sorry over some sofa.

Maybe Marjorie should say so to Gram. It was Marjorie who found Ma, quiet, cold, gray, blue, gone. But it was Gram who had the phone number of the People who would come, Gram who knew what to do. Gram who closed Ma's door and told Marjorie to stay away, to call the People to come and help. Gram who talked to the kind People in the white gloves who came to take what was Ma away. Gram who used her two hands against the wall to hold her bent body up. Gram, down-day Gram who got up to arrange all the arrangements. Marjorie who sat still on the sofa with her eyes closed, breathing, smiling and saying Hello to the People who covered Ma in white and carried her away. Marjorie who in darkness had pulled the bed out of the sofa as usual and Gram who pinched Marjorie's shoulder and made Marjorie push the sofa back into a sofa.

Gram who said, You finally got your own place, Margie.

Gram who said, No sense wasting a perfectly good bed.

And Marjorie who for these few days and nights now, since, has been sitting, mostly not sleeping, mostly staring, thinking, smelling the smell of Ma leaving.

Marjorie thinks that Gram would be happy to hear what she is thinking about the sofa bed. She sits and looks and sees the light in the room growing stronger, feels the day coming.

Once more, out loud, loud enough for Gram in her room to hear, Marjorie says it.

No sorry here for a sofa bed.

Today is coming. Today is already here. The room that was Ma's room is bright now with the cold light of another winter morning, and still, Marjorie is not sure if today she should take her vacation from the Store.

Because today the white-gloved People who took Ma away are coming back. Today the kind People who came to help are coming to bring Ma's leftovers back. Not leftovers. The reminders. No, the sand. The dust. No, the remainders. Today whatever is left of Ma is coming back and Marjorie is not sure if she should call the Store and tell them that today she is taking her vacation day.

Marjorie spreads her big fingers over her wide thighs and she presses hard down into her self until she can feel the huge heat of her self.

Lucy, she thinks.

For just one thought, for just one second out of all the seconds that will make today into today, Marjorie thinks, Lucy.

But stop. Stop, Marjorie says.

Let Lucy be.

Today there is enough to think about.

Marjorie is very good at walking down her aisles and watching the things in her mind and telling her self when to turn, when to look away. She sends Lucy back to the far-away department where Lucy lives and Lucy stays there, safe, shapeless, quiet, unseen. Lucy, there for only a second, and only in a blink of winter morning light that breaks into stars in the dark as Marjorie squeezes her eyes shut and holds them that way. No Lucy let into today and no harm done. No sound and no talking out loud. No squeak of sofa bed springs and no living room light.

Marjorie opens her eyes and sees that she is here, still, sitting, still, smelling the smell of Ma and watching the morning begin. The shape Ma left in the mattress below her is so soft that Marjorie feels sinking, feels almost sunk. She presses her hands to her thighs and moves slow, starts to move out of the deep sink of Ma in this mattress. Rocks her back slow and careful against the solid touch of the headboard. Marjorie breathes her breath, feels her heart blowing in the wind of Ma that moves through. Marjorie will get her self out of this worn-in bed. Marjorie thinks about the phone, thinks about Steve and the Store, is really thinking about taking this day for her vacation day.

4. MARGIE

Margie came out same as other babies. Raw, red, wrinkled. Bruised blue, screaming, shaking. Tiny fingers curled into tiny fists, mouth open wide, beating inside, breaking through.

Margie came out as a surprise.

Margie, for many months, ignored inside.

Margie, a pain in her ma's side.

Margie, forming and floating and growing and kicking and rising and falling and needing, needing, pushing, beating, fighting her way out.

Margie would not be ignored.

We said, Push.

We said, Fuck.

Fuck.

Fuck.

Margie came out same as other babies and different. Unexpected. Face up. Eyes open, watching, shocked by the light, the red, the bright of the world outside that place of dark where she had been before. Unwelcome. Margie came out looking for who was there. For who had done this to her. Margie came out screaming, writhing, wanting, watching.

We saw the brown eyes wide and we used our gloved fingers to clean them, to cover them, to protect them from the bright lights and all that blood.

It's okay, we said.

You're here now.

You've made it.

Margie came out eyes open, mouth open, ears open to all the sounds of the room in a world where she was not wanted. A world of too-bright lights and hands that touch and Fuck, Fuck, Fuck. Metal scraping against metal, the soft swish of sneakers moving quickly across a shining floor, the screaming that came from inside her and the screams that were coming from somewhere else.

Margie came into the world alone.

There's no other way, we said.

You have a beautiful baby girl, we said.

Fuck.

Margie came out smelling. Rubber gloves and metal and the thick warm mess of her ma. This world of blood and bleach and soap and body. French fries and sweet rum sweat. Herself and all of us.

No, we said.

There's no other way, we said.

Help, we said.

We don't need anybody's help.

We said.

What did Margie know her first day in the cold bright of the outside? That the gloved hands of the nurses felt good as they touched and washed and wrapped her in soft white blankets? Margie knew hands, neck, nose, lips, ears, toes, legs, fingers, tongue, lungs. Maybe Margie knew that there was a big emptiness inside her from the way her lips sucked air and her belly flopped fast in and out with her breath. She must have known pain then, long before she would know the word for it. We think Margie did not yet know about men. She could not have known that Ma did not know about her until it was too late. That pains, all pains, are easy enough to hide. Margie did not know that Ma did not know his name or which one he was. That he could have been any one of them. That the not knowing was probably for the better. Margie did not know that Gram had said a prayer for her every night before bed. She did not know that it was Ma's cigarettes that made the mucus in her lungs that made those first breaths so hard, that the beating inside her chest was called her heart and that this small bit of body was working harder than it should have been. Probably Margie knew pain and warm and cold. Air and water and the sound of Ma's voice, the screaming sound of Ma's voice. Her heart, beating, lungs, breathing, hands, grabbing, feet, kicking. The freedom and the loneliness.

She must have known.

We held Margie, rocked Margie, weighed Margie. We warmed Margie with our bodies while her ma watched the television. We ate our orange jello and wished for it to all go away.

We said, Quiet, quiet, calm down now.

We said, Is she normal?

We said, Yes, yes.

Everything's fine.

Fuck, we said.

We cried.

We prayed.

We screamed until our voice left and all that came out was air.

5. MARJORIE

Marjorie is making the smell of Ma go away. The shape, the sunk of Ma into the soft mattress is a thing that Marjorie cannot change. But the smell of Ma, the breathing-in of Ma, Marjorie is taking care of.

She has her yellow sponges and big brown bucket and her bottles of spray cleaners. Marjorie puts on her long yellow rubber gloves and her hands feel far away and different from her self. Ma's soft sheets Marjorie pulls off the bed and cuts into rags and with those rags Marjorie sprays and wipes away the gray coat of dirt and dust and Ma that cover all the things. She picks up dried balls of tissues that missed the wastebasket and candy wrappers that shine in the light and Marjorie throws away emptied-out bottles and bottles of pills. Little plastic round brown-red bottles of pills around the bed and under the bed. Round white caps on the floor look like stones like mints like mouths. Marjorie cleans quietly, uses Ma's sheets to wipe up all the Ma she can see, thick gray swirls of dust from a half-ripped-out Bible found far under the bed, dust from the top of the soundless television and dust on the top of the dresser.

The Bible, found, wiped, the pages torn, taken, Marjorie throws away.

Marjorie breathes her wind slow to help her knees bend through the pains. She puts her eyes close to the dust, to see what it is, really, what makes this gray that holds Ma's smell. Hair, small black Ma hairs, and cigarette ashes, and dirt, something like dirt, little bits of black and brown, and what else? Marjorie sneezes and the dust floats up and around her and she covers her nose, says, Excuse me, and tries not to breathe too much of this Ma dust inside.

Head hair, arm hair, nose hair, the secret hairs of the body, and skin, Ma's gray dry skin and her chapped lips and all the fingernails she must have clipped in this room. The cigarettes she smoked and the tissues she blew into and the crumbs she dropped from her potato chips. What happened before. This must be the dust of Ma. Marjorie coughs and covers her mouth and nose and moves her wind slow and small as she can through her self to stay clean and separate. Trying to keep Ma out.

Ma does not have many things. Things need money and time and care and want and all Ma wanted was television and cigarettes and bed. Marjorie puts her hands into every one of Ma's pockets and then pushes Ma's clothes to one side of the closet. She opens up all of Ma's drawers and feels her way slowly through the few things Ma has, the old soft t-shirts, the small white bottles of rum that Gram must have missed, the sweat pants and old packs of gum.

Marjorie is cleaning. Marjorie is looking for Him. Marjorie is wiping the Ma smell away and throwing Ma out of this room and Marjorie is looking for Him, for the clumps of chewed-up paper and the blue shirts and any other sign of Him in all this Ma. Marjorie is using her sponges and spray cleaners and paper towels to scrub away the last of the Ma dust and in all the pockets and under the bed far as she can reach and in all the drawers, Marjorie reaches and touches and looks, makes sure Ma kept none of Him.

The Bible, the torn-to-bits-to-chew Bible, is in the trash.

In one drawer, in the small drawer of the small table next to Ma's bed, Marjorie finds one picture. One faded photo of Ma, just Ma, alone, standing, unsmiling, wearing her black work pants and white cafeteria shirt, in front of the dark blue falling-down front steps of Apartment #2. Just that one picture of Ma, and across the front of the photo, on the bottom, the dark orange shadow of finger in front of lens. Every picture He ever took taken over by shadows of fingers got in the way. Took, taking, taken. But still, the photo is mostly of Ma, and Ma is not smiling but her hair is long and brown and her body is round and upright, how Marjorie remembers her, and the grass in front of the steps is green and long, how Marjorie remembers it, and Marjorie puts the picture back in the drawer and keeps cleaning.

Marjorie wipes all that she can wipe and throws the paper towels into the trash on top of the rags and the bottles and the dust. She cleans the headboard carefully, wipes the gray coat of dust away and moves her weight against it in waves to hear what sound it makes, to know if this is the wood-and-wall heartbeat she knew from before.

It is. Might be. Marjorie blows her wind hard through her and tries not to touch too hard to hear the sound. Is doing her best to make this place as clean as it can be.

Marjorie vacuums the thin gray carpet and waits for the sound to wake Gram but Gram's room is door-shut quiet. A down-day, probably. She ties up the garbage bag with all that Ma inside. Marjorie puts clean sheets on the bed and sits down for a rest.

Good. The room smells good. Marjorie sits and smells, closes her eyes to help feel her wind moving through. Ma is gone, almost gone, the air of her taken over by the sting of lemon, the sweet of Windex, the burn of bleach underneath it all.

Marjorie takes the rubber gloves off and shakes and squeezes her hands until they feel like hers again, until she can feel her whole body whole and together and warm and beating.

At first Marjorie does not know the dong-dong sound as the sound of the doorbell. The dong-dong sound makes Marjorie jump, makes Marjorie suck her breath in and hold it there. Marjorie waits maybe a minute for her body to settle, for her self to understand the sound, to understand that People are here, that someone is outside, waiting. She understands this and Marjorie squeezes her hands into fists and uses her fists to push out of and off the bed and Marjorie catches her wind best as she can. Quick as she can, Marjorie walks to the dong-dong of the door. Because Marjorie does not like to leave People waiting.

The People. The white-gloved People with Ma. Steve. The Store. Her vacation day. Marjorie, smelling of bleach, of lemon, of Ma, cleaned, remembers. Too late, Marjorie remembers how good she is at forgetting.

The man is short and thin and he wears a hat over a head that looks hairless and he says, Good Morning, and then he stands, quiet. Marjorie in the small doorway of the small apartment feels big and wide beside this small man. He uses his two hands to hold a cardboard box about as big as a shoebox and for a full minute, maybe more, he stands unspeaking, head down, waiting or thinking or praying. And when he does speak, when he looks up at her and smiles at her, his voice is so soft and far away that Marjorie cannot understand what he is saying. Words and words and a nod and then the man hands Marjorie the box so that he can reach into his coat for what is hidden there.

Marjorie's hands do not feel ready to hold the hard edges of this box that is not as heavy and also much heavier than it looks. The man feels around inside his coat and finds a paper and a pen and he places the paper and pen on top of the box and then opens his arms out toward Marjorie. In her mind Marjorie sees the ghost of her self hold her arms out to him. She can feel that unseen part of her, that other Marjorie that sits inside her skin, hold his small body close beside her. Her other Marjorie, the bright white lit-up shape of her self, wants to reach out and feel what his skin feels like and see how he moves with his wind and see if her wind and his wind could become the same.

Marjorie stares at his reaching arms and his small white hands and she breathes, brings the bright shape of her self back inside her skin, holds the box close to her chest. Blinks, blinks. The man nods and reaches and she understands that he wants to take the weight of the box back from her and Marjorie passes it back to the man. He nods his head again toward the paper and the pen on top of the box and in his low voice says words that Marjorie cannot hear over the inside sounds of her breath, her blood, beating.

But Marjorie can do it. Marjorie is not sure of the words the kind man is saying but Marjorie can see the pen there and paper there and Marjorie can understand what he wants from her. Ma in her room with her television had decided to go away from People. But Marjorie stayed her self. Marjorie is staying here in the world with the People and Marjorie understands how the world works. She understands that People hold special packages with two hands, with chins to chests, eyes down, and that to make a thing real you must sign your name. Marjorie is ready for what People will ask her to do. She has spent hours and hours of her life holding pens to paper, practicing exactly how to make her name into a name, into a shape that can be seen and read and known.

Marjorie picks up the man's pen and presses it into the paper on top of the cardboard box where Ma is. Maybe all that time spent practicing, all those afternoon hours, all those pieces of paper covered in the shapes of her, were for this. For this time, when Marjorie will sign her name perfect for this man, for Ma to come back home. Marjorie smiles, thinking this thought, feels good, feels right, as she makes her big round M and her smaller a-r-j-o-r-i-e. Marjorie, just this, just Marjorie, because the rest of her name is not hers, is theirs, is His, is nothing that People need to know.

Marjorie, signed.

The small man again holds his arms out to Marjorie and carefully, with her two big, soft hands she takes the box. He says words Marjorie does not hear and nods and takes the pen and paper and puts them back inside his coat. The man lowers his head one last time, touches his finger to the front of his hat, turns and walks away, closing the door quietly behind him.

Marjorie stands in the living room and holds the box. She watches the man out the window hold his coat close for warmth. Watches him light a cigarette and pull his short body up into the inside of a big blue pickup truck. Watches him drive away into the gray winter morning. A good man, small, kind, quiet, clean, gone.

Marjorie holds the cardboard box close to her body. It is heavy and light, light and heavy, thick and wide and so much smaller than she ever thought Ma could be.

What to do with this?

This box. A box of Ma. The cardboard shape of what is left of Ma.

Marjorie would like to talk to Dr. Goodwin. To see what People do with boxes of what People leave behind. But Marjorie has missed her chance for this month. She will have to wait for the days to go by.

Marjorie holds Ma in the middle of the small living room. She looks down at the brown sofa with the bed inside, looks up at the green clock passing the time. Today, still today, still the quiet of the early parts of today.

Marjorie puts the box on the floor beside the sofa. She has cleaned Ma up and signed her name and she cannot think of what else there is for her to do here in the apartment. Gram is quiet today, must be deep down in a down-day, must be sitting in her bed waiting for her Stories to start. Marjorie is here, awake, alive, and Marjorie has People who need her. Marjorie has her job to do, the Store out there, waiting for her. Today is a day like all the days, and like all the days the People need someone there to say Hello. And there are days and days to wait for her time with Dr. Goodwin.

Marjorie does not mind. She has things to do. Friends to see and People to help. Marjorie goes into the kitchen to begin the making of her toast with butter and grape jelly, the pouring of her milk over cereal.

Because there is nothing more to do here. No need, right now, and so, for now, Marjorie is going to forget about taking her vacation day.

6. MARGIE

Margie learned about lines. She did not know the word, *line*. But Margie saw lines all around her. Straight lines like walls, like pretzel sticks, like candy bars.

Lines curved all the way around to make circles. Circles, too, Margie saw. Margie started to see. To know and remember and recognize. Shapes. Margie, little Margie, began to understand her shapes. Curved lines all the way around like eyes and donuts and the brown centers of the yellow flowers that grew in the weeds at the end of dead-end Summer Street. Some up-days, Gram walked with Margie down to the end of the street, to the tall-grass place where the stones started, where the trees grew, where the street stopped and the cool wet-line curve of the brook was. Gram held Margie's hand and Margie squatted in the tall grass and there Margie saw green growing lines that scratched against her cheeks, her arms, her nose. Smooth gray circles of stones soaking wet and shining in sunlight. The changing white-light shapes of leaves cut out bright from the shadows of the great big trees that grew at the dead end of the street where they lived.

Margie saw circles and lines long before she knew there were words to say these things out loud. She touched her small finger to the four corners of Gram's book and around the box of cereal and Margie could not say square or rectangle, but Margie knew the shapes. Margie could feel the shapes inside her. The sweet crumbling circles of cakes Gram sometimes brought back from church. The shape of her sleeping ma seen through a door, cracked. Trunks of trees were a lot of lines touched together. The bent, broken-in-two circle backs of the hills that circled the town. Cakes cut up into pieces made small hand-sized triangles. Margie's stuffed bunny was made of lots of lines and circles and was soft, was a shape of its own that we still have found no name for.

We don't remember seeing the world this way.

Though we must have, we must have.

And colors. Margie's apartment, red-door Apartment #2, up the big dark stairs on the second floor of the old white-and-gray wooden house on dead-end Summer Street with the dark blue creaking front porch and the high glass windows the color of dust in sunlight. Inside Apartment #2, the colors were worn out, were the colors of what could be held, tasted, of Margie and Gram and Ma. White-powdered-donut white, the yellow box of cereal and the red box of cereal, the cakes another kind of yellow, a sponge yellow, a soap yellow, the cakes black, pink-frosted and the pink of the soft inside of the stuffed bunny's ears. The blue of the bunny's outside. The hard black of the bunny's eyes and nose. Ma's room painted orange and off-limits to Margie. The wooden floor brown, the carpet green, the rough red of the living room rug. The purple pillows and sheets on the bed where Margie slept beside Gram, the purple of

Margie's pajamas, the purple of pink lips pressed too long and hard and tight together.

For Margie, little, growing, big-boned Margie, the things made the colors. There was the dark red-book red of Gram's book and the gold shapes of letters, the B-I-B-L-E, each letter its own shade of gold, each shape shining in its own way. There was the pale blue of toilet porcelain and the gray of fingerprints on wall, a gray not the same as the gray of stones by the brook or the peeling-paint gray of the big wooden house that held up Apartment #2.

The colors of what was held in a hand, a mouth, and people, too. People and their colors. Ma, the brown-black and yellow of Ma, of Ma's long hair. The sun-brown of Ma's skin in the summertime, the pink of Ma in the winter, the orange burn at the end of her cigarette and the see-through gray smoke that curled up into shapes that disappeared as soon as Margie tried to touch them. The cafeteria-worker-white of Ma's shirts and the tight black of her pants.

The color of Ma getting ready for work was sometimes the color of a kiss. Sometimes Ma stopped to kiss her fat, quiet, smiling child. Sometimes Ma carried her to the kitchen sink and with her smoke-smelling fingers. Ma did her best to wash and comb and straighten Margie. This was the color of Margie, quiet, waiting, watching, being touched.

Stupid little pain in my ass.

Words were colorless. Sounds, rising, falling. The slam of front door same as Ma yelling at Gram, same as Gram's television turned up loud.

Gram and all her gray, her gray hair, the gray of her skin, the gray spots on her hands and the gray nightgown she wore down-days, most days. Gray all over except her eyes, the bright blue of Gram's eyes, like the plastic of Margie's cereal bowl, like the watery waves Margie watched on television, like the sky on a perfect yard sale day.

And Margie. The shapes and colors of Margie. Wordless Margie liked rolling, spinning, circling. Down low on the red living-room rug, Margie turned in slow circles and watched the colors of Apartment #2 bleed together. Margie's little legs grew into plump shapes that could bend, crawl, walk, but Margie liked the feel of the floor. Forced by Gram or Ma to get up and walk, Margie got up and walked, but left alone and in charge of herself, Margie moved in circles.

Picked up by Gram, held in front of the bathroom mirror, Margie smiled, saw, tried to see the colors of Margie. The light sun-dried mud brown of her hair, the red of her tongue stuck out. Margie lay in her place on the rug and looked at her hands, her body, at the shapes and colors of her. The pink of Margie's arms and knees and the white, not milk white or wooden-house white or powdered-donut white, but another white, a too-long-left-indoors white, a no-color color we might call white, the particular white of Margie's soft plump legs. Margie's fingers turned the color of whatever she touched, the pink and black and yellow of cakes, the red of Gram's lipstick, the brown of the dirt on the bank of the brook at the end of their dead-end street.

Margie, down low, rolling, becoming. Turning the colors of there, of where she was, of green insects squished, of strawberry pudding swallowed. Margie listened to the loud of Gram's stories and felt the shape of Ma's footsteps leaving. From her warm place in bed beside Gram, Margie saw the quiet dark of the inside. Left alone for the day to sit beside the big high-up bedroom window, Margie felt the cool flat glass against her cheek and Margie watched the bright alive of the outside.

Had we thought to look up, we might have seen the shape of her there.

Margie, moving her mouth, opening and closing, making circles and lines. Circles and lines with tongue and teeth and throat and lungs and up there behind the bedroom window was Margie trying to make the shape of the world into words. Margie, behind glass, looking out. Trying to make the sounds of the brook, the frogs, the sounds of the television. Margie, small mouth moving, circling, sounding out something like the shape of Gram, of Ma. Beginning to make the sounds of how we ask, of how we say.

7. MARJORIE

Marjorie stands here in her self in her pains in her place in front of the swinging door at the front of the Store and waits for the People to come. She smiles wide and holds her hands together behind her soft back. The door is long and glass and when the People step toward it the door slides to the side to let them through. Outside it is cold wind and gray ice and hills of black-spotted snow. Outside is home and the Club and Ma in a box beside the sofa and Gram and her Stories. Outside, the lined-up hills that surround the town are covered in white, are powdered, like donuts, coated, like white chocolates, round and circling like arms like walls. Outside there is the mountain rising. Inside it is bright white light and warm. Hot. Heat blows down from the light-lined ceiling right here right on the place where Marjorie stands. Marjorie stands here in the blowing heat because here is the first step the People take in out of the cold. Here is where the snow falls off boots and melts in pools. Here there is a puddle that Marjorie stands in, a puddle made by the boots and coats and hats of all the People who step into the warm around her.

Sometimes Marjorie sweats, a little, standing here in the hot air, but she does not mind. She does not move from the puddle, from her important place here by the door. Marjorie smiles her Store smile and thinks her Store thoughts. The People, the cold, the hot, the Hello, the things, all the things. Here, in her place, she is busy helping the People and so does not need to direct her self to the good departments. The registers beep and beep and beep and beep and the People pass by and the registers beep. Marjorie wears clean brown pants and black sneakers and a white short-sleeved shirt under her blue vest and when the door swings open she is red-faced, smiling, ready to Welcome the People. She does not need to remember or wonder or imagine. Marjorie needs to say the words she needs to say.

Marjorie says:

Hello.

Welcome.

Cold Out There Today.

Good Morning.

Good Afternoon.

Good Evening.

Come On In.

Marjorie holds her heavy shoulders still so that the People can see her name tag. Her name is very long, so long that the white stuck-on letters touch each other, so that her name is almost longer than the tag.

MARJORIE.

Marjorie stands up straight as she can and smiles and she is very good at keeping her eyes on the door and waiting and watching the People come in. She feels the straps of her bra under and inside, making a pain, holding her up. Marjorie moves her wind through slow and steady, in and out, down and up the length of her self. She is bigger than most. Marjorie takes up a little more space than most of the People but Marjorie knows this, Marjorie knows how to hold her self still, how to move her wind to make her self smaller, how to smile so that the People will smile and not notice how she has just a little bit more of the world than she should.

Hello.

Cold Out There Today.

Past the door is the parking lot and sometimes when the day is slow Marjorie watches the People park their cars and get out of their cars and pull their coats down over their belts and lock the car doors and check to make sure the doors are locked and walk from their car to the swinging glass door at the start of the Store where she is ready for them and waiting for them and smiling for them.

Welcome.

Hello.

Cold Out There Today.

Hello.

Sometimes Steve stops by to tell Marjorie to Mix it up a bit. Steve has a lot of long black hairs growing above his lips and he is big and wide like her. He wears his extra-extra-large shirts tucked into his black pants and often his shirts rise up when he bends over and often Marjorie sees some of Steve's white black-haired skin come up to the surface. Steve is big and wide like her but Steve is not quiet about it the way Marjorie is. Steve likes to talk loud and laugh loud and slap People's backs loud and Steve is loud about his big and fat, proud about it. Marjorie is not proud and not not proud, Marjorie is just Marjorie and Marjorie keeps quiet. Steve likes to push his huge chest out so that all the People will see the yellow pin on his vest that says MANAGER.

Try something new, Marge, Steve says.

Marjorie, she says.

Marjorie's name is important. She does not want to be called any name but her name. Before she had Ma and Him calling her all sorts of names and now that it is after, now that they are done and now that Marjorie is done with Him she is done with all the names except Marjorie.

My name is Marjorie, not Marge.

Sometimes she points to her nametag, just to make sure that Steve understands.

MARJORIE.

Okay, Marjorie, Steve says.

Keep it new, he says. Keep them happy. Get them in here so they'll empty those fat pockets. Keep it casual, you know, natural. And excited. Hey, I love that coat. Come check out these great sales we're having. Merry Christmas. Happy New Year. All that shit.

Marjorie smiles her big Steve smile.

I will try, she says.

Try isn't good enough. Try harder, Margie. You got to do, not try. You mind if I call you Margie?

Sorry, I mind. My name is Marjorie.

Okay, okay, no need to twist up those fat panties, Marjorie.

Steve squeezes Marjorie's shoulder with his big fingers with the small holes in them where the black hairs poke through and Marjorie stares at that hand as it squeezes. Steve squeezes Marjorie in the pained place where her bra strap cuts through, where her shoulder splits into two hills. The squeeze is just a fast squeeze, a moment squeeze, and soon as his hand has touched enough of her for her to feel it, Steve walks slow off to wherever he goes to do whatever he does in the Store. Steve and his squeezes. His dirty mouth. Marjorie rubs her shoulder at the spot where Steve's fingers were, rubs and rubs until she cannot feel his hand anymore.

The problem of Steve. Marjorie tries her best to see People as good and kind. Steve is fine and Steve laughs a lot and the People seem to like Steve. It is just that Marjorie is very particular about her touching. Down one of her inside aisles she has a list of People She Minds and a list of People She Does Not Mind. And the big ghost of Steve that walks around pinching those hidden parts of Marjorie is on her People She Minds list. So Marjorie always smiles and tells Steve that she will try and rubs and rubs at the place where Steve was, and then goes right on being Marjorie, staying right where she is, saying exactly what she feels is right for the People.

Welcome.

Cold Out There Today.

Good Afternoon.

Come On In.

The door swings open and Marjorie says Hello and just as she says Hello she sees that this is not just People coming in, that this is Benjamin. Her friend. Good. A good break in the People. The good of the outside coming in. Marjorie smiles big and waves.

Hi, Benjamin.

Benjamin is pushing a shopping cart piled high with small plastic red-and-green Christmas trees. He is tall and thin and not old and not young. Benjamin leans over the handle of the cart and his hair, dark blond, long, twisted into tangled braids, hangs heavy down around his head. His skin is smooth and such a good color, like cinnamon, like gingerbread man. Marjorie likes the color of Benjamin's skin and sometime Marjorie would like to reach over the space between them and touch Benjamin's arm. Not a big touch and not a squeeze. Just a touch, to see, to feel, what Benjamin is.

Hey, Marjorie, Benjamin says. How's it going?

Benjamin is good. Benjamin smells good sour, a green apple smell. Benjamin always stops by to say Hello and ask Marjorie how the day is. He works in the sides, at the back, in the belly of the Store, in hidden places where the People cannot go, doing important things. Benjamin is always busy. But Benjamin always comes by to say Hello and Marjorie always enjoys talking to Benjamin.

Good, Marjorie says. Good.

Marjorie smiles her best. She keeps her eyes on the door in case People come in. She keeps the gone of Ma to her self. Not because Benjamin is not good. Because she does. Because this is what Marjorie is doing.

How are you today, Benjamin?

Oh, hanging in there. We got a shitload of shampoo delivered last night and four of the boxes exploded somehow. Don't know what happened but it smells like fucking Hell back there. Like some lilac and strawberry and orange and vanilla orgy. Some fucking sorority massacre or some shit like that.

Marjorie nods and smiles. She does not always understand what Benjamin is saying, and so many of Benjamin's words are bad words, but Marjorie knows Benjamin is good. Marjorie understands that sometimes People cannot be blamed for how they talk, that People learn to say what the People around them are saying. That if it were not for Gram and television, Marjorie might also talk like Benjamin, like Ma, like Him, like People who say bad words because bad words are probably all they have ever heard.

Wow, Marjorie says. Sounds smelly.

Yeah, something awful. And then we got to get rid of all these asshole Christmas trees by the end of the day.

Marjorie nods and smiles and steps two steps sideways so that Benjamin can move his cart through.

Benjamin pushes past and stops and puts his hand gentle on Marjorie's shoulder. His long thin fingers feel fine there, feel warm and not hard or hurting. Benjamin is on Marjorie's list of People She Does Not Mind, so his hand touching her shoulder is fine, is good, feels good.

I'll stop by later, Marjorie. Stay warm, it's fucking freezing out there.

Okay, Benjamin.

Benjamin walks away into the long, bright deep of the Store and Marjorie turns and stands tall as she can and smiles at the People passing through.

Welcome.

Cold Out There Today.

Hello.

Benjamin and Marjorie and all the workers and even Steve are here for the good of the Store, are here to help the People. The bright lines of white light above Marjorie shine out for what feels like forever. Lights above shine out and out and down in long lines on the white shining floor, so bright Marjorie sometimes feels as if the whole of the Store is just light and light and light. The People pass through the swinging glass door, pass by Marjorie's Hello, and the People say Hello or the People do not say Hello and the People move on and into the Store to find the needed things. Spaghetti sauce and shampoo and t-shirts and tin foil and toothpaste and bottles of pills and boxes of tissues and bags of chocolate. So many People passing by and so many things out there to need.

And Marjorie, here, to say Hello.

Marjorie, here, to help.

Mostly Marjorie stands with her back to the Store not because she does not like the Store but because she likes it so much. This is a very huge Store and what Marjorie has come to understand after a long, long time of standing here is that a very huge Store is like very huge water. Not like the brook that sat low and still at the end of dead-end Summer Street. But big water, wide water, like the biggest lake, maybe, or like the sea, maybe.

Hello.

Marjorie has never been to the sea but she has seen it many times on television and she can understand how People feel about it. She knows that the sea is something People like to stand beside because it is so endless and beautiful and so strong that you have to stop thinking about your self because you are so small and finished. People start at their heads and end at their feet but the sea has no entrance and no exit. It just stretches and stretches and stretches. Goes and goes. This is why the sea happens so much on television. Because it is good, strong, and forever.

Cold Out There Today.

Welcome.

And this is how the Store is too. The very huge Store just goes and goes. It rolls out behind Marjorie, reaching so far back it feels as if there is no end. Marjorie keeps her eyes on the glass door and the parking lot beyond because if she were to look back into the Store she is a little sure that she might never be able to stop looking. Outside, there are hills touching hills in a circle against the sky that shows Marjorie where things begin and where things end. In the Store, here, behind her, there is just too much to see. Too many things. Baby clothes on baby hangers, televisions in love, big plastic plants, Bibles, bibs, sofas, fish food flakes, toothpaste, vitamin this and vitamin that, bras, tiny electric cars, dolls, cough drops, mops.

Good Afternoon.

Come On In.

Marjorie thinks this must be like what happens when People put their bodies under the sea and open their eyes. Down there they have so much to look at. Down there are all the colors of all the fish, the waving seaweed, the sharp gray lines of the sharks that cut through and how the sunlight comes down into the water and burns and disappears into all the dark under of water that does not end.

Welcome.

People open their eyes under the sea to see all of these things and this is why, Marjorie thinks, People are not made to breathe underwater. So many good things to look at down there that if People could they would stay under the sea forever. But People need to feel air and wind and sun in them and so no matter how much they want to stay and look at the sea, to live, to keep living, People have to stop looking, sometime.

Hello.

Cold Out There Today.

The Store is just like this, except the Store never closes. Except that People can breathe free and full in the Store. The Store is bright and warm air blows through and music plays and People laugh and registers beep. Just turn around and start looking and it is possible that Marjorie might never be able to stop watching all the things and things rolling out down the aisles and aisles and in those aisles things arranged in rows and boxes and baskets. On shelves on racks on tables on display. White-bread white and pink-panty pink and corn-flake yellow and orange-juice yellow and orange-cat orange and mint-mouth-wash green and purple-pen purple and angry-faced red. Every color People will ever see in the whole history of People is out there somewhere in the Store. All the shapes, too. So many smells, Marjorie cannot even begin to think about how many smells there are in the Store to smell. Blueberry muffins and coconut shampoo and black magic markers and chicken-liver cat food and coffee and roses and popcorn. Sea-scented candles and dried seaweed in packages and sand in hourglasses. The Store so huge that even the whole sea can fit inside it, if Marjorie stays too down deep in her thinking.

Welcome.

Come On In.

And above, there are signs. Big blue signs hanging down with their big white letters show the way.

HOME DECOR
BEDDING
JEWELRY
WOMEN'S WEAR

WINDOWS

ELECTRONICS

BABY

When Marjorie does need to turn, when Marjorie needs to walk out into the center of the Store, she looks up. She watches the signs to know where she is, to know where to go. The signs above and the things below and the People all around, searching, circling. Looking for what is needed.

Marjorie smiles and shakes her head from this side to this side. She stares so hard at the door her eyes almost cross. If she thinks too much about the very huge Store behind her, Marjorie begins to feel dizzy with the long beautiful lined-up life of all the things. It can feel good to be pulled and part of something so big, but the pull can also feel so strong Marjorie wants to sit down right here and close her eyes and be in her dark for a while. To spend some time sitting in her own departments, smelling the things she has stacked up on the shelves, touching the good she has saved from before and the new bright things she is finding in this after. The sound of the frogs singing in the dark in the brook at night, Dr. Goodwin and his shiny shoes, Gram on an up-day putting on her lipstick, and Lucy.

Lucy.

But here is the door to watch and there are always waves of People to say Hello to. The Store without the People is like the sea without the fish. Marjorie smiles and thinks about how good it would be if just for one minute of one day all the People in the Store – and Marjorie, too, Marjorie, too – could stop having to walk on their feet and instead float up light and free to swim around and touch and taste and hold all the beauty of all the things. Marjorie thinks it would be very good if sometime People could have a break from being People and be something else instead.

Good Afternoon.

Hello.

Cold Out There Today.

Marjorie stands her two feet hard on the floor and takes deep breaths and does her best to stop thinking about the big of the Store pulling her big self into it. So many departments inside for her to turn to, so many things she has to turn away from so that she can keep standing, keep smiling, keep giving the People her Hello. Marjorie bends one knee and she bends the other knee. Inside, her pains are here, are long, heavy, but quiet, but no different from usual. Sometimes she blurs her eyes so that the colors of the cars and the gray of the parking lot and the bright silver flash of the sun on the glass of the door become all the same, all shining. She smiles, she takes wind in, blows wind out. She waits. She speaks.

Welcome.

Hello.

The door swings open, slides shut. Cold air blows in and feels good mixed with the hot air on Marjorie's bare skin. Beside Marjorie are registers beeping and rows and rows of People lined up and needing things. Morning, night, always, the light in here is the same. Bright, white, beeping, everywhere. The light comes from long tubes up on the ceiling and sometimes when the day is slow Marjorie likes to look up at the loud lines of light and close her eyes and watch the ghosts of those lines cut across the black inside. Up, down, and across her departments. She does this now, looks up, stares until the bright lines hurt her eyes. Until she burns, until she needs to squeeze shut inside her self, to watch what happens there. Marjorie opens and closes, and closes. Because it is so cold outside that the People are few, because this is a different kind of pain, because this is something to do that belongs all and only to her.

8. MARGIE

Margie lived a long time without words.

We never sat with her and said, This is a circle, this is red, this is yellow. This is not a square. This is the shape of your hand held in your gram's hand. This is the color of someone crying in secret. We never said, Look, Margie, this is the size and color and shape of the whole wide of the world.

But Margie saw. Margie did not speak and no one said much to Margie, but Margie heard everything she wanted to hear. High up in Apartment #2, in the bedroom Margie shared with Gram, in the big loud bed where Margie slept beside the warm of Gram, night was the sound of Gram's snores, of her breath, loud, like thunder, like a storm, an engine, a monster, the sea, coming. The great big wind of Gram.

My wind, Gram said. I can't catch my wind.

Margie rolling to the side of the bed was the sound of mattress springs screaming and waking up was Gram's voice, low, whispered, reading from the red-and-gold of her book, one hand held over her chest. The sounds Margie knew best were the sounds of hearts, of her heart, beating, fast, light, and Gram's heart, slow, booming, out and out under the blankets.

Gram said, My heart.

My pains, my heart.

Gram's heart hurt her always. Maybe Margie could understand this, pain. Pain, the pinch of pain, pain a color of white unlike all the other whites. Pain was not something Margie learned or found or invented.

Did we? Did we learn about pain?

No.

Pain must be something we just know.

Pain was something Margie knew. Margie found out about pain by putting her fingers where fingers do not fit, by being picked up hard by the big black-haired friends her ma brought home. Pain was always there waiting to be let out and up and down and through Margie. She just knew, had, carried, understood, felt it. Pain. The never-ending lines and circles and ups and downs of pain.

We must all be born this way.

Born with it, with pain, that waits.

Margie's words came later. Much later, and slowly, and sometimes wrong. Margie, growing, rolling against the rough red rug, eating her triangles of cake, her squares of purple-frosted pop tarts. Margie, growing, getting bigger, longer, just a little more every day.

Showing her words slowly, Margie made slow sense of what she saw and felt and held.

Gram, Margie's first word.

For a long time, Gram. Gram and Gram and Gram. All that Margie heard and saw and felt and wanted, said with one long sound.

Gram.

And then, slowly, Ma.

Ma said mostly when Ma had gone away.

Ma, short, fast, the sound of Ma over before it had a chance to be.

Gram. Ma.

Words. Are these words? This naming, this calling out, this small sound of Margie down on the floor making her circles, making the shape of Ma, of Gram, with her lips, what was this? We don't know if Margie was wanting, if Margie was trying to say something important to the world outside herself, or if these sounds were just there, easy, known. Was Margie asking for something? For someone? Or was Margie just rolling around in the familiar, just making the roundest shapes of sound she could find?

But no.

But then, one night, under the warm of the blankets, Margie's first word.

Or third.

Margie's first word that did not belong to Gram or to Ma. The first sound

Margie figured out for herself, the first time Margie heard and knew and saw and said.

Heart, Margie said.

Margie, in the dark, in bed with Gram, with Gram's pains, heard the word and for the first time wanted to hold onto it, to feel it, to hear it inside and outside herself.

My heart, Gram said.

Oh, Margie, my pains.

Margie heard all the words. Pains and my and Margie and heart and oh. Oh. Margie heard Gram making these words again and again in the dark and Margie picked one and the one she picked was heart.

Heart, Margie said.

Yes, Margie, Gram said. Oh, I can't get my wind.

Pains, in my chest. My heart, I think. My heart, it's bad, Margie, it hurts.

Heart, Margie said.

Margie and Gram and the sounds that showed they were some parts of the same.

Heart, Margie started saying.

Margie, pointing to frogs sitting on stones in the brook, said, Heart. Pointing to blue paint chipping on the slanted porch steps, said, Heart. Up at the big black of the mountain, Ma. Heart. Touching her face to the blue soft of her bunny, her fingers into the centers of her donuts, her nose to the cool glass of bedroom window, Margie said, Heart.

A necessary word but not nearly wide enough to name the whole world.

We think.

Once Ma noticed Margie talking, she started teaching her the wrong words for things. We don't know why. Because she was bored, because it was funny, because she figured Margie would figure it out eventually.

Margie pointed to a circle and Ma said, Square.

The green carpet, Ma called, Red.

Dogs, Ma said, say Meow.

Cat, Ma said. Cat. Cats say Woof.

Say what a cat says, Margie.

And Margie, slow and smiling and always on the floor, learned to say, Woof. We laughed. A little fun. Some joy we did not expect from the day.

On an up-day, Gram might have tried to teach Margie the right way. That cats say Meow and dogs say Woof and that the kitchen table was a square, not a circle. To chew her cookies with her mouth closed and wash her hands after doing her business in the bathroom. Some days, Gram tried, but Gram had her pains to pay attention to. Gram had her book to read and her church to go to and her yard sales. Gram, like Ma, must have figured that Margie would learn. That Margie was fine, that Margie would catch up, that Margie would sooner or later find her way into the true, real, right of the world.

Margie learned to leave words alone. Ma said Cat and Gram said Dog and Margie stopped listening. Margie looked, instead. Margie saw small, big, soft. Noses wet, noses dry, ears made of lines and circles. Margie learned that making words made her loud. That she could only hear or see or taste or smell the world when she was quiet, when she did not try to remember the shapes of the sounds and the names for what surrounded her.

Margie sat on the floor of the bedroom in the hot of the sun coming in through the window and with her skin felt the different of this through-glass hot, different from the hot of hot dog on her tongue, different from the hot of hot water on her hands. She lay in bed beside Gram and felt the warm wind that came from Gram's mouth as she moaned and rolled and rumbled. Margie smelled the sour of Gram, the pinched-nose smell of Gram's sour different from the sour of milk left out, different from the sour smell that lived in the dark below the sofa.

At night, in the warm and sour air beneath the blankets, in the next-to of Gram, Margie put her small hand over her mouth and breathed out and in and smelled her own air, the nothing of it, the smell she could not match to any other smell, the smell of herself, what seemed to belong to her and only her. Margie felt her wind blowing through her and knew it was different from Gram's, different from the wind that shook the trees outside the window, different from the wind that went through Ma and the slow wind that moved from room to room in the open-window summertime of Apartment #2.

Margie shut her eyes and rolled slow from side to side, listening to her heart making sounds. Not words, but sounds. Her inside, sounding, pounding. Margie, little Margie, staying quiet, slowly building the world in her inside, the world that was only for her, a place built in shapes and colors and sizes that no one but Margie would ever know existed.

9. MARJORIE

Marjorie sits in the low pink and blue and yellow and green light next to the wall of signs at the bar at the back of the Benevolent and Protective Order of Elks and inside her sneakers she is secretly moving the pains down and out and through her toes. So many hours spent standing at the front of the Store, smiling, saying Hello, helping the People find what they need. A lady with three tiny crying kids needed to know where the popcorn machine was and Marjorie helped her with that. A man needed to buy socks for his wife and Marjorie showed him the way. So many People with so many needs and all day long Marjorie helps and helps, stands and smiles. Now, in the dark of the Club that is lit up by all of these candy-wrapper colors, Marjorie feels good and worked all over, and now Marjorie is waiting for her Shirley Temple that will show her that this day is almost done.

The Club is a special place. Members Only. The Benevolent and Protective Order of Elks. Marjorie likes to read the big white blue-lettered wooden sign above the bar quiet, inside her self. This is a name too big for her mouth to get right out loud. The Benevolent and Protective Order of Elks. A good name for a good place, the only place within Marjorie's walking from the Store and the apartment. Marjorie is not a member of the Club but Mac knew Ma from a long, long time before, and Mac always lets Marjorie come and sit and drink her Shirley Temples as his guest.

Today the Club is busy and it is taking Mac longer than usual to make her drink. Marjorie does not mind. She waits. She is good at waiting. Marjorie can see balloons and wrapped boxes with bows at the other end of the room and she is guessing that one of all these People here today is having a birthday. She wiggles her toes inside her socks, feeling the pains, releasing the pains, and kicks her sneakers a little against the big wooden bar and watches the birthday-party People talk and laugh and smile and drink.

Marjorie likes to be a guest. The Benevolent and Protective Order of Elks, the sign says. Members and Invited Guests Only. Marjorie is an invited guest. Members of the Club need to pay money and members of the Club need to be U.S. citizens who believe in God. This is what the sign under the sign above the bar says. Marjorie is a U.S. Citizen. God, Marjorie is not so sure about. Marjorie believes in the things she can see, the People and the Store. She can believe in the things she has seen, the blue-covered wall of her bedroom in Apartment #2, the grass wet at night. But God. Who knows about God? God is who keeps Gram company in Gram's room. God is a big unseen something to believe in. Marjorie has not yet made up her mind about God.

Except for in the Club. In the Club, where Marjorie is an invited guest, she can believe in God. Because why not? The People in the Club are kind, are good, and the People in the Club are here to help. And the bad of God in the Club. Always the good of God, the good of God, but what about the bad of

God? Marjorie waits for her Shirley Temple and looks at the faces of the People, at their wide-open happy mouths, how they touch shoulders and how their hands reach for each other and how some of the men put their arms around some of the ladies and how the ladies touch and touch their beautiful television hair. God in the pink and blue and yellow and green bar light. God in the drinks that make People laugh, that make People mean. Maybe there is God in here, in the pink light in the ice cubes, in the soft shining of the hair.

Marjorie puts her hand on her head and touches her hair and it does not feel hard and it does not feel soft. She rubs her hand over her whole head and closes her eyes to feel her self more. No, not hard, but a little stiff, dry, like drive-in grass at the beginning of winter. Marjorie's hair is shaped in waves, by its nature, and cut short, the way she likes it. Once a month, always before Marjorie goes to see Dr. Goodwin, she has her hair cut for a good deal by Sylvia in the small salon at the back of the Store. To take care of her self, to give the People something good to see.

Marjorie opens her eyes and looks around again. The Club. Marjorie has a huge history with the Club. The bar is long and wooden and it stretches out the whole length of the back wall and the wood is dark and smooth and feels good against her cheek. Marjorie sits here, at the end of the bar farthest from the bathroom, next to the wall with the signs that glow and buzz. A huge history with the Club. But before is before and this is the Club where Marjorie is an invited guest. The People at the birthday party are loud and laughing, are strangers. Marjorie squints her eyes and stares at the People at the other end of the bar, the quiet People who are looking at their hands, who are not here for the birthday party, who are drinking their beers and believing in God. Men, all of them. Mostly men, here, in the Club.

Hey, Marjorie, hang in there, Mac, from far away, yells.

Marjorie nods and waves. Mac there, in the dark at the end of the bar, calling out to her. Marjorie is hanging in, feels fine sitting here in her place by the wall, watching the People and taking her load off her feet for a while. Mac is big and strong and kind to her. So kind. If there is a good God in the Club it is Mac smiling and saying, Hello, Marjorie, and mixing her Shirley Temple and asking, How are you today? Mac there before, Mac here after. Mac who said her name. Mac who invites her in, who puts his big hand on her big hand, who lets her sit and stay and be.

Dr. Goodwin knows about Mac of course and of course Dr. Goodwin has asked Marjorie how she feels about him.

Dr. Goodwin's favorite words.

How do you feel?

How do you feel today, Marjorie?

How do you feel about that, Marjorie?

How do you feel about Mac, Marjorie?

Good, Dr. Goodwin. Good and good and fine and good. Dr. Goodwin's questions. Marjorie does not mind. She understands that Dr. Goodwin has a difficult job and just like how she is so used to saying Hello, Welcome, Come On In, Dr. Goodwin is used to saying, How do you feel?

And, Let go. Let go.

You need to let go.

How do you feel about Mac, Marjorie? Do you think maybe you love him?

Dr. Goodwin and his love. His feelings. Love this and love that. Love the things, love the People, love your self. Love your Lucy and Let go.

Good, Dr. Goodwin, Marjorie had said. I feel good about Mac.

That was the most truth Marjorie could think of for how she felt about Mac then and now this still seems the most she can say. So many words out there in the world, and People always wanting to hear new words and different words for what can just be said as good or bad, yes or no. For Marjorie, good is the right word because good can mean so much. Good is a big word, a wide word with lots of space inside it. Good can have love inside it. So many words. Good can hold on tight to warm and happy and Thank You and true and right. Even God, in there, in the good, if that is what People need to see.

Marjorie closes her eyes and sucks in her wind. She is going inside her departments now, thinking about too many things and forgetting what things she is thinking about. Wandering, looking at shelves and shelves of words and what she remembers. Marjorie does not want to get into a headache like she is into this footache. She keeps her eyes closed for a minute and for that minute she sits in her dark and she uses the light-outlined part of her self to go to her mind, to touch her mind, to pick up her mind and in that inside place Marjorie begins to wash her mind all over with soap and a little warm water. This is her way of keeping her self clean and free from any thoughts she does not need to be thinking. Marjorie, the other Marjorie, the inside Marjorie, rubs her mind, the smooth gray bumps and curves of her, gently. Gently scrubbing all the soft sides of her, rinsing her self with warm water and then letting her mind sit back down clean, alone, happy, soaking.

Marjorie opens her eyes and here is Mac, standing in front of her, smiling and holding out her Shirley Temple.

Here you go, Marjorie, he says. Gave you three cherries instead of two today. Sorry about the wait.

Thanks, Mac, Marjorie says, and she slides the tall glass close to her. The birthday People are laughing and now Marjorie can smell cake.

I heard about your ma, Mac says.

Oh. Yeah.

I was sorry about it, Marjorie.

Yeah. Thanks, Mac.

Marjorie leans toward the straw and takes a long sip of her cold, sweet, bubbling drink.

You and your gram getting along okay over there?

Yeah, Marjorie says. Good. Getting along.

Marjorie knows that Mac is like her, Mac is not a talker, and so Marjorie is not sure why he is still standing here in front of her. He seems to be waiting for her to say more, so Marjorie thinks of what more she can say.

Okay, Marjorie says. Not so different than before. Just quiet.

Mac nods and reaches his hand out across the bar and touches his hand to her shoulder. Marjorie does not mind because Mac is on her list of People She Does Not Mind. She is just surprised, a little. A touch. She feels her shoulder go stiff, a little. Mac keeps his hand there for a little while and once Marjorie is finished with her surprise her shoulder drops down again and she feels soft again and she smiles.

Where is Suzanne?

Marjorie's mouth asks the question quick, before her mind even knew she was wondering it.

Off today, Mac says. Some kind of family thing. Nothing too serious, don't think. She'll be in tomorrow.

Marjorie nods. She would like to see Suzanne. Suzanne, new to the Club. Suzanne is good. Beautiful and always smiling and always talking and always touching Marjorie's arm and hand and shoulder. Suzanne whose big, soft body makes Marjorie remember the heated-up good of before.

Hey, Mac says. That one is on the house.

Thanks, Mac.

He takes his hand away and Marjorie's shoulder tingles a little, remembering.

Okay, Marjorie, you enjoy yourself. I got a lot to get done.

Marjorie nods and she drinks her drink. She looks at the People and feels good about sitting here, about being together, out in the world, free.

Marjorie drinks her cold sweet drink down slow as she can. She sucks each cherry around in her mouth and squishes them between her teeth. The birthday-party People are having a very good time and Marjorie is happy about it and the sugary smell of their cake is making her hungry. She will go home and heat up some supper for her and Gram.

And Ma. Not supper for Ma. Just the remembering of Ma. Ma in the cardboard box beside the sofa. Delivered. Waiting. For what? Marjorie will go home and there Ma will be and what do People do with a box of their Ma dead in the living room?

Maybe Dr. Goodwin will know. Of course Dr. Goodwin will know. Probably all the People know. But Marjorie does not. Marjorie will have to spend some time in that department, will have to think about what place is the right place for stacking Ma.

She sucks hard on the straw and moves it around between the ice cubes and does her best to drink down the whole drink. Marjorie gets up slow from her stool, lets her toes stretch out inside her socks, bounces a few times on her feet to make sure they are strong enough to hold her up. She zips up her puffy purple coat and puts down two dollars on the bar, which is one dollar more than she usually gives. Marjorie puts her hands deep in her pocket and calls down to Mac at the end of the bar.

See you tomorrow, Mac.

See you, Marjorie, he says, and he waves.

Marjorie keeps her head down and her hands hard at her sides as she walks sideways against the wall of the Club, out of the way of the birthday People.

Get home safe, Mac says, as she pulls the heavy door of the Club toward her, as the cold air blows in.

10. MARGIE

The quiet of a usual day sounded like the television talking and Margie chewing. The not-there of Ma. Ma gone, out, away, at work or somewhere else far from Apartment #2. Usual days were down. Down-day Gram sat low inside the soft of her green chair and Margie laid out low and long as she could make herself on the rough living room rug. Gram watched her stories and did not speak. Margie rolled from side to side, looking up at the ovals of Gram's pink slippers, looking at the bright moving lights of the television. She put her eyes up close to the hard brown shining square of the coffee table and touched her tongue gently to the side of Gram's soft chair, just to know, to taste the taste of green–chair green. Margie put her small, thick fingers deep down inside the box of whatever Gram had given her to eat and felt the shape and size and weight of the food before she put it into her mouth. Margie with her fingers felt the small dry circles of chocolate chip cookies, the big rough circles of yellow potato chips, the bright orange squares of cheese crackers. With her tongue she tasted the sting of salt, the slow drip of sweet, the pain of the scrape of cracker against the soft spots inside her mouth.

Margie ate. Gram watched. Margie chewed and rolled and reached. Time went on and on. Slowly, steadily, potato chip by potato chip, one day by one day, Margie was growing, getting every day longer and wider and softer. This is how we grow, chew by chew by swallow, in secret, quietly, lying low on the living room rug. Margie living along with her usual days. Looking and tasting and touching and feeling and starting to understand. Eating and eating and eating.

Circle, Margie said.

Heart, Margie said.

Woof. Wind. Green.

Gram, Margie said.

Quiet, Margie, Gram said. I'm watching my stories.

Gram watched her stories and Margie made circles on the floor and Margie watched Gram watching her stories and Margie chewed and chewed. Margie felt her teeth hard and her tongue soft and her jaw, moving, her throat, moving, her breath moving in and out and in and her food sliding down. Down deep inside her, to the center of the circle of herself, down to where her chest beat, to all the small parts, to the slowly gaining shapes that together shaped Margie.

Usual days, Margie was left mostly alone and unseen.

Other days, the other-than-usual days, the sometimes-days when Ma came back to Apartment #2 after work, Margie was watched. Margie was poked and squeezed and touched. Margie was seen and told to get out of sight. Margie was taught.

Stop rolling. Stay put. Wash those hands. Don't touch. Don't eat that. Stupid. Stop staring. Act normal. Shutup. Sit up straight. Mind your own business.

Most days when Ma did come back, she came through the red front door loud and kicking and dusted white all over. Ma came home smelling like french fries and cole slaw and cigarettes. Coconut. Fish, if it was Friday. Ma came home, white dust all over her black coat in spots in streaks in shadows of handprints and the left-behind of shapes Margie did not yet know.

Ma came in and yelled and said, to Margie, to Gram, to no one, Stay put.

Mind your own business.

Don't look at me, Ma might say.

I'm not here.

The sometimes-days when Ma did come back to Apartment #2, she came back as a ghost, as white powder all over. Ma came back smelling like onions and ketchup and whatever had burned up that day. Ma yelled and banged and disappeared.

Ma worked in the cafeteria at the quarry. We all worked at the quarry. We all knew her. Or someone like her. Or something like this. We all came home dirty with white, with lime lining our skin, with grease, blood, sweat, with leftovers of days spent sifting through explosions. We picked up big white boulders and we smashed the rocks to pieces to dust. To make glass and cement and toothpaste and plastic and pills. We can understand the coming home a little angry, the not coming home at all. Her days were heavy with hot-washed cafeteria trays and the hard pinch of scarred fingers. Who cares what goes on behind the big silver buckets of cafeteria food? We can understand needing a drink at the end of the day. We can't say we really knew anything at all. We were all a little angry, all a little drunk. Whole long days spent watching the earth blow up and then picking up the pieces. Whole long lines of big-bellied men covered in white and calling for more chicken, more beans, more gravy, more coffee, more salt and sauce and skin fried crisp. We probably walked in rough and loud just like her.

Ma worked in the cafeteria at the quarry and even though she spent most of her time frying potatoes and pouring out heavy gray rivers of uneaten chowder, when she came home her black coat was always coated in white dust. Sometimes Ma came home with a friend and the friends were always heavy-footed and even more white all over than Ma. Friends with hairy faces, with circles of white in their eyebrows, their beards, with white blown into the scars carved into their skin. The friends never said anything to Margie or Gram, just banged doors with their big hands and the floor with their big feet and disappeared into the bathroom, the orange bedroom, to wherever Ma had gone.

Sometimes-days Margie closed her eyes and listened to the sounds of Ma and the friends moving through and around and inside Apartment #2. She did not stop rolling or wash her hands or sit up straight. Margie did not know about minding business. She did not know that she had her own business to mind. Days when Ma brought friends into their home, Margie stopped chewing so that her inside could be more quiet, so that when she put her ear against the hard of the floor she could hear the shapes the weight of Ma and the friends made inside Apartment #2.

The up-and-down of Ma and the friends. The long groaning lines of sound they made the rooms make. Margie listened to the floors, to the wood, to the wave-shaped sounds that came from Ma's room. Margie, waiting, listening, learning the slow sound of the heartbeat Ma and the friends made within the walls.

Who hasn't done such a thing?

Margie listened and Gram turned the television up louder. Margie stayed down low on the floor, feeling the alive of everything around her.

And when the inside was quiet, when Margie could not hear anything more from the smooth hard of the floor, when she had looked at Gram and was sure Gram was down deep in her television, Margie would crawl over to the place where Ma had dropped her black coat and there Margie would look for the white shapes of Ma. Margie's two hands small inside the big black fabric of Ma's coat would spread and hold and look. Margie put her nose into the black of the coat and smelled the fried of Ma, the sweet of Ma, the sweat of Ma, the smoke and burn of Ma. Margie held the coat as well as she could and looked for the white left-behind parts of Ma. The white slope of her shoulders where they had touched the inside, the white streaks in the shape of fingers or hands left on the outside. Margie touched her tongue to the white and tried to see what taste Ma had left behind. And Margie did not have the word for it yet, but what Margie tasted there, all Margie could touch and taste of Ma, was chalk, was dust.

11. MARJORIE

Marjorie is still standing in the living room in the dark, listening, waiting for a thing she cannot name. She still holds her arms stiff at her sides so her puffy coat will not make the swish sound coat makes when it touches coat. Marjorie moves her wind slow in and slow out, stills her self, holds her self still and waiting.

But what is the wait for?

Above her, Marjorie can hear Roberta's television and Roberta's coughing. Outside in the street she hears the slow slide of a car moving through slush. Marjorie turns her head toward Gram's room to hear what is there. Pages turning, scissors cutting, the television talking, bed springs squeaking.

But nothing. All Marjorie hears is her self breathing and the sounds of the outside small enough to call quiet.

Marjorie steps a few steps forward in the dark and her leg bumps into the sofa and here, in her, is the bright of pain. There is a lamp nearby here, somewhere, and Marjorie leans one hand down to rub her leg and with the other she reaches up and out and swings her arm in the air, looking for that lamp. When her fingers feel the thin cold plastic pole of the lamp, Marjorie stands up taller and turns on the switch at the top and the room is fast bright, white, naked with light.

God. Who knows how to believe? What Marjorie knows is that Ma did not believe in lamp shades. Too much money, she had said. Not needed. Dust traps. Ma did not believe in many things. Bras and crayons and the Bible and frogs. Marjorie's face is so near the small bare bulb that it takes some time for her to be able to see anything but the big bright round shape burned into her eyeballs. She breathes, closes her eyes, waits inside until the white-hot shadow has gone and it is safe to open her eyes.

Marjorie does not mind how the light looks. Bare, not so good, no, but the left-open lamps were what Ma wanted and so long as it was Ma making the decision and not Him, Marjorie does not mind. Marjorie feels fine with things how they are.

Now that she can see, Marjorie moves a little faster. Carefully, quietly, she takes her coat off and hangs it up on its hook in its place. She listens for Gram and hears only Roberta's television laughing above her.

Ma. Is it Ma she is listening for? Ma she is waiting for?

No. There is no Ma to hear. No Ma here anymore. A here, a place, an apartment, a life with no more Ma.

Marjorie goes to the side of the sofa and with her wind steady, hands steady, she bends down and picks up the cardboard box. The weight of it feels the same, strange, too heavy and too light. She holds the hard box close to her chest and moves fast as she can past the green chair, past the small kitchen, down the short dark hall and through the door. Ma's was-door, Marjorie's is-door. Through. In. Inside.

Marjorie puts the box down onto the clean sheets careful as she can. Across the hall, Gram's door is shut and the space at the bottom is dark.

Gram, Marjorie whispers, to see.

Gram, are you good?

Marjorie does not hear Gram's loud sleeping or the quiet sounds of the television. She hears just the nothing, and so she wants to see.

Louder, now, from across the small hall, Marjorie says it again.

Gram are you good?

Fine, Margie, Gram says.

Sleeping, Gram says.

Okay, Gram, Marjorie says. Goodnight.

Goodnight, Margie.

Better get that out of here, Margie.

No good holding on to it.

Marjorie says nothing, stands in the doorway and waits, tries to catch up with her wind and the quick of her heart. But nothing. Gram must have nothing more to say about it. Gram must be gone, asleep.

Goodnight, Gram, Marjorie says.

She shuts the door and turns on Ma's bare-bulb light. The room is the same, but clean, but white-lit, but Marjorie's room, now. Marjorie reaches inside her shirt and unhooks her bra. She moves her self in waves to let her self out, to get free of this painful thing that holds. Marjorie sits down into the Ma-worn shape of the bed beside the cardboard box of Ma but this room looks too naked, too bright. She reaches for the switch and sits in the dark.

This is a room that is better in the dark. More Marjorie's, in the dark.

She taps her fingers on the top of the box and whispers, Ma.

Ma.

Marjorie taps, taps, taps and says, Ma, Ma, Ma, each time her fingers touch the rough brown box.

Marjorie does not know what People do. What she should do. Marjorie did not make a promise to Gram. Marjorie just listened, Marjorie just heard.

In the dark in her mind she sees Dr. Goodwin in his nice red tie and his black pointed shining shoes and she tries to think of what he might tell her to do.

How do you feel, Marjorie?

Talk about what you are feeling, Marjorie.

Feel, feeling, Dr. Goodwin and his feeling. Marjorie walks slowly through her departments, through her main departments, through the places in her self where she can go, where she can see and know and ask.

Fine. Marjorie feels fine. Marjorie feels like Marjorie. Usual. Not special. Not not special.

Fine. Marjorie has got this box of Ma to figure out, but this box does not make Marjorie feel any one way or another. People dying, People's bodies burned up into People dust, this does not make Marjorie feel good and it does not make Marjorie feel bad. A little body gone before it had a chance to become People, a little almost-there body, maybe that is something to feel bad about. But Ma had a long enough life. Ma had her chance and her cigarettes and her Him and Ma did all the things Ma did.

This thinking is not telling Marjorie what she should do.

36

Well, Ma, Marjorie, soft as she can, says.

What do I do with you now?

In the dark, in the quiet, Marjorie uses her finger to make the shapes of Ma on the cardboard.

M-A.

Marjorie likes the feel of the box beneath her fingertip. She rubs her hand gentle against the surface and she keeps going, keeps making the shapes of names, all of the names.

G-R-A-M.

M-A-R-J-O-R-I-E.

L-U-C-Y.

Dr. Goodwin might not like that she has shaped Lucy's name so she rubs hard against the cardboard to erase the lines that were never really there. Or maybe he would not mind. Marjorie never knows what is going to be right and what is going to be wrong about her and Lucy.

Some days it is, Let go, Marjorie, let go.

And some days it is, Feel, Marjorie, you need to feel.

Marjorie does not know what is good and what is bad when it comes to Lucy. That department is dark and she does not like to go there and some days Dr. Goodwin wants her going there and some days Dr. Goodwin wants her to let that department go.

Okay, Dr. Goodwin. Okay. But Marjorie likes the rough feel of the cardboard under her finger and no one is here to know what she will let go. No one but Marjorie knows what the feeling is.

L-U-C-Y.

Marjorie likes the shapes there, even if the name is just felt with her fingers, even if the name is not real, is just hers, is just how she says it inside.

M-A-R-J-O-R-I-E.

G-R-A-M.

L-U-C-Y.

M-A.

No other names to make but these. Again and again, in the dark, on the box.

Dr. Goodwin would say, What about your father?

No, Marjorie would say.

Dr. Goodwin would say, Your step-father?

No, Marjorie would say.

No, Dr. Goodwin.

Sitting on the bed with this box heavy with Ma is making Marjorie walk down the aisles of these departments where she does not want to be. Thinking about things she does not need to think about. Marjorie shuts her eyes and puts Dr. Goodwin away. He is one of the good People but sometimes Dr. Goodwin says words about her that Marjorie does not want to hear. Sometimes he tries to make her go to departments in her self where she does not want to go.

No father, no step-father, Marjorie would say. Nobody but Him and He is just a nobody.

Nobody. No body. No.

Marjorie moves her fingers in lines and loops over the top of the box. She closes her eyes and makes the shape of the names of who is here, of who is not.

L-U-C-Y.

M-A.

M-A-R-J-O-R-I-E.

G-R-A-M.

Marjorie holds the box of Ma until the pains rise up in her knees, until both legs tingle, until she cannot feel the bottom of her self at all. She sits and touches the top and bottom and sides of the cardboard box. Still is not sure what to do with Ma. Should she get rid of Ma, like Gram said? Or keep Ma here, in her room, in her bed, here, beside Marjorie, where Marjorie is now?

No. Marjorie does not want to share this bed with the rest of Ma.

Marjorie puts the box of Ma back on the bed and bends one leg, slow, and her other leg, slow. Moves her wind in and down and deep into the places where the pains are, then puts her feet soft on the floor. She picks up the box and leans over and puts the box on the floor and slides the bits-of-Ma box as far under the bed as she can.

There. Done. Ma in a place, for now.

Marjorie puts her legs back up on the bed and leans soft against the headboard. Feels light and not so warm now with that heavy box gone under. She feels good, for now, for finding a place. Feels her body big and sinking into the soft-bed shape of Ma. Marjorie does only what she wants to do. She goes only where she wants to go. Her self belongs only to her. She cannot promise. Marjorie picks up pieces of her body and touches only what she wants to touch. In the dark, in the quiet, on the soft of her skin, on the cool clean of the sheets, with her finger, she keeps going.

M-A-R-J-O-R-I-E.

M-A-R-J-O-R-I-E.

L-U-C-Y.

12. MARGIE

And then, sometimes, less than sometimes, on a very, very not-usual day, Ma came home quiet and alone. Ma came home white-dusted all over and she hung her black coat up on the hook beside the door and Margie would not need to look for the shapes of Ma white on the dark fabric because there Ma would be. Sitting with them in the living room. Not just the shape of Ma, but Ma, big Ma, worn out, quiet, warm Ma sat on the brown sofa beside Gram's chair, above where Margie lay long and rolling on the red living-room rug, and together, all together, they watched the television.

Ma sat slumped back against the sofa and she watched the stories with Gram and Margie lay below her and watched the shape of her ma sleepy in the shifting television light.

Sometimes, in one of those once-or-twice moments that later feel like always, Ma might say, Let's see if there are any fish on tonight.

And Gram would nod and use her clicker to move through the bright channels of the television until she found some fish.

It happened that all they could find were the fishing shows, the ones with the big dark green lakes that stretched out forever around the quiet men who sat back and held their fishing poles still and watched, and watched, and watched until the moment when the fishing pole jerked and the men pulled back and the fish appeared. These fish were always big and dripping and dark green like the lake. Soaking up light like the lake. Out of water, the fish opened and closed the big slick circles of their mouths, stared out long and wild from their unblinking eyes. Gram watched, quiet, from the soft of her chair. Ma watched, body limp, relaxed, there on the sofa and almost not. And Margie, from below, watched, her small body rigid against the living room rug. Margie watched the light of the television glow bright and dark as the upside-down men held the big fish tight, as they reached their blackened fingers inside the mouths of the fish and gently pulled out the shining silver hooks. Again and again the big men held the fish and freed the fish and released the fish and flung their poles back out toward the big body of the lake and waited.

Just awful, Ma said.

What they do to those animals.

This was the time or two that we might call sometimes, these very not-usual days when Ma and Gram and Margie watched the fish pulled one after another from the dark green gape of a lake. This would do. These lake-bound caught-

and-released fish were better than nothing, but these were not the fish that Ma wanted.

The fish that Ma wanted Gram to find inside the low sounds and glowing light of the television were the underwater fish. The real fish. Sea fish. The swimming free fish. The clear-blue-sky blue of the television underwater, not the green under of the lake but the deep bubbling blue of the under of the sea. On these un, un, unusual days when Ma came home and sat quiet and white on the sofa, this unending underwater was what she wanted to see. The slow, silent moving through the sea, sunlight stabbing through in circles, in bright lines from above. Ma wanted to see the fish that lived down there, the limitless little orange ones moving as one, the round purple fish with red lips, the green fish, the square fish, the blind white fish and the big gray sharks cutting silently through the water.

Margie, Ma might say.

On a very, very not usual day, when the light from the living room windows had left and the room moved with the blue and the white and the purple and yellow and green and blue, blue, blue and silver of the television underwater, Ma might say, Margie.

Margie, get up here.

Margie, mouth sucking slowly on cracker or gummy bear or pop tart or chip, looked out from her place on the living room rug, out at the fish making shapes on the television, up at Ma there, above her, on the sofa.

Stupid Margie, Ma said.

Stupid.

And Ma would reach down and put her two hands beneath Margie's two soft shoulders and Margie would stop chewing and stiffen, would kick her heavy legs and do her best to make her body do what Ma wanted. Together, Ma pulling and Margie trying to push, Ma and Margie lifted little Margie up and off the rug, onto the sofa. And together, all together, sitting together in the deep sea light of the television, in the flashes of red and pink and orange and gold, Gram and Ma and Margie would watch the fish and feel the quiet weight of the water.

Heart, Margie said.

Fish, Ma said.

Woof, Margie said.

No, Margie. My own stupid fault. Fish. Fish.

Ma.

Fish. Stupid, stupid Margie. Ma don't swim. Fish. Say, fish.

Heart.

No, Margie, Ma said.

Ma looked at Margie and Ma picked up Margie's small hand in her big, boiled hand and Ma moved Margie's hand against Margie's round chest and Ma said, Heart.

Here is your heart, Margie.

Ma held Margie's arm and pounded Margie's hand against her chest.

Heart. That's your heart, in there.

Ma held Margie's arm out toward the television where a fat green fish floated through long brown arms of seaweed waving in sunlight.

Fish. Out there, fish.

Ma let go of Margie's arm and Margie put her hand back to her chest. Back to where she could feel herself warm and beating.

Ma watched. Not the fish, not the television, not Gram or the potato chips. Ma watched Margie.

What's that?

Heart, Margie said.

Good, Ma said. Not so stupid.

Ma put her fingers in Margie's hair and she rubbed Margie's skin and she said, Head.

Head, Margie said, and she tried to touch up on top of her, up where Ma's hand was.

Yeah, head. Good.

Ma touched her hand to the soft circle of Margie's middle and she said, Belly.
Belly.

Ma moved her hands back to rest on her own belly and Margie moved to sit closer to Ma. Margie put her hands up to her head and waited for Ma to say something, but Ma was back to the television, back to the fish. Ma, there and gone, gone and there.

Heart, Margie said.

Margie pounded her small thick palms against her belly and said, Head.

Belly, Margie said.

Heart.

Head.

Quiet, Margie, Ma said.

Heart.

Belly.

Ma looked down at Margie, two hands spread out against her chest, and said, Shutup, Margie. Quiet.

Head.

That ain't your head, Margie. Stupid Margie. That ain't your head you got. Those are your thingies.

Thingies, Ma said, and Ma laughed, a little.

Margie, can you say, thingies?

Big baby thingies.

Heart, Margie said.

Quit it, Margie.

Quiet.

I need it quiet.

I'm trying to hear the fish.

13. MARJORIE

Hello.

The workers work. Taking the old time down and putting the new time up. Christmas is over so the smell of Christmas trees and chocolate coins wrapped in gold foil and boxes of mixes to make gingerbread houses are long gone. New Year is not much of a time in the Store so the streamers and shining paper hats were here and not here so fast Marjorie hardly noticed them. Time in the Store passes in candy, in plastic, in things to show the People that time is going and going. Valentine's Day is next in the line of special days so today the workers are pushing around carts of soft red stuffed smiling bears and stacking heart-shaped boxes of chocolates on the shelves behind where Marjorie stands.

The entrance, the place where time is sure and stopped and known in things.

Today Marjorie is tired. Of time. Of things. Nights and nights of that soft bed, that feel of the box of Ma below, and right now standing here in front of the door Marjorie is having trouble keeping her smile a smile. Outside it is snowing so the People are few. Big fat blown-up pieces of snow fall down and blow around in the cold wind. Marjorie opens her eyes and closes her eyes. Watches the snow, the door. The bright red shine of foil-wrapped hearts lit up by white Store light. When she feels alone enough, when there are no People here to see, Marjorie holds her hand over her mouth and yawns, long, slow, smells the sour smell of her inside.

Steve keeps coming around. Steve's job. What Steve is. A come-arounder. Commander, Steve likes to call himself. When Steve comes around, Marjorie tries her best to keep her shoulders up and head high and Steve nods and Steve smiles and Marjorie smiles and Steve puts his hand to his forehead and kicks his big leg against his big leg, puts his big legs together, pushes his big belly out and waves his arm at her and Marjorie smiles.

Commander Steve, here, Steve says.

Hello, Steve, Marjorie says.

This is my ship and I expect my crew to be better than the best, Steve says.

Stand up straight, Marjorie.

Straighter.

Shoulders back and eyes out.

Eyes open, Marjorie! Eyes open. You have to know your enemy.

Back straight.

Like this. Tall. Proud.

Who is your enemy, Marjorie? Who?

Marjorie nods and smiles and steps one step backward, tries to get away from Steve's touching hand. But Steve is big-arm-out reaching for her. Marjorie can feel his fingers holding onto her back below her bra, to her soft sides that sit big beside her belly. Steve steps closer, squeezes. Steve and his games. Steve and his pretending. Extra-extra-large Steve and his always touching.

I asked you a question, soldier, and I expect an answer.

You look at your commander when you talk.

Who is your enemy, Marjorie?

Marjorie holds onto her wind and looks in the direction of Steve. She is tired and does not want to play the game. Here come the red-wrapped chocolate tulips on green plastic stems. Here comes Valentine's Day. Here come the People, passing by, all the faces same as all the faces. Marjorie wants to stand and watch the snow whiten the world, to feel the slow stacking of time on the shelves at her back, to say Hello to the People.

But Steve, here, holding on.

No enemy, Steve, Marjorie says.

There is! Yes there is! There is always an enemy, Marjorie.

Steve lets go and Marjorie breathes bigger, better breaths up and down and through her self. Steve lets go because he is using his big fingers on both hands to make the shape of two guns and Steve is pretending to shoot at her and shoot at the door and the People and the registers beeping behind where they stand.

Steve says, Aim and fire.

Aim and fire, Marjorie. Shoot to kill.

They're all your enemies, Marjorie. You want them all.

Kill them with kindness, Marjorie.

Get them in and get them happy and get those rich pricks spending.

Marjorie is not listening to Steve's words. She is watching the sweat coming up on his forehead. The thick black hairs above his lips and the big white bump that sticks out of his neck when he yells like this. Steve is not a real soldier. Marjorie has seen real soldiers in the Club and she knows that real soldiers are eyes-down quiet and polite. Steve is no commander. But here is Steve, wearing his yellow MANAGER pin.

Okay, Marjorie, Steve says, the sweat falling down now, darkening his shirt. I got better things to do.

Okay, Steve.

Make me proud, soldier, Steve says, and one more time he squeezes.

Marjorie nods and steps one step away. She holds her self very still until Steve turns and walks his slow, aisle-wide walk out into the deep of the Store. Marjorie's skin still feels the touch of Steve's skin but Marjorie has her ways of being. Marjorie has her things she does.

There is the Hello. When Marjorie is tired, like today, Marjorie is tired, she says only, Hello.

Hello.

Hello.

Hello.

Marjorie, taking care of the People. Taking care of her self.

And this. What Marjorie does to clean the stain of Steve on her skin. When the door is quiet and Marjorie closes her eyes and is alone inside the dark of her departments, she does this:

Marjorie starts up at the top of the inside of her head, up where it is dark, red, soft, warm. She holds her self shut tight and feels her whole head filling with water until there is so much water her head cannot hold all of it and the water pours down from her head through her neck and into the big dark empty rest of her. The water is warm and smells good. Maybe like salt, like sea. Marjorie has never smelled the sea but maybe this is the smell. Of clean and strong. Or the brook. The water Marjorie pours down through her departments and into her self is clear and shining, the water of the brook moving slowly in sunlight.

Marjorie feels all this water filling her and washing her, touching all her inside parts, stinging the underside of her skin just a little, just enough so that she feels a tingle all over, so that she feels clean and washed and light. Her bones float here in the water and with her eyes closed, with her whole self down deep in her warm wet inside, Marjorie feels so good and free she feels as if she can almost swim away somewhere. As if her big outside body has stopped holding her here to the ground and instead has let her go. Out of her skin, her body box, her holdings, out of the bright white lights of the Store.

Marjorie floats. Stands in her place and goes away, weightless, out. Out to the hills, out to that place where Lucy must be. Lucy in a little yellow dress in a whole warm body. Lucy out there, small, Lucy so small and Marjorie so wide and light and open.

Go, Marjorie. Let go.

Marjorie opens her eyes and blinks away the too-bright of the lights. Hears Dr. Goodwin's voice so clear it is as if he is here with her, in her.

Go where, Dr. Goodwin?

The snow outside blows and blows, blocks Marjorie's view of the hills. Out there is just cold and snow and a circle, a chain of hills. The mountain, gone in the white. A sky, gray and white, same as the ground. Cars covered, sitting cold and colder in the parking lot.

Where is there to let go?

Hello.

Hello.

Oh.

Benjamin.

Benjamin is here. Marjorie smiles and waves her hand at him.

Benjamin is white-flaked and shivering. He is pushing a shopping cart stuffed full of colorful bags of candy hearts. Thick bits of snow catch in Benjamin's hair, sit there, for a second, before disappearing into him.

How's it hanging, Marjorie?

Good.

Glad to hear it. Not so good over here. We got to put out about a million of these fucking heart bags.

Marjorie smiles and stands tall as she can and waits to see what more Benjamin will say.

Anything new with you, Marjorie?

Benjamin holds his arms together against his chest. He likes to stand this way, hugging himself, rocking forward and back on his heels. Marjorie has noticed that Benjamin is always moving, always rocking and spinning and jumping and moving his arms around. Like a kid, like a kid free and kicking on grass in sun in summer.

Oh, no new things, Marjorie says.

Just here, and home, and the Club, Marjorie says.

Yeah, Benjamin says. I hear you. Same old same old. Sunk down in the shit so far we don't even know we're in it.

Marjorie is not sure what Benjamin means so she smiles, so she says, Cold Out There Today.

Fucking freezing, he says. Rode my bike into work today and thought my balls were going to fall right off.

Marjorie feels her face get very hot and red. She understands what Benjamin is saying. Benjamin and his bike and what might fall off is something for Marjorie to think about. Marjorie is listening. Marjorie is not going to ask any questions, but Marjorie is not going to tell Benjamin to stop telling.

Hey, that reminds me of something I saw the other day, Benjamin says. You want to hear about it?

Okay, Marjorie, red-faced, says, and she holds her hands tight at her side and she smiles.

This was on TV I heard this, Benjamin says.

His hands are moving all over, hands rubbing his elbows and arms and scratching his head.

I saw on TV this show about this guy who is a long-distance runner who lives in a house on the beach. Right by the ocean, you know? You know, one of those rich guys with one of those big porches that wrap around the house and look right out into the whole fucking world, you know what I mean?

Marjorie nods and is almost sure that she knows.

Hello, she says.

The door. Even in the good of talking to Benjamin, Marjorie cannot forget her important place here with the sliding door.

Yeah, so, okay, Benjamin says. So this rich fuck is so rich and he has got so much time on his hands out there by the ocean that he starts running. Like, really running. Training for marathons, shit like that. Every day he gets up and he goes and runs on the beach and he runs and runs so much that he gets, like, addicted to it.

Marjorie smiles. Some People pass by, in, out of the cold, and Marjorie says, Hello. And Benjamin keeps on with his story.

The voice on the TV was all, THIS GUY – I forgot this dickhead's name – THIS GUY STARTED RUNNING AND BY THE TIME WINTER CAME HE WAS SO OBSESSED HE COULD NOT STOP. Something like that. Like this guy is actually fucking addicted to running on the beach. Like it's so necessary. To life, or whatever. Even in the rain, even when it started damn snowing. This guy, running.

Marjorie likes the sound of Benjamin's voice. Not deep and scratchy like Mac or wet and spitting like Him or low and kind like Dr. Goodwin. More like gentle and wide. Rolling. Not high and stopping like Steve's. When Benjamin talks his voice gets loud sometimes and soft sometimes and Marjorie likes that she can listen and not wonder too much about what words he is saying. She likes the up and down of Benjamin's sounds and how she feels good listening to him, how she can float her self in whatever he is saying.

Hello.

So the fucking crazy running guy keeps going into November and into December and even into fucking February. By February he is almost going to die he is running so much and it is so cold. And the whole time the TV guy is talking and they just keep showing this guy running next to the water. Big waves and all that. Then they fucking let the guy talk for himself, and you know what he says?

Benjamin is stopped and still and quiet and looking at Marjorie and she sees that he is waiting for her to say something.

Marjorie nods and smiles.

Yeah, so, he looks right at the camera and get this. Right at the camera and this guy has got this crazy face on and all he says is. This is what he says. Get this. In the winter, he says, I started putting seashells on my testicles to keep them warm.

Benjamin's eyes are wide and his mouth is hanging open a little and he has got his hands now up on top of his head and his elbows are out by his ears. He looks so surprised by these words he is saying. So happy. So here and living. Marjorie feels good just looking at Benjamin and watching the bouncing way People can be.

He seems to be waiting for her, again, so Marjorie shakes her head a little and says, Wow.

Wow, she says.

Seriously, Benjamin says. That's what I said. Wow. Holy fucking shit. Here's this asshole crazy rich guy and he has nothing better to do with his time than run around with god-damn seashells stuck to his nuts. Seashells! Fucking insane. Get that guy a job!

The door opens and a lady walks in with two little boys and one little girl and all three in the same blue sweater. The lady is trying to hold all six small, reaching hands and all of them are red-faced, talking, not looking, smiling.

Hello.

Right, Marjorie, Benjamin says. A job, right? Get that guy a job.

Right, Marjorie says.

The People pass by and Benjamin touches his hand to Marjorie's shoulder. Marjorie would like to know if Benjamin can feel her bra splitting her skin beneath her t-shirt. She would like to know if how Benjamin's touch feels to her is how the touch of her feels to Benjamin.

You watch TV much, Marjorie?

Oh yes. Some.

What shows do you watch?

Me, I watch the Stories. Commercials. The underwater shows.

Yeah, good. Good shit.

A worker walks up to Benjamin's cart and pushes it away, toward the growing red and pink and white of the display. Benjamin smiles and waves at the worker and takes his hand away from Marjorie and stretches his arms up high over his head. His shoulders stick out like wings against the tight thin blue of his t-shirt. If not for the little blonde hairs all over his chin and neck, Marjorie thinks Benjamin might look a little like a girl. Like a tall breakable girl you want to hold close to you and take good care of.

Man, Benjamin says. Shit.

Marjorie nods.

All this Valentine's bullshit makes me sick. Love and all that. Not the love, you know. Love is love, right? But all this plastic and shit. Love.

Right, Marjorie says.

You got somebody, Marjorie? A boyfriend?

Marjorie feels her face heat up heart-hot, feels her head big and beating. Hears her blood moving around inside. She squeezes her hands shut into fists. Marjorie believes in Benjamin. She believes that he is good and not as important about private things as she is.

No boyfriend, Benjamin.

Hey. Sorry, Marjorie. I didn't mean to embarrass you.

Marjorie knows her self. She knows that she will stay heated up for a while now. That her wind will need some time to slow down. Marjorie knows she has this big skin that blows up red sometimes when she sees things or People say things. Just her way. Just what happens inside Marjorie.

That's okay, Benjamin.

Okay, well, me neither. No Valentine. Stupid fucking holiday, anyway. Not even a holiday. Just another way to make us feel bad and get our money, right?

Marjorie nods and smiles.

Hello, she says.

Hello.

Okay, Marjorie, Benjamin says. Those piece-of-shit chocolate hearts aren't going to walk themselves off the truck. Don't want Steve the Sleaze coming around yelling.

Okay, Benjamin, Marjorie says. Good seeing you.

You too, you too. You doing okay here, Marjorie? Nobody bothering you?

Good, Benjamin.

Okay, he says. Don't work too hard. Remember there are all these assholes running around out there with nothing better to do than stick seashells on their balls. You don't do any more than you need to do.

You too, Benjamin, Marjorie says.

Say Hello. Watch the slide of the door, feel the cold meet the hot. Wait for her skin to fall back into the shape of her skin, for her wind to blow more slowly through. This is what Marjorie needs to do.

Benjamin waits for some People to come in and when they do and the door slides open he jumps through. Exiting through the entrance. Benjamin, his way, his cinnamon skin touched all over with snow. He jumps the wrong way through and turns and smiles and waves to her as he walks out and away. Benjamin and his bad words, his questions. Her friend. Marjorie waves and stands up straight. Still tired, still blown-up beating hard, but good, but fine, but more awake, now, more here, now. More outside, out of the departments that want to hold her in. Away from Steve, for now, the apartment, for now, away from what to do with Ma.

Marjorie, standing, smiles.

Hello, she says.

Welcome.

14. MARGIE

Gram called them her ups and downs.

I've got my ups and downs, Margie, she said.

Today I'm up, up, up.

Or, more usual, Today I'm down.

My pains, Margie. My heart. Keeps me down.

Margie looked for Gram's ups and downs in the shape of her shoulders and how she held her head. When Gram sat up straight in her chair, when she woke up early and stood in front of the bathroom mirror putting red on her lips and black on her eyelashes, Margie knew the day had started up.

Putting on my face, Gram said.

Get in here Margie and watch me put on my face.

Up days, Gram did not mind Margie around. Gram would put her nose close to the glass of the mirror and brush her skin with skin-colored powder, draw on her skin with pink and brown pencils, dust her skin with blue, green, gold shadows.

Up days, Gram talked.

Come on, Margie, Gram said one up day as she finished brushing her blush around her cheekbones. Your turn. Let's put on your face.

Margie touched her every-day-fatter finger to her face.

My face is on, Gram.

Your better face, Margie. Your best face. Get in here and give me your face, I'm going to show you how pretty you can be.

Margie did not want Gram to draw on her face. Margie liked her face, the soft of it, the skin smell of it. But Margie did not want to make Gram angry. Margie could see how high up Gram was, and Margie wanted Gram to stay that way. Up, tall, talking, happy.

Margie gave Gram her face. She stood in front of the bathroom mirror and closed her eyes and let Gram poke and tickle and rub her skin with brushes and pencils and things Margie had no words for.

Up days, Gram wanted to talk.

I worry about your ma, Margie. Out at those bars at all hours. With those men. Shooting pool, rough-housing, whatever it is they do. Down at Chick's, that's where she was last night. Chick's, the worst place out of all of them. I know about Chick's. Lord help me, I know about Chick's. Met the man who gave me your ma down at Chick's. Used to be you'd pay a couple of bucks and they'd let you drink all you want. Long as you want. All night. I didn't know any better, then. Used to be we'd drink and push all the tables away and dance. I tell you this because I know you won't tell anyone, Margie. We'd dance in a way that wasn't even dancing. Not the steps. Just pushing up against each other. I'm saying this now because I know you can't understand. We'd call that dancing, that rubbing and touching. Bad place, Chick's. You're too young to hear about it I guess. But that's where your ma's been and I'm telling you it's no good down there, Margie. I'm telling you because who else would I tell?

Margie kept her eyes closed and tried to stay still under the pull and push of Gram's fingers. The brush bristles tickled her cheeks and more than anything she wanted to rub her eyes, to wipe away the heavy coat of whatever it was Gram had painted on them. But Margie liked the rocking sounds of up-day

Gram talking and talking. Margie listened to Gram's voice and the only words she heard were hers, her name. When Gram's voice rose up the familiar mountain of that Ma-, Margie heard. Sometimes she stopped there, Ma, Ma, your ma, and sometimes Gram kept going, rising up to Mar- and then falling down softly into the valley of the rest of her, into the -gie, into the whole of Margie. This, her, Margie heard. Margie understood.

Your ma means to do good, Margie. I think so. I don't think she means to be as bad as she is. She's just tired. She needs to meet a good man. Needs somebody to take care of her. Because Lord knows I haven't done a good job of it. Our Lord would be a good man for your ma to take in but I know she's beyond that. And her father, she never even had a chance at him. God, he don't even know he's got a kid. Truth is those were my most down-days, Margie. I'm telling you because you're here. My brother, Frank, had gone off and gotten killed in the war. Bet you've never even heard of him, of Frank, Margie. Your uncle Frank. Would have been. Brown eyes like you but not soft and round like you. Tall, strong, always smiling, Frank. First day out, never had a chance. Blown up, killed. My stepfather drunk all the time and my mother sent off to the looney bin. I thought they were going to put me in there with her. Down-days back then, all of them, and it got so I had to be with people. Had to get out of the house, away from my stepfather, away from my brother. They sent him home to us in a box. The blown-up bits of him. I wouldn't say this to you if I thought you understood, Margie. Nobody ever opened the box, far as I knew. But my stepfather, there, in the apartment, and my brother there, in that box. I had to get away from it. Had to get out. So Chick's it was, days and nights I'd be there. Even asked Charlie for a little job washing dishes, picking up the place, whatever he needed.

Gram was still brushing dust on Margie's skin and using her fingers to rub around her eyes and chin and cheeks. Margie squeezed her eyes shut tight until stars appeared in her dark, tight and tighter so that she could watch the behind-lid fireworks bloom and burst to the sound of Gram's voice.

Whatever he needed, I said that. But Charlie said he didn't need anything from a drunk like me and so I just did what I did. All that time at Chick's, just to be with the people, and that's how I met your ma's father. That's how your ma came to be. Soon as I knew, I stopped going. Stayed home all the time. Stopped drinking. I did. Took it bad from my stepfather. But I didn't want him to know, the one who did it to me. I wanted to keep your ma as my own, my secret.

Make a kiss face, Margie.

No, not like that. No, keep your eyes closed.

Make a fish face, Margie. Fish face, make your lips like a fish.

Good, like that. Just going to get some color onto you.

Okay, Margie, now for your hair. Just keep those eyes closed. I want you to be a surprise.

Margie kept her eyes closed. She felt Gram's fingers on her scalp, moving out into the tangles, pulling at the strands, using the hard teeth of a comb to straighten out the knots and twists of Margie's hair.

Down, down-days then, Margie. But I learned. I saw how to be better. My stepfather sent me away to have my baby with the nuns. It was like that, back then. They wanted to take my baby away from me but I was on my best behavior. I learned. I stayed out there while your ma was real young. Big brick house, had my own bedroom, lots of old ladies around to take care of your ma and me. Lots of taking care of there. But then my stepfather died in an accident down at the quarry and I had to go back to take care of the house and things. And when I got back there, Frank was gone. The box of him, just gone. My stepfather must have done something with him but I never knew what. And I never spoke a word of it to my mother. My mother came home after a while, but she never got better. Just sat in her chair, waiting to go.

Gram sprayed something out into the air around Margie's hair and Margie breathed in the stinging stuff, the stuff that smelled like Ma, sweet, choking, like how the skin of Ma's friends could smell, and Margie coughed and coughed.

Keep your mouth shut, Margie. Almost done. Just going to set your hair now.

Margie kept her mouth shut and eyes shut and listened to the words flowing fast from Gram's mouth, the steady stream of sound that meant the day was still up, that meant that things were good, that they were together.

My mother didn't last long. She didn't want to live. I won't tell you how she died. Just in case you're getting any of this, Margie. Though I think you're not. Did it to herself, that's all I'll say. And for the best, I think. My mother didn't want to live without her Frank. Never even looked at your ma, her grandchild. But we got by. Got kicked out of the house, but we made it through. With the help of God, we got by. No more men for me. I was good. But your ma. I did my best, did as good as I could manage. But your ma, out at Chick's every night. All those men. She'll learn, Margie. She'll learn like I learned like you'll learn. Men are no good. Women aren't much better but men are just no good at all. Roaches, snakes, all of them. Devils. Just our Lord, only our Lord is worth a second look, Margie. Otherwise better to keep to yourself. Like you, Margie.

Quiet. A good girl. Too fat and this hair can't be helped but I think you are good. I think you'll turn out good.

Open your eyes and see what we've done.

Gram shook Margie's shoulder.

Open your eyes, Margie. Take a look.

Margie slowly let her face float away from the tight places where she had been holding herself shut. She opened her mouth a little and licked her lips which tasted bitter, like tin can, like left-out cheese sandwiches.

Don't make that face, Margie. Keep your tongue in and open your eyes. If you're going to be a woman you're going to have to learn to hide all the little sufferings that make us beautiful.

Margie opened her eyes. She looked at herself in the mirror and saw not herself, but all the colors and lines and powder that Gram had put there. Margie stared at herself in the mirror and she saw her, Gram. Little Gram. Margie looked at her face, at the bright red lips and the big pink cheeks and the purple and green and gold painted around her eyes and at her eyelashes, thick and black, and she saw Gram's face on top of her face. She saw them there together, in her, Gram's painted face put onto Margie's plain face.

You got your face on me, Margie said.

I put your face on you. Someday you'll learn to do it too. You look like a woman like that, Margie. Don't rub it. Don't touch your eyes. Keep your hands off your face and you can look like that all day if you want to.

Margie did not want to, but she did not want to ruin Gram's up. She did her best not to touch. Margie kept her fists squeezed tight at her sides and she spent the day wearing a face that felt heavy and thick and not like her own.

We saw or did not see the child playing quietly on the uneven front steps. The little girl painted into womanhood. We drove by, walked by, looked out the window, looked away. We saw and said nothing. We never even noticed.

Later, Gram sank deep into the down of her day. That was how it was. Days went up and down and up and down and there was no way to know if an up day would stay up or how long the down might last. Later, Margie sat eating saltines and butter at the kitchen table, and Gram walked shoulders-slumped into the room, stopped, and stared at Margie there, at how her cheeks glowed pink and her eyes sparkled purple in the white light.

Your face, Gram said.

Gram, up-day-turned-down Gram, had trouble saying even this.

Margie touched a buttery finger to her face. She smiled and said nothing. Margie could see that the day had turned upside-down. Even from her far-away place of however little she had lived, Margie could see that Gram's day had gone down.

Wash your face, Margie, Gram said.

You look like a little tramp.

Margie smiled and finished eating her stack of crackers. She nodded. To no one. Margie's face felt heavy and the powder and paint burned a little in places. She wanted to wash the weighing-down layer of Gram away. Margie wanted her own face back, her known face. She wanted Gram to come back up, for Gram to swim back up and through to the surface of Gram, to come sit with her and talk to her.

We wanted that too, in a vague way. For everyone to be good and all things to seem right. But sometimes the words we try to say to ourselves come out only as sounds. Sometimes no one is there to hear us make them, and sometimes we open up and nothing comes out at all.

15. MARJORIE

The Club is here in the middle of the long cold walk from the apartment to the Store, a good place to stop on a snowy walk from the Store to the apartment. Somewhere in the center of Marjorie's circle.

Marjorie is a walker. She holds her big purple coat close to her body and she blows her breath into the coat so that the air on her face is warm, is her own. Marjorie does not ride in cars. Marjorie does not ride in buses. Or airplanes. Marjorie goes where she goes in the big safe ship of her self.

The sidewalks are thick gray ice and old black snow. Marjorie is careful, is putting one foot down and one foot down, is moving her wind with her feet and keeping her eyes on her walking. Now is the time for the sun to set, and the sky all around is cold oatmeal sprinkled here and over there by bright holes of orange and red. Streaks of sun going down showing through. Streetlights buzzing above, turning on, helping Marjorie make her way.

Here is the Club.

Dark blue letters on a big white sign.

The Benevolent and Protective Order of Elks.

Halfway home, a good place for a stop, a rest, a warming.

Inside the Club is dark as usual, quiet as usual. No birthday party here tonight, as usual. Marjorie walks through the door and feels so heated-up from her walking and from the hot air blowing through the Club that right away she unzips her coat and gets her arms out of there. In the doorway, before she has even stepped all the way in, Marjorie is releasing. Getting rid of her top layer, letting her self out into the air.

Clothes are sometimes problems for Marjorie. She does not like to feel held in or smothered. Marjorie likes to feel as free as she can feel. And it is not that she does not want to wear clothes. Clothes are important. Because her bare skin, what she has got inside, is not for People to see. What Marjorie wants are clothes like pajamas. Clothes that are loose and comfortable and out-of-the-way. Covering and letting out. She does not like zippers and buttons and things that hold.

This is important. To know her self. To know what she likes and what she does not like. How to go about the living of her life.

Marjorie carries her coat into the Club with her and she wipes a little bit of sweat from her forehead. Her wind is fast and not so deep so she blows in as much air as she can and waits to slow and feel more like Marjorie.

Empty. The Club is very quiet and almost empty. As usual. Usual for the times when Marjorie stops in for a rest. Just men. A few men sitting heads-down at the bar, drinking bottles of beer and paying attention to their hands, to what is happening inside their heads.

And Suzanne.

Behind the bar is Suzanne and Marjorie feels good to see Suzanne. Not just men. Not just any People. Suzanne. Marjorie inside is still very heated-up from her walk and she can feel that her face is burning red and all the waters of her self are swishing. Waves inside, crashing. Marjorie smiles and looks at Suzanne. Marjorie smells Suzanne, the rose smell of Suzanne. And Suzanne has got her red curly-haired head turned down toward a magazine and Suzanne does not see Marjorie right away.

Suzanne is perfect.

Suzanne is Marjorie if Marjorie were Suzanne.

Marjorie sits down in front of and a little to the side of Suzanne and works hard on bringing her fast breath back to normal. On quieting her big loud heart.

Suzanne's shoulders are smaller than Marjorie's but not small. They are high and round in a good way. Skin swirling, skin like almond cake. Suzanne is big round circles all over. Skin showing all over. Shining and chewing gum. Good, beautiful, here.

Suzanne is down deep in that magazine and so Marjorie waits to speak. Marjorie looks at Suzanne looking at the pictures in her magazine and Marjorie tries to think what Suzanne is thinking. Marjorie would like to know about Suzanne.

About where she lives and what she does with her boyfriend. Where she was before and how things are with her when she is not at the Club. Suzanne must have a boyfriend. Or once, or before, Suzanne must have had a boyfriend. Marjorie knows this because Marjorie knows Tony. Little beautiful little-boned Tony who comes around the Club sometimes when Suzanne's baby-sitters can't make it. Suzanne's son, her other one of her, her baby, her little boy with little shoulders and little teeth and soft-looking hair like his ma. Perfect skin, like his ma, a smile like his ma. Times when Marjorie has seen Tony she has seen Suzanne, there, inside him, Suzanne painted all over his little body. Like Lucy. Like the feel of Lucy. Marjorie cannot look at Tony without seeing Suzanne or Suzanne without seeing Tony without seeing Lucy.

But these are secret seeings. Suzanne is a friend. A new friend, but a friend. And even friends don't say everything. Marjorie is sure that she and Suzanne are the same in some ways and so she always feels good to see her and talk with her. Suzanne, another kind of Marjorie.

Hello, Suzanne, Marjorie says once her wind is back, once the waiting seems long enough.

Suzanne looks up slowly from her magazine and smiles at Marjorie. A real smile. Not a Store smile or a Club smile. An outside smile, an inside smile.

Suzanne's eyes are so green that Marjorie can see them in full color even in here in this dark Club in the low orange glow of this bar light. Her hair, red, brown, gold, glows, too. And Suzanne has almost perfect teeth. Long, straight, white. Suzanne's nose is just the right amount of pointy and her ears are round the way ears should be. Television ears, ears like Marjorie sees in commercials. Suzanne is more beautiful than the ladies in the Stories. Marjorie sees all the People every day and Marjorie knows her People and Marjorie is sure that Suzanne is one of the best-made People in the world. Not too big and not too small and kind and smiling too.

Hi, Marjorie, Suzanne says. Sorry I missed you the other day. Mac told me you were asking about me.

Was just wondering, Marjorie says. Where you were.

Oh, yeah, home. Tony had some stomach bug. Had to take him to the doctor because he couldn't stop throwing up all over the place. But he's fine now, he's good.

Marjorie nods and smiles.

That is good, she says. Good.

Suzanne picks up a tall glass and says, You want your Shirley Temple like usual, Marjorie?

Marjorie's inside slows down fast and she blinks her eyes and she thinks. This is just a rest. A stop. A short time of sitting and not walking. Suzanne knows her usual. Her Shirley Temple. But Suzanne does not know her plan. Her need to rest. Marjorie is not sure that her Shirley Temple has a place here, with her, today.

But Suzanne is holding a glass, and Suzanne needs an answer.

Suzanne remembers what Marjorie likes.

Suzanne, so good.

Oh, Marjorie says. No. Thank you, Suzanne. I didn't plan on drinking a Shirley Temple tonight.

Okay, Suzanne says, and she puts the glass back in its place.

Hey, she says, stepping over to her right, in front of where Marjorie is sitting.

Hey, Suzanne says. I heard your ma died, Marjorie.

Suzanne puts her cold, gentle hand on top of Marjorie's warm, sweating one. Marjorie looks down at the hand touching hand and cannot think of what to say. Suzanne's skin is soft and she wonders how her skin feels to Suzanne. Marjorie hears these words Suzanne has said in her self as shouts as a stream, a scream that echoes in the empty aisles of the department she is making for what Ma is now. Inside, the words, sting. Outside, Suzanne's skin so soft and kind to Marjorie. Touching, holding on.

I heard your ma died, Marjorie.

Marjorie listens close to the words leaking down into her inside and she cannot feel what she is feeling about them. Died. Your ma died. Yes. The words are right and true and said. Died. Gone. Body sand in a box. No Ma no more.

Suzanne squeezes her hand and says, I was sorry to hear about your ma.

Marjorie stares at Suzanne's hand covering up her own and she says, Thank you Suzanne.

That is good of you to say, Suzanne.

Suzanne says, You've had a hard time of it, haven't you?

A hard time of it. Suzanne knows. Or, Suzanne does not know. Suzanne, someone to tell. About before. A hard time of it. Marjorie's secrets roll up against her skin, make her heart beat harder. Maybe Suzanne is someone to talk to but Marjorie will have to wait for the dark shapes inside to shape into words.

Suzanne takes her hand away from Marjorie's hand.

Not so bad, Marjorie says.

Marjorie's hand feels woken up and tingling cold in the places where Suzanne's skin touched down. She keeps her eyes there, on her skin, to feel Suzanne more, to remember where her fingers were.

Well, Suzanne says. I know you don't like talking, Marjorie. But I am sorry about your ma. Was there a service?

Marjorie brings her hand up to her face and presses her skin against the places that still feel like Suzanne. Not a talker, no. Things she would like to tell, yes, maybe. Maybe to Suzanne. But no, Marjorie is not a talker. She leans her cheek against the back of her hand and rolls her face just a little to wake her self up, to feel something different from what is happening inside her mind. The cardboard box pushed under the bed. This figuring out of what People do with a box of Ma burned to dust.

Marjorie smells the smell of Suzanne.

No, Marjorie says. No service.

Suzanne nods and says, Yeah, I know. I know how expensive it all gets. Dying isn't cheap. We didn't have one either, when my ma passed away. Just had her put in the ground and that was that. Alive, my ma was always mean so nobody felt like putting much time or money into her once she was gone, you know?

Marjorie nods and nods her head and rolls her cheek against her hand. Ma. Was Ma mean? Ma was mean. But the problem of Ma was that she let the mean of Him in. Opened the red front door. Ma's mean was different from His mean. Together they could be mean, yes, true, yes, but whatever mean Ma was did not compare with the mean of Him. Dr. Goodwin wants Marjorie to say who is bad and why. But by the time Dr. Goodwin came into it He was long gone and Lucy had come and gone and Ma was shut up in her room watching her no-sound television. What does mean matter once mean has gone away?

Marjorie is not sure if she knows about what Suzanne is saying but because Suzanne is looking at her, because Suzanne is so good, because she wants Suzanne to think that she knows, Marjorie says, I know.

I know, she says.

I know.

A man in a black cap at the end of the bar says, Hey, Sweetie, and Suzanne turns away from Marjorie. He taps his empty beer bottle against the bar to show them all that he is finished and in need of more. More and more and more. So much need to take care of. Suzanne laughs and turns again to Marjorie and winks.

A bunch of talkers, she says. All of them.

Marjorie smiles and watches Suzanne bend down to find a beer for the man. She watches Suzanne open the bottle and use two hands to carry it over to the man and in the light of Suzanne the man's face smoothes and loosens. Suzanne, the helper of the People. A worker, a giver of things, like Marjorie is, like what Marjorie does. Making the People feel wanted, Welcome, entered.

Suzanne puts down a clean napkin for the man and she leans over to him and smiles and Marjorie cannot hear what Suzanne is saying but she is sure that Suzanne is making the man's night into a good night. Even just the smiling, even a minute or two of talking. Sometimes it is good enough to have someone there near you, someone saying words to you, even when there is nothing to say back to them.

Suzanne is busy with the man at the end of the bar and Marjorie does not have a drink to drink so she stands up to put her coat back on to head home. A rest, rested. Suzanne's words swimming around now in her inside waters. Died and Marjorie and Your ma and Sorry and Service and Died. Mean. And mean. Marjorie zips her coat and walks toward the door. Maybe she should stop to wash off her mind. Maybe she should stay longer, here, with the People.

No. Time for Marjorie to go. She is going. Zipped up and held in tight against the cold. Marjorie does not say Goodbye to the People, just pushes her way out the door, going away.

But Suzanne.

The great good of Suzanne.

Suzanne, behind her, yells out, Bye now, Marjorie.

And Marjorie, because she can feel a small part of her self there in the Club, still, with Suzanne, turns and waves her hand.

16. MARGIE

Margie!

Where are you?

Stupid.

Get in here right now.

Where the fuck are you?

Margie was in one of her hidden places. Margie, on her belly, in the dark beneath her side of the bed, was making a world with her yard sale animals. Gifts from Gram, small soft pieces of comfort we had forgotten, given away, sold for next to nothing. The blue stuffed bunny, the favorite. The long orange tiger and the yellow bow-tied bear and the blackened white dog. Margie made worlds with whatever soft things we no longer wanted.

Margie!

You have ten fucking seconds to get your fat butt in here.

Ten.

Nine.

Eight.

Seven.

At six, Margie crawled out from under the bed. Six, her favorite number that year because six was how many years she was, total. More or less. Six or so years of being Margie and already some days she wondered about being something else. One of the big brown frogs sitting just under the surface of the water in the brook. A quiet, blue, mouthless stuffed bunny like her bunny, her best friend, her bunny who got to sleep in bed beside her, beside Gram. Or maybe a silver fish far under the sea, something living somewhere else, a place far away from Apartment #2 at the dead-end end of Summer Street.

Five. Four. Three. Two. One.

Now, Margie.

Margie heard Ma speed up her counting and she ran fast as she could out of her bedroom and down the hall, socks sliding on the slippery wood, landing on her side on the floor beside where Ma stood, angry, in the living room. Ma there, above her, big and swaying, long brown hair hanging, arms covered in dark brown spots, brown bloodshot eyes squinting. White cafeteria worker shirt splattered brown all around. Ma's face, red, spitting, angry.

Gram sat silent in her green chair in the darkening room behind Ma. Gram's eyes down, Gram gone inside the glow of the television.

Ma leaned down and over Margie and pointed at her hard in the chest with a rough finger and a sharp, shiny red fingernail. Margie tried to look, tried to understand Ma's anger, tried to think about what she had done, what had gone wrong, tried to see what was happening inside Ma's sweating, shaking head, but Margie was only Margie, was only something like six, and all that she had really figured out were the right smell of pop tarts perfectly toasted and how breathing hot breaths all over into the blue of her stuffed bunny's fur would warm her at night.

What do you want from me, Margie?

Margie did not understand Ma's question, so she kept quiet, kept still, tried to keep her face from looking too much one way or the other.

What else do you want from me?

I don't want, Ma. Nothing.

What is wrong with you, Margie?

Ma smelled like cigarette smoke and coconuts. We could not expect Margie to know that her ma kept a water bottle filled with coconut rum in her purse.

That sometimes she mixed it with orange juice or grape soda, sometimes she poured it in coffee or just drank it straight. We wouldn't think that Margie would understand how the stuff made Ma's heart beat fast and loud, that this was where some of the sweat and the anger were coming from. Maybe we whispered about how we couldn't believe she had a kid at home. Maybe we worried about her coming to work like that, or maybe we liked the smell of coconut on her and never noticed how her eyes moved so underwater-slow around a room. Maybe we thought she was sexy and maybe we thought she was trash. Whatever we might have been thinking, we never thought about it much. We had our own lives, our own problems, our own drinks to drink and jobs to work, people to fuck. We had too much of our own business to mind to care that there was a Margie out there, on the floor, in the world.

Ma squeezed Margie's shoulders and pulled her up to the full height of Margie.

I asked you, what the hell is wrong with you?

I know you can talk. I hear you in there with those stupid toys. So tell me. What the fuck is wrong with you?

Ma shook Margie and Margie understood that she needed to say something, even if she did not understand. Margie heard the rising of Ma's words and she knew a question had been asked.

I'm not wrong, Margie said. I'm fine. Good.

You're not fine. That's what your teacher said. You know that's where I've been? Down at your school. Two hours I had to take off work. They made me meet with that little bitch teacher of yours, Miss Whatever-Her-Name-Is. The little one who looks like a rat. Wants all this shit from me. And do you know what she said about you?

Margie's teacher was named Miss White, and she was young, thin, short, kind. Margie liked Miss White's high nose and light blonde eyebrows. She thought her teacher looked like a bird or a woman from Gram's stories, not a rat. Ma pinched Margie's arm again and more than anything else, at that moment, Margie wanted to get back down on the wooden floor and press her cheek to the cool, smooth surface and make her circles she liked to make to get the world spinning, to get to a place where she could understand what was happening in her, around her.

My teacher is Miss White, Ma. She's good.

Ma moved her fingers down to Margie's wrist where she squeezed hard, so tight Margie could feel Ma there between her bones. Ma, there, so close to the underneath of Margie.

She's a nosy little bitch. Wants to know all about us. Do you know what she said about you?

No. I don't know. She says I am doing a good job.

A good job, right. She says you are doing a good job of being fat, and lazy, and stupid. Good job, Margie.

We would have cried. Called out. If our mothers had yelled at us like this, if our mothers pinched us, screamed at us across a sea of sweet rum, held our wrists so hard they swelled up blue and black and purple. We would have cried if it had been us. We might have cried if we had been there to see Margie, small and fat Margie down there on the floor. Circling, so quiet, so unsure. We were never meant to be a mother. We cried, sometimes, in the mornings, in bed, maybe with a man there, maybe alone, deep inside that moment when the drinking goes away and has not yet begun again, when we thought about how this had happened, how our life should have gone some other way. We cried, we would have cried, but we were not Margie. We were not at all like Margie, who felt the pain from far away, who from the floor felt Ma raging all around her and who did not cry. Margie, slow, small Margie seemed not to know about crying.

Of course you have nothing to say. That's what your teacher said. Stupid. Always keeping quiet. Keeping secrets. She thinks you're stupid because you don't talk. Why the hell don't you talk, Margie?

I talk. See. I'm talking. Talking.

Ma slapped her hand hard against Margie's face. Margie's cheek, already always red, turned darker, redder, changed shades in the wake of Ma's anger.

Don't be a smartass. You respect me. You look at me, Margie. That teacher of yours says you're stupid. She says you're weird. Says the other kids see it too. Is that what you want, Margie? Everybody looking at us? She says you're still doing that spinning. Why the fuck do you have to do that, spin around like that? Show everybody how fucked up you are. And then they all think I'm stupid and fucked up too.

There was one more thing Margie had figured out besides the pop tarts and how to keep herself warm with her bunny. Margie had discovered that if she sucked her breath hard in and out, if she moved her air around inside her like wind, like a storm, she could stop listening to everything outside herself. Margie, who we all secretly or out-loud thought was slow, was stupid, had learned how to leave any place she was, how to take a trip down into the steady, beating, warm parts of her. We thought she was not listening, when really, it was just us out here who Margie did not hear. Inside, in there, in her, down in herself, Margie had her ears and eyes open to the beats, the breaths, the blood-moving music she made just by being her, by being here and alive and listening.

Ma could see that Margie had gone away somewhere. She could see that her slaps and her pinches were not working. That Margie was not going to answer any of her questions. Ma shook Margie a few more times, because she could, because she did not know any other way to touch her child. We would have helped, but we were old, we were tired, we were sunk down low in the dark of our own selves.

Just quit it, Margie, Ma said, letting go.

Quit the spinning and the stupid looks and whatever else you're doing to be so weird. I don't want people coming around here asking questions. I don't ever want to hear from that school again. You do what the other kids do. Those fuckers at your school say they want to help. I told them we don't need help. I told them you were just fine, so don't make me look bad.

Just be normal, Margie.

You understand?

Ma had tired herself out from all the yelling, first at the school, at the small, pale, busybody teacher, then at home with her stupid kid. Her stupid kid who got more stupid every day, who was too stupid even to keep the secret of just how stupid she was.

Margie, set free, made her face smile a little from that far-away place down under the warm, slow inside of herself. She bent her knees and used her arms to help her down, and she was finally left alone to lie down on the floor and feel the cold, smooth, wooden silence of it. Margie, off the hook. Ma moved loud around the apartment for a while and Margie could feel her there, the waves of stumbling footsteps rolling out and through the floor, the ripples of Ma that made their way through the wood and into Margie. She walked her feet one over the other and slowly, on her side, Margie turned in her circles.

Margie felt Ma walk by and maybe some part of her heard Ma say, Fuck.

Fuck, Margie. I'm sorry.

But what do you want from me?

Maybe Margie felt the wood sway with Ma's weight as Ma bent down to touch her forehead. Maybe, mid-circle, Margie felt Ma's hand, still rough and still smelling of smoke and coconut. Maybe Margie felt her ma touch her, just touch her, not pinch or poke or slap her, just touch, there, against her forehead.

Maybe she heard Ma say, Sorry, Margie.

Let's just all try a little harder.

17. MARJORIE

Oh, Dr. Goodwin. You know. Fine. Good. Some not good.

What was good, Marjorie?

I saw Suzanne and she is good. Lots of People coming into the Store in good moods, smiling, saying Hello back. Mac is good. Benjamin is good. The snow.

I'm happy to hear everyone is good. Any other good things happen?

Oh. Yes. A little boy got lost in the Store but we found him. Steve got on the speakers and put out the call and we all stopped doing what we were doing and me I stopped saying Hello. Me, I looked too. And we found him. We found the little boy near the fish tanks watching the fish. Not me but someone. One of us. His ma was so happy.

That must have been a little scary.

A little. The boy, alone.

It's been a long time since we last saw each other, hasn't it?

Yes, Dr. Goodwin. Very long.

You canceled your appointment last month. Everything okay?

I'm sorry about that, Dr. Goodwin. I had some things.

You said there was some not good, Marjorie. What was not good?

Well, Ma's gone.

Gone?

Yeah, gone. Done, you know. Passed by.

Your mother passed away, Marjorie?

Yes, Dr. Goodwin. That is what I am saying. That is a thing on my mind.

I'm sure it is. I'm very sorry to hear about your mother. How did she die?

She just went, Dr. Goodwin. I don't know. Just coughing and smoking and then quiet. Her time to go, I guess.

How is your grandmother?

Oh, you know. Gram is strong and quiet and just the same. Just Gram. Sitting in her room. Watching her Stories.

And how are you feeling, Marjorie?

Feeling fine, Dr. Goodwin. Feeling like my self. A little tired. Sleeping now is not so easy. But I have been thinking.

What have you been thinking?

The sofa bed. How it is not sorry. No. That is not what I mean to say. I mean to say that there is no bad in the bed inside the sofa. No.

I'm not understanding, Marjorie. Why have you had trouble sleeping?

No reasons, Dr. Goodwin. Sleep comes and sleep does not come.

Why is there no bad in the sofa bed?

Because the sofa bed is all folded up inside the sofa and no one sleeps there anymore. Gram made me move into Ma's room so I am in that place now.

Do you think you thought about not feeling bad about the sofa bed because some part of you was feeling bad about the sofa bed?

Marjorie?

Well.

Let me think about that for a minute.

Take your time.

Well.

No. No I was not bad about the sofa bed, Dr. Goodwin. I am good. I am fine. That was just thinking. Something to say.

Do you think you are having trouble sleeping because the room used to belong to your mother?

Oh no, Dr. Goodwin. It is the bed. The soft of this bed on my back. It doesn't fit me. The room I cleaned. Got the smell of Ma out of the room. Just a room.

What if you moved the sofa into the room where you are sleeping now and put the bed in the living room. Could you sleep comfortably then?

How about it, Marjorie?

Just thinking, Dr. Goodwin.

I need to think about that some more. How to know? I don't think Gram would like it. A bed is for a bedroom and a sofa is for a living room. What if Suzanne were to come by to visit and all I had for her to sit on was a bed? It doesn't seem right.

Do you feel sad about your mother's death, Marjorie?

Oh, Dr. Goodwin. You know Ma. Ma isn't someone to feel sad over.

I know your relationship with your mother was very complicated.

Not so complicated. Just Ma. Me. Him.

I know sometimes your mother said hurtful things to you.

That is true. But not so bad, really. Some People have it worse. I think.

Let's try not to talk about other people right now, Marjorie. Let's talk about you and your mother. Can I tell you what I am wondering?

Oh sure, Dr. Goodwin. It is good to hear your wondering.

I wonder if maybe you do feel sad about your mother. Maybe somewhere inside you, you do feel sad. But I wonder if maybe it is difficult to feel that because you are still angry with her about your stepfather.

You are always wondering about Him, Dr. Goodwin. But I don't know about angry. And I don't know why you want to talk about Him. He is mean and He is gone and Ma is gone so why talk about all that.

Because it is important, Marjorie. And that's why I'm here. To help you talk about what happened to you.

This is your mother. She should have taken care of you.

I take care of my self, Dr. Goodwin. I am good at that.

I know, Marjorie. But I have noticed something. Can I tell you what I've noticed?

You can tell. Yes.

I've noticed that when you talk about your mother you almost always talk about your stepfather, too. It sounds to me like you don't see much difference in them, in your mind.

Well, Dr. Goodwin. There is Ma. There is Him. Always together. People together too long and maybe they start to seem the same.

But there was your mother before your stepfather. There was your mother there with you after he was taken away. Can you think about your mother in that way? As your mother? Just your mother?

Before Ma. After Ma. Yes.

That's good, Marjorie. Keep your eyes closed.

Take your time and just think about it.

Try to see your mother as separate. Try to see them as two different people. How do you feel?

Like I am all split, Dr. Goodwin.

What are you split about?

Like I've got Him there in that department taking up all that space and then here's Ma over in this department and she's looking over at His side like she wants to get there next to Him, like she wants to walk down His aisles and touch the things of Him and put all of her things with His. And then Gram's got her department and Mac's over here and there is Suzanne and Benjamin and Steve and then, you know, I've got Lucy here all over. Lucy got out of her place and she is holding onto the stuffed bunny and she is not going to look at any of the other People and me, or me, she is not going to look at me either.

You've got a lot of people in there, Marjorie.

Yes, Dr. Goodwin. I shouldn't have said. I have got a lot of People in my mind.

And you've been thinking about Lucy?

I shouldn't have said.

What didn't you want to tell me?

66

Should have kept my big mouth shut.

It's okay, Marjorie. This is the place for telling. You need to tell.

It's just Lucy, everywhere, Dr. Goodwin. All over the place. In my mind here with all the People and in the Store running around and the People come in through the door and I say Hello and I think, Lucy, and at home in the light in Ma's room. And I know you say, Let go, Marjorie. Let go. I know. But look. Here is Lucy. And I don't want you to get angry, Dr. Goodwin.

You can tell me anything you like, Marjorie. I won't be angry.

Oh, good, Dr. Goodwin. Thank you. That is always good to hear.

Don't open your eyes. Keep them closed. Good, closed like that. Take some deep breaths. Stay there where you are in your mind. Can you still see the people there?

Yes, Dr. Goodwin. Always.

Open your hands, relax. What is Lucy doing?

Same, Dr. Goodwin. Standing. Being alive. Lucy is wearing a little yellow dress like that girl on the bread package and she has got the blue bunny in her little hands and she has got beautiful hands, and her hair is braided up so pretty and she is turned away from all the other People and I think that she is very angry. I know it. Little shoes, too. Lucy is wearing little purple shoes.

Let's try something, Marjorie. Just to try. I want you to try to pretend.

Okay, Dr. Goodwin. I don't mind trying.

Can you make a door in your mind, Marjorie? Can you picture a door and can you open it?

Let me see about that, Dr. Goodwin.

Take your time.

Is the door there?

The door is the big glass sliding door.

Okay, good. And can you open it?

Yes, Dr. Goodwin. The big glass sliding door opens. It is the entrance.

Good. Open the door and try to help Lucy walk through it. Can you help Lucy walk out of your head and away to a place where she might have some more space? Maybe there are places Lucy can go where she will be happy.

It's just a parking lot past that door, Dr. Goodwin. I don't think a parking lot is a good place for Lucy.

I want you to try, Marjorie. Pretend.

Are you trying?

Dr. Goodwin, I am very tired and I am done thinking of the People in here and the door and the parking lot.

Okay, Marjorie. Okay. Take deep breaths. Let's talk about why you are so tired.

I said so already, Dr. Goodwin. The bed is soft. Not the same as the sofa bed. But it is fine. It is a good enough bed.

Marjorie, I am worried about you.

No need to worry. I am good. Things are good.

I'm worried because you're bringing up Lucy. We haven't talked about this in a while. But it sounds like you are thinking about Lucy again.

Not again. Always. Don't worry about Lucy, Dr. Goodwin. I see Lucy for just one second and then I close my eyes and I tell my self, Stop. Stop seeing Lucy. Get her back to the department where she belongs. Same with Him. Stop. I see Him there and I say, Get out. Don't worry, Dr. Goodwin. I say the words you say. To my self, I say them. Let go, I say.

What if we tried something different?

I think things are fine how they are, Dr. Goodwin.

What if you try letting them stay there in your mind for a while?

Oh. No. I don't think so. I think I have got enough in here.

Just think about it, Marjorie. Sometimes sitting and feeling these things is important. Sometimes telling yourself to stop is only going to make the thoughts stronger.

Okay, Dr. Goodwin. I see.

I think you spend a lot of time taking care of the people in your head, Marjorie. And I think that you forget to take care of yourself.

My self is fine, Dr. Goodwin. My self is good.

Do you ever feel sad, Marjorie?

I said before. Ma is not someone to be sad about.

Do you feel sad about Lucy?

I feel fine, Dr. Goodwin. I keep saying. I go to the Store and I go to the Club. I see Suzanne. Drink my Shirley Temples. Talk with Benjamin. I watch the Stories with Gram.

It's okay to feel sad.

Yes, Dr. Goodwin. I know that.

I can see that you don't want to talk about this anymore.

Okay. Yes.

But I want you to think about it.

Okay. I will think, Dr. Goodwin.

Anything else on your mind, Marjorie?

I just need to know something that maybe you know about, Dr. Goodwin.

What's that?

Well. What is it that People do with other People's reminders?

Sorry, Marjorie. I'm not sure what you're asking.

The word, Dr. Goodwin. What is it? So many words. Ma's in a box under the bed and I need to do something with her. With her burned-up parts. Her dust. You know. But I don't know what People do. I want to do the right thing.

Are you talking about your mother's remains, Marjorie?

Yes. That's right. That's it. Ma's remains. Gram took care of calling and the People in gloves came by and took Ma away and then a kind man came back with Ma in a cardboard box about this big.

Did you open the box?

Oh. No, Dr. Goodwin. I did not open the box. I thought Ma might spill out everywhere and I thought I should know what to do with her spill before I open the box.

I'm pretty sure, Marjorie, that your mother's remains are inside another container, probably plastic, inside the cardboard box. If I remember correctly. And probably even inside another container, a sealed bag, I think, inside that other box.

Are you all right, Marjorie?

Just thinking, Dr. Goodwin. Fine.

Do you want to open the box?

I want to do what People do. I don't want Ma spilling out all over the place.

Well, I think that some families want to keep the person who has passed away close to them. So they find a nice container, like a vase. An urn, it's called. Or maybe a nice box, and they put their loved one's remains in there.

And then?

I think they feel comfort because the person is still near them. Maybe they put the vase or the box in a special place in the house and put a photograph of the person near it. It's important to remember. And of course some families don't like the idea of the person who has died sitting inside a container. Some people might choose to bring the remains to a special place and scatter them. Let them go.

Like what special place, do you think?

Maybe up to the mountain. Maybe if their loved one liked the outdoors they would take the remains to the woods or up on the mountain and let them go there. Or the sea, maybe. Usually the family thinks of a place that was important to the person who died, and they leave their remains there, where that person was happiest.

You look worried, Marjorie.

Not worried. Thinking.

What are you thinking about?

Suzanne said she put her ma into the ground and that was that.

Where do you think your mother was happiest?

Oh, who knows. Ma was never much happy or not happy. Chick's, maybe? But that's burned down now. Maybe Ma was happy in bed in front of the television.

Well, maybe it's best to find a nice container and keep her at home with you.

I will have to think about that, Dr. Goodwin.

Of course.

What do you believe happens to us when we die, Marjorie?

What? When we die?

I'm just wondering. We've never talked about it. Do you believe there's a good place where people go when they die?

I have not thought about that, Dr. Goodwin

Maybe it's a good thing for you to think about. Maybe it could help you to think about Lucy in a good place. And maybe your mother, too.

All I know is me, Dr. Goodwin. Here. Where I go. Alive. I don't know about where else there is to go.

Maybe you can think about it.

What time is it, Dr. Goodwin?

It is almost 5:00. 4:52.

Oh, okay. So eight minutes left.

Eight minutes left. Anything else on your mind?

Oh, you know.

18. MARGIE

Margie, alone, pressed her extra, extra sharp pencil tip to the thin gray paper and pushed. Not hard, not soft. Margie practiced. Another way for words to be. Written, read, seen, made. One line up. One line down. One line up. One line down. The thin gray paper had big blue lines to help Margie remember what way to push. Up. Down. Up. Down.

Climbing mountains, Margie, Gram had said, her dry, gray, wrinkled hand held around the fat, pink softness of Margie's hand.

M.

Margie.

Climbing mountains.

Margie, alone on the floor of her and Gram's high-up bedroom in Apartment #2, pressed her fingers against the smooth yellow sides of a long, perfect pencil and pushed against the paper with the rough silver downward curve of the sharpened, sharp, extra-extra sharp tip. Up. Down. Up. Down.

M. M. M.

Margie, alone with the sunlight coming through the big window, alone on the floor beside the bed with her big gray pad of paper, practicing what Gram had taught her. Margie, the smell of peanut butter and graham crackers and grape soda sweet on her breath, breathing in and out and in. Up. Down. Up. Down. Margie breathed in the smell of the pink, smooth, unrubbed, unsmeared eraser. The musty smell of the yard sale pad of paper. Margie pressed her pencil tip down.

Up. Down. Line.

M-A.

A break.

The point of the pencil pressed too hard, to breaking.

Margie moved the pencil in slow circles inside the small, pink, plastic sharpener. Circling, circling, unbreaking the tip, making her pencil sharp and perfect again.

Margie and all the time in the world for her to take. No place to go. No one there to tell her to go faster.

We would have liked to ask the world to always be so, for Margie. Warm, slow, purple pajamas soft in the sunlight. Making herself, there, quietly, in curving shapes on smooth paper.

Up. Down. Up. Down.

Margie's favorite. M. The mountain. Making her mountains.

Up. Down. Line. Up. Around. Line.

M-A-R.

Margie stopped to touch her tongue to the little metal circle that held the eraser to the pencil, to touch the rough, sour surface of it. She bit gently down on the eraser and made teeth marks in the soft pink of it.

Margie knew all the letters. She practiced slowly, stopping to sharpen, stopping to touch and taste and feel the sunlight. Sometimes Margie fit herself inside the lines and sometimes Margie filled a whole page with just one shape, one page filled with the huge mountain of M or the house of A or the lying-down lines of E.

M-A-R-G-I-E.

M-A-R-G-I-E.

Margie wanted to show Gram what she could do. She held her fingers tight to the pencil and held the pencil close to her chest and Margie rolled over her gray pad of paper and to the big white of the wall next to the window. Margie held the gray triangle of the pencil's point hard against the white square of the wall and there on the big bare wall she pressed and made huge mountains that could not fit inside the space of the paper.

M-A-R-G-I-E.

M-A-R-G-I-E.

Margie made the wall her wall. Stopping to sharpen, stopping to feel and taste.

M-A-R-G-I-E.

M-A-R-G-I-E.

M-A-R-G-I-E.

Margie was curled asleep on the floor when Gram came back and saw what she had done.

Gram, down, as usual. Down-day Gram had nothing to say to Margie. No words, only Gram's hand hard on Margie's shoulder, only Gram's arms pulling Margie up, Gram's fingers pointing to the wall, to the long gray mess of what Margie had done.

Gram, down, held her hand hard around Margie's hand, made Margie rub the pencil wrong-end up against the wall. Gram took the pencil away from Margie and pink-eraser-end rubbed gray pencil more and more into the white wall, made Margie's mountains into big gray rivers and clouds still there in the shapes of her.

M-A-R-G-I-E.

Your ma is going to kill you, Margie, Gram said.

And maybe Margie understood, maybe not, but Margie could see that Gram was down, could see what she had done was not right, knew that for down-day Gram to say any words at all meant that something was happening.

Margie, silent, stared.

Okay, Margie, Gram said, rubbing the eraser hard against the wall.

I'll keep this secret for you, Gram said. But just this one. One secret. No more, Margie.

Gram rubbed the wall until the eraser crumbled away. The big gray of M-A-R-G-I-E was still there, only softer now, bigger and lighter, floating, like a storm passing over the white of the wall.

By now the sun had set and Margie and Gram were alone in their room with Margie's mess in the gray-blue light of almost night.

No more, Margie, Gram said.

Say you are sorry, Margie.

Say, Sorry, Margie.

Sorry, Margie said. Another word. A long snake of a word. Not a shape, not a place to go or a thing to touch or a taste to taste. So many words expected of Margie.

Sorry, Margie said.

Sorry.

Sorry.

You better be sorry, Gram said. Now crawl under the bed and get me my magazines.

Gram pointed to the dark under the bed and pushed Margie toward it and Margie crawled and reached and pulled out what Gram wanted.

Gram shut the bedroom door and told Margie to get in bed and Gram pulled the covers up to Margie's chin. Gram took out her scissors and her tape from the top drawer of her dresser and sat down on the bed on the Gram side, the wall side, her bent back to Margie. Gram opened her magazines all around her and Gram licked her two fingers and flipped pages and Margie closed her eyes and listened to the sound of Gram's scissors slicing through the thin paper skin. Margie lay quiet under the covers and listened, and slept, and Gram cut and cut and cut and taped and cut and taped, covered, covering up the secret of what Margie had done.

M-A-R-G-I-E.

M-A-R-G-I-E.

M-A-R-G-I-E.

In the morning, when the bright sunlight opened Margie's eyes, the scissors were gone, the cut-up paper swept away, and Gram was there sleeping loud and slow beside her. Margie used her arms to hold her head up, to see beyond the rising shape of Gram, and there, all over what had been the white wall next to the window, Margie saw every color of blue the world had ever made. Squares of bright light swimming-pool blue, circles of deep-sea blue, white-cloud-spotted blue-sky blue, dark blue-painted-house blue, blue-car blue, blue-eye blue, globes of blue-and-green-globe blue, triangles of blue-fish blue and round snakes of running-river blue. Gram had found and cut and taped all that blue down on top of the secret M-A-R-G-I-E. A whole window of blue on the wall beside the window. And on top of the blue Gram had taped the cut-out shapes of people, fish, sharks, cats, cows, lamps, suitcases, televisions, chairs, shoes and crosses and coats and pairs of pants. Things, so many things and people and animals, floating or flying in the sea or sky that Gram had made over the mistake of M-A-R-G-I-E on the wall.

Margie, eyes heavy, squinting, still sleepy in the early-morning brightness, stared at the shapes and the shades of the blue and all the things that Gram had brought to live there. Margie stared, and smiled, and watched this whole world of color and life that lived now on top of the gray-smeared mountains of M-A-R-G-I-E beneath.

Margie, staring, smiling, put her hand on the slow up-and-down of Gram's shoulder and squeezed her, gently, and Margie said, Sorry.

Sorry, she said, and slow, dried-sleep-eyed Margie stared at all the colors that covered up her secret, her one secret that Gram had promised to keep.

19. MARJORIE

Marjorie sits in the chair beside Gram's bed and together they eat graham crackers with peanut butter and watch the television. Gram is quiet and chewing, a down-day, probably. Mostly down-days, now. Mostly down-days always, but, before, Gram could get around better. Gram went out to her yard sales and church and wherever else Gram went. Now Gram and her bad heart and her bad hip and her bad knees and bad ears and eyes mostly sits up against some pillows in her bed and watches television and does her cutting. Marjorie has her own no-sound television to watch now in Ma's room, but she likes sitting here with Gram. Marjorie likes hearing what the People on the television have to say and even on the most down of a down-day, Marjorie likes feeling next-to Gram.

Mostly they watch the Stories. Good ladies and bad ladies and good men and bad men. Many doctors and nurses and not many children and if there is a baby the baby is talked about but never seen, ever. Marjorie likes the way the People in the Stories talk. How strong they are about things. So angry when they are angry and so happy when they are happy. So beautiful. Bright white teeth in red, red mouths. Marjorie likes it best when the men with their big muscle arms grab the ladies in their short dresses and say words like, I want you, I need you, I love you. I must have you, they say. Sometimes Marjorie's face burns up and her heart beats fast and her hands shake a little when the Stories show men with no shirts kissing ladies in bed under the sheets. The men big as mountains and the ladies disappear in the shade beneath. And the sounds. Marjorie is very interested in the Stories at these parts. She knows what People do under sheets. The touching. Sometimes Marjorie's hands feel sweaty and she rubs them hard into her thighs and she feels very heated up rubbing her hands on her knees and watching the People kiss and roll.

Gram does not like the Stories once the men have no shirts and the ladies are in bed in high heels. Gram, commander of the clicker, always changes the channel and they watch commercials for a while until it is safe to go back to the Stories. Marjorie does not mind. She is interested in these things only a little and she has some pictures of these things already up on her shelves inside and Marjorie knows that any time she really wants to see something she can turn on her own television and there they will be. People, perfect and tall, soundless and together, touching.

Marjorie has a box of graham crackers and a jar of peanut butter at her feet. When the commercials come on she reaches into the box and takes a graham cracker out, breaks it in half and with a knife scoops out some peanut butter. Rubs the peanut butter onto the graham cracker. Makes a treat for Gram, two treats for her. Marjorie is young and always hungry. Gram is old and takes time with things. Marjorie makes a stack of Gram's extras on the small white table beside her bed, for later, for when Gram is ready for more. Her own treat, Marjorie chews slowly, lets the crunchy bits of graham cracker melt into the thick, warm pool of peanut butter in her mouth. Feels the heavy slide down into her center.

They watch the Stories and the room around them beats, breathes, waves. Marjorie licks and sucks and chews and while the commercials go on, Marjorie watches the walls of Gram's room for how they move. Here, all around them, are where Gram's cut-up pictures and colors and words and bits of the Bible are taped. Words, mostly. Some pictures here and here, photos of flowers and cars and horses and beaches white with sand, blue with sea. But mostly words, sentences, paragraphs and pages that Gram has found and needed around her. Gram keeps her scissors and tape and a stack of magazines and newspapers and her Bible next to her bed but Marjorie has never actually seen her do the cutting. Marjorie understands that Gram is very private. About the cutting. The choosing. The looking and reading and touching and feeling. The putting up of the cut-up pieces is not the private part. Marjorie knows this because sometimes when Gram cannot reach she will call Marjorie in and give Marjorie the roll of tape and a small pile of papers and point up at the places on the wall where she wants them put. And Marjorie tears the tape and sticks the pieces up on the wall and she never sees Gram choosing and she never asks why. Why this one? Marjorie never asks because Marjorie is very important about her private things and she understands that People do not always have answers to questions or reasons for wants.

But the moving of the papers on the wall is something that Marjorie would like to ask about. Why? Where does the wind come from? It is winter and the windows are shut tight and the air feels unmoving on Marjorie's skin and yet Gram's taped-up papers never seem still. The pictures and the words float up and fall down and were it not for the good job Marjorie and Gram have done taping them down, all that beautiful would just fly away. What is the wind in this room made of? Their wind, maybe. The in and out of their breaths. Marjorie puts the rest of her graham cracker treat in her mouth and wonders what else it could be. Lucy, she would like to say. Ma, even. The passed-along People. The never-got-started People.

Gram pokes Marjorie hard in the arm.

How does Gram always know? How does Marjorie look, that gives her self away? Her secrets always seem seen when Marjorie sits beside Gram.

Gram, her voice falling apart into cracks and ups and downs, says, Why don't you get out, Margie?

Get out where, Gram? I'm just watching the Stories.

Get out, to where the people are. To wherever the young people go.

Nowhere to be right now, Gram. I do go out. The Store. The Club.

That club is full of nobodies, Margie.

Not nobodies, Gram. The People at the Club are good.

Nothing for you there, Gram says.

Marjorie holds on steady to her wind. Blinks her eyes and rubs her arm in the place that Gram poked. Gram's face is shrunk up small and what is left of the blue of her eyes is yellow, wet, drowned, down, and what is left of her hair is gone beyond gray and rough and her body is a bony mess of skin under her nightgown. What is there to say?

You need a man, Margie, Gram says.

On the television, two ladies are sitting together in a car. One driving, beautiful, laughing. One sitting, riding beside, probably beautiful but hiding her face behind a brown coat. Marjorie cannot understand what the problem is.

I'm fine, Gram, Marjorie says.

You're not fine, Margie. I see you. I know. You're all shot to pieces.

I have lots of friends, Gram. I go places.

Gram takes one of her treats from the stack on the table next to her and holds it out to Marjorie. She shakes, a little, her hands. Marjorie takes the graham cracker and licks around the edges to taste the peanut butter before she bites it in two.

I wish you'd let Him in, Margie. I wish you'd let our Lord into your life. Him or even just a man. People can't live alone all the time like you do.

Marjorie chews and chews and crunches all the crumbs and swallows her treat before she speaks.

I've said, Gram. I'm not alone. I have Mac and Suzanne and Benjamin and all the People I help out in the Store. And you. You're alone all the time. In here.

I'm not alone, Margie, Gram says.

Gram is doing her best to sit up high and straight and to keep her eyes on Marjorie's eyes. To make her voice heard more than the voices in the television.

I'm not alone, Margie, because I have let our Lord into my life. All the time, I am not alone.

Know our Lord and know joy, Margie. That's what I know and that's all I need.

Okay, Marjorie says. I will think about that, Gram.

Think, Gram says. Margie and her thinking. Won't let no one into that thinking. Not even me. Not even our Lord.

Maybe Marjorie should say something about Dr. Goodwin. About how she has let People into her life. How she has got a good man let into her thinking. But Marjorie is important with her secrets. Everything Gram says Gram has said before and Marjorie stacks the words up on a shelf in the department of Gram. Marjorie is going to keep Dr. Goodwin to her self.

Help me, Margie. If you can't help yourself, at least do something for me.

Gram reaches slowly over to slide open the drawer of the table next to her bed. Marjorie keeps her eyes away so that Gram will not think she means to see her private things. Gram takes out a cut-out paper and a roll of tape and holds them out to Marjorie.

Okay, Gram. Where?

Marjorie wipes her hands on her pants and stands up. The paper is thin, so thin that the light comes right through, thin so that the room can be seen beyond it, so Marjorie knows that it comes from the Bible. So many Bibles and pages of the Bible cut and ripped and torn and taped and crushed and crumpled and chewed and sucked and stuck. So many ways Marjorie has seen the paper of the Bible touched. And why is Gram so sure that Marjorie should let our Lord in?

Marjorie takes the tape and tiny square of paper and Gram points to a spot to the side of her bed. Marjorie moves her big self carefully around the bed and in front of the television where a man and a lady are hugging and crying and hugging. The man, too, crying. Marjorie touches the spot that Gram points to, says, Here, and Gram leans and nods and watches.

I never meant to hurt you, the television says.

Marjorie tears some tape off the roll and looks at the paper to make sure she's got it facing the right way. She does not read the words, does not want to bother what is private for Gram. Marjorie, careful, rubs her thumb over the paper to smooth it down. To make it good and right for Gram.

That look okay, Gram?

Gram strains her neck to the side to look and she squints her eyes and looks and looks and then nods.

That's good. You're a good girl, Margie.

20. MARGIE

Lucy came with her ma and her ma's friend LD sometime during the long-day lazy sunlit-start of summer. The two big-bellied women and the pretty little girl came sometime during that time when chocolate-chip-cookie-hiding Margie was every day making a little more of herself. Her skin, slowly widening, reaching out to touch a bit more of the world. Margie was eight or nine or ten, or maybe younger, or older.

Margie from behind the dust and sunlight of the big window in her and Gram's high-up bedroom watched the three new people move in. She held her limp blue stuffed bunny by one ear and pressed her nose and cheeks and lips to the glass.

We have to wonder about that window. That high-up bedroom window. The shine, the streaks, the face and tongue and handprints left on that very important window. We have to wonder if there might be a little bit of little Margie still there. If even the smallest window-trace of Margie could still be found today.

Margie from the window watched the pale blonde girl turn cartwheels on the front lawn as the two women lifted big cardboard boxes out of the bed of a gray pickup truck. And with her other hand, her unholding hand, Margie slowly rubbed the smooth blue surface of the secret-covering paper sea Gram had made for her.

Margie had watched new people move in and move out of downstairs Apartment #1 before, but always a boyfriend and girlfriend or a husband and wife. The downstairs people had always come and gone quickly, had always played loud music and gotten into yelling fights with Ma. There had never been another kid living in the big peeling-gray house before.

We do not know why Margie waited so long to speak up, to show herself. For weeks, Margie watched the little girl below her, the small, smiling girl rolling in the overgrown grass around the big gray house. We cannot know why Margie stayed silent, sitting, pressing her cheek to the cool clear glass and waiting each day for the time when the golden-haired girl ran glowing out into the sunlight.

For weeks, Margie waited for Gram to settle into her chair in the living room with her stories and while Gram sat with the problems of the people on the television, Margie spent hours alone and free with herself, with her nose and forehead and sometimes tongue touching window glass. She watched the little girl skip on the sidewalk in front of the slanting blue porch steps and lie on her back in the middle of the road.

The more Margie watched, the more she saw the differences between the two big-bellied women who had come to live below. Margie watched the one woman with short hair and wide shoulders drive away in the morning in the gray pickup truck, wearing the blue clothes that all the quarry workers wore. She watched the other woman, shorter, hair longer, her belly just a bit bigger, her legs just a bit curved inward, sometimes come out into the yard to wave her arms and yell at the little girl. Margie, high up and behind the thick of the glass, could not hear what they said, but she watched how their bodies moved and she saw, maybe for the first time, that wide-mouthed yelling did not always come with the red of angry. Once, Margie saw them hug, there, below her, the big woman and the little girl, there, holding, in the sunlight, and Margie, alone in her place against the window, felt it, could feel it too.

Why not open the window to hear what they said, what they yelled? To hear what the little girl's laugh sounded like? We cannot understand how good the glass felt on Margie's lips, to Margie's small, warm, tongue. We were at work or watching television or at the bar. We did not know that Margie was made in a way that we were not.

There is a certain comfort that comes from assuming we are all the same.

Maybe Margie would have stayed quiet and happy watching from the window all summer long, but one day Ma came home in the middle of the afternoon with the friend Margie had seen once or twice before. The big, tall, black-haired, no-shirt, hairy friend smiled when Ma yelled at Margie to get out. A spitting, lip-moving, chewing friend who stayed quiet and smiling and holding on tight to the sides of Ma while Ma swayed and sighed and red-faced yelled for Margie to get out.

Margie by now was used to getting out. Gram had a headache and Margie got out. Ma came home angry from work and Margie got out. Friends showed up at the red front door with six-packs of beer and pretzels and Ma made Margie get out.

Margie got out into the thick, hot summer air and for a while spun in circles in the front yard. Spinning and spinning, standing up, feet moving in the slow shape of a circle, lying down on the soft of the grass, rolling. Margie, moving the world with her circles.

That was how Lucy met Margie. Spinning, in circles, world-upside-down, eyes closed, smiling, tongue and teeth flashing red and white, spinning and breathless and happy. Made by Ma to get out and Margie feeling nothing but good and free to be finally outside in the sun. Inside, we were pushed or let him push us to the floor to our knees and we kept our eyes closed and we waited for the warm moment when he would open and soften so that we could feel something too. Outside, Margie made a friend.

Hi!

The little girl opened her arms wide and started spinning beside Margie.

Hi. Hi. Hi.

Margie smiled but Margie did not, could not, stop her circles.

Hi.

Hi.

Hi, Margie said, and she opened her eyes, and swayed a little, slowed a little, and spun.

My name is Lucy.

My name is Margie.

We did not care about the two little girls spinning in the hot afternoon sun in front of the old house with the sagging porch. We figured they had names, and things they liked, things they didn't like. We could have guessed about what made them happy and what made them sad. Sun, swimming, dolls, frogs, boys, homework, and on, and on, whatever. We probably knew that each had a whole separate world of what they were afraid of somewhere inside their grow-ing, firming bodies. We might have walked by and seen them spinning and assumed they were friends. But we were busy, we were hurt and happy and afraid in our own worlds. We were teaching summer school classes, we were digging through piles of exploded rock at the quarry, stealing candy bars at the convenience store, fucking, getting fucked, driving our cars in drunk straight lines down Main Street, praying for babies not yet born. We didn't know that these were the first moments of Margie's first friend, and we didn't care.

Margie cared. Margie. Spinning, spinning, laughing. Lucy fell down laughing and got up and held onto Margie's bigger, softer arm with her two small hands.

Hey, Lucy said.

How do you do that?

How do you spin without falling down?

I don't know, Margie said, spinning slowly, letting Lucy hold onto her arm, spinning Lucy in a slow circle around her.

I don't know. I just do it. I put my arms out like this and I close my eyes like this and I stay here inside my circle like this.

Okay, come see this, Lucy said, and she pulled on Margie's arm to stop her mid-spin.

Come see these frogs I found.

We might have told Lucy we knew about the frogs already. We might have told her that we had cut-out frogs living on the blue-paper-water window beside our bedroom window. We might have said that we had been here from the beginning. That this was our place, that we had found the frogs in the brook at the end of the street a long time ago. We might have told the little golden twig of a girl that they were our frogs, not hers.

This is, after all, the usual division of the world.

What is ours and what is not.

But Margie was not like any of us. Margie smiled and let Lucy lead her past the dusty dead-end end of the street to the tall grass and smooth stones at the edge of the brook. Margie crouched low in the mud with Lucy and felt happy and surprised at the sight of these frogs she had seen so many times before. Margie looked at the little brown bodies of the frogs blowing up and down with breath and she made her heavy brown eyes into Lucy's light blue eyes and she smiled and felt all over again that she wanted to hold the frogs. Margie felt the cool of the trees that stretched out long and tall to protect the brook from the sun. She felt happy to see the frogs with someone else, happy to feel Lucy's small fingers cold around her sweaty wrist.

Lucy's thin body shook with excitement and she pointed and whispered in Margie's ear. Her breath, hot on Margie's skin.

Do you see my frogs? They're my pets, all of them.

Do you see my frogs, Margie?

I see them, Margie said.

I see your frogs.

We might have told the girls not to touch the frogs. To stay away from the mud, to stay clean, to stop rubbing their eyes and get their fingers out of their mouths. And besides, we would have said. Besides, little girls don't like frogs. We might have laughed and held them on our laps. The little one, at least. Maybe told them stories about good frogs and bad frogs and frogs that could turn into princes and about rich beautiful women in France who ate frog legs for breakfast.

But where were we? Sunk down drowned in ourselves and what mattered there. And what mattered there had nothing to do with two little girls making friends in the mud of a dirty brook at the end of a dead-end street in the bad part of town.

I love them, Lucy said.

I love them too, Margie said.

We all loved them. Or the idea of them, the frogs, the brook, the sun. The idea of little girls in the world will always be a good enough thing. The details of it, what they talked about and how the big one's skin seeped sweat while the little one shivered, the smell of the mud under their fingernails, seem less important, seem impossible to know.

But there they were. Margie and Lucy, shoulders touching, lying belly-down in the mud at the edge of the brook. Left alone and unseen. Watching the frogs watch them. Lucy told stories and Margie listened and laughed at all the wrong parts and Lucy laughed at her wrong laughing. Big sweating skin touching pale, thin skin, the thick, sucking feel of the mud and the scratch of the tall grass that hid them from view. This was the making of Margie's first friend.

21. MARGE

Didn't mean to surprise you, honey.

Your ma had to go out for a while.

Don't know where. The store I think.

She told me about you.

What's your name again?

Margie? What kind of name is that?

Margie Bargie Largie.

I'm just kidding, honey.

Marjorie? Wow what a name. Too much name for you. Too long for me to say.

How about I call you Marge?

I knew a Marge once. Worked in a diner near here. Had pretty little legs and pretty little titties. Wore a pretty little nametag. Marge.

Hey, I am talking to you.

You stay put.

That Marge knew just what I wanted. Sunny side up so they jiggle. Used to look down her shirt when she poured my coffee. Drank so much coffee over there.

What do you do? Do you pour coffee?

Dumb as a lump. I can see that. Not nearly as pretty and little as that other Marge.

Not nearly as pretty as your ma.

What you are is plump. Not as pretty but not too bad to grab neither.

Don't get that look I'm just playing with you.

How old are you, anyway, Marge?

That's it? I thought more. You had me fooled on that one. Look at those big titties you've got already.

Come on, honey, I'm just joking with you. Just noticing. Can't help it.

This is what men do, Marge. Men look. Nothing wrong with a look.

Bring me some of that paper you got.

I'm not going to bite.

Rip that up into pieces for me. My hands hurt today.

Good, like that. Like strips. Hand them over.

Look, Marge, your ma said for me to watch you so I'm watching you.

Nothing for you to be scared of, Marge.

Just me. Your ma's friend.

Good, give me them pieces of paper.

How about this? I won't even make you call me Mr. Mustang. You can call me just like your ma calls me. Just Mustang.

What's wrong now, Marge? You don't want to make friends?

Keep tearing that up. I want all of that. I want a mountain.

I'm watching.

Just like your ma told me to do, Marge.

I'm watching you.

I got my eye on you.

22. MARJORIE

Marjorie opens her eyes and she is sitting on the cold floor of the Store in the corner of the farthest department under the big blue hanging BABY sign. Again. Her wind, here with her. In and out and in. Marjorie stays sitting where she is, her back against two metal shelves of little baby shoes. Her legs spread out big in front of her, her black sneakers pointing up at a rack full of blue baby dresses on hangers. The lights, burning white bright lines above.

All the things.

All the things here smell sweet and soft like cakes like babies like baby powder like candy and flowers and Lucy.

All the things small and soft and waiting for babies not yet here in the world.

But coming.

It is not that Marjorie does not remember her self walking to Baby. She remembers, in her way. Marjorie is sure it happens like this.

Her shift ends. Marjorie finishes giving the People their Hello and she leaves her place and takes her usual path through the Store, to the back of the Store. Marjorie leaves her place and turns left and passes the rows and rows of beeping registers and then turns right to walk through the pinks and greens of Women's Wear and then straight and through the many moving bright lights of the televisions in Electronics.

She sticks to the wide center aisle. The main path. Where most of the People go.

Marjorie walks through the two big doors at the back of the Store and down a dark hallway and into the room with the gray box where she punches in. A special place. A place where the People are not allowed. Where the workers sit and eat sandwiches and candy bars and drink sodas. And Marjorie smiles to the room and says Hello to the room and she punches her card and she does not mind if the workers say Hello or do not say Hello. Marjorie takes her coat from the hook on the wall and she leaves the back of the Store as soon as she can because it is dark back there, many-roomed, back there. No bright colors back there and Marjorie prefers to be with the People.

Her coat. Her coat is here with her in Baby. Marjorie's big purple coat is on her, around her. Keeping her warm here on the floor. So she put on her coat. So Marjorie walked in her way to the back of the Store and Marjorie had her coat on and Marjorie must have been on her way to the sliding glass exit door when some part of her self decided to change departments.

This is always the problem, for Marjorie. The leaving. The going back home.

The tired end of the day. The day long and smiling with People. The many, many paths that open up to her.

In the Store, People have many choices. All the things, yes. People can choose one or two or ten perfect things out of the millions and millions of choices of things. The forever choices of what is wanted. Needed. But in the Store it is also important for People to choose which path they will take to get to where they need to go. The Store has so many paths. In the Store it is important to know your self and what you need. Look up at the signs to know where is where and know what is needed and find the right path. Some People need, first and most important, soup for warming and potato chips for crunching, so they start their time in the Store in Food. Some People need to feel beautiful and on display, so they start in Beauty or Clothing. The People who are in the Store to slowly enjoy the Store usually start by touching the things next to Marjorie, to see what the holiday is, to see what is special this time. Some People know just what they need and they walk fast and direct to Garden or Electronics or Hardware. In the Store each of the People can choose which way they will go and whether they will follow the signs up above and walk down the shining smooth path the Store gives them or if they will find their own crooked way on the carpet through the racks and shelves and things in the departments.

Usual days Marjorie walks to the front of the Store on the same path she took to the back. It is easy to move her self down the wide aisles of the center Store path and there are always many People there pushing carts and even though she has punched her card, Marjorie still smiles. Marjorie still says Hello.

Usual. The usual. A usual day, Marjorie stays on the path and leaves the Store and she does not need to open her eyes and see that she is sitting on the floor in Baby surrounded by racks and piles and baskets and boxes of tiny perfect things.

But here she is. It happens. Marjorie's mind goes to darkened departments where she does not want to go. She sits in a corner inside her self and watches her self walk where she walks. Marjorie sees that she does not smile and say Hello when the inside light-outlined shape of her self takes over, that she does not turn toward the front of the Store but keeps going straight and all the way to the end of the path and into the tight all-around of metal racks and plastic hangers and clean-smelling baby things. Marjorie is there walking inside her self, together with her self, wind moving, heart beating, legs, arms, swinging, and then suddenly her self is dark and far away and her self feels gone from her.

Another Marjorie here inside Marjorie.

A difficult thing to describe.

Something about Marjorie that only Marjorie knows.

What Dr. Goodwin would say if he knew.

You can't keep it all in, Marjorie.

Got to let it out sometime.

You need to feel.

Things.

Well. Marjorie is here. Feeling things. She has got her coat warm around her and a little soft baby shoe held tight in each hand. Baby shoes. Marjorie has got one baby shoe held tight in each hand. Little black ones. Sneakers, like hers.

Here she is. Again. Feeling. The floor hard under her legs and the shelves sharp against her back. It will be difficult for Marjorie to lean over and push her big self up so she stays sitting for a while. It will be difficult to put the baby shoes down. Marjorie knows. Marjorie is back in her self she knows. Marjorie knows the far-away part of her self that brings her to Baby is here because of Lucy. That she is here on the floor of Baby because of Lucy.

Marjorie knows.

This-Marjorie knows.

This-Marjorie does not need Dr. Goodwin to tell her why she is here.

This-Marjorie does not need Dr. Goodwin to know.

Because how can he?

How can any of the People know?

How it is to have had an almost-Lucy and not have any Lucy at all.

Marjorie knows how it is. She looks up at a small white dress covered in the smallest pink flowers and she sees Lucy small and perfect and wearing that dress. Marjorie looks at the little black shoes in her hands and sees Lucy wearing the shoes and at tiny hats and Lucy is in a hat and at soft yellow blankets and Lucy is pressed up close to her at night and they are keeping each other warm and safe and together. Dr. Goodwin knows that she sees Lucy sometimes in her mind but he does not know that Marjorie can feel Lucy too. That sometimes Marjorie touches her hand to her self to her skin to her big hanging breasts to her belly to her cheek and hips and heart and that she can feel there on her self what Lucy feels like.

Arms, legs, hair, eyes, eyelashes, fingers, nails, feet, sweat, skin.

Marjorie knows she cannot stay sitting, seeing, touching her soft warm self to the hard floor of Baby forever. Maybe she would like to. And maybe she could, if she really wanted. Because People are free to do what they want to do and the Store is open 24 hours 365 days a year and so sometimes Marjorie thinks about staying here. Sitting, thinking, feeling, being with the small soft things, forever.

But if she stays in Baby she would never see Dr. Goodwin again. Marjorie would not have any People to talk about the day with. She would not smile and say Hello and help. Mac and Suzanne might wonder where she went. Ma would stay in that box under the bed forever and Gram would have no one to tape up her words on the wall. Benjamin might come by and see her, here, in Baby, and Benjamin might not even ask any questions. Benjamin might understand. But Steve. The big problem of Steve. If Marjorie stays in Baby, she is sure that Steve would come around and make her answer questions. Steve would stand above her and pinch and touch and push at her and just because of the problem of Steve, Marjorie would probably want to leave Baby, anyway.

But the real of the problem is that Marjorie staying in Baby means that Lucy stays in Baby, too. Marjorie wants to sit and stay and think about the look of Lucy and the feel of Lucy but Marjorie knows that Lucy does not want to stay in the Store. Dr. Goodwin wants to know where Marjorie thinks passed-along People go but how can Marjorie know about that?

Marjorie has secrets. She has the want for Lucy to have made it. To have gotten the chance to become Lucy, to be with the People, to kick real, growing legs, to see frogs breathing brook water and be in a place even bigger than the Store. Marjorie wants to know what Lucy was and is, what Lucy felt like, what that small, unshaped part of Marjorie's own self looked like. How Lucy almost came to be.

You don't want to see, the People told her, but Marjorie wanted to see and Marjorie wants to see. Marjorie wants to see how Lucy will be, and Yes, Dr. Goodwin, Marjorie understands that Lucy is just there in her mind and that maybe it is better to Let her go.

Which is why Marjorie is going to get up off of the floor of Baby and stop seeing perfect Lucy in the perfect clothes. Why Marjorie is letting go of these two little shoes. Why she is putting them back in their package and stacking them back on their shelf. Because Marjorie knows she does not know what Lucy looks like because she did not know Lucy until it was too late. Marjorie knows that she does not know what Lucy feels like because Lucy could not be touched because Lucy was not perfect because Lucy was unpackaged and undone and all wrong.

Marjorie bends one knee and slowly rolls over to a place with enough space to push her heavy self up with her arms. Her heavy self, feeling heavier, feeling more like Marjorie. She puts her hand on the shelf to help pull her self all the way up and she keeps her hand there for a while to help her mind come back to where she is. Picks up what she can of the mess of her inside departments. Opens up the closed of her self, lets the warm water wash down. Comes back to her, to here, to where she is. In the Store. In Baby. In Marjorie. Bright lights all around so she does not know if it is day or night. Time in the Store might be minutes might be days might be never-ending and always. Tiny colorful things shining and kids crying, yelling, laughing, doing what kids do in the Store.

Lucy. Lucy.

Lucy.

Released.

Less here.

Leaking.

Away.

Lucy.

Marjorie washes up and down inside and makes her wind into a beat, a breeze. Says, Hello, just to hear a sound, just to touch the outside. Marjorie walks sideways on carpet past the racks and the shelves until she is through and out and past the danger of Baby. She moves slowly until she finds the wide shining center path through the Store. The People, the People are here. Pushing their carts and finding the things they need. Marjorie moves slow through the People, feels the pull and the roll of them and the things and the good. She walks head-up and more usual on her usual path toward the swinging door. Marjorie smiles and nods, breathes wide big-winded breaths, is doing her best to feel less and less Lucy.

23. MARGIE

Downstairs Apartment #1 where Lucy had come to live smelled sweet and a little sour, a lot like those white crackers packaged in plastic with the bright yellow cheese. Margie's favorite kind, the crackers that came with the little red stick for spreading the soft cheese all over.

Maybe we could have said something about how that cheese is not real cheese. About all that salt in those crackers. Something about chemicals, something like that. That a growing child should not be always eating out of plastic.

But we said nothing.

Minding our own business, we called this.

After that first day of frogs and spinning, Margie spent the whole long summer out, together, with Lucy. Margie, let loose to sun, her pale skin turning red and staying red, her clothes becoming more and more streaked with green grass stains and the brown splash of mud. Lucy inventing all the games and Margie happy to play along. They made grass salads on the front lawn and had contests to see who could hold a frog in her hands the longest. Looked out at the hills that circled the town, the dead-end street, the gray-paint-peeling house, and tried to find the center, the treeless place where every far-away hill could be seen. Lucy turned her tiny body in cartwheels and Margie moved slow and smiling through her circles. Out, outside, watching ants build mountains of sand in the cracks of the sidewalks, standing on one leg in sunlight, drawing with big pieces of pink chalk on the rough black back of the dead-end street.

M-A-R-G-I-E

L-U-C-Y

And when it rained, or when the sun dripped down too hot, or when they wanted to, they ran for cover into the good packaged-cracker smell of Apartment #1. Lucy had her own bedroom and Lucy's ma said Margie could come to play anytime. Margie brought most of her stuffed animals down to live in Lucy's room, where they would be warm and safe and surrounded by many friends. She left only her blue bunny behind in Apartment #2, because Gram let it share their bed, because Margie needed the bunny to help her breathe and be in the darkness.

There, on the thick blue carpet beside Lucy's small pink bed, Lucy made weddings between the yellow bear in his bow tie and the princess doll with dirt smudges on her thick rubber cheeks.

I now pronounce you husband and wife, Lucy said.

Margie watched, her arms around the group of Lucy's dolls and Margie's matted stuffed friends in the audience.

You may kiss the bride.

Lucy gently touched the soft brown nose of the yellow bear to the thin pink lips of the princess doll. She held the furry face pressed against the plastic face for a long time, moving them sometimes, slowly, from side to side, up and down. Lucy making fish faces with her lips and soup-eating slurping sounds somewhere down deep inside her.

Margie watched, mouth-mostly-open, smiling, in awe, always in awe, of Lucy and how much she knew about the world.

Okay, Margie, Lucy said. Now you do it, and I'll watch.

No, Lucy. You're good. I don't know how.

It's easy, just take two of the toys and stand them up at the altar, and you are the priest. Well, girl-priest. And you say some stuff about love and then they kiss and then they are married and in love forever.

I don't know, Lucy. You keep going.

Come on, Margie. Don't be a stupid baby. Just try it.

Margie did not want to be stupid and Margie did not want to be a baby. Margie wanted Lucy to stay her friend. Needed. Margie needed Lucy to be her friend. Ma had her big, black-haired, chewing, drinking friend and Gram had her stories. Margie had Lucy. Thin-boned tangled-blonde-hair Lucy. Talking, laughing, soft-touching Lucy. Lucy, her unstuffed friend.

So Margie picked up the black-and-white panda bear with the missing eye and the orange tiger. She did what she thought Lucy had done, held them close together and hit their heads slowly against each other, held them out in front of Lucy, in front of the other toys, and said, Now, today, you two are friends, forever.

Margie pushed the orange tiger's soft brown nose hard against the panda's flat circle-stitched mouth and did her best to make the soupy sounds like Lucy had made. Margie, free, talking, playing, out, trying to be like all of us.

Lucy wide-eyed watched and laughed and laughed so hard she flopped to her side on the blue carpet and rolled from side to side, one hand holding onto her tiny heaving belly and the other pointing to the toys held tight in Margie's hands. Margie smiled because she saw Lucy smiling, and laughed a little because Lucy was laughing, but Margie did not know what was funny.

No, no, no, Margie, Lucy said between laughs and rolls and breathless breaths.

You can't do it like that!

Margie looked down at the soft round panda and the long orange tiger and she did not understand what was wrong. But she could feel the weight of wrong in the air, so Margie dropped both toys and said, Okay.

When Lucy could finally sit up and speak again, she put both of her hands on Margie's shoulders and looked straight and close and long into her eyes.

Margie, are you stupid? Don't you know anything?

Margie felt her face blow up big and hot and red and she felt her sweat start up on top of her lip and she did her best to look into Lucy's eyes and smile.

I know things.

Okay, sorry, I don't mean stupid. But, don't you watch TV or movies or something, Margie?

I watch TV.

A tiger and a panda can't get married!

I know.

If you know, then why did you marry them and make them kiss?

I don't know.

Don't you know about weddings at all? And kissing?

I don't know.

Okay, Margie, well. Well, I will teach you. A tiger and a panda can't get married because they are both boys. They can't kiss in a church either. Only boys and girls can get married. Boys can't marry boys!

Margie looked down at the one-eyed panda and the stuffed tiger and she tried to see her way through the hot unknown of what she had done wrong.

How could we explain this? That bears are boys and tigers are boys and that boys don't kiss other boys. That these toys should not be married. Something we all just see, know.

Lucy was a good teacher. She laughed at what Margie did not know, but she showed Margie the right way and she said that Margie was her friend. Sometimes Lucy said stupid but Lucy's stupid was not the same as Ma's stupid. Lucy might say stupid but Lucy always said sorry and Lucy held Margie's hand and combed Margie's hair. Lucy, her small fingers always gentle. Lucy, always talking, always moving.

Sometimes when Margie's heart beat fast and her wind was hard to catch, she lay down on the floor for a long time, staring at the ceiling with her arms and legs spread wide, and when Lucy asked what she was doing, Margie said, only, Floating.

Floating.

Lucy might have pinched Margie's elbow to see if Margie could feel it, to see if Margie would move, might have called Margie weird, but usually Lucy would try to float, too. The two of them, bellies rolling up and down with their breath, floating and held down heavy on the floor by their own growing bodies. Margie and Lucy, friends, floated, and sometimes they fell asleep that way, together, waking up only when Lucy's ma told Margie it was time to go home, or, if it was a good day, asked if she wanted to stay for dinner.

Margie liked Lucy's ma almost as much as she liked Lucy. Lucy's ma was short and wide and smelled like flower soap, like a teacher. She had soft red shoulder-touching hair and a big warm chest and sometimes she would pull Lucy close and kiss her head and if Lucy squirmed away then her ma would open her arms and give Margie a long hug.

My girls, Lucy's ma said.

Margie liked Lucy's ma's smell and she liked how she was big enough to make even big Margie feel small. She liked how when she was close to Lucy's ma's skin she could feel her own body more. Margie's blood and heart and inside parts beat louder inside the close hold of Lucy's ma. Margie liked that

Lucy's ma cooked dinner and that in Apartment #1 no one ate in front of the television.

Lucy's ma's friend LD came home from work at six, same as Ma, if Ma came home. LD came home at six covered in quarry white. White all over her blue work clothes, white in her ears, white in her eyebrows and caught in between the spikes of her short brown hair. LD was big like Lucy's ma but not soft like her. LD, taller and big in a solid way, big in a strong way, big in a way that made Margie feel scared and safe at the same time. Big like the big of Ma's friends, but softer, quiet, easier to see and smell and hear.

For a while, times when Margie was allowed to stay for dinner, soon as LD opened the front door, Lucy's ma yelled out, Hey, Lucy's got a friend over.

And later, Hey, babe, Margie's here.

And finally, the more Margie was there, the more dinners Margie spent eating slow and quiet beside Lucy and Lucy's ma and LD, no more announcements were needed.

LD would walk into the kitchen and nod, smile, and Lucy's ma would sit in the bathroom with LD before dinner while she showered the white dust away.

Don't say anything, Margie, Lucy said.

But Margie had nothing to say. Margie liked the smell of Lucy's ma and the quiet of Apartment #1. She did not wonder about the sharing of a bathroom, about hushed conversations through shower curtains.

Margie sat quietly at dinner and ate macaroni and cheese and baked chicken and green beans. She was there at the dinner table to see Lucy's ma's hand slip under. Margie smelled slices of apples and butter melting over corn. She was there to hear LD and Lucy's ma laughing loud inside the steaming bathroom. And salad. At dinner in Apartment #1, Margie ate salad. Margie was allowed to stay for dinner, for the tastes and smells and hands held below table, and Lucy called Margie her friend.

You're my friend, Margie, she said.

So don't say anything.

It's a secret.

Margie nodded and squeezed Lucy's hand when Lucy squeezed hers. Margie did not know exactly what secret was happening, but Margie knew about secrets. Margie had her own secret, her one allowed secret, hidden away under the blue-paper sea on the up-above wall of her bedroom in Apartment #2. Margie listened when Lucy talked and Margie closed her eyes when Lucy told her to close her eyes.

We thought Margie was a good girl. We liked that she was so quiet. We liked that questions were not much a part of Margie's world. We might have said good girl but what we were really thinking was simple, slow. A safe place to hide what we wanted to hide.

Margie.

Margie lived in the world as Margie, as herself, never anyone more or less or different. Margie loosened inside Lucy's ma's occasional hugs and she did her best to play games the way Lucy wanted her to play them. Margie cut her meat into bite-sized pieces and learned how to eat corn on the cob. That summer, Margie was never again told to get out, because Margie was out, always, for as long as she could be, out and away and free and not alone. Margie felt for maybe the first time that she belonged to someone, to Lucy, that there was someone waiting for her, someone who wanted to play and laugh and touch and float.

That summer, we let them be. Margie and Lucy. Making their world. Keeping secrets they could not name. That summer they were happy. They were as free as we could let them be.

24. MARJORIE

Marjorie does not know how Gram found the box of Ma under the bed or how she was strong enough to pull it out and pick it up and carry it past the small kitchen and through the living room. Marjorie stands in the dark hallway that connects all the apartments and looks at the box here on the green doormat in front of their front door.

GOD BLESS THIS HOME, the doormat, under the box, says.

Yes. Okay. Maybe.

God again. Gram and her God. God in the Club, God on all kinds of things on sale in the Store. If God has got nothing else to do then maybe God will bless this home. But Marjorie has too much to think about right now and from what she has seen, God takes a long time.

Maybe it was God who helped Gram put Ma's remainders out here with the trash. Marjorie in her mind tries to see Gram holding the box and opening the door and throwing Ma out beside the dried-up paint cans and Roberta's big plastic duck statue. Gram, gray, in-bed-all-day Gram, must have asked God for help to get this box out here. Gram saving up her strength, her prayers, for this? Is this the right place for the rest of Ma?

Marjorie makes a fist around her keys and releases. Feels the small sharp pain of metal teeth biting into her soft skin. Marjorie feels and feels and lets go. Looks at the brown box in the low hallway light and wonders if it will weigh the same if she picks it up. When she picks it up. Marjorie and the light-out-lined inside part of her self sometimes looks hard at a thing or People and tries to imagine the weight of them if she were to hold them. Marjorie and the other part of Marjorie, arms open, imagines reaching out and holding him or her or it close against this light, lit-up, not-there part of her self. To feel the shape and the weight of what she is touching.

But no. This is not what Marjorie should do. Many times, Dr. Goodwin has told her that this is what she does so that she will not have to touch real things and real People. Marjorie blows her wind in and down and says, Okay.

Okay, Dr. Goodwin.

Living in the world means touching the world, Marjorie.

Yes. I know.

Marjorie unfolds her fingers and unlocks the door and pushes it open into the dark apartment. She bends down and picks up the box with both hands. Feels the pain, in her back, her belly, her knees and her feet. And her head. The cardboard on her skin is rough and the weight is the weight of what Ma is now.

Marjorie, alone, no help from God, brings Ma back to the apartment.

She puts Ma's box down on the sofa and turns on the tall white burning light in the living room. Marjorie blinks her eyes fast against the bright naked light.

What if she buys a lampshade?

A thought. A covering. For decorating. For keeping eyes safe from the bright and for keeping bulbs safe from the dust, the burned, the dirty of the world. Ma hated lampshades and Gram is gone off to her own place where things like lampshades go unseen in the light of the Stories. But Marjorie likes lampshades. How they look and feel and hide and soften. Dr. Goodwin's office has many lampshades. Some big, some small. Just a little thing to do to make the light easier to look at.

And Marjorie has this other what-if on her mind. What she said to Dr. Goodwin. Just a fast idea. What she thought when Dr. Goodwin said to put the sofa in Ma's room and the too-soft bed in the living room.

What if Suzanne came over, Marjorie had said. And the only place for her to sit was a bed in the living room? And Marjorie would have to sit on the bed too, with Suzanne.

Marjorie saw it then, in Dr. Goodwin's office, and Marjorie can see it now. Suzanne in her mind, in her living room, coming in through the door and smiling and saying Hello, stopping by for a visit. To sit and talk together. And there would have to be a sofa. Marjorie thinks Dr. Goodwin is wrong about the bed in the living room because Marjorie wants to do what People do and People sit on sofas in living rooms. With lamps in shades. Bare bulbs covered. Suzanne could come by and they could sit together on the sofa and drink grape sodas and eat graham crackers with peanut butter and look at the yellow soft of the light. Talk. Mac can come, too. Marjorie can see this in her mind. And now that she is standing in the living room looking around at the bare white light on the gray walls and the big shadows on the gray carpet and the burned-in pain of the ghost of the bulb on her eyeballs, Marjorie is more sure that she should buy a lampshade to make where she lives look more like a place where People live.

And even if Suzanne never has the time to visit, Marjorie will be here. Gram will be here. Ma won't be here.

Ma will be, where?

Ma, the rest, the left-behind leftover Ma.

Lampshades are a good idea but right now Marjorie has more important things to do and things to think about. She has got this box of Ma to hide or open or put out with the trash. Gram moving around the apartment when Marjorie leaves it. Gram and her shut door, her Stories, her scissors. People and all the secrets they do when they are door-closed left alone.

The living room is small and the only place Marjorie can see to put Ma is on the sofa or next to the green chair or underneath the uneven card table in the corner. In the little square of the kitchen the cabinets have no doors and are stacked with cans and boxes anyway. The cold, thin, pink bathroom is just toilet, shower, sink. The only places Marjorie can think of for Ma are places that People can see. Out in the open. Where Gram will know. Marjorie understands what Dr. Goodwin said about People wanting to be near their loved-gone People, but she is still not sure what she wants to do with this box of Ma. Better to wait and think and know. For now, Marjorie just wants to put Ma away somewhere where her container will be quiet and unseen.

No noises from Gram's room and no light coming from under the door so Gram must be sleeping. Marjorie takes the box back to Ma's room. No. To her room. Marjorie takes the box to her room and closes the door and in the dark gets down on her knees and pushes Ma's box back under the bed. Breathes her breath in beat with her pains. Reaches her arm far as she can under the mattress and pushes the box to where she thinks Gram cannot go.

Gram will think that the box of Ma got taken away with the trash. Good, fine. Marjorie free to do what she will do.

Marjorie uses the side of the soft bed to help her stand and she rubs her knees with her hands. Her wide knees are too big for her palms. It feels good, to feel her self. Marjorie holds handfuls of her heavy skin and feels how warm hands feel on skin through pants. She takes her bra off and moves her shoulders free, slow, in circles. Marjorie sits down on the side of the bed and the springs squeak beneath her and she moves her hands down, around and up and down her legs. This is good, sitting, looking at the dark, rubbing the blood and bones and meat around inside her legs. Not thinking, not talking, spending some time with her self after another long, long day with the People. And Gram does not need to know that Ma is still around. Marjorie alone can know. Marjorie has her secrets and Marjorie can keep her secrets. She rubs hard against her legs, into her legs, starts at her knees and moves slowly up her thighs and squeezes all around her thighs and then rubs slowly back down to her knees and squeezes all around her knees.

It is good. To feel and touch. To know all the big beating-heart-warmed parts of her self.

Marjorie thinks about Dr. Goodwin and how he sometimes takes off his glasses and rubs his eyes. Dr. Goodwin is a good-looking man and when he takes his glasses off Marjorie thinks he looks like he could be on television, on the Stories. Dr. Goodwin has very smooth skin and clean shirts with collars and straight ties and shiny shoes and he always smells like peppermint. Most men Marjorie knows do not care so much about how they look and smell. Mac and Benjamin are People She Does Not Mind but their faces are always full of little hairs and their shirts are always t-shirts and their t-shirts are almost always stained or ripped. Steve is worst. Steve is on her People She Minds list because of the touching and because Steve is always showing his huge white skin. His hairy face. Steve smells like sweat, like french fries. Steve tries to keep his shirts tucked into his pants but his belly and sides and back always slip through.

But no. He was worst. The worst. He almost never wore a shirt. Even when He went outside the apartment to wherever He went He did not wear a shirt.

Look, Dr. Goodwin. Trying. Letting in.

Marjorie would like to clean out His department forever but there are some things she can still see. The thick, black, curly hairs on His big hanging belly and how the hairs were all over His chest and how He would sit in Gram's chair and hold His beer in one hand and with the other rub and rub and rub those hairs. Put His fingers into those hairs and comb and pull and twist and smooth. Little black hairs left on Gram's chair in the sink on the living room rug in Marjorie's room on the kitchen table in the everywhere, the all over of Apartment #2. And He was a paper chewer so between beers He would tear up pieces of whatever paper was around and make a mouth-sized paper ball and He would put it in His mouth and chew and chew. Sometimes spit dripped down the sides of His mouth and onto His chest and into the black of the hairs, there, but He never noticed and if He felt it He did not care. Newspapers, napkins, letters, bills, homework, magazines, tissues, pages from books. He did not care what kind of paper He was chewing as long as He had His mouth full of paper. Paper or beer. Both. His big lips opening and closing, the long black hairs on His jaw moving up and down, chewing on the paper until there was almost nothing left to chew and whatever was left He spit out and stuck somewhere. Thick little black hairs and wet paper stuck. The inside of Apartment #2.

And when His mouth was not busy with beer and paper, when He finished his six-pack or could not find a book to rip up, He talked. Not talked. Yelled. Words. At the room, at nobody, at that name He made up, that name He made her hear. Marge. Marge. Marge. But Marjorie had her ways of not hearing Him. Marjorie had her self, her inside. The sounds of her body breathing, beating, being.

Going to the departments where she does not go. Trying, Dr. Goodwin. Her wind, moving hard, fast. Her fingers, holding tight, holding on.

Him and His dirty paper and beer and bad-words mouth. Marjorie knows that People use bad words and usually she does not mind. She knows People like Benjamin cannot help themselves. That words are hard. That there are just too many words to know. Marjorie knows that sometimes bad words help People say what is hard to say, like I am sad or I am angry. Or help. Help me. Marjorie can see this on television, that the bad words start to come out when People feel things that are real and need to say what they need to say and what they need to say cannot be let out in any other way.

But He was not People. He was just mean. Marjorie does not think that He could feel any feeling except angry. When He had stuffed His mouth with all the beer and paper He could take, He yelled, and the words He yelled were always bad words and when He yelled He always yelled for Marge.

And the yelling and the chewing and the drinking and spitting not even the worst, worst of it.

The quiet. The bad of quiet.

The worst of no sound.

Gram, gone, where?

Ma, quiet.

Ma did her best. Ma tried to make Him quiet down. Ma did not want anyone to hear. Ma would sit on the floor next to Gram's chair and light cigarettes for

Him and hold them to His lips when He was too far away to hold them for Himself.

Leave Margie out of it, Ma might say.

Yell at me if you want to yell, Ma might say.

But yelling was not the worst of Him.

Marjorie believes that Ma did the best job she could do and Marjorie knows that He was too long gone to hear any of it. Ma got His paper for Him. Ma took home napkins from her work so that He would have something to chew on. Ma took Bibles from the church because He liked thin sheets best. Because Gram could not watch. Because He liked messing up the words of the Lord. When He chewed He could not yell and so many nights Ma spent on her knees on the floor in front of Him there in Gram's chair. Ma ripping and ripping, crushing, making little paper balls so that His mouth would have something to do.

Marjorie rubs her knees harder. Shakes her head. Feels her self.

Here, she says.

Here in the bedroom.

Here, alone.

Now. Here, now.

Marjorie needs to catch her wind. Marjorie cannot be Marjorie without her wind. Her heart, beating against her inside. Wanting out. Wanting away. Marjorie tries to catch hold, to stay here.

Dr. Goodwin wants Marjorie to spend some time in these darker departments, but Marjorie has reasons why she does not go to them. Private. Private. Private. What Marjorie has got in here. Marjorie must think her way out, away from Him. Marjorie feels good thinking about Dr. Goodwin and his smooth face and nice suits and she does not mind thinking about Benjamin and Mac. Suzanne is good, Suzanne is a face for her to hold and touch and feel. Lucy is a place she wants and does not want to go to. Lucy is too big, too unknown.

Marjorie is not going to go to the place in her where He is.

Ma. Marjorie does not mind thinking about Ma if Ma is the Ma coughing in bed watching her no-sound television sneaking her secret cigarettes. That Ma, the after-Ma, is fine. But Marjorie is not going to spend her time in her mind with Him-Ma. That Him-Ma was still Ma but different, the mean of Ma, a Ma who did her best but whose best meant ripping up Bibles and going away to get more beer. Dr. Goodwin wants Marjorie to think about Him and Ma as two different People but the best Marjorie can do is think about Ma as different departments of Ma. The before-Ma, the Ma who sat with her and watched the fish float across the television. The Him-Ma, a Ma she will stay away from, and after-Ma. Not really even Ma, then, after, just someone sitting alone in her room with her salt-and-vinegar potato chips, feeling what secrets she was feeling.

Enough.

Away.

Get away.

Go.

Marjorie's legs are very warm from all her rubbing. Sometimes when Marjorie goes into these departments she forgets that she is her self, now, here, in her body. Marjorie breathes, to feel her self, to remember, rubs her skin, to remember. Squeezes, softly, to feel. Feels her solid self big and alive beneath her. Says some words to stop all the quiet.

Hello.

Welcome.

Cold Out There Today.

It is good to hear good words. Marjorie looks around the room and sees that she cannot see. Sitting in the dark. This is not what People do. Marjorie leans over and turns on the bare bulb lamp and the room lights up too naked and bright. People use lampshades to quiet the light.

Marjorie has her wind back here with her. Her heart, back in time with her.

Is this what Dr. Goodwin wants?

Too many things to know.

Marjorie sits back down into the warm soft circle she has made here and looks around at the big shadows this let-out light makes. Maybe she will buy some lampshades. Make the living room into a room where People might want to live and come and talk. Make this room more into a room where Marjorie wants to be.

Ma won't mind. Ma can't mind. Ma, gone under. Out of the trash and back under the bed. Under the bed, as good a place as any, for now.

Marjorie will keep thinking about it. She will stack this lampshade idea in her mind with all the others. She will see how and what and if she feels.

25. MARGIE

At recess Margie waited for Lucy by the wall. In the still-strong sunlight of back-to-school, Margie stood, Margie waited. Quiet and patient, for her friend.

The wall was not a wall. More a fence, really. Hexagon holes in green wire and silver poles holding it all together. We might even have called this a chain-link fence.

A cheap way to separate this from that.

Us from us.

But Lucy called it the wall so Margie called it the wall, and though these particulars of language seem important to us, Margie did not care about the words. Margie and Lucy walked to school together and in the morning they went to the wall and at recess they went to the wall and after school they met at the wall. A wall, a fence, a place. All Margie seemed to care about was Lucy and the world they had there together.

Meet me at the wall, Lucy would say.

Margie would nod and all through math class and silent reading time, Margie's mind would crawl out through the rectangular classroom windows, across the dried-up kid-feet-killed playground grass, to the wall.

Lucy said that small people lived in the tall grass that grew around the bottom of the wall. Small people with small houses and small furniture and small animals they walked on small leashes. A whole small city going on around the wall. Small lives so much better than the big, normal, boring life they had on dead-end Summer Street. Lucy said that she had seen the small people a few times. Eating small dinners, singing small songs, a small man dancing slow and close with a small woman. Lucy had seen the small people, but Margie still had not.

Stuck in her classroom, at the back, big belly pressed against small school desk, Margie stared out the window and thought about the wall and wanted. Wanted to be out there, to wait for Lucy and look for the small people. Margie wanted to be away from the words and papers and pencils and raised hands and questions and whispers of school. To be outside where she could feel and touch and see a small place better than where she was.

When we called Margie's name, it was as if she wasn't there. Her body, the soil smell of her body, was there, but where was the rest of her? We cannot say. We cannot say we wondered much about it. All we knew was that we called on her. We tried. We did what we could manage, and because Margie did not look up, because she kept quiet and caused no problems beyond the absence of her eyes, we soon stopped calling, trying, caring. We soon stopped seeing Margie much at all.

But Lucy, we saw.

Pretty, little, wild, light-haired Lucy could not go unnoticed.

Lucy, who belonged to Margie.

Though we would have said it was the other way around.

Lucy was almost always late for their daily recess meetings at the wall. Lucy was loud and touched too hard and teachers liked to make her sit inside to make her learn not to pinch or push or sing or swear. Margie waited at the wall for Lucy, half of her watching the grass for any signs of the small city moving and half of her watching the school doors for the moment when Lucy would break free. Margie liked to put her fingers through the wall, to feel the smooth, hard hexagon shapes against her skin. She held on there, waited, watched.

Maybe, in the beginning, we tried to help Margie play with the other kids.

Maybe we said, Go run around, Margie.

Once or twice we might have asked her what she was doing there, but Margie only smiled and shrugged and it was easy enough for us to forget. To leave Margie alone and free to hold and stare and wait.

And then there were those of us who did see Margie. Or, not see her. There were those of us who sometimes thought to look at Margie and we did not so much as see Margie, we smelled her. We smelled cigarette smoke in the knit of an unwashed sweatshirt. Maybe we felt sorry about it, or probably we held our noses and giggled. We smelled powdered cheese dust eaten directly from the packet from the box of macaroni and cheese. If we did see her, maybe we saw Margie put her head down on her desk at the end of the day. Margie, rolling her forehead in slow circles. The shine of her hair, how it fell in slick strands that touched her shoulders. We smelled the smell and maybe we did not know what it was or maybe we did, the smell of what were once chicken nuggets dipped in honey and the soft skin of cafeteria french fries kept in a pocket.

Days when we had nothing better to do than look, we laughed at Margie's pilly purple sweatsuit. We asked each other why she didn't just wear normal clothes? If we thought no one was looking, which was almost always – almost always no one was looking – we threw dried leaves or sticks or lunch leftovers at Margie. We said all the bad things we say to each other when we are young. Now, maybe now, a very few of us will remember what we said and we might wonder about Margie. Why was she like that? Whatever happened to her? Were we at all to blame?

Margie did not mind the teachers who blew their whistles or the kids who threw things. She stayed quiet and calm inside herself and almost never felt angry or sad. Felt, in fact, less and less and less. Margie was busy with the wall, with the smell of the sap releasing from the trees, the feel of the grass against her skin. How the light changes as clouds move through. Margie rolled and looked out far away to where the hills were, to where the hills sloped into hills and more hills. She was happy to be with the wall, with the idea of the small city out there, down there, all around her, somewhere. Margie did not mind the loud world outside and above her because Lucy was coming, because once Lucy was there, everything else went away.

Lucy did the talking that Margie did not like to do. She knew all the words. Lucy could fit her body into spaces much smaller than where Margie could go. She would lie down low against the wall and squint through the grass and tell Margie what was going on down there, in there. Lucy had all the words and Lucy could see all sorts of things that Margie could not.

There's a small hat. A very small hat. Like a boy's hat. And I see a tiny pink dress too. Definitely a small dress, with straps, and a big bottom part, like a ballerina, like a ballerina's dress. I can see them for sure, Margie. But no small people. I don't see the small people but I can tell that they're there. They're back there, I think. Behind those dandelions, see? The grass is moving a little and I know they're in there. The boy and the girl, and she doesn't even have her dress on. They're naked in there. Do you see, Margie?

Margie held herself up on her elbows and knees and tried to see what Lucy saw.

I don't see.

You know what they're doing in there, Margie? Do you know?

I don't see. I don't know.

They're doing it. I bet they're doing it back there. Behind the dandelions, in that tall grass there. The boy and the girl, they're naked and it feels really good and they're doing it.

Margie liked to stare at the ground and through the grass and to think about the small people out there. She wondered if the small people looked like her, like big people. If there was a small Margie and a small Lucy and a small Ma and a small Gram somewhere down there around the wall. Or if the small people were new and different and not like them at all. Margie wondered, but she did not ask. Margie lay down low and looked and waited and listened to hear what Lucy saw.

One day Lucy told Margie that she had gone back to the school at night and that she had caught a small person. Lucy had not taken Margie with her. Lucy said it was a thing she had to do alone. She had waited until her ma and LD were sleeping and then had run all the way to the school. Lucy said that the streetlights were strong enough for her to see. She said that the small people had been out having a party. Small cups and plates and small men in bow ties and small women in only their underwear. Lucy said she had seen a small man in a suit laughing and climbing the wall and that she had taken him. She said she had taken the small man home with her, and that he lived with her now, and that someday they were going to get married and have babies.

Margie wanted to see the man. Margie wondered about the man. More than anything, Margie wanted to smell and see and touch the small man in the suit who lived somewhere secret in Lucy's room.

But Lucy said, No.

Lucy said that there were some things she had to keep all for herself.

It's private, Lucy said.

This is private.

Lucy talked about the small man for a few days, and then she stopped. Margie understood that private meant not asking questions, but long after Lucy stopped talking about the small man, Margie kept thinking about him. She wanted to see him, to see how his small body moved and to watch how Lucy took care of him. What did he feel like? How did he eat? Some nights, lying awake in bed next to the slow snores of Gram, Margie thought about leaving Apartment #2 and running to the school, like Lucy had done. She thought about going to find her own small person to keep in her room, under her bed, to take care of and watch and touch.

But Margie stayed in bed. Margie did not know anything about the town at night. Lucy said there were streetlights, but when Margie looked out the high-up window of Apartment #2, she saw only black, dark, black. Margie thought that the streets at night might change shape, that she might lose the school, Lucy, herself. And Margie was not sure if a small person would want to come and live with her. She did not know if under the bed she shared with Gram was a good place for a small person to be. Margie wanted to meet Lucy's small man first, to watch him eat pieces of candy bars and ask him if he liked living in a world where everything was so big.

Because sometimes even Margie wanted to live somewhere else. Sometimes Ma's yelling and the slamming front door and the loud of Gram's stories and the sounds of Ma's friends who came in the day, in the night, in the in-between and all the time, made Margie want to be somewhere else. Even school might be better. Margie wondered if maybe she could live with the small people at the wall, instead of bringing them to live with her in the banging and yelling and cigarette-smoking of Apartment #2. Maybe the small man liked living with Lucy because it was quieter there. Better air, down there. Margie very much wanted her own small person, but Margie worried about it, about what a small man might feel if she were to take him to live with her.

So Margie stayed in bed. At school, at recess, she stayed alert and looking for the small people. Margie was afraid Lucy might have forgotten about the small man. That Lucy had forgotten to bring food and water to the small man, that the small man forgotten under Lucy's bed had no air to make wind, that the small man's small heart had stopped beating. Margie was afraid but Margie said nothing, because this was Lucy minding Lucy's business.

But in secret, another secret, secretly, Margie worried about him.

Margie thought hard about his small, soundless heart.

Maybe we should have worried about Margie. Maybe we should have asked what was on her mind. Small people? What would we have said to that, anyway? What kid doesn't stare out windows? And how were we supposed to know that the school lunch we found in her pockets, the smeared meat and carrots and potatoes, were not there because she did not know enough to eat her lunch. We just could not have known about it, about how Margie was trying hard to save some food for the small people, to keep a whole small world alive out there by the wall.

But there she was. Breathing her breath as slow as she could, watching, waiting for Lucy. Margie, keeping her secrets, wanting things that could not possibly be.

26. MARJORIE

I think you know more than you think you do.

Love is not for me, Dr. Goodwin. I am happy to be with my self and the People. Doing what I do.

I know, Marjorie, and I'm happy that you take such good care of yourself. But talking about love can't hurt, right?

I don't know about all that.

What do you love, Marjorie?

Me?

Oh, I don't know, Dr. Goodwin.

Too many things to say. I will need to think some more about that.

How do you see love happening around you, Marjorie? In your life?

The People. I see love happening with the People who pass by.

What do you see?

Oh, the People see a shirt and they say, I love that shirt. Say to each other, I love that shampoo, I love that lamp, I love that pen. Lots of things to love in the Store.

That sounds like a certain kind of love. Affection, maybe. For objects, things that we feel somehow make our lives better.

Yes. A lot of love of things.

Any other ways you see love, Marjorie?

Animals. Suzanne's son Tony has a pet puppy he has brought to the Club and he carried that puppy close to him and he kissed the puppy's head and was saying I love you, I love you, I love you, like that.

Okay. Anything else?

People love. Friends. Moms and babies. Not so much the dads. People come in holding hands but not in that way. As friends. Some families seem nice.

Sure. In a good family there is a lot of love. And maybe people from bad families make new families with their friends. Do you feel that way, Marjorie?

I feel fine, Dr. Goodwin.

Some people say that in families or with very close friends the kind of love they have for each other is unconditional. Have you heard that before?

No I have not.

It means that the love between them stays forever. That no matter how good or bad someone is, they will always be loved and accepted. Many mothers feel unconditional love for their children.

You don't feel cold in here today, Dr. Goodwin?

No, I feel comfortable. Are you cold, Marjorie?

Yes Dr. Goodwin, I am cold today. I am going to put my coat on if it is okay with you.

Sure, Marjorie. I want you to be comfortable.

Feel better, now?

Better, yes. Good.

So that's what I mean by unconditional. Even when a child is bad, and even when a mother is angry, there is still a lot of love between them.

Yes. Good.

Do you think your mother felt that way, Marjorie?

Not again with Ma, Dr. Goodwin. Ma's gone. Put away.

I don't want to upset you, Marjorie, but I do think we need to talk about these important things. Your mother is gone but I think she is still very much alive inside your mind and I think that's why we need to talk about her.

She's pushed under. The bed. Right now I have no Ma on my mind. Nothing to say about Ma.

Okay. We don't need to talk about your mother right now if you don't want to. But sometime.

You have a very beautiful office, Dr. Goodwin.

Thank you, Marjorie. I'm glad you feel comfortable here.

I do. Four lamps and four lampshades. A lot of light.

I like to keep it bright. But I think you are trying to change the subject, Marjorie.

Just saying what is in my mind, Dr. Goodwin.

Can you think of any other ways you see love happening around you?

Valentine's Day. People love hearts and chocolates. But all that is over now, in the Store.

Any other ideas you have about Valentine's Day besides chocolates and hearts?

It's a love day. Men and ladies together. Kissing. That kind of love.

Romantic love, you mean? Between married people. Or with a boyfriend. A girlfriend.

Yes Dr. Goodwin. I watch the Stories. People and what they do in the dark. I know about that.

I think it's best if we try to say the right words, Marjorie. Are you talking now about sex? How people in romantic relationships often use their bodies to show love? The love in a healthy sexual relationship.

Oh Dr. Goodwin.

You don't need to be embarrassed, Marjorie. We've talked about this before.

I don't know anything about that. I just go to the Store. See the People. Watch the Stories.

I'd like to ask you some direct questions, Marjorie. Try to answer them if you can. If you feel ready.

I need to get out of this coat now, Dr. Goodwin.

Take your time.

Relax, Marjorie. Open your fingers. Good. Take some deep breaths.

Good. Can I ask you some questions now?

You can ask, Dr. Goodwin. But I don't know.

Do you ever think about sex?

Oh Dr. Goodwin. I already said. I watch the Stories. I see the men and the ladies. The no clothes. What is moving around in the dark. I think about what I see.

Do you ever feel like you want to have sex, Marjorie?

No, Dr. Goodwin. That is not for me.

Breathe deep. In and out. Slow. You don't need to worry.

You okay?

Okay.

Marjorie, do you remember having sex?

No, Dr. Goodwin. I have said so before. No, I have not done that. That is not for me.

You are a smart person, Marjorie. I know you know that to make a baby a man and a woman must have sexual intercourse.

Yes, Dr. Goodwin. I know you know I know that. Yes, I know.

What about Lucy?

Dr. Goodwin, I do not want any more of these questions. Lucy is let go. Like you said. Why talk about Lucy? Too hot in here. All these lamps. And bright. I don't want to talk about Lucy.

Calm down, Marjorie. Deep breaths. Good. I don't want to upset you.

I am not upset. Fine.

We don't need to talk about Lucy any more today but I think this is something you must think about, Marjorie.

Think about and don't think about, Dr. Goodwin. Let go and let in and go away and stay. Always another thing. And I am fine.

You aren't fine, Marjorie. Inside, I think, you aren't fine. Am I right?

I said fine and I am fine, Dr. Goodwin. Inside. Outside. Under.

Can I tell you something I've learned from talking to a lot of people, Marjorie?

Sure, Dr. Goodwin.

I've learned that people are very strong. That when people have been hurt or when people have some reason to protect themselves, they build walls inside their minds. That people's minds are very powerful and that our brains are very good at pushing away what we don't want to think about.

Good. I see. People are strong.

But people can't live that way forever, I don't think. Our walls usually aren't as strong as we think they are. They can break. Thoughts and images and feelings start to come through. Do you know what I mean?

Like a leak.

Yes, like a leak. And a small leak builds and builds until there is so much pressure built up inside that something breaks. The leak becomes a flood.

Sounds bad, Dr. Goodwin. So much water, everywhere.

But one way to prevent that from happening is to talk about these things that are hiding in there. The things we don't want to talk about. What hurts us. What bothers us. What we need to remember and what we need to feel.

Okay, Dr. Goodwin. But I keep my mind very clean. I wash the bad things away with my waters and I feel fine. No leaks. Not a flood. Like a shower, warm.

But maybe you need to think about some of those things, Marjorie. Maybe you need to feel the bad things. What if you didn't wash them away?

People have to wash, Dr. Goodwin. People have to be clean to go on with the day.

And people also need to be honest with themselves.

Yes. Right.

Even when the feelings are bad, even when it hurts to remember, our minds can't push things away forever.

Okay.

I have a question and I want you to answer me honestly.

Okay.

Where did Lucy come from, Marjorie?

Lucy, Dr. Goodwin.

Yes. Where did Lucy come from?

From me, Dr. Goodwin. Lucy came from me. I know that. I am remembering. From my self. Never had a chance.

And where else?

I want you to think about this, Marjorie.

Breathe.

Breathe.

Good.

Let's just sit here for a while, Marjorie. Until you feel better.

Better?

Marjorie?

Okay, Dr. Goodwin.

Did you think of what you love, yet, Marjorie?

I am thinking.

I am still thinking.

What is it you want, Marjorie?

I don't know, Dr. Goodwin.

From life, I mean. From the world. What do you really, really want?

I just want, Dr. Goodwin.

I just want.

27. MARGIE

It's because of my time, Margie, Lucy said, and she held her head in her hands and held her arms around her legs and made a ball of herself in the hot shade at the edge of the brook.

Summertime. Summer, the time for Margie and Lucy. Sun-lit, school-less, outside, let out, unwatched, unheard, free.

It hurts, Lucy said. Because it's my time.

You don't know about it yet, Margie.

You're still a kid.

Margie sat beside in-time, in-pain Lucy and Margie put her hand soft as she could on Lucy's hair and Margie rubbed Lucy's head slow and gentle, the way Lucy had showed her. Margie, out-of-time Margie, did not know what time was giving Lucy this pain. But Margie would do anything Lucy asked her to do. If Lucy said she was sad, Margie would put her two arms around Lucy and squeeze her tight like Lucy told her. When Lucy was angry, Margie sat still beside Lucy while Lucy screamed out all the bad words she knew, while Lucy threw rocks against the sidewalk and kicked ant hills to dust.

You've got those, Lucy said, pointing to the rise of Margie's big chest. But you haven't started your time, yet, Margie.

Thingies, Margie said.

Boobs, Lucy said.

Yours are already bigger than mine and I bet once you start your time they'll get even bigger.

You're lucky, Margie, Lucy said.

Ask your ma about it, Margie. I've got cramps hurting me bad and I don't want to talk right now.

Thingies. Boobs. A time. Pains.

Margie did not want to ask Ma about it. Margie was growing, always, but more, now. Not just wide but up, out, hanging down. Hairs, Margie was growing hairs. Breasts. Lucy and Margie, one summer day, suddenly, or over some time, slowly, by magic, by surprise, had breasts. Not the round, sexless hills that had been there before. Not just fat there in those outmost places but breasts. Breasts that bounced with touch. Breasts that stood up small and hard and pointed on Lucy's thin chest, that grew out heavy and long above Margie's big stomach. Lucy's ma bought her soft bras to keep her breasts contained and Margie stretched her t-shirts out bigger, big as they could go so that hers would fit inside, so that they could hide.

Margie did not ask Ma about it. Margie hid herself quiet and away as much she could and once the weather warmed and summer started, Margie got out. Away, always, as much as she could be, from Apartment #2. Margie pulled her shirts out big as she could make them and slept with her arms stiff, still against her sides, as if Gram might forget she was there at all. Margie kept quiet, kept herself as hidden as she could, tried to be as much as she could out, away, with Lucy.

Because now there was the returning friend. The black-haired friend there every night shirtless with Ma beside. The always-there friend who Ma let in who Ma let have a key. The low, deep voice of the loud friend seemed slow coming at first, just a rumble, now and then, through Apartment #2, and slowly, slowly Margie heard more of him, and more, until she knew him, knew the sound and smell of him. Him, his voice, the loud of him, thump of him, his sounds so different from the rest of them up there in Apartment #2.

Margie was so used to Gram's high, nails-in-a-bucket voice she hardly heard it anymore.

My pains. My heart.

Lord, hear our prayer.

Gram's voice was part of Apartment #2, was lost in the sound of the television, the screams and sighs of the stories. Ma's voice, too, loud and strong and ripping as it was, only hit Margie with its longest wave.

Big as a fucking house.

Stupid Margie.

Margie, always listening, eyes so often closed, concentrating, had learned the sounds and voices of Apartment #2, the pounding, the out-of-breath sounds, the behind-door laughing, the long watery flush of the toilet, Gram's snores, the holding sounds of the pains. Margie had learned how to stay where she was and go away, how to breathe her breaths into her hand, her bunny, how not to hear. She knew how to go inside, into her wind and blood and heartbeat, where the sounds were always the same, where everything belonged only to Margie.

Ma's sweating, shirtless, more-and-more-there friend was not like the others. The others, Margie had learned how not to hear. The others came and left and did not come back. But this friend, this chewing, huge-hairy-handed friend, was there in Apartment #2 and would not go unheard. His voice broke through, into Margie. The big, black-haired friend, his sound, his footsteps, the feeling of him in her home, sat down heavy on Margie's wide shoulders. This friend was a staying friend, and that made Margie want to leave.

We might have stepped in and said, Go, Margie.

Get away.

Get out.

But where was Margie going to go?

Lucy. Almost every day, Margie went downstairs to Lucy's good-smelling Apartment #1. Or outside, on the sidewalk, by the brook, and as much as possible, with Lucy. Out watching the circling hills that did not move. Even with breasts, even though we would have called them too old for such things, the two growing girls sat together by the brook with the frogs or played the pretending games Lucy wanted to play. Margie always the salesman, the doctor, the priest, and Lucy always herself, grown up, beautiful and rich and wanting and getting.

Lucy gave the speeches and Margie listened.

Forgive me Father for I have sinned, for I have bought the biggest boat and all the seas and from now on all the blue on the globe belongs to me, to Lucy, Queen Lucy, and Margie, too, Margie can have some too, and we are big, and we are sailing and we are dressed in diamonds and rubies and pearls.

Good, Margie said.

No, Margie. You're the priest. You have to think I am bad and you have to say you forgive me for it or I'll die.

Don't die, Margie said.

You have to say, I forgive you for all of your sins.

I forgive you, Margie said. For all of your things.

Margie said what Lucy told her to say and Margie did what Lucy asked her to do. When Lucy said she was lonely, Margie held Lucy's hands the way Lucy said boys should. Lucy pretended, and Margie laughed and played along. Margie saw everything Lucy wanted her to see, Lucy tall and beautiful, dressed up and sailing, shining.

How could we have guessed that Margie knew about diamonds or rubies or pearls? Or that she could see herself there, beside Lucy, bigger and darker but glittering all the same. Sailing away, together, on a sea as smooth as the brook in summer. We might have laughed at all that Margie saw inside her. Slow, soft Margie, in her purple sweatsuit, sidekick to skinny, loud-mouthed Lucy, might have shocked us with how bright and clear she could see all these beautiful things inside her. What with the stares, the circling, the rubbing her head against whatever was cool or soft, we could not imagine all that Margie was imagining. How Lucy made the worlds, but Margie was the one who really lived in them.

You just wait for your time, Margie, Lucy said.

See how different you feel.

Grown up.

And it hurts a lot.

For some time, Margie played the pretending game with the returning friend. She closed her eyes and sat down inside herself and imagined that he was not there in her home, the town, the world. She stayed away, outside, with Lucy, playing as best she could the part of all the people Lucy wanted to play with. Margie tried and tried and tried to squeeze herself shut, to keep the sound of the chewing, rumbling, yelling, laughing, pounding friend out, to forget the smell of his cigarettes and spit and white-dusted boots kicked off at the door.

He knew her name. He knew something like her name. A part of it. He knew Margie only in the parts of her she could not hide. He knew Apartment #2 and he knew where to find her inside it. The black-hair-spitting friend left pieces of himself everywhere. Dark hairs on the white bathroom floor and stuck to the toilet bowl, chewed-up pieces of paper stuck to the kitchen table and all around Ma's bed and even on Gram's chair where he sat sometimes to drink, to yell, to watch the television and take over the room. Ma's friend, there, in Gram's chair, and Ma, there, below, beside him. Gram, wherever Gram went, and Margie, who did not need anyone to tell her to get away. Margie, who did as best she could.

We didn't know.

Or, we knew, but we didn't know any better.

We were left alone and lonely and we liked the way he raged and pounded and wept and held us.

We were powerless, thin-boned and living out the long, slow life of our stupid mistakes.

We asked for forgiveness.

We minded our own business.

Had we noticed those breasts Margie was growing, maybe we would have told her to cover them up. Maybe we would have told her about becoming a woman. Her time, what to expect. Tried to lessen the surprise, the shock of what her body would do.

Margie, a woman.

Maybe this was difficult for us to see. Fat little Margie. Slow-moving, slow-eyed Margie sitting alone in the kitchen eating saltines smeared with butter. Margie, body ballooning out in every direction, a woman, an almost-woman. Her time, coming any minute. Had we sat with Margie, talked to Margie, held Margie, helped Margie, maybe we would have seen that all the extra Margie, all the eating and eating and growing was a wall being built. Another Margie in the making. Maybe we would have seen how she hid herself with herself, how her breasts hung same as the rest of her, how her shoulders hunched in and her stomach stuck out.

But even if we saw, even if we noticed, what would we have done?

Margie was Margie and we were us, all of us, and much as we fucked and lied and pretended otherwise, there was no way out of us.

There we were, together and absolutely separate.

Here we are.

Together with Margie. Down low, away, in the shade of the trees beside the brook. Body-doubling and sunlight leaving. Margie, waiting for something, for her time, for the time that Lucy said was coming.

28. MARJORIE

Rough day, Marjorie?

Oh, Mac, you know. A day. Good. Rough.

Shirley Temple?

Yes. The usual.

The usual, coming right up.

Marjorie sits in her usual place and today the barstool feels not big enough for her self to get comfortable. She moves her weight from side to side to find the best spot for sitting. Suzanne waved to Marjorie when she came in but she did not stop to say Hello and Marjorie has not seen Suzanne for some minutes now. She has not yet said Hello to Suzanne so Marjorie is sitting up straight as she can, making circles with her eyes around the Club, looking for where Suzanne is. There are more People than usual in the Club this afternoon and the smells are strong and not usual. Marjorie kicks her feet a little against the bar and puts her nose up high and when she brings her wind inside she keeps it there to see what smells she can see.

Marjorie is almost sure the new smells are the smell of food. Roasted like meat cooking. Warm and thick like butter like potatoes. Light like crescent rolls. Clean like steamed green beans.

Marjorie brings the smells inside her and lets her mind taste them and the smell and the taste of the food goes right to that department where she most does not want to go and Marjorie coughs, chokes on her wind, blows hard to get the smells out, holds her hand up over her nose to keep her self safe and it may be too late to stop the remembering because inside she is lighting on fire and outside Marjorie is starting to sweat.

Mac brings the Shirley Temple over and puts it down in front of her.

You all right, Marjorie?

I smell something, Mac. What's the smell?

Mac tips his head back, big nose up in the air, and takes some deep breaths. He smells and smells, looks like nothing, like Mac, normal, and smells, and then something happens to his face, his eyes get a little bigger and he looks right at Marjorie's eyes and his whole face has fallen down soft and sad.

Oh, sorry, Marjorie. I thought we told you about that.

About what?

Prime Rib Dinner. We had to change it to Wednesdays.

I go here on Wednesdays.

I know, Marjorie. I'm sorry I forgot to tell you.

I don't go to Prime Rib Dinner.

I know. I couldn't help it. The meat guy's schedule changed and he can only get it to us on Wednesdays now.

Mac pulls his face up so far his eyes and nose and forehead wrinkle in tight and sorry. Marjorie looks at the wood of the bar so that she does not need to see. Marjorie watches People all day long and she knows the ways People's faces can look. Faces get bunched up hard when they are angry and spread out wide and warm when they are happy. Sorry mostly squints around the eyes and sad is falling. Marjorie all day looks at People and Marjorie knows how to see the feel on faces. Mac's face is squinting-falling-squinting and this is not what Marjorie wants to see. She looks down at the tiny bubbles swimming up the sides of her light pink drink. The bright red cherry that alone floats inside.

Well, Mac. I go here Wednesdays.

Sorry, Marjorie.

Thursdays is Prime Rib Dinner. I don't go here Thursdays.

Yeah, I know, Marjorie. I should have remembered to tell you.

Marjorie knows that Mac has to do what he has to do for the good of the Club. Just like how Marjorie has to do what she has to do for the Store. What Steve says. What the meat guy says. People want to have their own ways but People have to always think about other People. Marjorie holds her hand tight over her nose and moves her wind through slow and small to keep the smell out.

Well I am going to go, Mac.

Okay, Marjorie. Are you sure you don't want to try to stay?

Sure. I am sure.

We could get you set up at a table away from where we'll put the food out.

No thanks, Mac. Not today.

I feel bad about this, Marjorie. I should have remembered to tell you.

Okay, Mac. Now I know. Wednesdays.

Yeah. Prime Rib Dinner Wednesdays.

But I would like to say Hello to Suzanne before I go.

Oh, sure. She's in back, cooking. I'll go get her and tell her you're headed out.

Thank you.

Marjorie takes a deep breath in through her mouth and pinches her nose. She puts her lips around the smooth straw and drinks her Shirley Temple down fast as she can. The usual. Not the usual. Marjorie sucks her lips tight around the straw and swallows the sweet bubbles and tells her departments to taste that and feel that. The cold, the sweet, the expected. What should be there. Marjorie closes her eyes and pinches her nose and drinks her whole drink in three big-breath drinks. No one remembered to tell her. Not Mac, but not Mac's fault. Marjorie puts her fingers inside the cold of the ice in the glass and with two fingers picks up the cherry. Mac working hard. The cherry, the soft, sugary round of the cherry, Marjorie swallows down fast and whole.

What Dr. Goodwin would say.

Smell, Marjorie, smell.

Take it in, let it out, let go.

Marjorie will try, Dr. Goodwin.

But all day Marjorie smiles to the People and Marjorie is tired and Marjorie cannot try every minute of every day. Marjorie is not open and working 24 hours a day, 365 days a year. Her self is not bright and shining and on display like all the things in the Store. These rows and shelves and boxes and things inside Marjorie are not all stacked up neat and clean and known. Ma is in pieces in the box under the bed and Marjorie still does not know what to do. Gram is shut up quiet, the words of the Lord flapping all around. And here Marjorie is with the smell of Prime Rib Dinner.

When she squeezes her eyes shut and looks down and up and around inside like she is doing now, Marjorie sees dark. All the dark. A lot of things she does not want to think about. Marjorie will try, sometimes, for Dr. Goodwin, to stay some with before-Ma and Him-Ma and maybe even Him, and Lucy, if she can, but Marjorie will not stay in the Club for Prime Rib Dinner. Dr. Goodwin wants to talk about unconditioned love but what about the problem of Prime

Rib Dinner? Too much in this department that she does not want to look at or think about or touch. The smell of meat and bread and butter and the dark and the glowing wall of colors and the sound of forks and knives and bottles touching bottles and Mac and the swinging bathroom door and the pains, the pains, and the cold smooth floor and the eyes of the buck black up above and the People talking People chewing People laughing People quiet People screaming.

Marjorie's face is on fire and her forehead is wet with the sweat of trying to stay under and she knows Dr. Goodwin does not want her washing off her mind but Marjorie is burning and this is a need she has. This is Marjorie taking care of her self. Eyes shut tight as she can Marjorie goes deep inside, up to where her mind floats in its boiling sea of all these things she does not want in here, in her. To where the departments have opened up and spilled over. Marjorie holds her mind gentle in one hand and with her other she is careful, very careful, as she tips her opened-up head to the side and lets the bad thought water pour out. And the things with it, all those things let out of the departments where she does not go.

Her wind. Marjorie holds on to her wind and her heart. To her self. Her want. Head tilted sideways, ear down against the hard, cool of the bar. Holding her nose safe from the smells. Pouring out the bad she has got inside.

And when Marjorie is empty as she can be, she moves her head slow, puts her mind soft and safe back inside its place up on top of the mountain of her. Lifts her self up higher and higher until she is back to sitting on the barstool, her mind a baby, new and pink and clean and unused and good as a baby.

Hey, Marjorie.

Marjorie is still down deep inside her closed eyes and she is almost but not yet done with what she needs to do. She feels the soft of skin touch her skin and her hand tingles and Marjorie is not ready to open her eyes but she is being touched and so she must. She must.

Suzanne is out there. Here. Suzanne, thick red hair pulled back into a pony-tail. Brown-stained dishtowel over her shoulder. Smelling like meat roasting like the smells. But Suzanne, still. Smiling, pale bare arm out and hand touching Marjorie's hand. Suzanne's hand a little warm, a little wet, washed.

Marjorie, you okay?

Suzanne. Okay. I need one more second.

Okay. Take your time.

Marjorie closes her eyes and goes back to her wide-open waiting mind. To finish what she started. She pours some warm water down over the smooth hills of her self and with the gentle hands of that inside-outlined other one of her,

Marjorie uses a soft soapy sponge to massage the bad things away. Marjorie takes some deep breaths to help with the washing and when she has scrubbed her mind clean enough, she pours some more warm water into the dark. Not a leak. Not a flood. A washing. A bath. A swim. Taking her time. Her self, new, clean, finished, ready to get her home safe.

Marjorie opens her eyes and smiles at Suzanne and by accident a burp rumbles up from inside her and gets out loud into the air.

Excuse me.

Suzanne laughs and picks up Marjorie's empty glass.

Wow, Marjorie. Thirsty today?

Yes. Thirsty today. And in a hurry. I am headed home. Just wanted to say Hello.

Are you sure? But I'm back there cooking. It's Prime Rib Dinner tonight.

I don't stay here for Prime Rib Dinner.

Oh no? But I promise you I've cooked up a lot of good food tonight. And it's cheap, only $8.95.

$8.95?

Yep, all you can eat.

But Prime Rib Dinner is $6.95.

Oh, well, I think it used to be. But, you know, things get more expensive every day.

I know.

Sure you don't want to stay?

Yes. Sure. Sorry.

Okay, well, it's good to see you, Marjorie. How are things?

Good. Things. How is Tony?

Tony's good. Always into something. Up trees, down holes, you know. How they are at this age.

Running around the Store.

Yep, Tony does that too. He runs everywhere he can. Wish I had his energy.

Okay, Suzanne. Good seeing you.

You sure you don't want to stay for Prime Rib Dinner? It's going to be tasty tonight. I'm mashing those potatoes with lots of butter and salt and pepper and just a little sour cream.

Marjorie's face begins to feel hot again. She knows Suzanne is good and new and unknowing. Marjorie does not know if Mac has ever said anything to Suzanne. Mac is very important about what is private, so probably he has never told. Suzanne is smiling and her face is wide and unworried and Marjorie thinks she must not know. If Suzanne knows, Suzanne will not ask Marjorie again to stay for Prime Rib Dinner. If Suzanne knows, she will know the deep-down secret departments of Marjorie. Suzanne will be more here, with Marjorie, in her self. Someone inside to sit with. Someone who will know.

Suzanne, Marjorie says.

Yeah?

No, thank you. I do not go to Prime Rib Dinner.

Okay, then.

But ask Mac. It is okay. With me.

Sorry, Marjorie, I'm not getting it. Ask Mac about what?

Prime Rib Dinner. Me. Mac knows. Mac can say.

Okay, Marjorie. I'm not sure what you mean but I'll talk to Mac. You sure you're okay?

Okay. I am going now.

All right. Take care of yourself.

You too Suzanne. Take care of your self. And Tony.

Sure will. See you soon.

Mac can tell. You can say I say it is okay.

Suzanne squeezes Marjorie's hand and then lets go. Marjorie likes the way Suzanne's skin feels, not so soft and not so rough. Warm. Suzanne smiles and turns and walks back toward the kitchen and Marjorie slides slow and careful down off her stool. Suzanne will know. Suzanne, more and more here with Marjorie, a more and more friend. Uncontained. Marjorie drank her drink so quick that when she stands up straight on the floor she can feel her inside free and floating and crashing. The smell of meat and potatoes and beans is still here all around her. Stronger, but so is Marjorie. Stronger, now, knowing now. Her mind is washed clean and now she knows that Wednesday is Prime Rib Dinner night in the Club and now Marjorie knows not to come to the Club on Wednesdays. Maybe she will tell Dr. Goodwin, but Dr. Goodwin will probably tell her to go. Go and smell the smells and eat prime rib and remember.

Dr. Goodwin, in his nice tie, his shiny shoes, his bright lampshade-lit office, can say all the words he wants to say.

But Marjorie, here, in her self, moving through the smells of the Club, through the world, through her departments, is the one who has to do the things. The one who is trying, the one who is doing her best to stay here, holding on.

Marjorie pulls the door of the Club open and walks out. Stands for a while in the cold yellow late afternoon air. She holds her coat close around her to keep warm and breathes and breathes until the smell of the air of the Club feels gone from her inside. Marjorie looks up past the sidewalk and the Club and the lines of the telephone poles to the place where the hills touch the sky.

Sorry, Dr. Goodwin, she says.

Marjorie moves her wind with the outside wind, lets in all this good open air and raises her finger up to trace the backs of the far-away hills. She follows the white snow lines of the slopes, turning her body big in a slow circle.

I do not go to Prime Rib Dinner, she says.

Marjorie moves her finger slow, making the shape of the chain of the hills. She leans a little to the left, moves in her containing circle, draws the hills in a whole ring all the way around her. Follows the tall of the mountain up high and back down to the long curls of the hills. The circle of hills, keeping in, keeping out.

Marjorie makes fists with her red fingers and puts her hands inside her pockets. People pass by and into the Club and Marjorie can see how they walk fast and heads-down and hungry for Prime Rib Dinner. Marjorie turns and starts walking. The Club at her back, Marjorie, surrounded by hills, by blowing, clean air, moves the mountain of her self slow and free in the cold direction of home.

29. MARGIE

L-U-C-Y
L-U-C-Y
M-A-R-G-I-E
M-A
M-E
A-G-E
R-I-G
G-E-M
G-R-A-M
R-A-G-E
L-U-C-Y
M-A-R-J-O-R-I-E
M-A
J-A-M
J-E-M
L-U-C-Y
J-A-R

R-O-A-R

R-E-A-R

O-A-R

A-R-E

I

A-M

A-I-M.

L-U-C-Y

L-U-C-Y

R-A-M

M-A-J-O-R

E-A-R

R-I-M

M-O-R-E

A-I-R

A-R-M

L-U-C-Y

L-U-C-Y

L-U-C-Y

30. MARJORIE

Middles of the nights Marjorie, free from her bra, from Gram, from the Store, rolls over to lie in the worn-in place Ma left in the soft sinking mattress and presses the button on the clicker that turns on the soundless television. The set is an old brown box with only two channels that come in clear enough to see People inside all the dots and waving lines of light. Marjorie lies in the shape of Ma, held by the mattress of Ma high up above what is left of Ma, Marjorie's arms and legs curled up near to her to feel warm to feel the whole big whole of her. She is careful with her self, careful not to make the headboard sounds. Marjorie holds her hands close to her chest and slows her wind, slower and slower until her skin is so still she can feel her heart beating beneath her fingers.

Marjorie holds her self close and warm under her blankets and from inside the very dark of the room she watches the way People move through the television light. The men and ladies on the screen smile so much. Their mouths move quickly, teeth flashing bright white and their lips are big and red and wide and open and closed and open. Marjorie stares at the light lines of the television that take the shape of lips and when the television People smile, she smiles, and when

Marjorie sees the People laughing she hears laughing in her head. When the television People are sad Marjorie follows along with the falling curve of their lips. She does not ask what the People are sad about. Or wonder. Marjorie just watches, just moves her face together with the light.

The People on the television are mostly involved in very long commercials. They hold up gold-topped bottles of shampoo or strong mops or big containers of soap that can clean up any and every mess. Marjorie watches the People smile and touch their hands to the things, rub the things, watches them hold the things up close to their noses to smell the things, showing how much they love the things so that People will buy the things.

Some People go to the Store, some People go to the television.

Marjorie lies very still inside her self and watches the People move their small bodies inside the bright shifting colors. The light leaks out quiet and always changing on the walls of the small room and Marjorie feels far, far under the water, at that place where the light comes through only in pieces, where the People float and touch and do not speak.

Sometimes the men and ladies in the television kiss and push their bodies together and Marjorie watches, breathing and beating from inside the big warm bounds of her self. Gram does not like People together and touching. Dr. Goodwin wants Marjorie to talk about it. But Marjorie just wants to see. Marjorie watches. She watches the big hairy hands of the men and the smaller surprised hands of the ladies. The men grab and rub and hold with their hands with their whole bodies. The ladies squirm and laugh and push and push away until something must change inside and they give up and in and move with the slow hands of the men. Marjorie watches the men and ladies touch skin to skin and she touches her own soft skin of her chin and her belly and her neck. Her heart, Marjorie touches. Marjorie watches the People touch lips to lips and Marjorie touches her finger soft and gentle to her lips.

Yes, Dr. Goodwin, Marjorie thinks about this.

But some things are for night and quiet.

Always a man and a lady touching in the long late-night commercials and Marjorie has never seen them do anything except kiss and lean and rub and hold. Afternoons when Gram falls asleep or is too slow with her clicker, Marjorie sees the People in the Stories move around the bed under the sheets. Marjorie sees the sheets roll up and down and in Gram's room she can hear the sounds the People make and Marjorie does not need any more than this, what the People want her to see and hear and know. Here, the People in the underwater light of the television in this middle-of-the-night room sometimes kiss and touch but they never roll or rub because they are the commercial People, are workers, there to sell things.

Marjorie understands. Marjorie does not mind. She watches the People in love with their things inside the television and she watches the colors of the light burning bright around the People and she watches the light on the walls rise and fall and rise. Ma is here but held in by her box under the bed. In this deep middle of the night Marjorie's departments are closed down. She does not need to think or remember or try. Marjorie just watches, just feels. She is warm and soft and surrounded.

Marjorie stays very still in the soft bed where Ma used to sleep. The only sound let out into the room is hers, is the slow, big, warm beating of her heart. And inside, sometimes Marjorie hears the People laughing. Marjorie watches the light of the lines of the lips and if the People on the television have their heads thrown back, hair swinging, mouths wide open and no-sound scream-ing, this is something that Marjorie can feel, a sound she can hear loud inside the uncontained love of her self.

31. MARGIE

And then the day Margie came looking for Lucy, and Lucy was not there.

He was there, now, always. There in Apartment #2, sitting in Gram's chair with Ma beside him. Chest bared, chewing. Gram, down, always, gone off to somewhere else to be with her stories. Him making his sounds and Ma making her sounds and Margie getting out of Apartment #2 as quiet as Margie knew how.

We do not know where Lucy was.

We did not hear Margie or see Margie or smell her.

Margie, gone down deep inside herself, did not think to knock or call or say, Hello, I'm here. Margie wanted only to get out and away. Margie ran quiet as she could down the stairs to Apartment #1, to where Lucy should have been. Margie turned the doorknob and let herself in.

Margie walked through the doorway into Apartment #1, walked down the hall and into the living room. She might have called Lucy's name like a ques-tion, like, Lucy? But Margie stayed quiet because she was listening, because she heard sounds like running, like lost breath, like snoring or crying or whispers. Fighting sounds, pain sounds, waves of sound creaking through the wooden floorboards. Margie heard these sounds, and Margie saw.

Lucy's ma, her skin, all of her skin, her whole body laid out naked and rising and rolling on the sofa. Lucy's sofa, where Margie sometimes sat. The green of Lucy's sofa beneath the slow-moving freckled skin of Lucy's ma. Her breasts, big, held up high and hard. Not by her hands, other hands. Lucy's ma's hands lost in the white-dusted hair of a head there against her skin. Two bodies, moving, making these sounds soft and serious like secrets. Margie watched and did not know that she should not be watching. The two big bodies pushing together, rising and widening and falling and flattening. A new smell in the air, something like the wet mud below the stones in the brook, like Margie's licked skin. Margie watched and wanted to understand, to know what she was seeing. Margie, wanting. To see skin and breasts and hands moving, to see the shapes of bodies like freckled mountains against the dark green of the sofa. To see Lucy's ma, her short body spread out long and open. Margie watched to see the face that was turned down, away from her, to see the other body pressing there against Lucy's ma's body. To smell, to know, to see what was happening.

Margie watched.

Margie held her breath, held the new smell long as she could inside her, held her arms against her breasts, against her hard heart beating.

Margie, keeper of so many secrets.

Margie watched until Lucy's ma heard or turned her head or opened her eyes. Until Lucy's ma screamed. A high scream, surprised, a louder scream than any seen on Gram's stories. Margie did not hear what she screamed, or if there were words being said. But Margie saw Lucy's ma's skin turn red. Her freckles burned up all over. Margie heard her name, the only sound in that screaming sound that Margie could understand. She saw the two bodies on the sofa pull apart. Margie stood and stared at Lucy's ma and her big breasts hanging, shaking, as she reached for clothes, for coverings. And Margie saw the other body, the breasts, the face that had been hidden from Margie. The kind, calm face of LD. LD smiling at her, LD sitting back bare and open and quiet.

Lucy's ma moved fast, screamed, hid what she could hide. Made some words in between and out of her screaming sounds.

Get her out of here, Fuck, Margie get out, Go away, Margie, God, Fuck, What is she doing here?

Margie heard. Margie knew she needed to get out. She understood that what she saw should not have been seen. Why, Margie did not know. Wrong, Margie could see, Margie could feel. That she had done something wrong, that something wrong was being done. That bodies are not meant to be seen. That we must hide most of what we are from the world. Margie could not speak or move but she understood, almost, this.

Come on, Margie, LD said, big body rising slowly from the sofa.

LD did not try to hide herself the way Lucy's ma did, behind shirts and pillows and the F-word and Margie's name. She walked slowly to Margie and put her hands on her shoulders and moved her halfway through a circle and softly pushed her away from the living room. LD's hands, gentle on Margie's shoulders, helped her walk back down the dark hallway to the still-open front door.

It's okay, Margie, she said.

Don't worry.

Margie, her heart beating her up, her wind coming fast, the sounds of Lucy's ma's screaming still loud inside, could not speak.

Don't be scared, Margie.

It's just us, just playing around.

LD used her hands to turn Margie toward her. In the dark of the hallway Margie could see LD only in pieces, only the outline of bare there before her. LD's hands touched Margie's shoulders and even though the rest of her body did not touch Margie's body, Margie could feel her. The heat of her, the hills of her breasts in the dark air between them. The big smell of LD's body there in the hallway.

And behind them, Lucy's ma was still saying it.

God, Margie, get out.

LD squeezed Margie's shoulders. Not hard, not soft. Just to show that she was there, touching, talking to Margie.

What did you want, anyway, Margie?

Margie?

What do you want?

Just, Margie said.

Lucy.

Lucy's not here. She's out.

I'll tell her you were looking for her.

Okay?

Okay, Margie said.

LD helped Margie turn back halfway around in her circle. She pulled the door the rest of the way open and pushed softly against Margie's back. Margie, feeling hot, feeling things she could not name. Feeling, for once, the unfamiliar feel of feeling. Margie let herself be let out.

Better keep this to yourself, Margie.

Pretend you didn't see.

LD closed the door and Margie was left alone in the flashing-bulb-lit hallway outside Apartment #1.

Margie heard LD lock the door. She stood there in the hallway, beside the creaking wooden stairs, in that place between her home and Lucy's, that dark downstairs space they shared, for a long time. Margie put her arms inside her t-shirt and held her breasts in her hands. She touched them, squeezed them, pretended. That her hands were not her hands. That she had not seen.

But this touch, this grab, this needing to feel, this was Margie. Margie, alone, left behind by Lucy, let out by LD, feeling the soft heat of herself, of her body. Margie on the outside, feeling. Finding out what was there, what was hers. This was Margie shut out, alone, with nowhere she was wanted, nowhere safe from the sounds of other people living lives that had nothing to do with her. Margie, heavy in her own hands, keeping this to herself, giving herself over to the soft, safe care of Margie.

32. MARGE

What's this, Marge?
I see you.
Playing with your big titties down there in the hallway.
Trying to hide.
Your ma is going to crack up.
Marge the Barge caught red-handed.
Titty-handed.
Squeezing her big balloons.
Those dykes get you all worked up, Marge?
How do they feel?
Good, right?
Maybe I won't tell your ma.
Maybe this will be between me and you, Marge.
Me and you and your big bags you've got.
Our secret.

33. MARJORIE

Spring Is Here.

Marjorie stands in the center of it, in the People-pushing-carts heart of the Store, next to a big yellow cardboard display with huge orange letters that say

Spring Is Here. She turns in a slow circle. Marjorie looks up at the hanging signs, trying to know where she should go.

Benjamin is coming, pushing a shopping cart stacked with boxes of sunscreen for the display. His eyes are red and kind and he is wide-smiling like usual.

Where's your vest, Marjorie? You working today?

Hello, Benjamin, Marjorie says, turning her circle toward him. Not working today. Just needed to look at some things.

Oh, he says. Okay, but it's too bad you had to come in on your day off. Me, I can't fucking stand being here when I don't have to, you know?

Marjorie nods.

Sorry, sorry, Marjorie. I know you don't use bad words or any of that shit. Shit. Sorry. But, yeah, I feel so trapped in this place, you know? These walls and the ceiling and the shelves and all this plastic bullshit everywhere. And the lights, they drive me nuts. I forget what the world outside really looks like when I'm in here, you know, Marjorie?

I know, Benjamin. Outside there is more air.

Exactly, Benjamin says, starting to open the boxes of sunscreen. More air, all the air. And this piece-of-shit sign is wrong. Lies, all of it. Spring isn't here. Spring is coming, you know, but not here. This place has no respect for what's true, you know, Marjorie? I was out last night to see it. The snow is finally melting down off the mountain. You ever go up there, Marjorie? Up to the Glen, right at the bottom of the mountain?

No, Marjorie says.

Marjorie has never been up close to the mountain. Or a mountain. She has never seen the real sea. Or a lake. The brook, yes. The park, yes. Marjorie goes where she goes and where she goes there is always a sidewalk. No sidewalks go all the way to the mountain.

You should, you should. It's beautiful up there. Fucking unreal. I ride my bike up. Or borrow a buddy's car. Just go up there and sit in the dark and wait to see what I am going to see. So dark up there. You can really think, you know, in the dark. In here, all these lights everywhere, you just can't think. But up there, it smells like life, you know? Like shit growing and shit dying and grass and air. And the dark is like something you can touch. Like you could take it home with you.

Good. Sounds good.

Benjamin closes his eyes and takes some deep breaths. Like he is there, now, in this place that he loves. Marjorie watches the bones of his shoulders move up and down in his wind. She can understand this, the need to be in some dark for a while.

Okay, okay, okay, Benjamin says, opening his eyes and staring at the rows and rows of blue bottles of sunscreen in the boxes.

Okay, Marjorie says.

Shouldn't think about it too much or my head might just explode right here. Don't think Steve would like that, much, my head popping open. I hope he'd have to clean it up himself. Asshole.

Marjorie stands still. Today she is here in the middle of the Store for a reason. For a problem. Not to say Hello to the People, not to walk down the center path to punch her card. Her day off and here Marjorie is deep inside the Store, where she almost never goes, surrounded by the waves and the pull of things.

Marjorie, standing in the heart of it, ready to go.

Because of need. A need.

Sorry, Marjorie. I don't want to keep you. You look busy. And me, I'm just killing some time. Killing some time thinking about killing myself. This store, killing me, all of us, all the time. Dying right now as we stand here and stack up bullshit and pick out bullshit and use coupons to get our bullshit cheap as we can. I'd laugh but it's not funny, you know. But I don't mean it that way. Just going one minute by one minute, you know? Hoping the day goes fast and the night slows way down.

Take care of your self, Benjamin, Marjorie says.

You got it, Marjorie. You too.

See you soon.

Yep, I'll be here, opening up boxes, putting out the shit.

Marjorie raises her arm up to wave to Benjamin and then steps some steps away. She closes her eyes and turns again in her slow, slow circle. Spring Is Here. Almost. The ice and snow in the parking lot are melting down into small dirty lakes that steam up white when the sun comes out. Time happening and Marjorie holding on. Marjorie and her question, still, the question of Ma in the box under the bed and how Dr. Goodwin said that some People find a nice thing to hold their dead People dust.

Marjorie opens her eyes and lets the light burn in. Steps one step by one step around in her circle. Looks up and again at the signs that show her how to know the Store. So many departments all around. Lines of light leading to this center of the Store like roads like veins like all the words for what goes to and from the heart. All the things stacked exactly where they should be, where they belong. Aisles and aisles to choose from. Marjorie stands as close to the center of the center path as she can, to see all the departments, to feel less of the pull of things.

So many things that would be fine for holding Ma.

How can Marjorie know where is the right place to go?

She stops her circle and looks up and away. Out there, ahead of her, is Electronics. Ma loved her television, but Marjorie does not think that television is the right place for People's remainders. Televisions are expensive, and loud, and Marjorie would not know how to open one up and pour all that Ma inside. Or if this is even something she could do. Marjorie is not sure if there is enough empty inside in a television to hold a whole pile of Ma.

Next to Electronics is Auto Care and Marjorie does not even need to think about trying those aisles. Cars are not part of Marjorie. Big loud things that take People places. Marjorie has never had anything to do with cars and except for her first day in the Store when Steve gave her a tour of the whole place, Marjorie has never been to Auto Care.

A small turn in her circle and there is Lawn and Garden. Dr. Goodwin said that some People use a vase or a nice pot or a box. Lawn and Garden has these things, Marjorie thinks. But Lawn and Garden is another department where Marjorie never goes. Lawn and Garden has its own sliding door. There is a big part of Lawn and Garden that happens outside. Marjorie knows from Benjamin that they even sell small trees in Lawn and Garden. Sometimes Benjamin stops by to say Hello and his hands are dirty black with dirt and he smells like the sidewalk on a rainy day, like how Gram's nightgowns can be when she has not washed in a while, and when Benjamin stops by like this, Marjorie knows he has been in Lawn and Garden.

Today is not the day Marjorie will go to that department.

Today is not a day for too much new.

Marjorie closes her eyes and turns, lets her self guide her self. She opens her eyes and sees all the bright pink-purple-silver stacked colors of Beauty and closes her eyes again. Beauty is not where she will find the right place to put Ma. All the powders and sprays and creams of Beauty. Things to put on, not put in.

And out there, in the corner of the Store, out far beyond Beauty, is Baby.

Today is not a day that Marjorie will end in Baby.

Marjorie has her question picked for today. A question of Ma that has an answer here in the Store, somewhere. The other questions, she stacks up high on her shelves. The other questions are not questions for today.

And out there, Marjorie sees the big hanging sign for Home Decor.

A department that might have an answer for Ma.

She walks slow and long past Food to get there. Down the wide center path, not too close to any of the aisles on the sides. Marjorie keeps her eyes on the bright light lines on the floor because the pull of Food on one side and Beauty on the other is strong, because she needs to stay here close to her self. Today is Marjorie's day off, but still, she smiles and nods and says Hello to the People she passes.

Marjorie stops at the first aisle of Home Decor and looks down its long, shining throat but does not step in. After all this time in the Store surrounded by all of these things, Marjorie knows that the best way to stay her self in the middle of so much is to stay away from the things. From here, from the top of the aisle, Marjorie can see that here the things are big and seem shaped more like furniture. Things like desks and chairs and tables for holding televisions. Their apartment is small and what Marjorie has got left of Ma is small so Marjorie moves on.

Home Decor has an aisle for curtains and another aisle for rugs. There is an aisle for lamps. She would like to buy lampshades for the living room, for Gram's room, for her room. Marjorie sees all the lampshades stacked on top of each other on one side of the aisle, on shelves and hanging from hooks. Big white ones, small colorful ones, medium-sized cream-colored ones with little ridges, some with wire inside, big light green ones with pink polka dots. So many sizes and colors and shapes. Always the problem of too many decisions to make.

Marjorie has bigger problems.

She knows to move on, to pass by, to leave the lampshades for another day.

The aisle next to the lamps and lampshades looks like it has more things that Marjorie might be looking for. Smaller things. Candles and candleholders on one side of the aisle. These are beautiful but too beautiful, not necessary, wrong. The other side of the aisle has big cloth albums for photos and silver picture frames and some boxes that must be for keeping photos. Dr. Goodwin had said something about People putting a frame with a photo next to where they put their loved person's leftovers, but Marjorie does not think she will do this with Ma. The only photo she knows about of Ma is the one she found in the drawer of the table next to Ma's bed, the one of unsmiling Ma and the shadow of His finger.

Marjorie turns and takes three steps toward the next aisle. This one might be the one.

But this aisle is all vacuum cleaners and vacuum bags and small plastic vacuum parts. Marjorie looks up at the signs to see where she is and she sees that she has stepped out of Home Decor and into Home Living. Sometimes this is what the Store does to People. People think they are right where they need to be, right about to find what they need to find, and the Store suddenly changes. The Store is a very huge wonderful place but the Store is not an easy place to be. The Store is strong pulls and rolls. Marjorie looks at how the light reflects red, purple, silver off all the different vacuums and she feels bad that this is not the aisle with a thing for Ma and good that People have so many vacuums to choose from. People need to feel free and open and allowed to decide. People need to look at a vacuum or any other thing and People need to look down low into their most self part of their self, down into their furthest department, and find out which thing of all the things, which vacuum of all the vacuums, is the one they were made to have.

Excuse me. Excuse me. Jesus, lady. Move it.

Marjorie feels her body burn up red and she sees that she is standing here in the middle of the wide aisle and that the People cannot pass by her. She smiles at the yellow-haired lady with her cart who wants to move on further into the Store and the lady is eyebrows-together angry.

Excuse me, she says. Get the fuck out of the way.

Hello, Marjorie says.

Now, the lady says. God. Some people.

Marjorie steps a quick step back into the aisle with the pictures and the candles so that the lady can keep going. The lady is quiet, does not smile or look at Marjorie again. She holds on hard to the plastic handle of her shopping cart and pushes forward fast. The lady is not so big as Marjorie, but not so small either. Not so old, but red in her face and wrinkled, probably from a lot of angry. Marjorie sees a lot of faces like this lady's face, like Ma's face, the pulled-in wrinkle of a living gone on with a lot of angry. Lots of different kinds of angry and the very known, very different look of long-felt angry. The quiet angry, the angry that lives just under the skin, the down-deep angry, the angry that will come out in small pieces.

Stupid god-damned cow, the lady says once she has passed by.

Marjorie will not mind. Does not mind. Is not minding. She holds her arms close over her chest and finds her wind and on her wind is the smell of all the candles, the clean of the sea and the deep of gingerbread cookies. Marjorie knows she takes up more space than most People and she can understand that this might make People let a little bit of their anger out. Dr. Goodwin wants to talk about all the different kinds of love, but what about all these different kinds of angry? Undone love, okay. How about undone angry? Marjorie sees a lot more angry than love pass by. Some moms hug kids but many more pinch and drag and squeeze. Red is the color of angry and red was the color of the boxes of heart-shaped chocolates for Valentine's Day. Red is the color of blood and angry and the heart. And love, too?

Marjorie does not know. Too much to know. Marjorie does not know where all the angry comes from or the love or the red and what that means. All Marjorie knows is her self. The sound and the smell and the feel of her wind flowing through. The loose of her skin and the rough of her hair. Marjorie knows her self and she knows that today will not be the day she finds a thing for Ma.

Marjorie moves her legs with the in and the out of her wind and looks out and up and down the wide center path before she steps back onto it. The biggest bright vein, where most of the People pass by. Marjorie looks up it and down it and up it. She wants to be sure the way is clear, sure that she will not see any more of the angry of the People today. She needs to get back to the heart of the Store, to find her way fast as she can, to get out, out of the way, away.

34. MARGIE

Margie waited cheek-down on the ground, her round back pushed up against the wall, watching the pounding feet of the playground. Margie, too big to play, too big to lie there like that, like a little kid, looking. Too-big Margie looking carefully through the dry, beat-up grass for any sign of the small people.

The teachers kept Lucy inside longer and longer now that they had moved up and through and to the almost-end of middle school. Same building, same wall, but different recess time. Kids no longer playing, groups of kids standing in circles laughing and kissing and watching, always watching, for what was not the same.

Sometimes Lucy was not let out at all. Something about her, the lean, loud shape of her, made the teachers eager to keep her in. Still, Margie waited for her every day. Sometimes she stood and bent one knee and then the other knee, keeping herself warm. Some days Margie rolled slowly from side to side, lying down in the grass or standing up against the wall. Margie, making her circles. Growing up but not out of it. Margie, with every change of the seasons growing more and more down and in.

We had stopped noticing Margie and her circles a long time ago.

But not us. We saw. We noticed. When we were bored, when we thought to look, we watched Margie. We stood in our own circles and laughed at hers.

We oinked at Margie.

Rolling around like a pig, we said.

Big piggy Margie, we said.

We cannot be blamed for what we said to Margie. The sounds we made. What we might have thrown. We saw huge Margie bulging there inside her pink skin, rolling there beside the chain link fence she still called a wall, face set in something like a smile, eyes half closed as if she were somewhere else, as if she had taken a trip away from the school, out of the town, off to a place we could not know about. We saw something surfacing there in Margie's face as she rolled that looked something like happy, like something we could not say.

Stupid, we said.

We were young and cannot be blamed.

Some days Margie rolled slowly up and down her spot of playground, and sometimes Margie was still, floating. Sometimes Margie waited, held her wind, watched and hoped that the small people were safe from the kids. And on a good day, sometimes with only ten recess minutes left, the teachers let Lucy go.

Hey, Margie, Lucy said.

Hey, Lucy.

Margie kept her cheek on the ground, her eyes on the grass. Lucy sat down gently on Margie's side, on that hard-soft spot of her hip, right above her bottom. The part of Margie that Lucy liked best. Where she fit, where she could sit without hurting her friend. Margie felt Lucy sit down and sink a little into her. She looked up out of the grass and at Lucy there, sitting up high on top of her. Lucy had been there before, but each time Margie felt Lucy warm and new. Each time Margie watched Lucy sink into her and each time Margie waited for the extra weight to hurt. But Lucy was small and she did not hurt and Margie liked how the place where they touched felt warm and solid. Margie liked feeling her body rise and fall with Lucy. She turned her eyes back to the grass and with each big breath that moved through, Margie felt the light weight of Lucy.

What are you doing, Margie?

Looking.

At what?

The kids.

What about them?

Their feet.

Why?

The small people.

What?

They need to be safe.

What? Seriously, Margie?

Serious.

Eighth grade is almost over, Margie. I can't believe you're still thinking about the small people.

Sometimes I think about them.

Lucy would have said more, but this was when we saw them there. When we saw them there that way. When we saw Lucy up there on top of Margie. Lucy rising and falling in Margie's breeze. Their bodies touching, bottoms touching. Lucy's skin rising, riding up there on top of the soft fat mass of Margie.

We knew it, we said.

We knew it.

Dykes, we said.

We yelled. We screamed. Laughed. We ran over and pointed. We made pretend cameras with our fingers and took pictures. We surrounded.

Smelly Lucy riding a stupid big pig, we said.

Sluts.

We threw pebbles at them and kicked clumps of grass. If there were any small people down there, we took care of them.

We looked away.

Fuck you, Lucy screamed.

These things happen.

We let this happen.

Margie stayed still, beating, watching, holding the weight of Lucy still and safe as she could.

We stepped in and told them to scram and they scrammed.

We couldn't say who started it.

No swearing, we said.

No touching.

Lucy slid down slowly off of Margie's soft side and sat with her thin back up against the warmth of Margie's thighs. Her small face was lit up red and sweat dripped down from Lucy's tangled blonde hair. She cried, a little, and Margie tried not to see.

Margie looked down into the grass. Closed her eyes. This, Margie could not watch.

I hate that, Lucy said.

I know, Margie said.

You know what?

That you hate that.

Fuck, Margie, Lucy said.

She leaned down lower into the soft sink of Margie's body. Lucy put her arms around Margie's leg and rested her head on Margie's knee and she squeezed. Margie felt the heat of Lucy move up and down her body in waves. She felt her face burning hot and she felt the wet of Lucy's forehead heavy against her knee. Margie put her hand on Lucy's head and kept her eyes closed tight.

Lucy's voice, when it came, was far away and low and sad, was a sound, a pain Margie did not want to hear.

I can't believe it, Margie.

You still look for them?

Margie?

You still look for the small people?

I am still looking, Margie said.

35. MARGE

Look out there look there, you see that?

That's mine. New wheels. My new baby.

Look at it, would you look?

Marge, I'm telling you to look so be polite and look.

See there, that baby? That's mine. My new baby.

Good? You think that baby is good?

Good is nothing. That baby is the fucking best.

I'm going to show you, Marge.

I'm going to show you how much better than good that sweet baby is.

Get out there. Let's go.

Yes, into the car.

Too stupid, Marge.

Now.

I'm saying so. Your ma don't care.

Out. Now.

Go, Go, Go. Move those fat legs.

See how the sun hits her? See those curves, that shine.

All mine, Marge. Mine and nobody else going to fucking touch her.

Don't touch that handle. I don't trust you.

No. You are not going back inside. You are going for a ride.

Good, fuck.

Don't touch anything. Get in.

Get back there. I don't trust you up here.

Can you fit? You fit back there, Marge?

Life hurts, Marge. Deal with it.

Now listen to her. This baby purrs. Like a little kitty cat. Like a fucking woman, Marge. Listen to this baby moan.

You hear that?

What's wrong with you back there? Like you never been in a car before.

Your ma don't need a car. She's got me. I'll take her where she wants to go.

Okay, Marge, hang on tight. Here we go.

No belts back there, Marge.

Just hold on.

Fast? You think this is fast? Fucking fast my ass.

I'm going to show you fast, Marge.

You hold on and you watch. Fast is coming. We're getting to fast.

See that? You hear that? Get your stupid fucking head up out of your lap and look.

I told you to look.

Look at me, Marge. Look at this baby.

I'll decide when we go home. You just fucking sit and watch and like it.

We'll drive around all day like this if I say so.

Tell me you were wrong. Good is fucked up. Good is an insult to this beautiful baby.

Say you're sorry, Marge.

Louder. Say you're sorry for what you said.

Not to me, stupid. Say it to my baby. Say it to her.

Apologize. Now.

Say it. Tell my baby how fucking sorry you are for insulting her.

Now lean down and kiss her.

Do it, Marge.

Do what I fucking say.

36. MARJORIE

Angry. A lot of angry.

Do you really think it's the store that makes people angry? Or do you think the store is just a place that might bring out anger that's already there?

How to know, Dr. Goodwin? But a lot of angry passes by. A lot of angry happens in the Store.

What do you think makes people angry, Marjorie?

Oh, many things. The wrong color pants. Bad words. Touching. Not enough money. Not being beautiful.

Those sound like very different reasons.

Well, lots of different kinds of angry.

What do you mean?

I mean what I say. All the kinds of angry. I don't have a good way to say it like you, Dr. Goodwin, like a psycho-doctor, but what I mean is different kinds of angry. Like, little boy angry, like red faces and little cheeks popping out. Like little girl angry or men's angry. How they carry it around. Like lady angry. In the forehead. The eyes. Like a lady's angry in the Store.

This is a specific woman's anger you're talking about, Marjorie?

Yes. In the Store. That lady's angry. Hers was all in her face. Held tight in the lines of her cheeks, you know? Between her eyebrows, like her eyebrows were holding on hard to the angry there. And her shoulders. All of her. All angry, but held in, under her skin.

What was she angry about?

I don't know. Just angry.

Was she angry with you?

I don't know, Dr. Goodwin. I can see the People and talk with the People but I can only know my self and what I am thinking about.

What do you feel angry about, Marjorie?

No angry, Dr. Goodwin. I am fine. No more angry with me.

I don't know if I can believe that. You've just told me that everyone has her own kind of anger. What is your kind?

I am no kind of angry, Dr. Goodwin. I am done with all my angry.

So I should believe that you are different from other people? That you don't feel any anger at all?

I am different, Dr. Goodwin. Yes. I am not like People. I like People and I am like People in some ways but like I said. I am my self and my self is not the same as People.

Okay, Marjorie. I don't mean to upset you.

I am not upset.

You look upset. You're sweating.

I am not upset. Sweating is hot, not upset.

So who else around you is angry, Marjorie? It sounds like you spend a lot of time watching people and thinking about what kind of anger they carry.

Steve. The manager. At the Store.

The man who sometimes pinches you? The one who you don't like to be near?

Yes. Steve.

What kind of anger do you think Steve has?

Fat man angry. Sorry to say but it is a kind. I know I am big too, Dr. Goodwin, but not like Steve. Steve has his big huge belly. His skin shows. He has his fat all around him and the fat makes him angry. You can see it when he walks away, how his arms move fast next to his big belly. Like he is pretending he is not how he is. And how he puts his head to one side when he talks to you and he spits when he talks and he never says, Sorry. Steve's angry comes out all through his body in this. This.

This.

What is the word, Dr. Goodwin?

What word are you trying to think of? Describe it.

Boom. Breaking open. Like a firework. But bad.

Like an explosion? You mean his anger seems explosive?

Exploding. Yes. It is exploding out of his body and Steve tries to seem like the men on television but his body is not that way. And he pinches my arm and tells me, Try. I try, Dr. Goodwin. I am a good worker. And People walk in and Steve tries to put the big of him on display. And I know all of that is his angry. And he is exploding.

He doesn't sound like a very safe person for you to be around.

No, Dr. Goodwin. Steve is not safe.

What do you do to protect yourself from Steve?

I stay quiet. Step away. Hold my arms tight around my self like this.

You know that you could file a complaint if you want to, Marjorie.

I don't want to complain, Dr. Goodwin. I like my job. Steve is just Steve in his angry.

Well, I know you make good decisions, Marjorie. But I hope you will continue to stand up to Steve.

Yes.

Anyone else? What about your mother? What kind of anger did she have?

Ma again, Dr. Goodwin. You know I don't know about Ma. Ma is much harder.

But you know so much about Steve's anger. Why not your mother's? You've known her for so much longer. You must have spent a lot more time watching her than Steve, right?

Ma was always so up close, you know? Like you look at a thing up in front of your eyes and all you see is color. You don't see the thing until it is far away. Ma is like that I think.

What color is your mother, then? What do you see when you think of her up close, as you say?

Oh. I don't know. Red, I guess. But red is not just angry. Red is all things.

Is your grandmother angry?

Gram? Gram is just old-lady angry. Shut-in angry. Watching the Stories angry. Yes. Some. Angry that she does not have long hair like the ladies in the Stories. Angry that her body is all bent up. Angry about all the men.

What men?

All the men. Gram's angry is about all the men. The big of men and the strong of men. How they yell. Ma's men, mostly. Television men also.

Was your grandmother often angry at your mother for the men she chose?

Gram has her Lord. She says that the Lord is the only man she will let in.

What kind of anger did your stepfather have?

Dr. Goodwin, you know I don't like to talk about Him.

I know you don't, Marjorie, but that's why you come here, isn't it? To talk about the things that are difficult?

I come just to talk. Just to say Hello to you and talk about the day.

But you also come here because you have some problems you need help with. You have painful things that are difficult to deal with alone.

And don't say father. Even with a step in front.

What do you prefer I call him, Marjorie?

Nothing. No name. Better not to talk about Him. Not worth the time.

I think we have to talk about him, Marjorie. What kind of anger did he have?

All of it, Dr. Goodwin.

Can you explain what you mean by all of it?

All of it. How to say? The angry-dog angry the little-boy angry the shark-eating-fish angry the boiling-water angry the spitting angry the television angry the hissing-cat angry, even, even old-lady angry, man angry, Ma angry, even.

That's a lot of anger for one person. Where do you think all that anger came from, Marjorie?

Came from. It is just there.

I think anger usually comes from things that have happened to us in our past. Do you know what I mean?

From what People remember.

Yes, from what we hold on to. What has happened to us. Do you think your stepfather had some things happen to him that made him angry?

I don't know, Dr. Goodwin. I don't care.

I'm just trying to ask questions that might help us understand him better, Marjorie.

Nothing there to understand. Just Him, sitting in Gram's chair. Chewing. Angry.

If he were sitting here in this room with us right now, how would I look at him and know he was so angry?

Oh you would know. Because of the curled-up skin lines on His forehead. You can watch those. How they are deep and they wave and get deeper. The black hairs on His chin and cheeks and chest. And His hands. Always moving, even a little, even just to rub His hands together or make a basket out of his fingers like this. His hands have that angry like Steve's hands but Steve's hands are always clean and pink and His hands are dirty and white. Lime everywhere and He leaves ghosts of His hands on all the things. Him always touching and touching and He touches a thing and it has Him on it, his ghost, the dust of Him. And chewing. The angry in the chewing. Watch His mouth move. Teeth and tongue sucking paper from dry to wet to not there. Chewing and chewing at His paper all day. A whole full mouth and when there is no paper there are dirty words. Bad words. And when there is paper He opens up and His mouth is wide and chewing and sucking and He makes all the paper disappear. And starts again. Or spits it out. Says the bad words He has to say. Spits out His wet paper ball and says it and always angry things, mean things, and around Apartment #2 there are all these white places He touches and touched and is touching and bits of paper He's spit out and stuck around and they stick to the walls and the windows and under the bed.

I can see that you are very upset, Marjorie.

Not upset. Fine.

You're shaking. I know these are hard things to think about.

I said I do not want to talk about Him, Dr. Goodwin.

I know, Marjorie. What are you thinking right now?

I am thinking about what you made me think about. Him in the chair. The color of Him. Up close.

What color is he?

White. Wet, chewed paper. Lime dust. Ghosts of hands. And Him. White touched all over Apartment #2. White. The worst.

Breathe, Marjorie.

Let's just sit here a minute.

Breathe.

Take your time.

Are you angry right now, Marjorie?

Not angry, Dr. Goodwin. Fine.

Your face is very red.

I already said. Red is not angry. Not always angry. Many things.

Here's some water.

Breathe.

I can see that you are suffering, Marjorie.

Take deep breaths.

We can breathe together.

Follow me, Marjorie.

Breathe.

Breathe.

Breathe.

I can breathe, Dr. Goodwin.

I can breathe by my self.

37. MARGIE

Gram, down, a down-day, did not want LD to touch her and Margie did not know why.

We might have guessed. The short hair spiked stiff with gel. The chapped lips, the hard flat jaw and the way LD swung her arms when she walked. Her arms, alone. Those thick muscles curving out against her tan skin. We saw all the effort LD put into looking strong. We saw her men's jeans hanging low and her big black t-shirts and how she hid whatever she had beneath. We saw her eyes, her eyelashes, the far reach of them, curling out, betraying the parts of her she tried so hard to pack away. We saw how she looked long and sad and wanting at Lucy's ma. We could not know for sure, but we knew.

But Margie. Margie had witnessed it. Margie carried their secret inside. But Margie, slow, world-less Margie, did not even know there was something to know.

And Gram, deep in her down-day, moving fast, trying to get out, away, had fallen down the sagging front steps.

Summer was over. The warmth was leaving and the wind was every day less gentle. Leaves on the trees drying up into themselves, turning colors, waiting to go.

Margie and Lucy sat on the dead-end sidewalk, Lucy using a stick and dirt to show Margie how to shave her legs. Even from there, from where they sat, far below Apartment #2, on the sidewalk, they heard Gram and Ma yelling. Gram's voice high like a bird and repeating like a bird.

Something like, He has to go. He has to go.

And Ma's voice low and loud like a train coming, yelling bad words.

Fuck you old bitch.

Jesus.

Whore.

Words Margie heard without understanding, words Lucy pretended not to hear.

Look, Margie, Lucy said, rolling up the leg of her pink-gem-dotted jeans. Put the shaving cream on like this.

Lucy picked up two handfuls of sidewalk dirt and dust and pebbles and poured them over her pale calf. She took a small stick and rubbed it slowly up from her ankle to her knee, pressing just enough to make her skin ripple in the wake of the wood.

And then you just rub the razor up your leg, she said.

Just like this. Hard but not too hard.

Careful.

And then the ugly hairs disappear and your legs are smooth and really sexy.

Lucy wiped her hands on her thighs and she put her arms around Margie's leg and Lucy pulled on the stretchy fabric of Margie's purple pants.

You try, Lucy said.

But the yelling above them rained down harder and in the storm of Ma and Gram. Margie heard the low, the even lower than low, the deep bottomless voice of Ma's friend. The rolling thunder of him. Margie could not hear his words, but inside, in Margie's head, in her body, she heard him, his laughing, the long up-and-down rumbling of Ma's moved-in friend, laughing.

LD had pulled into the driveway, then, as Lucy tried to pull up Margie's pant leg and Margie tried not to listen to the voices in her apartment pouring down.

LD, turning off her truck's engine, sitting still, hands on the wheel, listened.

What's going on up there, Margie?

Margie, ears wide, eyes on asphalt, did not move.

Margie's gram is pissed at Margie's ma, Lucy said.

Don't use that word, Lucy, LD said, opening the door of her pickup to let more of the words in. And I asked Margie, not you. What's going on up there, Margie? Why are they fighting like that?

Margie turned her head in a slow circle, from side-to-side, and moved her shoulders up and down.

Gram's down, she said.

Lucy had rolled enough of Margie's pant leg up to show some of Margie's skin, the white skin stretched out big and soft and sagging, the blue veins that branched up under the surface, and the long black hairs that grew there. Lucy poured sidewalk dust over Margie's skin and slowly rubbed the stick on the part of Margie's leg she could reach. Margie felt Lucy's touch spread up and out from that spot on her leg, felt the slow rubbing of the stick in her spine, along her shoulders, making her heart beat faster, making her shiver there in the sunlight, there in the angry sounds-falling-down of Apartment #2.

It's because they got married, Lucy said.

Margie's ma and that gross guy.

Her gram hates him.

Margie, listening, feeling, shaking a little with good shivers from the slow up-and-down feeling of Lucy's stick, stopped moving.

For a second, Margie stopped.

A heartbeat, skipped.

Breathing, stopped. Seeing, stopped. Hearing, feeling, stopped.

Margie's heart stopped beating, for just one second, just long enough for the whole of Margie to come to a complete stop.

Margie, for one second, empty, still, gone, away.

Gone.

Was how it felt.

And when Margie came back, she had a question to ask.

How do you know?

Lucy, still slowly rubbing the stick against Margie's skin, said, What do you think they've been fighting about, Margie? Are you deaf? You didn't even figure out you've got a dad now? Well, whatever, a stepdad. A pretty weird one too.

Lucy, LD said, stepping down out of her truck and slamming the door behind her.

Be nice.

LD walked over to where Lucy and Margie were sitting. Above them, the yelling had stopped. Margie was trying to hear, trying to understand. A dad. A stepdad. Margie's heart beat out pains and her face lit up on fire. She could see Lucy's fingers moving the stick against her leg, but Margie could not feel it. Margie could not feel the sidewalk under her or the air blowing cold around her. All Margie felt was her, herself, inside, her blood moving, running all around inside with nowhere else to go.

It's none of our business, LD said, and just as she said it, the front door was flung open, the screen door exploded out, and Gram came running, falling down the front porch steps. LD ran to help and Lucy and Margie stayed where they were, still, wide-eyed, watching.

And Gram, fresh from fighting, on fire, down, Gram in the middle of a down, down-day, fell down and did not want LD to touch her.

No, Gram said. Get away.

Leave me alone.

Let me help you, LD said, leaning over Gram's small body curled up at the bottom of the steps.

Can you stand?

I can stand, Gram said. I can stand. Don't touch me.

Are you hurt? Is anything broken?

Don't touch me, Gram said.

You're bleeding.

LD took some tissues out of her pocket and pressed them against Gram's elbow. Margie watched the white wad of tissues turn red, turn the color of Gram's insides.

Gram tried to move her arm away from LD.

I said not to touch me. I don't know you. I don't know you people.

Margie, get over here and help me up.

Get these people away.

Margie stood up and stepped closer to Gram. Sidewalk sand poured down from her leg into her sock. Margie, doing her best to take hold of her wind, did not know what to say or how to help. What to do.

This is LD, Gram, Margie said.

I don't care who this is, Margie, Gram said. I don't want strangers touching me. Get over here and pull me up.

I live downstairs from you, ma'am, LD said. We've seen each other many times. Margie's always down at our place.

Margie's business is her business. I don't know you and I don't want you touching me.

Fine, LD said. Then I'm going inside and I'm calling an ambulance.

LD stepped away from Gram and Gram, shoulders slumped and heavy from the down-day, from fighting, from falling, put her hands on the ground and started to push herself up.

Don't you dare, Gram said, her breath coming in short bursts, her voice high and pinched.

You go inside and stay away.

Devil in you, all of you.

Leave us alone.

Margie, Gram said.

Margie, move.

Lucy, LD said. Get inside. Now.

Lucy, scared quiet by the sight of the old woman on the ground, by the bright red blood drying brown on white tissue, by the words, ran past Gram's bent body, up the uneven steps, through the doorway and inside and away. LD followed, her big arms stiff at her sides, her eyes steady, looking forward, calm, away from Gram.

Sorry, Margie, LD said, shutting first the screen door and then the heavy wooden front door.

And Margie, left alone with broken Gram, did not understand. Why LD left, and why Gram did not want to be touched? Where all this quiet had come from, so quickly? How could she help? What did it mean, what Lucy said, this yelling, this word, dad, stepdad?

We could have answered some of Margie's questions.

Maybe.

We might have had a guess.

But there are some questions we could never have known how to answer. What has to do with these most private parts of life. What happens inside. The answers that come slowly and must be lived out.

Like Margie. What was happening to Margie.

What happens out there that we cannot do anything about. What we do not want to see or hear or know. All the ways it was just not possible to help.

Come here, Gram said. Get over here, Margie, and let me hold on to you.

Margie did what Gram asked. She bent her knees and crouched down low so that Gram could hold onto her shoulders. Margie stood up slowly so that Gram could rise with her. Gram held tight to Margie's skin, so tight it hurt, so she

144

would not fall down again. They stood still for a long time, the light leaving, shivering, slowing their wind, waiting.

Just a minute, Margie, Gram said. I'm just waiting for my legs.

My heart. Giving me pains.

This will kill me, Margie.

My heart.

Just wait for my legs to come back.

They waited. Margie and Gram, breathing their breaths, holding tight. Looking out at the hills, circling, closing in, out at the far-away hills that kept them in.

We watched from inside, from outside, from the windows of cars passing by, or not at all. We saw, or we did not see, or we pretended not to see. The giant girl, plain-faced, the old woman white with pain, red in the places where her blood broke through.

She's done it to us, Margie, Gram said, squeezing.

The Devil, she's taken him in.

No, Gram, Margie said. LD is good. LD isn't bad. She's good. I like her.

Devil. No, not that one.

Your ma, Margie.

That man. Your ma did it.

Married him.

Brought that trash into our home for good.

Margie looked up at the high gray windows of Apartment #2. The wood, gray paint chipping, looked the same. The trees around the house shook their long green arms in the breeze, same as always. The air smelled like grass and gasoline and the air was quiet. Cold, blowing, dried leaves scraping, but this happened every year, this was normal. A down-day, but this was normal.

But inside, things had changed.

I tried, Gram said.

I tried to tell her. But your ma has to have him.

Has to have that man.

Stay quiet, Gram said.

Stay out of his way, Margie.

Stay like this a while longer, wait until my legs come back.

Best as you can, Margie.

Get away.

Today Marjorie cannot understand the story of the Stories. She sits in her place next to Gram and watches the People on the television move slow and floating. Opening their small circle-lit mouths to speak or yell or cry or laugh and the sound rolls out to Marjorie not as words but as waves. Ups and downs of People sounds. Today the television feels far underwater and Marjorie has so much in her mind to listen to, so much work just to move her wind through, is so busy staying unsunk inside her self that she cannot enjoy the Stories.

Gram seems up today. Sitting up in bed, saying, sometimes, Yes, Yes, to the People on the television.

Yes. Bless you.

Gram in her up-day has a bag of gummy bears open on the table beside her and she eats them one at a time. Waits until the end of a commercial break to pick a new one out of the package and then sucks on it slow as the People in the Stories do what they are doing.

Marjorie is not sure. Marjorie cannot understand what is happening. She sits, shoulders slumped, eyes toward the television but not really seeing. Not eating the gummy bears. But here. Most of her is here. And even with the drowned sound of the television and even with the noise of her inside moving, breathing, working, Marjorie can hear Gram's mouth slipping slow and careful around each gummy bear. Licking, sucking, and if there is any part left by the next commercial break, chewing up the rest.

Prime Rib Dinner Wednesday. Marjorie said for Suzanne to ask Mac about Marjorie's most private thing and by now Suzanne might know. The brown-stained meat-smelling dish towel thrown over Suzanne's perfect round shoulder. Suzanne's hair, how does it feel? Dr. Goodwin and his talk. Too much talk of Him. The white. The white has been gone a long time. So many things gone a long time. Him gone. Has it been long or short? Long, seems better. Long gone and far away. Ma gone a short time. Ma also long gone and far away, but forever. Benjamin and how he asked if Marjorie has a boyfriend. And what to do with Steve? Where to put Ma?

So many People. The Store, the world, even in this room, with Gram. People everywhere and how can Marjorie ever know anyone but her self?

People and their outsides. So different. So hard to know.

But Lucy, soft. Lucy was inside. Is inside. Lucy, there, unknown, growing, grew. Not all the way and not the right way but perfect in her way. Lucy. So short a time but important. Marjorie's. A part of her self she did not know. A warm and beating, unbreathing part of her self unknown and unseen but loved. Unconditioned. Even for just a minute. Even for what was never really here. A feeling of it. A good thing inside Marjorie that must be like what Dr. Goodwin means when he says that word, Love.

So much far away. Before. After.

Now.

Which is when?

After. And before.

Both?

But Marjorie is fine.

But then Dr. Goodwin asks questions about love and angry and all of these things and Marjorie has to look down the long dark stretch of departments where she does not go and Marjorie might look fine and like her self on the outside but Marjorie is awake and feeling and afraid a little of the storms that happen in here, how she is not clear, how she is puffed up full of clouds, how sometimes she feels her own thunder, how too much talk of before and what is stacked up and away in the dark in Marjorie makes her afraid of what could puddle up, of what might leak through.

How to stay floating?

How to keep going on and on and on with the days?

Sometimes Marjorie wants to know. About someone outside her self. What they are thinking and feeling and remembering and wondering. Not always. Most days it is hard enough for Marjorie to know what Marjorie is thinking. Even when she closes her eyes and pours her warm waters over her mind, even when Marjorie washes her mind all over and clears out the departments, even when inside she is her most clean and easy to see, it is hard for Marjorie to think of how it is to be in any body but her self.

But some days.

Some days, lately, Marjorie would like to be able to know these things more. How it feels for Suzanne to watch Tony run or what Benjamin sees when he rides his bike to the bottom of the mountain.

I know what you're thinking over there, Margie.

Gram's voice is so loud and cracked and cutting through that Marjorie's whole body bursts up into shakes. A high tight wave of surprise rises up from her belly to her heart and for a moment she feels almost afraid. For a moment, Marjorie does not know what is happening to her. In her. Her heart beats fast and one breath becomes three breaths and her mind is for just a moment the bright white of all the colors burned up together. The terrible, terrible of white.

But this is just Gram talking. A voice from before. And after. Now.

This will pass. The feeling is passing by.

What, Gram?

I know what you're thinking.

I don't know what you mean, Gram. I'm just watching the Stories. Not thinking.

Gram picks a gummy bear out of the package with two thin fingers and takes her time getting the treat to her mouth. She starts sucking on the gummy bear and while she does she keeps her small, cracked-egg eyes on Marjorie's eyes. Marjorie looks at the rivers of wrinkles of skin around Gram's eyes and at the many small hills of Gram's cheeks that move up and down as she sucks at her gummy bear.

I know you, Margie. I see you.

What do you know, Gram?

I know you're thinking about your ma. And you're right.

I wasn't thinking about Ma just now, Gram. Not much.

You're right about it, Margie. I didn't want to say before. But she was all done. All she was ever going to do, she did.

Gram, I don't know. About what?

What she did was right. Not in the eyes of our Lord, but for her.

What do you mean, Gram? What did Ma do?

You know what your ma did. I might have done the same, if I were her. If I was done like how she was done. With what she'd done. And what she didn't do, for that matter.

Ma did a lot of things, Gram. You need to say what Ma did that you are talking about. Because I don't understand what you are saying.

Stupid, stupid. Stupid.

Stupid? Me or her?

You, Margie, stupid. Sorry. But look how stupid you're being. Not listening. Not seeing. I know you know and here you are so stupid you forgot or so scared you won't say it to me now. Holding it in. But I know you know. You cleaned up her room after.

Marjorie sits and watches Gram suck her face slow in and out around her gummy bear. Gram's lips, chapped, thin, not any color anymore except the same color as all of her. Pale, pink dried and wrinkled away into gray. Almost no hair left on her. Some pieces of white, gray, dried-up white, not enough to cover the skin of her head.

Stupid, that word. A word heard so many times, said by so many People, but not much from Gram. Ever from Gram? The sound of stupid coming from Gram sits down loud and heavy in Marjorie.

Think, Margie. Lord, help Margie to see. Think about your ma. Think about all that you threw out from her room. All those bottles of pills around the bed.

She was sick, Gram.

Nobody dies of a cough, Margie.

Not just coughs. Ma had her pains.

Her pains. Your ma's pains. Maybe you are too good, Margie. Still thinking good thoughts about your ma.

I try, Gram.

How many pains and how many pills, Margie? How many bottles did you pick up and how many pills? All gone, right? Just bottles, empty. More than enough to put all the pains to bed for good.

Marjorie presses her palms to her thighs to feel her self and moves with her wind, down and up, up and down. She remembers. Marjorie remembers the small plastic circles of bottles of pills she had put in the trash on top of Ma's candy wrappers and cigarette cartons and the dust of Ma. Ma's pills that she had needed so much. The pills that took the pains away. And how Ma must have loved them, how this must be a kind of love that Dr. Goodwin never talked about. People and the love of what makes the pains stop. Marjorie remembers. The small round shapes of Ma's pill bottles. The orange-brown of them, the half-peeled labels scratched at, the thick white caps all around the floor, the bed. The caps opened up and thrown beside the bottles. The bottles emptied out.

Your ma wanted out, Margie.

Away. She got away.

Probably thought she was getting off easy. Should have been made to stay longer in her own mess of herself.

But she's with our Lord, now, Margie. And God won't let her get away with it. He will make your ma answer for what she's done.

Gram swallows whatever is left of the gummy bear she's been sucking on and turns her eyes back to the television. Marjorie keeps looking at her. Marjorie's body feels gone. She cannot turn or stop or move or move away. Marjorie watches Gram reach into the package and bring another gummy bear up to her mouth. Small and yellow. Lemon, maybe. Sour.

Don't worry, Margie. She's not off the hook. Our Lord knows. Your ma will pay.

Back again at the dead-end department of Ma. Marjorie closes her eyes to be more with her self. Pay, and with what? And how? Marjorie inside sees the big bright shape of the Lord there ready at the cash register and the bent-over pale of after-Ma and what has Ma got to give?

Marjorie does not know. She hears the voices from the Stories only as sounds, as whispers far away and underwater. Marjorie does not know if she knew what Gram says she knows. Here inside the wide dark space of her self, Marjorie can see that even now, even after so long spent living here inside her body, inside her mind, there are still whole shapes of things she can see only in shadow, in parts. Things that she cannot see at all. Big dark shapes here in the departments, on the shelves, pushed back and away but here, heavy, not known but felt. And here in the dark around where Marjorie's heart beats, even here where it is so hard to see, there are big bright holes of light. Things unseen in the dark and then things bright and white and so burning that Marjorie cannot come near. The darkest of black beside the big unending white of white. What Marjorie knows, and what she does not.

I shouldn't say these things, Margie. But this is how I feel. They say that God is more willing to forgive than we are to ask. But I don't know if that's true in the case of your ma.

I don't know, Gram.

It's gone on long enough, Margie. Time for you to get your ma out from under your bed.

Your ma's made you suffer long enough.

Get her out of here, Margie. Get her to our Lord.

So that we can go on.

So that you can get away.

Gram says what she has to say and goes back to her quiet, her gummy bears, her Stories. Marjorie sits beside her with her eyes closed and breathes. Inside it is too dark and too bright and here, now, there is no place to sit back and let loose and feel. There is no Hello, no Welcome. There are pains, long, packaged, white and beating.

This is not how People should live.

Marjorie squeezes her eyes shut tight and tighter and tight as she can. The stars come out bright and bursting on the big wide dark of her inside. Marjorie opens up the huge black sky of her and begins to let the warm water wash down. She understands what Gram is saying. Most of it, Marjorie understands. Marjorie can feel the shapes of things she cannot fully see, and she can see the lit-up shadows at the edge of the blinding bright white of where she cannot touch. Marjorie sits and waits to see and feel what she is feeling. She moves her hands slow and warm down her thighs to her knees and back up again. Moves her self, with her self, in the washing warm waters of her self. She feels fine. She will feel fine. Inside she will float up light and free in the warm and the touch of the water.

This is not a storm.

Here it will not storm.

This is a wash, a shower, a bath, a way out.

This is a flood that Marjorie is making, a flood from her self to fill her self to let go of her self to help her self to drain her self of what is dark, shaped, blinding, white, of what is known and not known and what should not be.

39. MARGE

Here, Marge, here. Get here.

Get your ass over here.

Here, a toast.

This is the good stuff.

Some real champ-pain. And whiskey. The good stuff.

Toast. Cheers.

To us, Marge. Me and your ma. Hitched.

Get that glass up.

To us. Say it. To my ma and my old man. My new old man.

What the fuck is wrong with you?

Stupid.

Can't you talk? I know you can talk. I hear you talk.

Talk out there with your girlfriend. I hear you, Marge. I watch you two out there. Big ugly you and your pretty little friend.

Say it. To Dad. To my new daddy.

Come on, Marge. You can get one out. Just one word. Just one little word out of that big fat mouth of yours.

Pop. Daddy. Father. Dad.

Sir. You want to call me Sir, Marge?

Keep that glass raised up there. High above your head.

One word and you can drink that down.

I know you know my name, Marge. Let's hear it.

I will help you. Move those big lips of yours for you.

Too lazy to do it yourself.

Here.

Fa-ther.

Da-ddy.

See, Marge. It ain't so bad, talking.

Mus-tang.

Mus-tang.

Now drink.

Fuck it, you know what?

You know what I just realized, Marge?

Fuck, I don't want to be nobody's daddy.

Mustang. That's me.

You call me Mustang.

Cheers, Marge. To us.

Drink.

Say it. To us. To Mustang.

Louder.

Drink.

You drink that now.

That's good shit you've got in there, Marge.

I bought that for you.

Drink it now or I'll pour it down myself.

40. MARJORIE

Marjorie likes babies. She stands and watches the swinging door and does her best to smile and she waits for People and she waits for babies. Shoulders high as she can make them go. Standing. Watching. Waiting.

And sometimes babies pass by. Babies dressed in bibs in pink dresses in purple pajamas in blue tiny t-shirts in blankets in little puffy coats in strollers in seats put in shopping carts or in the arms of their ma.

Marjorie likes babies so much.

She smiles. Wider. More. As best she can.

Hello, she says.

Welcome.

Marjorie makes her voice loud. Moves her arms and her legs. Would open the door for the babies, if the door did not swing open and closed on its own.

Because Marjorie likes the babies even more than the People.

Marjorie likes babies the most.

Of everything.

But babies do not like Marjorie.

Marjorie makes her voice loud and she opens her arms wide. Welcoming the babies with all of her, with the whole of her big self. Waving her arms out wide to the babies and moving her legs toward them.

Marjorie would like to hold a baby.

Marjorie opens her arms out wide to Welcome a baby to the Store and she steps fast toward the baby and arms-out-wide stands close as she can to the baby and looks down on the little feet, the little nose, the little bald head and the little hands making fists.

And the bright other inside Marjorie reaches for the baby and touches the baby, brings the baby up to her self and holds the baby close.

And the outside Marjorie stands arms-out wide over the baby and always, and now, the baby cries.

The baby is crying.

The perfect baby face, the soft baby cheeks balled up red and tight, the little baby eyes squeezed shut and pouring down. The baby nose running. The ma moving fast past Marjorie and into the deep of the Store.

Babies do not like Marjorie.

And this, only this, Marjorie minds.

The ma moves the baby away and Marjorie is left alone. Pains in her arms from the long holding out.

Now, and always, when the babies come and the babies go, Marjorie feels bad.

Not good. Not fine. Not okay. Not usual.

Bad. The cold empty alone of bad.

The arms-out wanting to touch, wanting to smell and hold and feel, of bad.

The bad unending alone feeling of long-lost and never-here Lucy.

Lucy the almost of unpacked love. Lucy who would have wanted to be held. Lucy who would have needed to be warmed and fed and carried and washed and loved and loved and loved. Lucy and all the possibilities of Lucy. Lucy with legs kicking in grass, with a little body wearing a little yellow dress. Lucy with hair like Marjorie's, eyes like Marjorie's, heart and blood like Marjorie's. The endless on and on of Lucy.

The most good that Marjorie almost made.

Lucy.

Marjorie, alone, making Lucy.

Inside, in the dark, the secret putting-together of Lucy.

Belly, hands, lips, heart.

Half finished, half here.

The imperfect Lucy.

What Marjorie, alone, must have done wrong.

Lucy.

What Marjorie did not know.

Marjorie, alone.

Arms held out wide, ready to touch and hold and feel and know.

Catching her wind when she can.

Marjorie, alone, stands out of her place.

In front of the swinging door, beside the air where the baby is not.

Blown-up big, beating, feeling bad.

The gone of Lucy.

The never here of Lucy.

The pains.

People passing by, through, in, into.

In need of the needed things.

And Marjorie stands.

Wanting.

But what?

41. MARGIE

Gram, in darkness, said it like this.

Time to get up, Margie.

Time to get up and face the day.

Margie got up and faced her days. The part of the day she spent in Apartment #2. Big and chewing and hiding. She got up and got on with her long, slow day at school. Margie's day made longer, now, slower, now, because Lucy was not there. Lucy took a bus now. Lucy, still below, in Apartment #1, but moving on, up. Margie still walked. Lucy left, Margie stayed.

Separated. We had no choice. For school, that's all. And not because they touched, not because of what the other kids said about them. Because this is the natural course of events. This is the truth. What we all could see. That Lucy was normal and Margie was not. Lucy was lazy, maybe, and had a mouth on her, for sure, but she was quick, she was smart. Margie was slow, quiet. So stuck in her own world the easiest thing for us to do was let her stay there. In, down, wherever she was.

That's what happened. That's what we did.

Lucy moved on, moved up, and Margie stayed where she was. In the room at the edge of the school where we left her alone, where we saw and did not see all the signs of things we did not stop to name. There are so many needs out there. So much need, so much help being asked for. How could we choose which one to pay attention to?

How could we have answered what was never asked?

Margie made her way through her days at school by staying quiet and inside herself. She heard the voices of her teachers and ate all of her lunch and thought about Lucy. Went to the wall when she was allowed. Waited for the teachers to say, Time to go home.

Time to go home, Margie.

Margie took her time going home. All day she waited for the time, and when the time came, she moved even more slowly than her usual slow. Margie put her pencils and her notebook and her packages of crackers into her blue backpack one by one, each one into its separate place. She walked slowly so that the other kids would pass by. So that we would not notice Margie in her t-shirt with holes, her pants stretched tight and starting to tear, in her cigarette-smoke and school-lunch smell. Margie, slow, floating, weighed down by all that she had built up against the outside.

Usually, it worked. Usually, we didn't notice Margie. We were looking at girls and how they bounced and bent over and pulled each other's hair. We were passing notes to boys. Tongue-kissing behind the school. We were driving home. We were passing through.

Margie took her time going home because more and more Lucy was not there. Every day, long before making the slow, creaking climb up to Apartment #2, Margie knocked on the door of Apartment #1 to see if Lucy had made it home yet. Every day Margie knocked, because Margie knew, now, about knocking, about showing the people inside that she was there, outside, waiting. Wanting to come in.

Days when Lucy was home, they sat together on the sidewalk or in Lucy's room or in the shade of the trees at the edge of the brook. Lucy, grown taller, her breasts grown bigger. Blonde-haired becoming-beautiful Lucy who rode the bus, who went to another school, now, who sometimes did not come right home after. Lucy told Margie stories about the kids in her school, what they did, what they said. Margie listened and nodded and smiled when Lucy smiled and laughed when Lucy laughed and at the end of the story Margie did not remember how it had begun. Sometimes Lucy drew pictures for Margie of boys in her class or showed her the notes they wrote. Sometimes Lucy gave Margie candy bars the boys took from the store on the corner.

They think this is a present, Lucy said.

But they stole it. They didn't even bother to buy it.

What's that supposed to mean?

Margie ate the candy bars and sat beside Lucy when Lucy was there. When Lucy said she was sad, when Lucy wanted her to, Margie put her arms around Lucy and squeezed. When Lucy asked Margie about her day, Margie always said it was good.

Good. The days were good.

But the days with Lucy dwindled. Most days, Margie knocked, and Lucy's ma opened the door and said something like, Sorry, Margie.

Lucy's busy. Lucy's not home.

Lucy's out.

For a long time, Lucy's ma held the door only half open and said just these few words.

Sorry, Margie. Lucy's not here.

Okay, Margie said, and in her mind Margie could see Lucy's ma inside, could see how Lucy's ma had looked out of her clothes. Margie would think about her big, round, white body, how she had rolled off the sofa and tried to cover herself with pillows. Her freckles, the roll of them. Margie remembered. Lucy's ma's body, moving in waves, breathing hard. Let loose. What Gram said to LD. The bright red drying to brown where it had soaked into the white tissues. All the bumps and thuds and scrapes and creaks of Apartment #2, above.

Margie said nothing.

We said nothing.

And time was hard to tell.

Until that day in the almost-winter, one sunless day when dried leaves blew up the steps and into the hallway, when Margie needed help and Lucy was not there.

What, Lucy's ma said, opening the door. Margie?

What's wrong?

Me, Margie said.

Margie could see her breath big in front of her in steam when she breathed, could see her words as a cloud when she spoke.

My pains.

Lucy's ma opened the door a little wider, put her warm fingers around Margie's cold wrist, pulled her closer. She looked up Margie and down Margie, all over the whole of Margie.

Where are you hurt? What happened?

Margie, red-faced, put her hands around her belly and looked down at herself.

We knew. We had seen.

Out in the dark of the hallway Lucy's ma could not see, but once she had let Margie inside, once she had Margie in the warm yellow light of the living room, she saw.

You're not hurt, Margie, Lucy's ma said.

It's normal. It's just your time.

I don't know, Margie said, and she held herself tight, closed her eyes because she was not sure where to look, what to do.

Your ma hasn't talked to you about it, Margie?

Ma's busy.

Busy, right. God, Margie. I keep hearing things up there.

But it's not my business. Come on, Margie. Come into the bathroom, you've got to learn.

Margie listened to what Lucy's ma said and did what Lucy's ma told her to do. She learned, let Lucy's ma tell her about her inside. Herself, her body, what was happening in there. How to watch it and listen and know it. What would happen. What could happen. What should not happen. Not to be afraid of it, the bright red of it, the heat of it, the touch of it. The blood-letting-loose of it. Margie sat with Lucy's ma a long time in the bright white light of the bathroom and Margie understood.

Her time.

Margie, catching up to Lucy.

Releasing.

Margie, her body, leaking.

Margie, this is what we call growing up.

This is what we call becoming a woman.

This is the smell of it.

This is the look of it.

This is how to hide.

This is the danger.

This is the pain.

This is normal.

42. MARGE

Where's Marge?

I know you're here.

Where else are you going to go, Marge?

I know you're in there.

I can hear you.

Smell you in there.

Let's talk for a while. I'm sorry I called you fat. I mean fat is a good thing.

You know we're friends, Marge. Sometimes friends say things they don't mean.

I'm sorry about that.

Will you open up the door and talk to me?

I miss you, Marge. Been spending a lot of time with your ma and shit can that woman talk.

I don't want to talk to your ma right now. I want to talk to you, Marge.

Why are you making all those sounds in there?

Getting your panties in a twist.

Is that old bag in there with you?

I bet she is. I bet the two of you are in there together.

I bet you're rolling around in there. I hear you. I know what you're up to.

Open this fucking door Marge.

This is your father out here, Marge.

Your friend.

Open this piece-of-shit door or I will break it down.

You want your ma to come home and see a broken door? Who do you think she'll blame, Marge? Think she'll blame me?

You get your pretty porker ass over to this door now and you open it and you let me in there.

One.

Two.

This is no joke, Marge. You hear this?

You hear my fist out here on this door?

Don't be stupid.

Two-and-a-half.

That's it, Marge.

Three.

Fuck.

Look at my fucking hand.

Look what you made me do.

Stupid.

Get over here and pick this door up.

Get over here and say you're sorry.

43. MARJORIE

Marjorie sits alone in the afternoon dark of the almost-empty Club and eyes-down nods when Mac says, The usual, Marjorie?

The usual. So many days and days and weeks and months gone by and Marjorie is tired from so many things that have nothing to do with her usual. What Gram says Marjorie knows about Ma. Ma and what she did. Ma, sick, sick of being Ma, sick of the light of the no-sound television, of the quiet of Gram, of the bare-bulb apartment, of Marjorie, of the night sounds of the sofa springs, of before, and after, of all the things.

Lucy running free.

Departments leaking into departments, things falling from shelves faster than Marjorie can stack.

And does it matter?

About Ma?

If it is not your self who does it to you, who is going to do it?

Marjorie leans forward and crosses her arms on the bar and lays her head down on her arms. Hears the sound of her coat all around. She closes her eyes and waits for her drink and does not even feel thirsty, does not even want to talk to Mac today. Spring Is Here and Marjorie's coat is not even off. No usual at all. This day, these days, Marjorie, so far away from the usual.

Marjorie, sent home early from the Store today. Two hours early, because Steve said so. Because Steve pinched her arm and punched her card for her and said that People want to feel Welcome, not scared.

You're scaring them, Marjorie.

Get out of here.

Not her usual. So much time spent in her special place in the Store and Marjorie has never left before the end of her shift. Not when she was sick, not when it was her birthday or Gram's birthday or on any of these days with that box of Ma at home waiting. Never gone on a vacation day. Even on every one of those days in the life of Marjorie that might not have gone as usual, she has held on hard, has made sure that the hours of the day happen where they should happen, that the day, the things, her self, stay usual.

And then today happens.

Today Marjorie sits in the Club with her arms hugging the bar, with her head sunk down into the soft coat that covers the soft skin that hangs around her self. Today it is two hours early and here Marjorie is in the Club. Not her usual time and because the outside is more bright than usual the inside looks more dark than usual and because Steve said Marjorie was scaring the People and because Steve punched her card and told her to Get out, here Marjorie is with her head down and coat on in the Club that is much darker, and quiet, and more empty than usual.

But here is usual Mac with her usual drink. Her Shirley Temple. Her someone like a friend, Mac. Her wind, her dark, her heart. And Mac's not usual, but not minded, hand warm on her hand.

Marjorie, you okay?

Marjorie lifts her head and blinks her eyes and tries to sit up straight on her stool.

Yes, Mac. Okay.

Mac reaches down into a big jar of red circles floating and pulls out two extra cherries for Marjorie's drink. He drops them in and her Shirley Temple breaks into waves of more and more small bubbles. Explodes. Exploding. The ice moving, pink liquid crashing up the sides of the glass, making room for something else.

Marjorie stares hard at her drink. Her usual turned not usual with two drops. Today is not a day for Marjorie's face to smile but she makes her mouth move in circles around the words, says, Thanks, Mac.

You seem low today, Marjorie. How's life?

Another question.

How many questions are there in the world?

Marjorie can only see her self from inside her self and in here seeing is difficult, in here is too much dark and too much bright, too many things being thought. In here is low from all that Marjorie can feel big and shaped but cannot see. The high pain of the light holes so white Marjorie cannot turn toward them. Marjorie sees the mess made in her inside departments and because of Mac asking questions and because of Steve and his Get out, because of the People with their eyes who see her who see that Marjorie is not her usual Marjorie, it must be that her inside has come out. Marjorie, opened up. The People can see in. Her door, slidopen, her self puddling out.

Marjorie puts her head back down on the bar so that Mac will see less of her. So that she can keep the inside in. Because Marjorie does not want to answer any questions. Because Marjorie does not have the answer to Mac's asked How of life.

160

And time is beating.

Time inside is slow, is heavy.

But sometime during this head-down time, this moment or minute, these quiet breathing breezes of Mac's waiting and Marjorie's dark not wanting, Suzanne comes. Suzanne who knows, now, or does not know. The flowered smell of Suzanne. The warm wind of Suzanne. The sound of Suzanne, the perfect here of Suzanne. Suzanne comes into the Club laughing, singing some song, and with her Marjorie hears Tony, small-boy-beautiful Tony, singing that same song in his high baby voice.

Not usual. But not a bad not usual. A good time for Marjorie to try again to pull her self up out of her self.

Hey, Suzanne, Mac says.

Marjorie turns to look at Suzanne and Tony. Suzanne is smiling and her red hair is pulled up high and tight at the top of her head and she is wearing pink lipstick and a green shirt and even in the dark of the Club, even on this day when so many things seem so far gone from usual, Marjorie feels a little good to see that Suzanne is still her perfect, pretty, perfect self. That she is here. And Tony, with his soft-looking hair so bright it looks more like light on his head than hair, like he is a boy who even in a dark place like the Club has got his own little sun on him. Tony, here, too. Tony and his small legs in small blue jeans, his thin arms swinging as he sings, his arms pale and bright and stuck out wide like wings from the sleeves of his red t-shirt. The usual is Tony taken away by a babysitter by the time Marjorie gets to the Club. Tony, little Lucy-like Tony, is all Marjorie can see. His little fingers and how he curls them into claws and calls himself a monster, how fast he runs between tables and stools through the Club, the way his small mouth sends out so many big, loud words.

Hi, Mac, Suzanne says. Hi Marjorie. How's everybody doing?

Marjorie cannot make her self smile but she can make her head nod and mouth say, Okay.

Mac puts his hand again on Marjorie's hand.

I'm good, he says. But Marjorie seems down in the dumps.

Marjorie feels her face and arms and neck go hot and red and her legs she cannot feel and her belly squeezes up and behind her eyes and nose there is a feeling like a sneeze, a pressure, a painful tingling like being pinched like being underwater like not being able to breathe. Departments tipping into departments. Water moving through, fast. Not the warm of Marjorie's water but cold, holding under.

Tony's little feet running around the Club and his little loud voice scream-singing.

Look At Me, Mommy! Look At Me! Look At Me, Mommy, Look At Me. I'm An Airplane Mom I'm A Jet I'm A Submarine Look At Me!

Marjorie puts her arms around her ears and holds her head in her hands and bends forward until the sticky cold wood of the bar touches her skin. She holds on tight, presses her self into her self.

Quiet, Tony, Suzanne says. Just a second, honey.

Marjorie feels her skin against her skin making her warm skin warmer.

Let it go, Marjorie, Dr. Goodwin would say.

Let it out.

You have to let yourself go sometimes, Marjorie.

No.

No.

Dr. Goodwin knows a lot of her self and Dr. Goodwin is good and kind and right about many things, but Dr. Goodwin is wrong about letting her self go.

Because where is there to go?

But gone, gone, gone.

Marjorie can hear Mac and Suzanne whispering. Tony singing. Inside, she is moving, falling, pushing, beating, flooding, holding on.

Marjorie needs her self. Marjorie needs what is inside to stay in. Let it out, let her self go, and Marjorie would not be Marjorie. A leftover, the skin, the body big and empty, just another person in all the People of People. That would be Marjorie if she let go. That would be Marjorie with the inside all let out. Marjorie, an invited guest in the Club. On the bathroom floor with her inside out and Lucy laid out red, drowned, soundless, beneath her. Marjorie with that most secret part of her self let out and not allowed to see. With the shape of what would have been Lucy, that shape of the hidden part of her self that grew in her self that Marjorie did not know until it was let out, let go, until her inside pushed what was there through and out and away. What is not the usual. That day. This day. That time. Before. That biggest secret part of her self, her self so big already, the secret hidden inside, her self so big, big enough for Lucy, big enough for Lucy to be and grow and live.

And live?

Was Lucy alive inside?

How much is not usual hiding inside the skin of the usual?

Look At Me Mommy Look At Me Watch This Look At This Look At Me Mommy Look At Me Now.

That shape inside that Marjorie felt and did not feel. The pains. But there were and are and always will be pains and how do People know when the pain is usual and when the pain is not?

Marjorie might have known.

The pains that piled together. The pains of that day. The pain in her knees her back her belly. The pain of piling green beans on her plate. The private pressing pains of Prime Rib Dinner.

Suzanne's arm around her shoulders is warm is a pull is heavy is a touch Marjorie feels from down under and far away.

The pool of pain inside her so big so pressing and pushing that Marjorie had nothing to do but lie down and open up and let it out. To let go of Lucy. What was warm and unknown and unshaped. Unfinished.

What was $6.95. What is now $8.95 and on Wednesdays. What was $6.95 and a good deal on Thursdays. What was Marjorie's usual. Before. When meat was cheap. Before Suzanne and Dr. Goodwin. When Mac charged only $6.95 for Prime Rib Dinner. For all-you-could-eat mashed potatoes, green beans, cooked carrots, rolls, dark red soft meat. Where Marjorie was every Thursday. In the Club. With the People. Cutting up her meat, smiling, drinking her Shirley Temple. Away from Gram, Ma, Him and the little bare-bulb apartment they split all between them once there was nothing else to blow up in the quarry and Apartment #2 became more than they had to give.

Suzanne's voice is sound sent through so much lake of before of what is inside and underneath, of what is Marjorie spilling department into department that Suzanne's voice is here and heard but is not heard here by Marjorie, is heard from far away, from where Marjorie is, heard from somewhere below the bottom of her self.

It's okay, Marjorie. I know. Mac told me.

I'm so sorry. It's okay.

Okay enough to pile her plate high as she could without spilling. Marjorie always ate more green beans than carrots, more meat than beans, more potatoes than meat and always two rolls. Sliced in half, buttered. That day the pains pushing inside, popping inside, more pains than usual but pain, but pain. How could Marjorie know? Pain was pain is pain is pain. Gas. Her time. Too much soda, two-day-old pizza for lunch. Pain all day that day but pain all day all the days. Marjorie all day that day felt her insides squeezed and pinched and punched and probably more than usual. But pain, pressure inside. This was the usual of Marjorie, before.

Mommy I'm Bored I'm Bored Can You Watch Me One Minute Mommy

One Minute Watch I'm An Airplane I'm A Truck I'm Hungry Mommy Play
With Me.

I said quiet, honey. Mommy is talking to Marjorie right now.

Breathe, Marjorie. Calm down.

Mac told me and I can't imagine.

Breathe.

It's okay. I know. I can't imagine.

How you must have suffered.

The usual and Thursday and the usual for Thursday was to go to the Club
to eat her Prime Rib Dinner to be free and with the People, together with the
People, not as a worker, not to say Hello and to Welcome, just to be, to eat,
to be out and away. And in her pain Marjorie piled her plate high and brought
her plate to her table and every step she stepped sent more pain and more and
Marjorie put her plate down on her table and held her belly in her hands and
felt the pain not just there but everywhere inside, felt the waves of pain so high,
so hard, that Marjorie put her food-steaming meat-smelling plate down on her
table and holding her belly in her hands she walked as fast and straight and usual
as she could to the bathroom.

Marjorie? Do you want to come with me to the bathroom?

Let's wash off your face. Get you cooled down.

Marjorie, her hot red head-down face hot against her hands, does not want
to go to the bathroom.

Marjorie does not go to the bathroom in the Club.

In Marjorie's mind there is a department for the bathroom of the Club. Aisles
and aisles she never goes down. A white-tiled unseeable department deep inside
her dark. Flashes of bright white lines of light that Marjorie cannot look at. A
place she pretends is not there. Here. Blinding white flashes she pushes away.
Lights that push back, aisles of bright holes of light that for terrible moments
let the unseen be seen. Things still, stacked, what Marjorie remembers and does
not want to see, the Club, the bathroom, the pain, in pictures, in flashes, inside.

I Hate You Mommy I'm Bored I Want To Go Home I Want You To Play
With Me Watch Me Mommy Watch Me I'm Flying.

All of the things Marjorie saw and the one thing Marjorie wanted to see and
was not allowed to see. What was all hers, all wrong, all gone.

The black glass eyes of the big brown buck head above the mirror above
the sink. Plastic yellow tulips in a green vase beside an ashtray gray with cigarette butts, some lipstick-stained, bent and cold, some still orange, still spinning
thin ribbons of smoke into the soap-smoke-prime-rib-potato-scented air. The

square mirror Marjorie's fist broke into pieces when the pain waves hit too hard, too high, when her insides started to push through. How even inside all of her pain Marjorie felt bad about the mirror, felt bad about how Mac would have to see what she had done. How Marjorie tried hard to keep her hands on her self, to hold her insides in, to hold on. How before Marjorie laid her big self down on the bathroom floor she saw the dark wet leak of her self in pieces in the mirror that was all her fault.

Tony, I said stop it.

Marjorie will be okay, Suzanne. Give her some time. Let her be.

You're making me worried, Marjorie. I've never seen you like this.

Can you at least say something?

No Marjorie cannot say anything. Marjorie is inside the department where she does not go and Marjorie does not know how she got here. But here she is. Too much thinking. A day gone different from usual. Too many things. The pain still here in this bathroom in her mind, still as a photo, whole white and blinding pain like a bulb looked at bare and up close. White pain so white it is a little blue. The exploding. The white life of stars. The pain of the burn of light burned into eyeballs and how even in the eyes-shut dark the shape of what was there is there, here, still.

People. Inside in the department in the bathroom, People. Not just Marjorie and her self and her pain. People's voices calling for Mac, calling for the ambulance, calling for God, for her.

To Hang In There.

To Push.

Calling, Marjorie.

Marjorie.

The thick wet down her legs on her skin on her clothes under her fingernails on the silver-blue-speckled floor where Marjorie lay. Where Marjorie's hands were, her hands that hold her head here on the bar, her hands that hold her ears that hold her self in, Marjorie's red wet hands held red-stained toilet paper. She remembers. Marjorie remembers she tried to wipe it all away. The smell of blood and potatoes and prime rib and what she had kept inside.

The spoiled smell of Lucy.

Can Lucy, the good idea of Lucy, really smell so bad?

In the aisles of this department a lady's voice looks like the long cold white of a sink seen from below. A man's voice is high and thin and watery as the sweat and the wet that became the whole world of what Marjorie saw. The pain, the smell, the bottomless white terrible of what she remembers.

This Is Boring Mommy I Want To Go Home I Want To Play A Game.

Suzanne's arms around Marjorie on both sides now, Suzanne's hands rubbing her shoulders, Suzanne's hands making the sounds of coat, the sound of Suzanne's voice far up at the surface where Marjorie is not.

I know, baby. I know. Just a little bit longer.

Suzanne, red-haired perfect, soft, warm, and after. Mac there, Mac here, Mac was there, watching, but not Suzanne. People before and People after and Suzanne, perfect in her after.

Suzanne should not know.

But Suzanne knows.

The great big secret of Marjorie.

The People around. Down this aisle of Marjorie is a bathroom crowded by People. People watching, People helping. Voices and the smell of warm bread buttered and even in so much bad, in all that pain, Marjorie and what she knew and knows.

That People are good.

People care about People.

Hands holding her, touching her, helping her find a place in the pain where there was air and space and a way to lay and breathe and feel. The soft of someone's t-shirt beneath her neck. Her pants, soaked, taken, gone. Marjorie opened-up there for all the People to see.

But the good, the good.

Coats put over and under her to hide what could be hidden. People. Soft rubber-gloved fingers pressing hard down on her belly down into her. People come to help. Hands and hands touching. Not bad touches, hard touches but not angry. Touches that Marjorie did not have time to Mind or Not Mind. Careful touches, caring.

Voices.

Mac's voice.

Jesus, Marjorie, Jesus.

Mac praying, for her. Mac and the Lord, talking.

God.

Marjorie in the Club must believe in God and so Marjorie on the cold bathroom floor of the Club in her pain in between waves of it, when she heard Mac saying her name and could feel the People helping, when she felt the great big weight of her self pushing through, believed.

Loud voices praying, telling, helping.

Come On, Marjorie.

Push.

Marjorie, who was it?

God, Marjorie, God.

F-Word, F-Word, F-Word.

Who did this?

The words smelled like metal, like the big metal smell of blood. The words felt wet, cold, hard as bathroom floor. Looked red and brown covering the white of gloves. Words black like blood, bright like blood.

And People. So many People. Marjorie on the floor letting go of what she carried inside, of what she did not know, of what would have been but never was Lucy, looked up. Marjorie looked up high and saw People shattered in the mirror above her, People standing in a circle around her, protecting her, helping her. Marjorie, in the long and high-as-hills moment of her most pain, looked back and up, up above the ruined mirror, looked up above and into the dead black glass eyes of the buck and in there she saw the shadow shapes of the People, her self, her inside out and all over, and Lucy, what was or is or would have been Lucy. The one look Marjorie had of her most hidden, round, drowned part of her self. All Marjorie ever saw of what she named Lucy, of her secret, of what she made and carried and did not know, spilled out onto bathroom floor, cut away, contained, wrapped in soft white dishtowels.

Unshaped, unseen, not allowed.

Unconditioned.

What Marjorie did.

Taken.

Marjorie breathes. In and out and in and out and in and out. By her self. With Suzanne's hands soft and warm on her shoulders, with the sounds of Tony's feet running around the Club, with Mac somewhere nearby, quiet, watching, breathing.

The worst of the department visited. The rest bright lines of light tubes and eyes closed and the blurred ghosts of the light. Of Marjorie gone under. The light-ghosts going from white to yellow to black to dark to nothing. The pain, her body opened up and emptied out. But pain is just pain and Marjorie knows pain and it is important to bring her self back here, back to usual.

Tony's small body beside her. Marjorie, head-down, beating, breathing, coming back, can feel him next to Suzanne, next to her.

Mommy I Said I Am Bored I Want To Go Home I Want You To Play With Me Now.

Back, back, back. To now. To the Club. To after. To Marjorie. To where there is no Lucy. To the stool. The hard wood of the bar. To here where Marjorie knows her self and how Marjorie can surprise, can see, to Marjorie who knows there are secrets inside.

So many possible things.

To after. To the hospital where doctors asked her questions and nurses wiped her face with cold towels and gave her little cups of apple juice, where Marjorie lay alone in her white hospital bed in pain. The worst over and never over. The hours, or days, the long, long minutes into minutes into gray light through hospital blinds into the fluorescent-lined darkness of night. The slow inside stacking of things up high on shelves. Building and rebuilding and finding ways around the departments where she will not go. Marjorie in and out and in and inside the big cold belly of empty. The most empty Marjorie could ever be. A phone call from Mac and what she understood of it. Her name, Marjorie, Marjorie, and God.

And Dr. Goodwin. The first of Dr. Goodwin. The Hello and the How are you of Dr. Goodwin. Dr. Goodwin in his tie in his black pointed shoes, shining, sitting in a chair beside her and asking her what he will always ask.

How do you feel, Marjorie?

Dr. Goodwin sent to her from somewhere, from his office, from the Department of People Who Help. Telling her what happened. Telling her, I'm here to help you.

Dr. Goodwin, even then, sitting beside her, so interested in his favorite thing, his word, her understand.

Do you understand, Marjorie?

Do you understand where you are?

Do you understand what happened to you?

They've taken him away.

You won't have to see him.

Do you understand?

Understand, understand.

Like a song for Marjorie to stand under. Marjorie, lying under, there, for that day, or days, for that time in the early of after, listening to the People, saying words, nodding, trying to smile, to say Hello, from there, from under, from far inside the warm waters of her self. Not wanting to leave. Nowhere to stay.

They've taken him away.

Do you understand?

I'm here to help you, Marjorie.

You're safe now.

Nod if you understand.

Marjorie shakes her head slowly back and forth against the soft of her arms and the warm she has made here with her wind, her coat, her skin. She nods because her neck is stiff from so much leaning over the bar, so long spent so deep inside her self, because behind the dark of her shut eyes the flashes and pictures and smells, sounds, voices, the aisles, all the aisles of the departments Marjorie never goes to, are loud and bright and right here. Marjorie nods her heavy head into her hands because she is letting go. Because inside, the waters of before and after are settling down into now. Right now.

Because Suzanne says, You okay, Marjorie?

Because Suzanne knows.

And here is Suzanne.

Sure you're okay, Marjorie?

And Mac says, She's okay. Let her be, she'll be okay.

Mac who knows.

And Tony is here, screaming.

Mommy Play With Me Play With Me Please Please Please Please This Is Boring I'm Bored I Want To Go Home I Want You To Look At Me Watch Me Fly I'm An Airplane Mommy Please.

Marjorie is taking steps closer and closer toward Marjorie. Toward after. Now.

Inside she is swimming away from the departments, away from the pull of before, away from the places where pain still lives in glass bottles on shelves in things in places she will not touch. Marjorie breathes her breath, brings her self up through her self to where her heart beats, to where her heartbeat feels usual.

Usual. Usual. Usual. Usual.

Marjorie opens her eyes and sees the dark of her skin up close. She thinks. She can think. She thinks that this is now, this is after. That she knows her self. How all the People, and Marjorie too, have secrets inside that are secret even from their selves. Too many departments. Too many things. And maybe Marjorie does not need to see the shape of all these secret things inside her self. Maybe it is fine to leave some things unknown, untouched. Maybe Marjorie does not need to understand.

Because how can she understand this whole of her?

Isn't it enough just to be here in this body, beating?

Marjorie breathes. In and blinks her eyes. Out and wiggles her shoulders. In and pushes her arms into the bar to make her stronger here on her stool. Out and lifts her head.

Marjorie looks around and moves with her wind and smiles. Sees. The colorful lights of the signs in the Club, the dust falling through the light coming in
around the windows. Mac wiping the bar with a white towel. Suzanne standing
next to her, her warm hand rubbing Marjorie's back. Suzanne's hand-through-
coat rubbing the hurting place where Marjorie's bra digs in. And Tony, running. Flashes of Tony, so fast, his small legs, his perfect pale skin and small arms.
Warm, alive, running, screaming. Shaped, here, now.

Little beautiful Tony running up close to them, to Suzanne with her hand on
Marjorie's back, Suzanne who is here helping. Tony running up beside them,
to Suzanne, to Marjorie. Marjorie whose head is up, who is nodding, blinking,
coming back.

Now Can We Go Can We Go Home Mommy I Am Bored I Am Hungry I
Want To Go Home I Want You To Play With Me.

Tony up close to them, near Marjorie's knees, next to Suzanne's body, Tony
coming in close to the soft of Suzanne, the wide ma parts of Suzanne where
Tony fits in, where Tony puts his arms, where Tony squeezes and cries and
wants.

Suzanne takes her hand off Marjorie's back and what is left behind feels
pained and without weight. Suzanne takes her hand off Marjorie's back and puts
her hand on Tony's head. Suzanne puts her perfect hand on Tony's head and
Tony cries and cries and even more cries.

It's okay, baby. Mommy's just helping Marjorie out.

Tony's little lit-up head turns to look up at Suzanne, at Marjorie, and his face
is red and white waves. Thin wet lines of tears run from his eyes to his chin and
in his eyes there are little pools that shine. And Tony's small mouth opens, and
Marjorie sees Lucy, sees in Tony's mouth the mouth that Lucy might have had,
hears Tony's crying as Lucy's crying as a sound let loose from the department
she has just left. Marjorie turns on her stool so that she can see more of Tony.
Turns her shoulders so that she can reach her hand out, across the Club, from
the far-away of her self. Marjorie's arm lifted and held out wide and reaching to
touch, to feel Tony, to touch the real of the tears on Tony's small, perfect face.

Stupid Marjorie Mommy I Want You I Want To Go Home Stupid Stupid
Marjorie Stupid.

Tony's small hand is fast, flashes up, slaps Marjorie's big arm out there in the
space of the Club between them. Marjorie feels Tony's little hand hit her hand,
sees the little-boy angry all over his face, hears Stupid Stupid Marjorie, and feels
Lucy, feels the not-there of Lucy, the never-was of Lucy, the lost chance of
Lucy, the hot of the things inside Marjorie that she cannot see, the size of all

of these shapes of her self that she does not understand, and Marjorie, Stupid Stupid Marjorie, big, smiling, wide-open, let-out Marjorie, bends her knee and with the pains that live inside, and hard as she can, fast as she can, with all the weight of the things she has got stacked away inside, swings her leg at Tony, at his little crying chest. Kicks Tony, kicks her black sneaker at his small perfect body. Marjorie kicks her leg with all of this angry she cannot feel, one kick, one fast kick, one hard kick at Tony's chest into Tony's chest and with one cracking kick Marjorie kicks Tony over and down and onto the floor.

And for the first time in a long, long, long, long time, Marjorie is crying.

Marjorie is burning hot, red, angry.

Her whole body alive, angry, shaking.

Hot water boiling over from her inside to her outside.

Suzanne screaming.

Tony coughing, crying, screaming.

Mac running, saying, Jesus, Marjorie.

What did you do?

Fuck.

Mac running around the bar toward Tony, Suzanne, Marjorie.

Suzanne screaming, saying, Tony, saying so many bad words to Marjorie.

Suzanne covering Tony's little body with her big body, her soft, perfect, red-haired, beautiful, beautiful ma-shaped body.

Marjorie trying to stand, trying to see, trying to understand her self, her crying, her big fat foot that kicked, her angry, this angry that Marjorie did not know was down here inside her self.

Tony coughing, crying on the floor.

People coming over.

People standing in a circle around, watching, come to see what Marjorie did.

Suzanne's voice loud, Suzanne's voice angry, saying, Get out, Marjorie.

Now. Get out.

Suzanne's voice soft, kind, for Tony, saying, It's okay, baby.

I know, I know. You're safe. You're okay.

Suzanne's body, gone from Marjorie, bent over Tony, lifting his shirt to look close at his little body, looking for broken parts, looking at what Marjorie did.

And Mac's hand hard on Marjorie's arm. Pulling Marjorie up off of her stool. Not helping. Hurting. Hurting her. Holding on.

Mac, saying, Come on, Marjorie. You got to go.

Mac pulling Marjorie away from the bar, away from her Shirley Temple with the two extra cherries. Her usual, untouched. Mac pulling Marjorie away from

Suzanne, away from Tony, away from the People. Holding on to her and moving her around the tables and chairs, through the Club, to the bright of the light coming in through the door.

Fuck, Marjorie. Why'd you do that? What the fuck? God.

Mac opening the door, pulling Marjorie's arm through the door, Marjorie's body following. Marjorie not feeling, not thinking, not seeing, going where Mac makes her go. Out of the Club, out through the door, out into the cool air of the almost-spring outside.

Get out, Marjorie.

Don't come back here.

And quiet.

Then quiet.

The empty without end of quiet.

Mac gone back inside. Marjorie left alone and breathing and fast-heart-beating outside. The black backs of the hills out there on all sides. The brown brick walls of the Club, beside her. The sidewalk underneath, her legs, shaking, the pain inside and all over, the pain and her self and what holds her up.

Marjorie looks up at the cold rolling gray clouds. Around at the small Club windows, high up, too high up for her to see through. Marjorie wants to look in. To see Tony. To see him stand up. To see Suzanne hold him, to see his body held against Suzanne's body. To see him safe, to see the angry go away. Marjorie wants Mac to come back outside and say that he made a mistake. To say that Marjorie is still his invited guest. To let Marjorie back inside. Marjorie wants Suzanne to open her arms up and let Marjorie walk inside the circle they make and be there and safe and be sorry.

For all to be undone.

Marjorie is standing outside in the bright gray light in the cool wind inside her self in the cold of the empty of her hot angry let go. She stands still and sunk inside all the parts of her self she does not know how to feel. Lost. Stuck.

Alone and cold and sorry.

Usual, usual.

Gone.

Marjorie sits down on the hard gray of the sidewalk and feels the crying come back. The pressure, the pains, the pushing. Marjorie's head, down in her arms. Marjorie deep down inside her self. Angry and sorry and bad. Marjorie holds her self tight and to Suzanne and to Tony and to her self, Marjorie says, Sorry.

Sorry.

Sorry.

Sorry.

44. MARGIE

After, Lucy's ma's voice was softer, was easier to hear. She told Margie to sit down on the sofa and Margie sat down on the sofa. The green sofa and what had happened there. Margie sat down and Lucy's ma brought her a burning mug of hot chocolate with white marshmallows floating on top. Margie put her tongue carefully down on each marshmallow and sucked each one up slowly, feeling the sweetness take over her mouth.

Lucy's ma asked some questions about school and Ma and Gram and Margie answered in her Margie way.

Good. Fine. Good. Yes.

What could we do with words like these? So big and empty. Words, just words. Words with nothing to do with the life being slowly, quietly, carefully lived.

Lucy's ma sat beside Margie on the sofa and said, You want to watch some TV, Margie?

Okay, Margie said.

This was how it started. Margie, her time come, and Lucy's ma there, the door opened. Hot chocolate and television. Sitting together on the sofa. Inside, warm, away from the autumn wind. What terrible parts of life have not been made even a little bit better by this?

Margie kept up with her every day after-school knocking on Lucy's door and Lucy's ma started letting her in. Lucy's ma did not watch the stories or the fish. She watched talk shows and cooking shows and shows about animals and people and the inside of people's bodies. Shows with people in suits talking about things that Margie did not try to understand. Margie watched the way the little circles of light inside the television glowed all together to build the picture, the person, their blue eyes or green eyes, the shadows on their cheeks, and how the circles of light changed constantly, moving to make the picture move. She sometimes looked away when the men and women on the television pushed close. Margie, her face red, knew, now, about what was private and should not be shown. The secret of the body that should not be known.

The secret of Margie downstairs in Apartment #1.

Sitting on the sofa close beside Lucy's ma.

What had to be kept from Apartment #2.

Sometimes Lucy came home and sat between them on the sofa and they all watched television together. Sometimes Lucy came home crying and went to her room and shut the door and Lucy's ma told Margie to let her be. Sometimes Lucy did not come home at all.

One of these days, a Lucy-less day, Lucy's ma walked out of the living room and came back with a plastic shopping bag. She put the bag down on Margie's lap.

Here, Margie. I picked this up for you.

Margie looked in the bag. Inside was a bra, white, big, shiny, stretchy. A bra like the bra Lucy wore, only bigger. Two big circles and two long, wide straps and little metal hooks at the back. Margie touched the soft, smooth fabric, picked it up, put it to her cheek. Margie put her nose to the white and smelled. She breathed hard, tried and tried and could not think of what the bra smelled like. Like peppermint and bleach and bread and soap all at once.

I noticed you don't wear one, Lucy's ma said.

You know what this is, Margie, right? What it's for?

Thingies, Margie said.

Breasts, Lucy's ma said.

I noticed you don't wear a bra. But I think it's time.

And I know your ma is busy.

Lucy's ma took the bra from Margie and pressed the circles to her own chest and showed Margie how to put her arms through the straps and how to hook the hooks at the back together. Again and again, Lucy's ma showed Margie how it worked. This difficult thing people have made. This complicated, hard-and-soft system of straps and bands and cups. For keeping the body in, away, unseen. For the sake of others, this thing, a bra, barely a word, more a sound, a thing made to keep Margie's breasts safe from the world and the world safe from Margie's breasts.

It's easy, Lucy's ma said. Once you figure it out.

Just practice, at home. In private. You'll get it.

Lucy's ma put the bra back in the plastic bag and told Margie to put the bag in her backpack. Margie did not have a special spot for a bra in a bag in her backpack, but she made some space, she fit the balled-up bra in between her notebook and her markers.

Margie, Lucy's ma said. If anybody asks you about it, it's better not to say I gave it to you. Just say Lucy did. Or you bought it on your own. I don't think your ma and your gram would like me giving you things like that. But I know they're busy, and it's time. It's really long past the time you should've started wearing one.

Okay, Margie said.

Margie understood. A secret. Another secret. A piling and piling of secrets. Margie understood secrets.

Time. Long past the time. Margie's time. All that time Margie spent in Lucy's Apartment #1, Lucy was off somewhere, escaped, growing up. We didn't notice. Did anyone? All that time, the hours, the days into days into months into years. All that time Margie spent away, downstairs, out. Was anyone watching? Wondering? Waiting for her?

And this is to wonder nothing about the time she spent at home.

We, like Margie, understand what must be private.

We will not ask about Apartment #2.

We do not want to know.

LD came home every day at six, but for Margie, no-time Margie, it was not six when LD came home, it was the end, when Margie's time was almost up. When Lucy's ma would go away. LD came home, blue work clothes speckled white, same as his. But LD did not yell and spit and chew paper and say bad words. LD smiled and kissed Lucy's ma on the cheek or the nose or the lips.

And LD said, Hi, Margie.

Hiding out, again, Margie?

Margie smiled and nodded. Smiled and nodded and kept her eyes on the lights of the television.

Should we have called someone?

We should have.

We knew.

But we had our own hiding out to do.

And we were scared.

We were in love.

The truth.

We were scared of him, too.

These were Margie's afternoons, stretched as long and as far as Margie could manage. Sometimes Margie still stayed for dinner, days when Lucy was home, but this was less and less the usual. Most days, soon after LD came home, Lucy's ma would tell Margie it was time.

Time to go.

Time to get up.

Time to go home.

Margie's days, marked by time, by words, by movement, by change. From here to here to here. If Margie had had her way, she would have stayed put. Margie would have stayed still with Lucy. She would have stayed seven and sitting beside the brook with Lucy. Margie would have stayed out on the side-walk in sunlight, in summer. School-less, secret-less, breast-less, time-less, free. Margie would have stayed with Lucy, warm with Lucy, little with Lucy, him-less and happy with Lucy.

But the world works on time, and Margie, mostly of the world, mostly there, went where time told her to go.

Margie went home.

And we went on.

45. MARGE

I found your secret, Marge.

In your room.

I saw what you did.

Fucked up that wall.

I knew that old bag was helping you hide something. All those ugly pictures she taped up there.

I knew there was something going on.

Behind my back.

I knew the two of you were up to something.

You're going to pay for that wall, Marge.

Thought you were being cute, putting your name up there for everybody to see.

You look me in the eye when I talk to you.

You think that makes this your house, Marge?

You trying to make problems for me? Trying to get that landlord to come in here and yell at me about what you did?

Stupid, Marge.

I'm smarter than you.

I know what's going on.

You want to know where all your pretty pictures went, get over here and look down my throat.

Look down in here, Marge.

This is what I did with your secret.

Can't hide it anymore.

Now everybody knows what you did, Marge.

46. MARJORIE

Marjorie remembers.

Today Marjorie does not want to talk to the People. She wants to sit in her quiet with her self. Marjorie wants to sit in her self and not talk and not think and not see.

But the Store. The People entering. The swinging door opening and this old lady in her blue raincoat who wants to talk.

The lady stands beside Marjorie. Small and old and bent-backed and dripping, here, beside Marjorie.

Do you, the lady says, her words coming slow as she catches her wind. Do you remember when all this wasn't here?

I remember, Marjorie says.

The day outside is warm, warmer, but wet, but gray clouds cover up the underwater sky. The display beside Marjorie is yellow and pink and green. All the red of Valentine's Day long replaced by candy eggs and smiling Easter Bunnies.

My first date with my husband was right here. God rest his soul. Right here, can you believe that? Back long before this store was here. When this was the drive-in movie theater. Are you a local girl? Do you remember that?

Marjorie is far away. Dug-into by the straps of her bra. Still and quiet and sunk down inside her self. But here is the door, here are People passing by.

Hello.

Here is this old lady stopping to talk, to pass the time. Holding her dripping coat close to her thin body. About the size and shape and bent of Gram. And yes, Marjorie remembers.

I remember.

It was so lovely, here, back then. That wide-open field. Silver poles holding speakers. I remember those speakers were heavy. But so clear. And that enormous screen. The tallest thing in town. That huge white square and behind it just black sky and stars. And we'd park our car and sit together in the backseat and with the speaker there in the car the sound was just for us. And it felt so good, nothing else all around but trees and sky and those handsome actors a hundred feet tall looking down on us. Right there, it was, that beautiful screen. Right out there where the parking lot ends.

Marjorie looks out beyond the glass of the swinging door to where the lady is pointing. She remembers. But all that is gone, now. People sit inside to watch their movies. The screen and the field and the trees taken away to make room for the Store. What People did People cannot not do.

Hello.

I can see that you are busy here, the lady says. I won't keep you.

Marjorie nods. Another day she would have liked to stand and talk to the lady. She would have liked to hear about what it was like to sit and watch giant People lit up against the dark sky.

But today Marjorie cannot talk to the People. Today Marjorie is gone inside.

Just saying Hello, Marjorie says.

Well, it's good of you to do, the lady says. It makes all this feel like a friendlier place.

The lady starts taking her slow steps into the Store.

And, she says, turning back toward Marjorie. And, you know what I'm remembering? Before the drive-in was here, this place was just nothing. Just trees. When I was a little girl, there was nothing here at all. My sister and I used to walk here and look at the birds and build little houses out of branches.

Sounds good, Marjorie says.

Yes, good, the lady says, holding tight to her coat. But what use was all that nothing? I couldn't come to the trees to buy my detergent on sale. That's for sure.

The old lady walks slow away into the Store and Marjorie stands in her place. Outside, the belly of the sky hangs heavy and dripping. It is hard to see, now, what was here before. But Marjorie, mostly, remembers.

The day, the rain, is making Marjorie feel her pains. And what is happening inside her, all this thinking she cannot think, is giving her a kind of hurt in her mind. This sorry Marjorie has is like the rain, something she feels inside and outside her body. Marjorie moves her neck in a slow circle and picks her legs up one by one. In her knees and her elbows she can feel this rain. All sorts of pains inside her self and outside her self. Sorry all around.

Hey, Marjorie, hey.

Benjamin. Here again. Two times already today Benjamin has been by. Stacking Easter Bunnies and mopping the floor. Benjamin, today, too, seems far away and quiet, for Benjamin. No whistling, no singing, no stories.

Sure you're okay, Marjorie? Sure?

Yes. Sure.

Today a day to make People stay inside the warm quiet of their self. Out of the rain and away from the People. Marjorie does not know what Benjamin has got inside him. But she knows that all People have things inside that make them sometimes quiet and far away. Even Benjamin, long-haired, singing, swinging, always moving, laughing Benjamin, must have things inside he does not want People to know.

Hey, Marjorie. Did you hear me? I said, Hey.

Hi, Benjamin.

What was that lady talking to you about?

I don't know. What was here before.

Weird. Probably lonely. Just wants somebody to talk to.

Benjamin is pushing a cart of plastic-wrapped boxes of foil-wrapped chocolate eggs. Marjorie steps to one side so that he will have more room to work.

Hey, Marjorie, he says. I know I asked and I don't mean to be annoying but are you really sure you're okay today?

Sure, Benjamin. Fine. Just some pains. You know, the rain.

Really? Because, I don't know, you seem different today, Marjorie. Sad or something. You've always got that big smile and you always seem pretty happy but today, I don't know, you seem different.

Marjorie smiles as best she can. For Benjamin.

But today Marjorie does not want to be seen.

Today Marjorie has nothing she wants to say.

In the quiet between Marjorie and Benjamin there is no quiet. There is the sound of the Store, the carts wheeling, People talking, registers beep, beep, beep and beeping. Benjamin puts his hand on her shoulder. Lays his thin, soft hand down warm and gentle on Marjorie's shoulder. Marjorie tries to rise from her self, to feel the feel of Benjamin here.

Hey, Marjorie, I'm sorry. I know how it can be. Some days the shit just rains down and piles up. Some days you don't know your head from your asshole, right?

Marjorie holds on to the smile she has made and hopes her face will turn away from red and back to the usual color of her face. She does not want Benjamin to think that she is angry. Marjorie wants Benjamin to be Benjamin, even with his bad words, even though today she wants to be only with her self.

Sorry, Marjorie. Sorry. My big mouth.

It's okay, Benjamin. I don't mind.

How about this, Marjorie. I have this idea. Remember how I told you about the Glen? That place I go to check out the animals and the hills and the bugs and ponds and trees and shit? Where it's quiet and you can think, you know?

I know. I remember.

Well there is this one great spot up there. This, like, I don't know what it's called. Like an opening. Like this place where there are trees all on the side but this one spot is open and you can see out into this field. What do they call that, Marjorie? Like, a clearing? You know what I mean?

Marjorie nods. In her own way, inside, she can see what Benjamin is talking about. She does not know the word for it, but Marjorie thinks she can see.

Yeah, okay, so this spot. This place. Fucking amazing. Sorry. Amazing. Beautiful. The trees all around and this wide-open place and the hills out behind the trees and around you on all sides. And these fireflies. I don't even want to tell you about it, Marjorie. I want you to see it. I want you to come up there with me. You said you've never been, right?

Okay, Benjamin. Sounds good.

I'm serious, Marjorie. I really want you to come and check this out. Something different. Get both of us out of this shithole and into the air, you know, the woods, nature, the sky. Freedom and all that good shit.

Benjamin and his plans. Benjamin is always thinking about how to be out, away. He needs the air and the woods to feel free from the Store. Marjorie understands this about Benjamin and Marjorie knows it is different for her. She does not need the air and the outside. Marjorie is fine in, inside, in the Store, in the Club, down in her self with the good things, with what was good about before, with Lucy. With what good of her self is left for her to be with.

Promise me you'll come with me sometime soon, Marjorie. Once it dries out up there. Once it gets a little warmer there are going to be so many beautiful things to look at and you can just sit out all night up there. You look like you need to have some fun, Marjorie. I think you're sad, or something. I'm not going to ask about it. But it's been a long bastard of a winter, right? So tell me you'll come up and check it out.

Okay, Benjamin. Sure.

You promise? I got your word, Marjorie?

Her word. Marjorie and all the words that are not hers, all the words unheard by Marjorie. People and their plans. Marjorie knows Benjamin is good and she knows that Benjamin says many words he does not mean or does not think about or will forget. But even on this bad day Marjorie can almost feel the good feeling of sometime going somewhere with Benjamin. Just an idea to put away inside, to hold and touch and remember.

Okay, yes. Thank you.

Great. I'm going to hold you to that, Marjorie. I'm going to take you up there and you won't be able to be sad. You'll be so fucking in awe you won't be able to talk or feel bad. You can really think. And no people around up there, either. Just quiet, and the trees, and those fireflies. It's going to blow your mind.

Good, Benjamin.

All right, Marjorie. I know you want to get back to that door. And I have these asshole eggs to put out.

Benjamin lifts his hand from Marjorie's shoulder and her skin under her vest under her shirt feels cold and tingling. All this time, Benjamin had been touching her. And Marjorie, so far gone inside her self, is only now noticing. Only now feeling these cold little fires, here, where Benjamin's hand was. Marjorie, feeling what was there only after. This huge feeling of what has already gone.

47. MARGIE

Margie kept the secret under her side of the bed so that Gram would not see it.

Her secret, pushed just far enough under so that it could not be seen, but close enough for Margie's fingers to find in the dark.

When Margie was alone, at night, or during the day when Gram was out, away, when Gram was gone off to wherever she went, Margie reached her arm down under the bed and felt for the secret. Margie felt for it and when the smooth fabric of the secret touched Margie's skin, she put her hand tight around it, pulled it out from under the bed, and held it.

Margie held the soft secret Lucy's ma had given her close to her nose and breathed it inside her. She rubbed her cheek to the soft-hard circles and twisted the springy straps around her fingers. Margie held the secret close and thought about Lucy and Lucy's ma and LD down there, below her, moving or sleeping or eating or talking, living, slow, quiet and safe in the good of Apartment #1.

Alone, at night, when Margie could not sleep inside the rise and fall of Gram's snores and the sounds of Ma's bedroom, Margie held on soft to her secret and went down with her breath into the slow, steady beat of herself. And down in there, inside Margie's inside parts, was Lucy. The smell of Lucy's grape lip gloss spread out strong and warm inside Margie. Lucy's colors, her pinks, the light blonde of her hair, the brown of her freckles, were painted up and down and all over the inside of Margie. Sometimes when she listened to her heart beating, Margie wondered about Lucy's inside, about what she smelled like in there, about how her heart sounded. Margie wondered if they sounded the same, her and Lucy, if friends could beat their blood to the same beat.

Can any of us be expected to understand what Margie felt?

Are we all really as separate as we seem?

Yes, we think so.

We think it is easier this way.

We think this is the way things are meant to be.

48. MARGE

Show me, Marge.

You love this cute little bunny so much, you show me.

I see you and him.

How you sleep.

Fat arms wrapped around his bunny neck. Lips on his little bunny face.

Do you love him, Marge?

Tell me how much you love your little faggot bunny.

Why don't you talk, Marge?

You tease.

Why don't you move?

Are you scared of me?

Too stupid, is what I think.

Stupid like your ma. Ugly like your ma.

But don't tell her I said so, Marge.

I don't mean it.

I love your ma like you love your blue faggot bunny rabbit.

Hold her close and feel her mouth.

You won't tell nobody, I know.

Maybe just that bunny. I bet you tell him all your secrets.

Well you know what, Marge?

You tell that bunny to watch out.

You tell him I'll rip him up and swallow him whole.

Come on.

Can't take a joke?

It's just too easy with you, Marge.

You got to learn to put up more of a fight.

49. MARJORIE

Marjorie, again, always, again sitting back up against the hard headboard, feet, knees, thighs, belly, self sunk down into the soft, too-soft bed. The shape of Ma in the mattress becoming every night more and more the shape of Marjorie and still she cannot sleep. Marjorie, again, breathing, blinking in the seeping blue light of the soundless television. Marjorie, here, again. A day, a night, a night, her life in things thrown off shelves, of departments leaking into departments. Marjorie, again in her inside, again and again watching her big black-sneakered foot fast-kick Tony's little chest. Again hearing Mac's Get out. Suzanne's Go away. Marjorie alone. Watching the People on the television walk and touch and nod and sway. Marjorie wanting. The hard, the holding, the remembered feel of the springs of the sofa bed. The good of the usual.

Marjorie with both hands squeezes her skin more alive. Behind her knees, in her neck, under her armpits and in her head there is pain. Waves and pokes and pools of it. Marjorie feeling so much she cannot say. She opens her mouth to whisper, to speak to her self, to Ma or Lucy, just to speak, just to see what she will say, and Marjorie says nothing. Marjorie squeezes her shoulders and arms and opens her mouth and moves her lips and she is quiet and unknown as the People on the television.

She rubs her rough elbows and her hands take turns touching every one of her fingers. Marjorie puts her hands in the warm place under the big of her soft breasts and makes her hands into shelves to hold her self. Thinks. Feels. Sees. Suzanne's body covering Tony's body. Benjamin and his braids and his bicycle. Mac and his angry, his hand hurting her arm. His prayer.

Jesus, Marjorie, Jesus.

Lucy.

Marjorie rubs her hand down to her belly that rises and rolls with her wind.

Where is Lucy?

Ma, real Ma, burned up into dust in a box under the bed. Ma is here.

But Lucy.

Marjorie remembers.

Marjorie remembers the shape, the dark, the red quiet of Lucy. Real Lucy. What was not shown to her. Who never had a chance. Special, secret Lucy. The surprise of Lucy. The small body, almost body, the becoming body messed up by Marjorie's body. Lucy, who did not need to be so wrong. Lucy, but Lucy, Marjorie did not know. Until Lucy had stopped becoming Lucy. But now, and now, Marjorie wants to know.

Where is Lucy?

Taken. Lucy was taken. But where? Marjorie holds on hard to her belly to her big empty feeling. Marjorie is trying to remember. Looking hard into the bright of the lights inside, trying to see, trying to know. So much time she cannot touch. Things she wants and cannot remember.

Where is Lucy?

Marjorie rolls over onto her side and rocks her self until her legs are off the bed and on the floor. She wiggles her toes and waits for her blood and breath to slow.

There must be ways to know the things she does not know.

Marjorie stands up. She steps into the hallway quiet as she can and across the hall hears Gram's snores loud and slow. Marjorie uses her hands to help her walk through the dark apartment to the kitchen. She switches on the bright white light. The sudden shock of things, dark shapes, shadows, shaped into what is known by the light. Marjorie blinks until her eyes can see, and then she picks up the telephone.

Probably Dr. Goodwin will not be there. Marjorie does not know the time but she can see from the dark and the quiet that she is somewhere in the deep of the night. But Marjorie wants to know.

The ring. Ring. Ringing.

This is the sound of Marjorie looking for People. Wanting to know. To get out of her self, away from her self, free from what she does not remember.

The rings are long and unanswered. Marjorie's heart beats fast and faster. The pains of her body will not rest.

A ring. A click. An answer. A machine. A message Marjorie does not hear.

A beep.

Her voice, too loud in the too quiet kitchen.

Marjorie needs to know this.

Where is Lucy?

Hello, Dr. Goodwin. Here is Marjorie.

Where is Lucy?

50. MARGIE

This was a new place for Margie, this huge open abandoned place where Lucy said the people in the town used to sit in their cars and watch movies. A long, gray-green lot stretching out all around, bordered by almost-leafless trees on three sides and a giant white square screen at the front. Gray poles stuck into the ground in rows. And the wind, the cold hard wood-burning wind of autumn, blowing.

Those poles were for the speakers, Lucy said.

That's how you hear the movie from your car.

Margie walked slowly, Margie followed. Big, bloated, belly-down clouds rolled out and up and behind the tall white rise of the screen. Thick gray clouds that cast shadows over the slopes of the hills behind. Cold clouds about to open like mouths, clouds the dirty nothing color of the place where they were, where Lucy had let the boy lead them.

Lucy told Margie to keep quiet and just watch.

You're my bodyguard, she said.

You protect me.

Okay, Margie said.

I'll watch.

I'll protect you.

The boy held onto Lucy's hand so hard Margie was afraid he might break it.

Who is she?

He asked the question and in the middle of asking, he spit, big and white and heavy, in Margie's direction.

She's my bodyguard, Lucy said.

The boy laughed and pulled her hand and tried to make Lucy walk away from Margie.

You don't need a bodyguard. I'm your bodyguard.

We walked by and saw the boy holding onto Lucy. We saw Margie watching and we laughed and we wondered who was going to get it. We looked away.

Margie's here to watch. She's just going to watch.

Fuck that. I want you alone. I want you to myself.

She'll stay quiet. She's just going to watch.

The boy tried to pull Lucy away again and Lucy leaned toward him and bit into his arm. She stuck her tongue out and licked his freckled skin. Margie watched, her wind moving through her in fast waves, her heart beating loud in her chest in her belly in her ears, her legs.

The clouds heaved a long low sigh and let out some drops of wet that hit cold and hard against Margie's skin but she did not look up, did not move or look away.

Margie, guarding.

Margie waited for the boy to hit Lucy. She watched Lucy lick her tongue up and down his arm and she was sure the boy was going to hurt Lucy. She was sure she would need to protect Lucy from what was coming.

But the boy got quiet. The boy let go of Lucy's hand. He stepped closer to her and said something low in Lucy's ear.

I know you like that, Lucy said.

And if you want more, you let Margie stay where she is and watch.

The clouds continued to cough and Margie stood where she was and watched. In the middle of that empty place, surrounded by cold gray poles, by trees, by hills, beyond, circling. Margie watched the long body of the boy slump and soften around Lucy's small body. She watched the boy bring his face down to Lucy's face and she watched their tongues touch, lips touch, watched their mouths swallow each other, watched their bodies push closer together.

The rain seemed slow to come.

Margie watched the boy put his hand on Lucy's t-shirt on Lucy's breast and she watched his fingers touch and squeeze and rub. Margie watched, and she felt, she did not feel good. Her body felt hot, all over. Her breath came hard as her heartbeat and Margie was afraid her head might float up and away from the rest of her. When she blinked, she saw black spots, she saw the boy trying to touch inside Lucy, trying to make his body into the shape of Lucy's body, trying to make Lucy less herself and more a part of him.

Margie walked up next to where Lucy and the boy moved mouths-open slowly together and Margie used both of her big shaking hands to push the boy as hard as she could and loud as she could, Margie said, Stop.

Again and again, Margie said, Stop.

The boy laughed and held on harder to Lucy. He put both hands on her breasts and he pulled and held Lucy's body as if Margie had not tried to push him away. As if Lucy liked it. As if Margie was not saying, Stop. As if this was the way people loved. As if Margie was not there at all.

It's okay, Margie, Lucy said, her voice small.

You said to watch and protect you.

Yeah, Margie. You just stand over there and watch.

The boy dropped to his knees in front of Lucy and put his head up under her white t-shirt. The big shape of him moved inside there, moved over Lucy's body, looked to Margie like a robber trying to break into her friend. The boy, eating Lucy alive.

He's hurting you.

Lucy lifted up her t-shirt so that Margie could see, so that she could see what the boy was doing to Lucy.

See, Margie. Just watch.

It's good for you to see.

It feels good.

You need to learn sometime.

Margie watched the boy move his mouth and his hands and his nose and his tongue up and over and down and around Lucy's skin. Trying to find a place, a way, into Lucy. She watched Lucy put her fingers into the boy's hair and she watched how Lucy held the boy's head in her hands. Margie looked at Lucy and Lucy smiled and looked at Margie and her blue eyes looked far away and gray like the clouds above them, like the dusty field around them. Margie watched Lucy, thin, beautiful, tangle-haired Lucy, move the boy's head slowly over her body.

As if Lucy knew where she wanted him to go.

As if Lucy had done this before.

As if we were not watching.

Wide-eyed, wanting.

Margie watched until the rain, for sure, had started. She watched until she saw Lucy close her eyes and go somewhere else. Margie watched for as long as she could, until the water dripped heavy down from her hair into her eyes, until the shape of the boy and the shape of Lucy became the same big, blurred shape. And then Margie turned away from Lucy, away from that twisting shape of them and the sounds their bodies made. Margie turned away and Margie, eyes-down, walked slow and wet and quiet toward home.

51. MARGE

Your ma's gone, Marge.

You know I don't know where.

Probably out fucking some asshole. Making him fish sticks and buying his beer.

Just kidding, Marge.

Your ma knows who's boss.

Who cares where she is? Maybe this time she won't come back.

Then we can live just us, Marge.

That old bag won't last much longer. Maybe your ma's run away and it'll just be me and you and your pretty friend.

I like her hair, Marge. That friend of yours.

Why don't you do your hair like hers?

I like her jeans too. She's a tease, that little one.

Still won't tell me her name, will you, Marge?

You like making me guess.

You got some of that tease in you, too.

Why won't you introduce me to your friend, Marge?

I just want to tell her how pretty she is.

Are you ashamed, Marge?

Are you ashamed of me?

Are you?

Say so.

Say you aren't ashamed.

We're family, Marge.

We got to take care of each other.

52. MARJORIE

Gone, Marjorie.

Gone where? I want to see Lucy, Dr. Goodwin.

She was born dead, Marjorie. She was cremated.

Where is Lucy, Dr. Goodwin?

I don't know, Marjorie. I just know that the baby's body was cremated.

Marjorie?

What happened?

What made you think about the baby all of a sudden?

Not all of a sudden.

Always thinking.

Did something happen to make you think about the past?

I think about the past, Dr. Goodwin.

All the time I think about the past. Not all of a sudden.

I'm sorry if I angered you, Marjorie.

My angry is just angry. Here it is.

I think it's good for you to express your anger.

They burned Lucy up? Like Ma?

Yes, Marjorie. The baby was cremated.

And nobody asked me.

People did ask you, Marjorie. You were in the hospital. They called me to come and help. There were papers for you to sign and we talked about what would happen to the baby's body. Do you remember that?

No, Dr. Goodwin. I don't remember that. I don't remember any papers.

It was a very stressful time for you. Sometimes when bad things happen our minds shut down. We don't remember as a way to protect ourselves. What do you remember from that time?

Do you remember talking to the police?

Do you remember them telling you they took your stepfather away? Marjorie?

I remember I want to see Lucy. I remember nobody let me.

You were in shock, Marjorie. You were in a lot of pain. Do you remember?

I remember. The pain. I remember I don't want Lucy burned up like how Ma's burned up.

Have you been thinking about your mother?

I am not thinking about Ma, Dr. Goodwin. Ma, I know where she is. I want to know where is Lucy?

That's what we've been talking about, Marjorie.

So creamed up, burned. But there's still the dust. Where's the rest of Lucy?

I don't know, Marjorie. I wasn't there when you signed the papers. But when we talked, that first time we met, you said that you didn't want the baby's remains.

I don't remember that.

Do you remember me telling you they took him away? That you would be safe?

I can't, Dr. Goodwin.

It was a terrible time for you, Marjorie. Try not to blame yourself.

I want to know where Lucy ended up.

You could call the crematorium and ask them what happens to unclaimed remains.

Marjorie?

Dr. Goodwin, there are too many words for all this. I don't know how to say it. All I want to know is, where is Lucy?

Would you like me to try calling, Marjorie?

You will do that for me, Dr. Goodwin?

Sure. I can try calling right now. I think it's important that you know what happened.

Thank you. Thank you.

It's no problem, Marjorie. I'm going to step outside and use the phone in the main office.

Okay, Dr. Goodwin. Thank you.

Done.

Dead.

Gone.

Creamed. Claim. Unclaim.

Remembers.

Just a little baby.

A half of Lucy.

What did you say, Marjorie?

I didn't say, Dr. Goodwin.

Okay, well, I just spoke with someone at the crematorium. This information might upset you, Marjorie. He told me that the baby's remains were claimed by your mother.

Ma?

Yes. Her signature is on the form he has.

Ma took Lucy?

Yes, Marjorie, that's how it seems.

But Ma never said so.

Ma never talked about it.

Do you have any idea what your mother might have done with the remains?

No. I cleaned her room. I don't know.

Maybe your grandmother will know?

Gram just sits. Gram stays out of it.

Well, maybe you should ask her, anyway. You never know, Marjorie. And sometimes people need to be asked. Sometimes it's hard for people to be the first one to talk about something.

I want to see Lucy. I want to be asked. Nobody asked, Do you want a Lucy? And then I have a Lucy and nobody asks, What do you want done with your Lucy?

You look very sad, Marjorie.

I hate to see you suffering in this way.

I am sorry, Dr. Goodwin.

What are you sorry about?

About Tony. Suzanne. Mac. Tony.

Why are you sorry about Tony?

I am bad, Dr. Goodwin. I am sorry. I am all bad. The worst in People.

No one is perfect, Marjorie. We are who we are and sometimes we do bad things and sometimes we do good things. But I don't know anyone who is all good or all bad.

I am very sorry. Lucy. Tony. I was not my self.

Did you tell them that you are sorry?

I said, Sorry. Sorry, Sorry, Sorry.

And what happened?

I said Sorry to my self, Dr. Goodwin. No People around to hear it. Just me outside the Club and my sorry.

Yourself is a good place to start. But if you did something you need to apologize for, there need to be people there to hear it.

Nobody asked me about it, Dr. Goodwin. Pains. A Lucy. Little baby burned up.

Sorry.

I am sorry, Marjorie.

I am sorry.

53. MARGIE

I'm sorry, Margie.
I'm really sorry.
Can you forgive me?
Okay.
Will you say it? Just so I know.
Say, I forgive you, Lucy.
I forgive you, Lucy.

54. MARGE

Marge.
I see you there.
Your big fat ass.
I see those titties swinging.
Get your fat ass over here now.
Those dykes downstairs.
What are their names, Marge?
You tell me.
I see you with them, Marge, those dykes.
All smiles with those dykes.
Laughing.
I bet you let them touch you.
Lick you all over.
Do you, Marge?
Answer me.
Fucking dykes.

I can't stand dykes, Marge.

My ma was a god–damned dyke.

Made my old man beg for it.

Are you a fucking dyke, too?

I bet you are.

I see you.

I catch you with those dykes Marge and you're dead.

And them too.

All of you.

You hear me?

55. MARJORIE

Marjorie stands outside the Club and breathes hard and fast. Wind in and out in beat with her heartbeat. The hills around her are beginning to change from brown to green. Waking up, the brown bones of trees more and more coming alive. Today, there is sun, white-holed sun at the top of the dark blue sky. The day cloudless, windless, the hot sunlight burning into Marjorie's coatless shoulders. She moves most of her weight from her left leg to her right and wipes the sweat around her ears and above her eyes. The black mounds of snow that were here have melted down and away into dirt, into sand into sidewalk. Spring here. Marjorie down deep in her days of sorry.

I am sorry.

Marjorie says her words out loud to the hills around her. Up into the too-blue sky. Marjorie in a usual day does not want things. The usual Marjorie is fine. Wants macaroni for dinner, maybe, wants the People to feel wanted. The usual, the small wants, is what Marjorie is used to. But the usual is not the usual. Not now. This want that Marjorie feels, now, out here in the hot of the afternoon sun, is a big, important want. This want has weight and it sits heavy on Marjorie's round shoulders and it digs down into her skin. This want is strong and loud and here and beating.

Marjorie stares at the white in the spaces between the dark blue letters.

The Benevolent and Protective Order of Elks.

Marjorie wants to go inside.

Marjorie wants to say, Sorry

Marjorie wants to sit and talk and drink her Shirley Temple.

Marjorie wants to be back in her usual.

But the People need to want her. Mac and Suzanne.

192

Marjorie pushes her wind out hard to the warm air and pulls it back in again. She puts her hand on the handle of the glass door and pushes her way into the Club. The bright of the outside for a moment lights up the dark of the inside. Marjorie is here.

The Club smells like the Club. The sweet and sour of spilled beer, the baseball caps of the People sitting and the long, heavy left-behinds of cigarette smoke. Marjorie blinks her eyes fast to make the bright of the outside become the dark of the inside and for a moment she cannot see but she can hear.

Quiet. What is called quiet. The sound of a swallowed drink. A scrape of clothes on clothes. A sigh. The scratch of skin against skin. The sound of air moving around People stopped moving.

The big dark room of the Club comes to Marjorie in pieces. The colorful glow of the signs on the wall and the lines of light they make on the shiny wood of the bar. The People, their dark shapes slumped at tables and on bar stools. And the shadows of Mac and Suzanne, seen last, standing here, there, unspeaking, watching.

Marjorie says, Hello.

Her heart beats hard and fast and very alone under the waves and waves crashing against the sides of the inside of her self. Marjorie smiles and looks at Mac, not smiling, and at Suzanne, not smiling. Quiet.

Cold Out There Today.

Marjorie says what Marjorie says. But what she says is wrong.

Warm, I mean.

Marjorie stands still in her place next to the door. Not her door, this other door, this Club door. Big and glass and handled. People have to push this door open if they want to come in. So many doors out there, how many doors to pass through just to finish a day?

Marjorie wants to step away from the door and closer to her place at the bar but Mac and Suzanne are standing there, quiet, staring. Mouths small and eyebrows down and squeezed and arms crossed tight in front of chests.

Marjorie sees their angry and holds her wind and says what she wants to say.

I am sorry.

Get out, Marjorie.

Beautiful Suzanne with her red hair held up high on her head with her lips not smiling with her mouth made small from all her angry says it. And says it again.

Get out.

Get the fuck out, Marjorie.

A fire starts in Marjorie's face and she feels her body stop. Her ears shut and the sound of the outside is lost inside the crash of the blood in her head, the waves of sorry inside her body, the collapse of her self into her self. The exploding. Marjorie blinks her eyes fast and holds her arms tight around her belly and when she says what she wants to say her voice is too soft, her voice is a sound sent from far below the sinking surface of her.

I am sorry.

Go away, Marjorie.

Marjorie holding on to her self and staring at Suzanne's arms-on-hips wide-eyed angry. The People turned to look at her, hands held to glasses, to beer bottles, watching, waiting. Mac walking from behind the bar toward her, Mac walking up to Marjorie to see Marjorie to talk to Marjorie to touch Marjorie with his big hand on her arm, holding on, pulling her out and away.

Mac saying, Come on, Marjorie. You can't come in here anymore.

Mac's hand is hard on her arm but not angry, not not kind. His fingers sink into the soft parts of Marjorie. Mac with one hand holds her and with one hand pulls the glass door open. Pushing to enter is easy, just a hand, the weight of People wanting to come in, this is enough to enter. But leaving the Club is not so easy. Leaving the Club means pulling the huge weight of the door away from the wall. But here is Mac, one arm pulling the weight of Marjorie, one arm pulling the weight of the door, standing between the inside and the outside, pushing Marjorie out into the bright of spring.

Marjorie stands on the sidewalk in the sunlight and Mac stands in the dark doorway surrounded by all that glass.

What do you want, Marjorie?

I want to come in. And say, Sorry.

Sorry, Marjorie. Sorry's not good enough. You can't come in here anymore.

Marjorie tries with her whole self to catch her wind, to blink her eyes into seeing in the blinding light, to say what she wants to say.

I am sorry.

Well, okay, Marjorie. But still, you can't come back here.

Mac turns and walks away into the dark inside the Club. The glass door swings shut behind him and for long, long seconds Marjorie listens to the beat of the door banging closed. Marjorie covers her eyes with her hands so that she does not have to see the bright, the day, the spring, the growing, the place where she cannot be. She cannot look up and out at the holding of the hills. Marjorie sinks down low into the hot of her dark and breathes, breathes, breathes as if she is running away.

56. MARGIE

Help me, Margie.

Margie held her hand up and out so that Lucy could balance, so that Lucy would not fall. They walked slowly in the last cracked yolk of sunlight, slowly, so that Lucy could balance on the smooth metal rail of the railroad track, so that Lucy, hovering there, those few inches above Margie, would not fall. Margie held Lucy's hand and they walked side-by-up-high-side along the tracks through the woods, not toward school and not toward dead-end Summer Street. Just walking, together, to places Margie did not usually go, to wherever Lucy was going. The two girls, arms bared, the autumn air warm enough for walking but the wind a threat, the wind a hard line of cold cutting through.

We can get there through the woods, Lucy said.

There's a cool spot I want to show you. At the way-back of it.

Margie nodded. She listened for the crashing sound of a train coming behind them. Margie held tight to Lucy's thin hand and felt her heart pulsing, softly, just below the surface where her skin touched Lucy's skin. She did not care where they went. Margie just liked being beside Lucy.

I can't believe you believed me, Margie.

Why?

Not why. Ask me, about what?

About what?

The small man. Remember, you believed me when I said there were small people? When I said that I had a small man living in my bedroom?

I believed, Margie said.

I know, it's funny. It's funny that you believed in him. I don't know, I wanted to believe it too, I guess.

I wanted to see the small people.

Me too, Lucy said. I wanted the small man to be real. I wanted him to be mine. To be my boyfriend.

Margie and Lucy followed the train tracks through the woods, across the road that led to the quarry, past the red abandoned brick factory. Lucy stepped slowly, so that she could balance, so that Margie could keep up. Margie, putting one foot in front of the other, her big thighs brushing together, rubbing together, creating heat, and her heart, moving, beating, bringing sweat up to the surface of her skin.

Do you want a boyfriend, Margie?

Margie shook her head. Moved her shoulders up and then down. Let go of Lucy's hand just a little and breathed her breaths in beat with her heart.

No, Margie said.

So, what do you want? A girlfriend?

Margie's heart in her chest like a ball, bouncing, fast, and faster, and faster, sounded in her ears like thunder, like the train that would come and eat up those tracks.

I'm just kidding, Margie. Chill out.

But really, Lucy said.

What do you want?

No wants, Lucy, Margie said.

Just friends.

No school.

Quiet.

Lucy laughed.

Easy enough, she said.

Lucy pointed to a place where the trees opened up and a little limestone path went through.

It's here, Margie.

Lucy jumped down off the rail and pulled Margie's hand, gently, not letting go. Margie followed, held tight, did her best to keep her wind steady, her heart, steady. The bright white rocks crunched and slid beneath their feet, made a low white cloud of dust where they stepped.

At the end of the path was the place Margie had seen before, the big empty place with the rows and rows of gray poles rising from the ground. But this time, Lucy had taken them to the behind of it, to the place farthest from the white sky-tall screen. They walked out of the woods and behind the boarded-up building that used to sell popcorn and candy and condoms to a place at the back that had once been a playground.

Lucy led Margie past a rusted set of swings and a small red slide to a big metal merry-go-round. To the big circle with four iron handles, the circle that spun in circles, that could be pushed, that could whirl you around, around, around.

Sit down, Lucy said. I'll spin you.

I'm too big, Margie said.

The wind was stronger here, out in the open. Colder, here, than it had been in the woods in the protection of the trees. Lucy pushed Margie's shoulders down onto the metal merry-go-round and Margie let her big body relax, release.

You're not, Lucy said. Just sit there and put your legs up and hold on.

Margie sat and pulled her legs close. She pushed her knees up near her head, made herself as small as she could, held on tight to the cold metal. Lucy pushed the arms of the merry-go-round slow, slowly, at first, and then faster. The circle moved Margie around slow, slow, slow, and then the weight of Lucy pushing, the wind, the momentum of Lucy's hands, of Margie spinning, moved Margie faster and faster around. Spinning and spinning. Margie coming around to Lucy again and again and faster. Margie, a white soft moon passing by, passing by. Margie, orbiting.

Lucy pushed until the merry-go-round was moving too fast for her to keep up, and then she put her two hands on the metal arm and pulled herself up onto the fast-spinning circle. Margie and Lucy spun, and spun, fast at first, the world around them a blur, a whirl. Laughing, holding on tight, afraid, and alive, and laughing, together, turning and then slowing, slower each time the circle completed a circle, losing speed, losing strength. And Margie and Lucy laughed, held on hard, watched the world come to a stop.

Everything is spinning, Margie, Lucy said. Lucy laughed and laughed.

Lucy crawled beneath the merry-go-round arm that separated her from Margie. She rolled over close to where Margie was, Lucy's thin body pressing up against the big curled-up ball of Margie clinging to metal.

Lucy crawled and rolled her small, curving body close to Margie's body, closer, so that Lucy's body covered Margie, so that their skin, where it showed through, touched, so that the warmth could be felt, the warmth of skin under the thin layers of their cotton shirts, the warming that happened through Lucy's jeans and into Margie's worn purple pants. Lucy moved quickly, slowly, quick and slow at once, was how it felt for Margie. Lucy put her leg over and between Margie's leg and her head on Margie's shoulder and her hand, her small, warm hand, Lucy put her hand gently down around Margie's big, soft, beating, braless breast.

She squeezed. Lucy squeezed, slowly, her fingers firm and slow, squeezing, feeling. Lucy touched Margie gently, but hard enough for Margie to feel it. Margie held her wind inside and felt Lucy feeling. What should have been private. These parts of Margie that no one should know.

It felt good. Margie felt good. All over, warm, spinning, her wind coming back to her hard, fast, her heart, hard, fast, trying to break out. Margie felt Lucy there feeling her, felt the weight of Lucy and felt fully, and only, good.

Lucy put her lips to Margie's cheek and pressed. She put her lips to Margie's lips and she stayed there, pushing, pressing. Lucy's slick grape-scented lips holding on to Margie's thin, chapped lips. Margie more and more uncurled from the ball of herself and Margie lay back and felt the softness of Lucy, felt Lucy's tongue, warm, wet. Margie stayed still, open, feeling, letting Lucy move, touch, feel.

Lucy put her mouth near Margie's ear and she made the warm, whispered shapes of words there.

I love you, Margie.

And she laughed. Lucy laughed and rubbed her hand up and down Margie's body, squeezing Margie's thigh, her knee, her breast and her cheek.

How does that feel, Margie?

Good, Margie said.

When Margie caught hold of her breath, when Margie could speak, she said, Good.

Good, Lucy said.

She laughed.

Lucy's laugh, kind, low, a different laugh from all the other laughs.

See, Margie. Now you know.

Now you know about boyfriends.

How they feel.

What they do.

Margie knew her inside was warm, liquid, spilling, boiling, feeling good. Margie knew Lucy's fingers, now. The shape of them, the length, the smooth sharp of her fingernails, the weight of them on her skin. Margie knew the smell of wind in Lucy's soft blonde hair and the warmth of Lucy's legs, Lucy's belly, the everywhere smell of the grape of Lucy's lips.

Get up, Lucy said, pushing her small body up to sit cross-legged on the hard circle of the merry-go-round.

Margie rolled slowly to her side and put her hands beneath her body and pushed herself up.

Stand up, Margie. Stand up there in front of me.

Margie did not ask Lucy questions. Margie wanted Lucy to feel good and happy. Still spinning, her eyes trying to focus, trying to catch hold of something that was not a circle, Margie slid along the metal surface and stood on the soft ground facing Lucy. Margie, in the losing-yellow-light, stood in front of her friend.

Take your shirt off, Margie, Lucy said, sliding closer.

I want to see.

I want to see you under your clothes.

Why? We want to ask. Why ask such a thing of Margie?

There is so much we will never know.

Big, gone-inside Margie who put her pajamas on in the dark, who squeezed her eyes shut when she dried off with her towel. Margie dressed with her back to the cracked bathroom mirror. Margie saw herself in pieces, in white flashes of soft skin, in patches of rough dark hair. Margie in her unwanted body slept as stiff and far from Gram as she could. She knew the inside of her, the slow current of her blood moving up and down and through, the tides of her breath and the beat of her heart in her ears, her chest, her belly. That inside place, where Margie lived, she knew, she could see, hear, feel. But her outside, the skin that kept her in, was a secret Margie kept from herself.

A secret every one of us but Margie could see.

Don't be scared, Margie.

I just want to see.

You know, if you are like me.

What you look like under there.

Here, Lucy said, pulling her arms inside the sleeves of her shirt. I'll do it too.

Lucy wiggled and used her hands inside to push her shirt up and off her body. She sat, small, white, and open, in front of Margie, in the going-and-going light of the almost night, to Margie, Lucy glowed like television. Her skin was thin, soft, smooth. Lucy's skin like skim milk, white, watery. Lucy's breasts rose up above her chest like cupcakes, vanilla cupcakes that ended in small pink points. Margie stared, not just at Lucy's breasts, at all of her, there, uncovered, let out, in front of her.

Margie pulled her purple shirt over her head and let go of it, let the stretched cotton she wore outside fall to the ground. She did not look down at herself, at her big body hanging there, her breasts heavy on her belly, her dark nipples big circles on the end of her big round chest. Margie felt the wind blowing cold on her, on parts of her kept so long secret, hidden, covered. Margie looked at Lucy, at Lucy looking back at her.

Wow, Margie, Lucy said. You've got big ones.

Margie did not nod, or smile, or say anything at all.

Margie looked, breathed, stood, showed.

Jump, Lucy said. For fun. Just a couple of times. Jump up and down, Margie. Like, jumping jacks. I just want to see.

Margie jumped, once. Jumped, again. Margie jumped and her whole big body went with her, rising up into the air and falling back down to the ground. Margie did not jump high and she did not think about why or how she looked as she did it. Margie jumped and felt herself for a moment weightless and then heavy with the weight of all that she carried. Margie jumped because Lucy had asked.

Okay, Margie. Okay. You can stop jumping.

Come back, Margie.

Margie stepped closer to Lucy.

Lie back down. It's cold but it feels good.

Margie lay back down beside Lucy and felt the rough metal circle cool and firm under her back. Her breath blew hard through her chest from the jumping, from the feeling of being there, bare, beside Lucy.

Lucy moved as close to Margie as she could get, and then closer, pushing her small body again against Margie's big body, finding space for herself in the big soft gaps of Margie. She put her hand back on Margie's body, slower now. Lucy's hand, warm, moving slowly, in circles, rubbing. Squeezing, slowly, circling. Margie's heart beat up against her skin in the valley between her breasts and Lucy moved her hand there, to touch the beating parts, to feel Margie alive beneath her. Margie closed her eyes and felt Lucy feeling her, felt the air blowing across her wide, open skin, felt good, safe, touched, held.

Margie felt and beat and felt and breathed and felt and felt and felt until Lucy took her hand away.

I know, Margie, Lucy said.

It feels good, right?

You can do it too, if you want, Lucy said.

If you want to.

To me, I mean.

Lucy moved her body away from Margie and lay out small and bare beside her. Lucy, spread wide, open, waiting. Eyes closed, Lucy's white, freckled, beautiful belly rising up and falling, in the cool of the wind that blew through. Margie stayed where she was, pounding, looking at Lucy. Margie did not understand, did not know that Lucy was waiting for her, waiting for her touch. Margie knew only the loss of Lucy, felt the cold of Lucy's body pulled away. The pain of autumn air stinging skin so recently touched, warmed, revealed.

They lay there a long time, in the abandoned playground at the back of the soon-to-be-torn-down drive-in, in the deep-yellow-sinking-into-slow-blue light, in the rising wind, in the quiet of uncertain desire. Margie, deep inside herself, cooling quickly, feeling, feeling where Lucy was. And Lucy, thin back resting against the cool metal merry-go-round, knees spread wide, feet just barely touching the ground, open, offering, waiting. The two girls, grown up and away and out and almost into women, lying together, still, waiting for what would come.

Dykes, we might have said.

Do it, we might have said.

Come on, Margie.

This is your chance.

Your moment.

Who hasn't done such a thing?

Let loose, we might have said.

Touch her, we might have said.

Feel her.

Show her.

Love.

Love.

Try.

It'll be dark soon, Margie, Lucy said.

We better go home.

57. MARGE

What's this, Marge?

Another fucking thing you're trying to hide from me.

You think I don't go into your room, Marge?

This is my house. I go where I want.

I like this. Feels soft.

Smells like you, Marge. Like fat titties.

Why keep it secret? All the way under your bed.

This what you touch at night, Marge?

I bet that's it.

I bet this ain't even yours.

I bet you stole it from those dykes downstairs.

You are a dyke, aren't you, Marge?

No? It's yours? I don't believe you.

I think you stole it. I think you smell it and you look at it and you touch yourself and you think about those dykes.

Is that it, Marge? Is that what you do? Why you tried to hide this from me?

I'd like to take this down there and tie it around their necks.

Watch those dykes beg for their lives.

You think I wouldn't do that, Marge?

Disgusting, them.

No? You expect me to believe this is yours?

I don't believe you, Marge.

Why don't you wear it, then? Why hide it under your bed like some porno?

Prove it, Marge.

Prove it to me or I'm going down there and I'm going to show those dykes what you did.

Put it on.

Put this on and show me it's yours or I'm going down there and I am going to teach those dykes a lesson.

Teach them to stay out of our business.

Make them pay for turning you into a dyke, Marge.

Five seconds, you got.

I'm waiting.

Put that on or I'm going down there.

I'll kill them, Marge.

Think I won't? Think I can't do it?

Show me.

Five.

Four.

Three.

Two.

One.

58. MARJORIE

The pains are bad today. So bad that down-day Gram does not want to eat the graham cracker and peanut butter treats Marjorie is making for her. Gram has one thin, shaking hand held against her chest and one against her belly. Her eyes are open and on the Stories and then squeezed shut against the waves of pain when they come.

My heart, Margie, she says.

Marjorie is careful not to break the graham cracker as she spreads more peanut butter across its smooth surface. She wants to help Gram but she does not know how. Marjorie does not know if Gram can be helped, or if this is just what time will do to People. She wants to ask Gram about Lucy, but here are the pains.

What can I do, Gram?

Nothing. Not a thing. Nothing to do but feel the pain.

The Stories seem more and more far away from Marjorie. She sits here and watches and sees the People only in pieces. An elbow the color of milk, a man eating meat, a lady crying. Always a lady crying. What happens on the Stories is always so important it stops seeming important. Nobody in the Stories looks like Marjorie, or Gram, or Ma. Every few minutes a bad thing happens to the People in the Stories, but the bad is always fast and not really felt. Nobody on the Stories knows about the feeling of a Lucy taken away.

Marjorie puts another graham cracker sandwich next to Gram and gets up from her chair. She walks around the bed to the window and pulls open the blinds. Clouds of dust float down on Marjorie's head and she holds her wind to keep it outside. Marjorie with two hands pulls the window halfway up and open, letting the warm, cut-grass-smelling air inside. Gram's taped-up words and pictures rise and fall in the quiet that circles through.

What are you doing that for, Margie?

To get some new air in here, Gram. The same air all the time can't be good for your pains.

Pains don't care about the air. Pains come from inside. What has the air got to do with that?

It won't hurt, Gram.

It smells. How can I watch my Stories?

You can still watch your television, Gram. Just try it for a while.

Marjorie walks out of Gram's room and across the hall to where she sleeps. This room, too, is dark and old-air-smelling. Marjorie goes to the window and opens the blinds, pulls the thick glass up to let the spring air in. Outside, there are trees, hills, roads, apartments, grass, People walking dogs. The sun, the sky.

Marjorie puts her nose up close to the screen of the window and feels it rough against her skin. She moves her wind smooth as she can and still her heart beats fast and hard. The not knowing is all she has got inside. All the departments overflowing with it, with the big, the black of not knowing. The bright blinding light of wanting to know. And Gram across the hall. Gram who might know. Gram, the only one left to ask.

And here are the pains. Marjorie, nose, forehead pressed against the scratching wall of the window screen, feels the pain passing through. Staying. The pain living here in her. All over are the pains. But living has to keep going on. Marjorie has to ask Gram the question.

Gram, Marjorie says.

Louder, she says, Gram.

Margie, Gram says, her voice from across the hall low and small. If you want to talk to me get back in here.

Marjorie walks quick as she can back to Gram's room and stands in the doorway. Someone in the Stories is screaming. Marjorie pushes the button to turn the television off. She does not know how to say what she wants to say. But the want is strong and here, now.

Gram, I need, Marjorie says, and stops.

And says, Gram, I need to know about it.

About what, Margie? Close that window, it's cold in here.

I need to know about that time.

What happened.

To me.

Marjorie knows that Gram will not understand the Lucy of Lucy. That this is only how Marjorie says it to her self. Her self, here, shaking, her heart beating up against her skin, in her head, her belly. Her wind moving fast. But Marjorie has to do it. Marjorie has to put together the right words to make Gram understand.

About the little baby, Marjorie says. That got burned up. That paper Ma put her name on.

Gram is quiet and listening. Holding one hand on her heart and one on her belly.

You want to know about that, now, Margie?

Yes. I want to know.

Sit down. But shut that window first.

Marjorie, heating up, breathing hard, goes to the window and pushes it almost the whole way down. But leaves the bottom open just a bit, just enough to let the smallest outside air in.

She walks back around the bed, sits down in her chair beside Gram, and waits.

I wasn't sure if you'd want to know, Margie, Gram says, looking at the black of the turned-off television.

I didn't think you remembered all that. So terrible.

Better for you to keep it forgotten.

I remember, Gram. Some things.

I should have helped you, Margie, Gram, slow, quiet, says. But I didn't know how. What to do.

I am fine, Gram. I want to know about what happened to the baby's dust, after.

If you ask me, the only good your ma ever did in her whole life.

Gram takes a break from talking to think, to hold her heart and her belly harder.

Well, and you, Margie. You're a good thing your ma did. But going to get that poor little baby's ashes, that was a good thing. That was a good enough thing.

Ma took them?

You weren't in your right mind, Margie. I couldn't blame you. Said you didn't want them. Said you didn't want to see.

I want to see, Gram.

I think I did want to see.

Well, that may well be but you said you didn't want them. At the time. And I didn't blame you. I don't blame you. Don't know what I would have done myself. I had Frank taken from me, I had the burden of that. What was left of him just up and taken by my stepfather, put God-knows-where. I don't think I've ever gotten over the loss of that. First Frank, gone, and then Frank, gone, again.

Your brother?

Your uncle. I know you never knew him, Margie. But what I'm saying is I knew the feeling of losing the same thing twice and that is why I think it's good that your ma did what she did.

What did Ma do?

She went down there and she got the baby. This was after the police and all that. After they took that man away. Your ma went down herself and she got the baby. The ashes. Just a little pile of them. Not even a pound.

And nobody told me.

Nobody talked, then, Margie. That time. And you, the most quiet of all of us. Like you weren't even here, for a while. Doctors and social workers, whoever they were. Coming by, poking at you. You were quiet for a long time, Margie.

And then you came back and I wanted you to stay. I was afraid if I said something you might go away again.

I'm here, Gram.

I thank our Lord every day that you've got that doctor of yours. One good thing this state has done for us. A saint, that man must be. Worth the paperwork.

You know Dr. Goodwin, Gram?

I don't know him. I just know he's out there. Helping you. Helped you get that job in that store you love so much.

God fulfills our needs in unexpected ways, Marjorie.

Good, Gram. But what did Ma do?

Where did the baby go?

Here, Margie, Gram says, moving her hand from her belly to the bed. Your ma didn't know what to do with them either so I took them and I've been keeping them under here. For you. For when you were ready for them.

Marjorie's departments, for the moment, are quiet, still, listening. Marjorie looks at Gram's thin hand here on the bed. Lucy here. All the times Marjorie has sat beside Gram, watching the Stories, eating graham crackers and peanut butter. Lucy here, too. Under the bed. Here. Waiting.

Take them, Margie. They're yours for you to do what you want.

Marjorie pushes herself down from her chair, puts one knee and then the other on the floor next to Gram's bed. The papers on the wall above and around her move in the thin wind that passes through.

But Margie, Gram says. I mean it about your ma. She's mine and I say what happens to her. And I want her out of here. I don't want her hanging around anymore.

Gram knows. Marjorie does not know how Gram knows that Ma is still here with them. But Gram knows and Marjorie will do what Gram wants her to do.

Okay, Marjorie says.

She puts both hands on the floor and leans down low to look under the bed. It is dark and dirty under here. Big gray balls of dust and hair and whatever else falls down from People as they live out their living. Little pieces of paper all around. Words without sentences, words come untaped and at rest under the bed.

And a little purple plastic box. A box about as big as Marjorie's hand with two little hooks that keep it closed. Purple, Marjorie's favorite. A little purple box of Lucy under Gram's bed. Here the whole time, all the times. Saved by Ma. Watched over here by Gram. Lucy, waiting for Marjorie to take her back.

Marjorie moves as gentle as she knows how. Pulls the box of Lucy toward her and holds Lucy close as she unfolds her big body toward standing.

Lucy, known.

Lucy, found.

Lucy, saved.

Lucy, safe.

Lucy, here with Marjorie.

Thank you, Marjorie says.

Gram, one hand still spread out over her heart, with her other reaches for the clicker.

Don't thank me, Margie, Gram says. And don't thank your ma, either. One good thing doesn't cancel out a million bad.

Okay.

Thank our Lord, Margie. That's who you ought to thank. We can't know His plan for us but we have to have faith that He is there watching. That good will come.

Gram turns on the television and the Stories start talking.

Okay, Marjorie says. Good. Thank you.

Marjorie holds the small, smooth purple box of Lucy close to her chest. It is light, easy for Marjorie to touch and feel and carry. She steps careful steps toward the door.

Margie, Gram says. I told you to shut that window. Shut it all the way.

Marjorie puts the box of Lucy down on the television and goes again to the window.

Sorry, Gram, she says. I just thought it was good to get some new air in here for you.

I don't want new air. I want my air. I want to know what's getting into me.

Okay, it's shut. See? It's shut all the way.

And the blinds, close them. Too bright, I can't see my Stories. Nothing to see out there.

Marjorie does what Gram wants and when the room is dark and closed, Marjorie steps back around the bed, picks up the box of Lucy, walks across the hall. Marjorie feels the long pull of need hanging from the beat of her heart. To be free and quiet and alone with the box, with Lucy, with her self. The high, hard-to-catch-her-wind feel of wanting. Marjorie wants to see Lucy. To know what Lucy is now. To see what Marjorie made and what was taken away and come back.

Marjorie stands in the doorway of her room and smells the afternoon air. Inside, her aisles wait, her heart waits, her wind is strong, is waiting. Marjorie holds the little box of Lucy close to her belly, her chest, her cheek. She feels the smooth of the box against her lips, smells the sweet plastic smell of things contained.

Marjorie needs to see Lucy.

She wants to be alone with Lucy.

Marjorie does not want the People, even Gram, even her People, to see.

Marjorie is very important about what should be private.

Marjorie, holding, beating, wanting, shuts the door.

59. MARGIE

Margie sat heavy and quiet on Gram's side of the bedroom, on the floor beside the window, her arms sometimes on the chipped gray sill, sometimes at her sides, sometimes held tight around herself, her head against the cold glass. The pain in Margie's head a slow, steady pulse, the pain from skin too long touching cold, the pain of so long spent inside. Margie's heart moving in beat with the pain, pumping blood up, around, into, through the pain.

Outside, it was snowing.

Flakes fat as potato chips, big flakes of snow falling from an unending sky. Circles of snowflakes swirling outside the high-up window of Apartment #2. The ground giving in to the white.

Outside, they were leaving.

Lucy's ma, LD, carrying white-dusted cardboard boxes to the bed of the gray pickup truck.

Stacking, laughing, moving quickly.

Lucy, leaving.

Lucy, going away.

Lucy, getting out.

Because the big gray paint-peeling house on dead-end Summer Street was not a place for staying. Because of the dark hallway, the upstairs sounds, the rotting-leaf smell of the brook. Because of him and what he said. All we heard and did not say.

Margie understood. Margie knew why they wanted to leave.

But nobody had asked Margie about it.

Nobody had said, Margie, we need to go.

Margie, we have to get away.

And so should you.

Get out.

Go.

How could we say such a thing? Margie was never ours. Never our responsibility. We did what we could. We watched and we saw and we gave what we were able to give. We felt as much as we could feel about it.

We had ourselves to worry about.

We had each other.

We cannot be blamed.

Margie held her arms around herself and her head against the smooth, cold window. She moved her nose to the side, moved her mouth just so, so that her wind would not fog up the glass, so that she could see out and down. Margie watched the snowflakes fall from the big nothing white of the sky, down to the big nothing white of the ground, onto the blue tarp that covered the bigger and bigger stack of cardboard boxes piled in the bed of the pickup. Margie saw the snowflakes sit down white on top of Lucy's ma's red hair, saw LD's skin turn a burning color out there in the cold.

Margie saw Lucy only once.

Long blonde-haired Lucy, thin and tall and perfect in her green wool coat. Lucy, grown up, grown into the shape of a woman, almost. Lucy did not carry boxes or come outside to talk to her ma. Margie watched and behind-window waited and Margie did not see Lucy. Lucy, who must have been down below, inside, moving below Margie, moving through the huge space between Apartment #1 and Apartment #2. Lucy, who did not climb the dark wooden stairs to say goodbye.

Margie understood.

And Margie, alone, watched from the cold, cloudy glass of her bedroom window. Margie watched, stayed quiet, let the pounding of Apartment #2 roll out behind her. His footsteps heavy on rug on carpet on bed on wood on chair. Cigarette smoke and television turned up loud and baked beans burning in the kitchen. Apartment #2 swelled and breathed and rocked and grabbed and held and contained.

Margie, snow-bound, did not hear Gram come back to the room. She did not look up at Gram and Gram, down, did not look at Margie. Gram got into bed and held her hand to her chest, rocked slowly with her difficult breath.

My heart.

Oh, God.

My pains.

Margie stayed still, quiet, watching the world outside move on. Holding herself, feeling her pains, feeling her body inside moving in its circles.

What could we have done?

We didn't even know she was there.

We would never have thought she was watching.

Margie, her time. Margie, her face pressed to the cold glass of the window, could feel her time warm inside her. Her time, going, losing, slowly. Moving from the inside to the outside. Margie's time, leaking out. Her pains, staying in.

Where was Ma?

That's what we would like to know.

Isn't she the one who started all this?

Margie kept her face pressed to the hard window, to the thick icy glass that rattled in the wind, that kept the outside out. Ma always there, somewhere. Sitting beside him, beside where he sat in Gram's green chair, beside where he sat leaving hairs on what used to be Gram's chair, beside where he sat tearing, chewing, spitting, shedding, spreading himself out from what had been the good of Gram's green chair, out from that place in the center of Apartment #2. The smell of him, the hairs of him, the chewed-up, spit-out, wet-paper inside of him all over and up and out and around, covering, covering up Apartment #2. And Ma, too. Ma, part of it. Ma, swept up, away. Ma, gone under. The sounds of Ma, the smells of Ma, the touch, taste, shape of Ma drowned out by what Ma had let in.

We have nothing left to say.

We did what we did.

We wanted.

We needed.

We loved.

We tried.

And did not.

Beautiful, warm, blonde-haired, small-boned, summertime-smelling Lucy appeared once below Margie. Lucy did not carry cardboard boxes or come outside in the snow to talk to her ma or LD. Lucy must have been down there, below Margie, waiting to go, but Margie did not see Lucy or hear Lucy or feel the weight of Lucy moving through the wood of the house they shared. Margie waited, waited, and Lucy did not show herself to Margie.

Margie saw yellow headlights and the long brown of a car drive slowly down dead-end Summer Street. She saw the car turn around at the end near the frozen brook and pull up close to the sidewalk in front of the big gray house. Margie watched the headlights flash once, flash twice, watched the snowflakes circling down. Margie kept her forehead pressed to the cold pane of the glass, kept her eyes on the brown of the car disappearing into the piling white.

And then Margie saw Lucy. Tall, green-coated, beautiful, going-away Lucy. Lucy ran head-down, shoulders-up, through the snow, through the cold, to the waiting car. To the door of the car, to the warm of the car. Margie saw Lucy run small-step carefully past the place where Gram had fallen, past the place where Lucy had turned cartwheels and Margie had made her circles, past the sidewalk where all the good that could ever happen had happened.

Beautiful Lucy ran through the snow to the warm waiting car and opened the door. She did not stop, did not look up. Lucy opened the door of the car and moved her body inside it. She was quick, she must have been cold. Margie watched Lucy get into the car and close the door behind her. Margie pressed her face harder against the cold of the glass and watched the white-covered car cough out gray smoke. Margie watched the car drive slowly away into the swirling white.

What is left to say?

We have nothing more.

We've said it.

All of it.

60. MARGE

Marge.

Marge.

Marge.

Marge.

Marge.

Marge.

Marge.

Marge.

Marge.

Marge.

Marge.

Marge.

Marge.

Marge.

Marge.

Marge.

Marge.

Slut.

61. MARJORIE

Forgiveness can be so difficult, Marjorie.

Yes.

Especially when a child was hurt. I'd imagine it might be hard for your friend to forgive you.

Because I am bad.

Because you did a bad thing.

But I was not me, Dr. Goodwin.

You were you, Marjorie. A part of you hurt that little boy. How does that make you feel?

Bad. The dumps.

Sad.

It's okay to have these feelings. Sometimes we have to sit and feel sad to feel better.

Are you okay, Marjorie?

Okay, Dr. Goodwin.

You said that you tried to apologize, right?

Yes. Mac and Suzanne said to Get Out.

It sounds like you won't be able to go back there for a while. And maybe never again.

But if they forgive.

If your friends can find a way to forgive you, maybe they will invite you back. But, Marjorie, it's important for you to think about the possibility that they might not forgive you.

I know this is hard, but it's the truth. And if you can accept it, maybe you won't need to spend so much time worrying about what might happen.

Maybe they can't forgive me. Maybe the bad was too much.

What about you, Marjorie?

What about me what.

Can you forgive the people who have done bad things to you? Can you forgive the people who have hurt you?

How do I do that, Dr. Goodwin? What do I have to do to forgive?

That's a good question. I don't know the answer. I think it's different for everyone, it's a feeling. Sometimes it means that you can find a way to understand the person who hurt you. Why they hurt you.

No, Dr. Goodwin. I don't understand that. Bad. Just bad, is all I can think of.

Maybe that's your answer, Marjorie. Maybe you can't forgive the people who hurt you. And maybe you don't need to.

Good. I don't forgive Him.

But it's important that you find a way to forgive yourself.

My self.

You. I think you are the one person you must find a way to forgive. Or else you'll spend all your time thinking about the past.

But I hurt Tony. I am bad.

You did a bad thing and you apologized. Your friends don't need to forgive you. But you need to forgive yourself.

How?

I don't know, Marjorie. That's for you to figure out.

Just keep going. Be good.

That sounds like a start.

Keep going with the days. Be good as I can.

I know you will find your way, Marjorie.

Forgive my self.

But not Him.

62. MARGIE

Well.

Except this.

We're sorry, Margie.

That's one thing left to say.

63. MARGE

Nowhere to go, Marge.

Snow out there is high as your tits.

Your girlfriend, gone.

I'll miss her, Marge.

That tight little ass out there running around.

Used to like watching her right out there. Right out your window, Marge. Best view in the house from up here.

Everybody's gone, now.

Big fat Marge left all alone.

What are you going to do now?

Dykes don't want you.

Your ma don't want you.

I still do, though, Marge.

Mustang's here for you.

Look at you, getting fatter every day. Keep eating like that and you'll never leave this house.

But that's okay, Marge.

I don't mind.

You're still pretty to me.

You think I only go for the skinny ones but that's not true.

I like to hold on to them, Marge.

I like something to squeeze.

And you got a lot of you to squeeze.

You got a lot to hold on to.

64. MARJORIE

The day is not day and the night is not night. The light is warm, is slow to leave, is the blue light left behind after the sun goes down behind the hills.

Marjorie stands still in her self outside the Club. Resting. At rest. Listening to the whoosh sounds of the cars whooshing by on this side, the People-soup sound of the People laughing and yelling inside the walls of the Club on this side, the beat, beat, beat sound of pounding down deep in her under.

The sign.

The Benevolent and Protective Order of Elks.

The brick walls of the Club, protecting, holding.

Keeping the People in, keeping Marjorie away.

Marjorie does not try to open the door of the Club. She stands in the middle of the sidewalk and she steps two steps to the grass on the side to let the People pass by. Resting, here, in her place, halfway between the Store and home, not inside, but here. The air is deep into spring air, warm wind leftovers from a wet-parking-lot-steaming-in-sunlight day. Marjorie moves slow inside with the come and go of her wind. She will not go into the Club. Marjorie knows that Mac and Suzanne are set in their angry. Marjorie knows that Mac and Suzanne are not going to open the door. But here Marjorie is, at the Club, outside the Club, sorry, in the center of her circle, because this is her place.

And where else is there to go?

The soft round backs of the hills all around her sometimes surprise Marjorie because they are always here. Green to orange to yellow to brown to snow to brown to green. People get so used to looking down into their own selves that they forget to look up and around and away. Marjorie turns her head up and the whole world looks bigger. More sky, more space, more hills, the mountain. She turns in a slow circle so that she can see the whole huge blue-to-brown-to-green place all around her.

Lucy, everywhere.

Marjorie, from the pocket of her too-warm purple puffy coat, takes just a little bit of Lucy and lets her out into the air around the Club. Lucy here inside Marjorie and let go. Let out. A little bit of Lucy gone to the top of the Club, to the sidewalk, to the trees. Lucy up on the tops of the hills and into the open windows of the Club and in the grass and in the gray streaks of cloud and in her hair and nose and mouth and in her skin and in her inside. Lucy, all over. Marjorie opens her lips up wide to take the biggest breaths she can take. The air warm and cleaning. Marjorie moves her wind through her in waves that roll out long like the sea, tall like the hills. Taking in and pushing out. More and more Lucy in and in and in.

And Ma under the bed. Ma in that box. Ma will come next.

Marjorie spins slowly inside this big circle of blue-light-lit world inside the hills and feels so much Lucy and not much at all of Ma or Him or before. There is the bad inside, the kick, the little bent body of Tony, the Bible torn to chewed-up bits, but time is time and those times have passed by. Marjorie turns slow to see all the things she can see, moves slow and safe through the departments inside. Alone in her self, quiet, free to be and look down her aisles, stacking up high what is too much to feel.

A man's voice.

Excuse me. Hello. Can I ask you a question? Can I ask you what you're doing?

Marjorie stops her circle and turns her head to look at the man. He is short and fat and wearing a shiny red jacket and barely haired and wearing glasses and not very old and not at all young.

Some departments inside close and Marjorie catches hold of her wind before she speaks.

Hello. I am just resting here. Looking around. Nothing much.

The man smiles and Marjorie cannot see any angry at all in his small round face. His lips stick out a little farther than his nose and there are small sharp brown hairs all over his rolling chin.

Oh, good. Good. Today is a beautiful day. Me, I am an outside guy too. I just walk and walk.

Marjorie presses her lip tight to her lip. She puts her hands deep and careful into her pockets and nods.

The man raises his arm and waves at Marjorie and keeps his smile up high on his face. His hand is the dark of dirty and his skin looks smoothed over hard in places.

Excuse me for not introducing myself sooner. My name is Mister Norman. Mister Norman for most people because Mister is how you get respect in this world, you know? But you look different to me. You look nice. You can call me Norman, just Norman. What's your name?

Marjorie. My name is Marjorie.

Good name! Mar-jor-ie. Mar-jor-ie. Strong. Three syllables. I used to be an English teacher. College. No, little ones. Third graders, maybe. We'd clap like this. Mar-jor-ie. You can clap to know the syllables. What do you do, Marjorie? Me, I used to be a doctor too but before, you know. Long time ago. And now I walk. I'm a walker. I'm good at walking.

All these words. This man is a little like Benjamin. Marjorie looks close at his eyes, his big chin, his smile. Like Benjamin but not good-looking like Benjamin. A fatter, faster-talking Benjamin. But smiling, and kind, and stopped here to talk with her.

I work in the Store. I work with the People. Say Hello, help People if they need help.

Oh, I love stores. I walk all around in stores. Hey, Marjorie, do you want to walk? We are just standing here talking and this sidewalk is starting to hurt my feet. I need to walk. I need to move, you know? I don't walk fast. I walk slow. I walk so I can know what is happening, you know? So I can figure out where I am. You can walk with me. Let's go.

Marjorie looks at the Club and wants to be inside with Mac and Suzanne and the People, with her Shirley Temple, in her usual place. She looks at Norman and he is moving from foot to foot, side to side, slow, still smiling.

Well, Norman. I am sorry. This is where I go.

Where? Here? This? This sidewalk? Okay, that's okay. We can walk here. I just need to walk some. Here, this is good. We can walk up this sidewalk and then back down it. How does that sound?

Marjorie feels around inside her self and her departments seem fine, quiet, still. No hot waves or heart banging around or blown-up parts.

Okay, that sounds good. But just here. Just in front of the Club. This part of the sidewalk here.

Great, sure. You can walk miles just in one small spot, just putting your feet in place, forward and back and forward again. You can take a whole long trip just in that little part you're walking on. I took a trip to Egypt and England and China. The whole world, I've been to. In Egypt they ride camels and if you want to walk, everywhere you walk you walk on sand. And in Japan I ate a giant live fish and I was walking next to the sea and I jumped into it and just swam and swam.

Marjorie is gentle with her hands in her pockets. She walks slow and looks down at her feet while Norman talks. His sneakers are white and wide and have holes in places where she can see his red socks underneath. Marjorie steps her right foot down and then her left foot down and she sees that Norman is watching their feet too and she sees that Norman's feet are moving the same as her feet.

What do you think about that, Marjorie? About all those places I go and the fish? Where did you take a trip to?

Marjorie is not sure what Norman is saying. She is watching their feet meet the sidewalk together and together.

She says, Oh, yes. Good.

Good, yeah. Yeah. Where did you take a trip to?

A trip? No trips. I don't take trips. Just here. I live here. I just take trips to where I go. The Store, the Club, home. Just lots of small trips.

I know, I know what you mean. Cash, right? Need a lot of cash to take trips. Better to just be where you are and be happy there, right? I am really happy here. Really happy walking here up and down this sidewalk. Feels like we're going somewhere special. Going somewhere and here.

Marjorie tries taking her steps a little faster and when she does Norman also steps a little faster. She slows way down and Norman does the same. Together, the same, they turn and walk back and forth on the sidewalk in front of the Club. So much time of her life spent inside the Club sitting on her stool and not even one time did Marjorie ever think that she would walk so far and for so long outside of it. Something new. Something different.

I am happy here. I am happy just walking and talking. Very good to meet you, Marjorie. Are you happy, too? Are you happy here too, Marjorie?

What? Sorry.

Are you happy?

Happy. I don't know about that.

Norman stops his steps and Marjorie keeps walking alone. Maybe Norman needs a rest but Marjorie is not tired yet. Marjorie likes feeling her legs strong and alive under her. Seeing the same squares of gray, the same hills rising around again and again. Marjorie wants to keep walking, so she does, up the sidewalk, and back down. Norman stands in the place where he stopped, big-lipped mouth open, staring at her. When Marjorie's steps take her close to him again, he reaches his hand out and taps her shoulder.

Hey! Hey, hey, Marjorie, hey. I feel sad right now. I was happy and now I'm sad. I feel sad that you said you aren't happy here. Why aren't you happy?

Marjorie stops and looks at Norman. She moves her shoulder down and away, closer to her self, because she does not know yet if Norman is People She Minds or People She Does Not Mind. But his face is what he says. The fallen-down low of sorry, the opened-up of sad.

I'm sorry you're sad, Norman. I just said that I don't know about happy. That's just me. My self. Too many things. You know, life.

Oh, life. Life. I don't mean life, Marjorie? Are you listening? I want to know if you are happy here on the sidewalk walking. You know, right now. If you are happy out in the air here taking this walk with me. Life is too long to be happy, you know? But in small parts you can be happy. Like now, on the walk. Are you happy here on the sidewalk?

Marjorie hears what Norman is saying. Not happy about the whole big whole of life. Happy in just one little piece. A good department, an aisle easy to walk down. The hills around Marjorie are much darker now. The light is deep underwater blue and the day is almost sunk down into night. Marjorie feels her body warm and living and even as she stands here, still, she can feel her self inside move with the beat of their walking. She breathes the air clean and deep into her. Lets Lucy in, and out, and in, out. Marjorie bounces on the fronts of her feet, wants to keep walking. Feels empty, light. Feels good.

Okay, Norman. I see. Yes, I am happy. Here walking on the sidewalk, I am happy too.

Good. Good, good. I feel better now. Not so sad. Happy. Hap-py. See, you can clap for any word. Two syllables. Hap-py. Like stepping. One foot, the other foot. Hap-py. Okay, good. Let's keep going. On our trip. Let's walk some more. I walk all day and I can walk all night too. I can go forever. Until I get tired. Until I need to sleep and then I sleep and then I walk some more. Want to keep going, Marjorie?

Sure, Norman. I will keep walking with you. For a while.

Marjorie moves one foot in front of the other, not too fast, not too slow. Feeling her inside soft and strong and painted over white and clean by the warm almost-night air. The lights of the Club glow brighter and brighter as the air darkens and Marjorie looks there and then does not look there. Marjorie keeps her eyes down on the sidewalk, on her feet, on Norman's feet here next to hers, on the to and from of the trip.

Above them, a streetlight buzzes alive, so that even in the dark, the walk can keep going. Marjorie might understand Norman's idea of happy. She does not know if what she feels right now is happy or not, but Marjorie knows that here on the sidewalk, in the warm-air end of the light, she feels close to good.

Step and step and step and step and step and step and turn and step and step.

Going somewhere and coming back and going again. Moving. Keeping with the going, the coming.

The man named Norman is talking and Marjorie is not listening. Marjorie feels good enough here, walking, in her self and out in the air. She wants Lucy to feel it too, the sidewalk beneath, the hills around. Marjorie lets Lucy a little more out into the world. She looks up while she walks and in the light of the streetlights Marjorie sees the chain of the backs of the hills holding all around her. Marjorie turns and feels and looks and where it is dark out there Marjorie sees the forever of all the empty, the open, and the stars, the far-away bulbs of the stars slowly switching on into life.

65. MARGE

I'm so lonely, Marge.
You don't know what it's like.
People need people.
Your ma leaves me. All alone.
And what does she expect me to do?
I got needs, Marge.
It's normal.
You don't know because you're a big dyke.
Or maybe you do.
I just can't be alone all the time.
You and me, Marge.
Do me a favor.
My mouth hurts. My mouth needs something. My tongue gets antsy.
You know, Marge? I know you know.
Go get me that old bag's book.

The big fat one she keeps under the bed.

I know all your secrets. Everybody in this house.

Get me that book she loves so much and we'll do it together, Marge.

You and me.

Together.

Teach her a lesson.

Do what I say. I'm sick of her thinking she's so much better than the rest of us.

Who cares what God thinks? God never gave me anything.

No? You won't do it, Marge?

Don't want to upset your dear old gram and her heart, oh, her heart, her heart?

Fine.

Then you come over here and keep me company.

You go and get your gram's book and we have some fun with it or you come over here and keep me warm.

It's so cold out, Marge.

I can't be alone all the time.

Your ma would want you to take care of me.

Your ma understands that men got needs.

66. MARJORIE

Lucy in her small purple box is here beside Marjorie. What little is left of Lucy, not much, but more than enough for Marjorie. More than Marjorie's one hand can hold. Lucy, seen, now, the soft, thin silver of Lucy dust that Gram kept safe for Marjorie inside this purple box. Here for Marjorie to touch and see and know. Marjorie, with just a pinch of the sand of Lucy kept in her pocket, now, does not need to go through her departments looking for Lucy. Lucy is all around, and inside, and here on the table beside Marjorie's bed. Lucy is here and carried and safe and can be felt with Marjorie's fingers, felt in the inside way Marjorie can feel the good of things.

Marjorie says Hello to Lucy in her box beside the bed and turns on the bare-bulb lamp. The room lights up bright with shadows and Marjorie goes to the window to shut the blinds. It is good to feel the new air, to smell the exploding spring, but Marjorie does not want the People to see in. Marjorie wants to be unseen and safe here inside with these important things she needs to do.

Marjorie has three big plastic bags with her, one white lampshade in each of them.

She has done it.

Marjorie feels good.

She takes the lampshades out of the bags. Each one is protected by plastic that Marjorie must unwrap, plastic that must have protected the white of them from the dangers of dust and dirty fingers on the shelves of the Store. The lampshades are big and thick and wrinkled. Marjorie touches her finger to the shade's hard outside and draws a long circle around it. A thing made to protect the light. To hold the light. To hold the light in and make the living a little softer, easier to see. Three bare-bulb lamps in their tiny apartment and now these three beautiful lampshades.

Marjorie takes a lampshade into the living room and puts it on the lamp in there. It is easier than she had thought. Hold the big circle of the lampshade above the bulb and push down careful as she can. Push down careful and the thin wires inside the shade open up and let the bulb inside. A perfect home for the light. Push, push, gentle, push, until the whole round body of the bulb fits right inside the wire inside of the lampshade. Marjorie switches on the lamp and the living room glows soft and yellow and safe. The sofa is there, brown and hiding the bed inside. Not needed and left alone. This light, here, now, is something good to see. The room looks more like other rooms. Warm. A place People might want to be.

Gram's room is next. Marjorie knocks soft at Gram's door and there is television inside but no answer. She pushes the door open wide enough for her head to fit through and says, Gram?

Gram?

Gram's answer is a cough and the scratch of nightgown against sheets and the voices of the television being turned down so low the words are not words, are only sounds. The light of the screen glows blue and red and yellow on the paper-breathing walls of the room.

Marjorie holds the lampshade behind her back with one hand and pushes the door open with her other.

What do you want, Margie?

I want a place for People to be, Gram.

I brought you something.

I don't want nothing, Margie. No people for me.

Gram sits up small and straight as she can against her pillows.

I don't want nothing except for you to get your ma out of here. That's what I want.

Okay, Gram, Marjorie says, stepping sideways toward the lamp so that Gram will not see the surprise. Okay, I know. But I brought you this anyway.

And for you to get yourself a friend. That's what I want, Margie. For you to be less alone all the time.

Okay, Gram.

You need someone with you.

I know, Gram. I have People. I am good. Just watch.

Marjorie takes the lampshade from behind her back and gently presses it down over the bare bulb of the lamp in the corner. This one easier, now that Marjorie knows how to do it. She turns on the light and Gram blinks and blinks and closes her eyes and then slowly opens her eyes back up and looks from the lamp to the television to the lamp.

Makes it hard to see the television, Gram says.

Marjorie turns the light off so that Gram can go back to the dark of her Stories.

Okay, Gram. But now when you want some light you won't have to squint at it. You can see and feel good. Look around.

Gram nods and Marjorie walks back around the bed to the door.

It's good, Margie.

Good, Gram.

You want to sit and watch some Stories?

Not now, Gram. I'm busy. Got to do this. Maybe later.

God bless you, Margie.

Thanks, Gram.

You too.

Gram nods and sinks back into the soft of her bed. Marjorie walks out of the room and closes the door behind her. Marjorie is moving. Marjorie is doing what she needs to do. She does not want to sit in Gram's room right now. Marjorie does not want to be in the dark with the television People and the sad and the happy of the Stories. Marjorie wants to be with Lucy, and her self, and the good and the new of these lights she can look at with no pain.

Back in the too-bright of the bare bulb lamp in her room, Marjorie picks up the last of the lampshades. She pushes the big white circle down gently on top of the bulb and the scream of the light goes away. Marjorie looks around the room and she is not in the bright white of the Store and she is not in the dark and she is not in the shifting underwater blue of the television light. Marjorie is in the room, in the quiet yellow glow of light held and let out slow. In her room, in her self, alone, alive, different, and the same.

Here with Lucy.

And Ma.

Marjorie puts her hands on the edge of the bed to help lower her big self down to her knees. Puts her hands on the floor and presses all the way down to the floor, to the black under of the bed. Marjorie reaches and reaches and moves her arm around under there until her fingers touch the rough edge of the box of Ma. Big gray balls of dust and hair and under-the-bed roll out around the box as Marjorie slides the cardboard toward her. She brushes the box off and sits down with her legs crossed, the rest of Ma here inside the cardboard walls, resting on top of her lap.

Marjorie is going to see what is inside. What is inside is not Ma. Inside the box of Lucy was not Lucy. Just dust, sand, left-behinds. Soft and crumbling. Inside the box of Ma is just, what? A thing. The bits that People leave behind. Just that, just burned-up things, not People.

Marjorie stays down low on the ground. She does not want Ma spilling out and onto the bed and into the good air of the room. Marjorie slides her fingers underneath the wide tape that holds the box together and pulls it back and away. The top two flaps flop free and Marjorie moves her wind through her, feels her heat here, alive, beating. Here in the soft yellow light rolling out from the lampshade, Marjorie opens the box and looks inside to see the whole of what Ma left behind.

Inside, like Dr. Goodwin said, is another box. A box of Ma inside a box of Ma. This one is black and plastic and a little smaller than the cardboard one, just small enough to be held inside it. Inside the purple box of Lucy was just the dust of Lucy. Gram must have opened Lucy up, must have held her carefully and found the right safe place for her to rest. And Ma has just been in cardboard under the bed. Catching the dust and hair as it blows through. Marjorie picks the plastic box of Ma up and holds it close to her chest for a moment, just to feel it, just to know the weight of it. Then she puts it down on the floor and flips up the two hooks that keep the box shut tight.

Marjorie is done with all this thinking about Ma. Her inside aisles feel wide and easier to walk down. She knows where to find Lucy. What departments to visit and what departments to pass by. Marjorie is here in the room, in the light that can be looked at, in her self, her warm, safe self who is ready to see.

Marjorie opens the plastic box and inside is a thick, clear plastic bag and inside the bag Marjorie can finally see what is left of Ma. Dust, like she thought. Dust, like Lucy's dust, only darker, heavier, more. Marjorie holds the plastic bag in her two hands and moves the weight of Ma from hand to hand. Inside the plastic is what Ma is now, a million little burned up pieces of Ma. All that Ma ever said or thought or did or felt or loved or hated all burned up into the two-hands of dust Marjorie holds now, here, close to her. All that red-faced angry and the white quarry dust and so many colors of pills inside there, all burned to black, to gray. All the sounds Ma ever made from before, from her bedroom, from the living room sofa, from after, from where she sat closed-door alone and coughing. What Ma brought into Apartment #2. What Ma brought to Marjorie. Him, in there in the dust of Ma, in the black of what Ma left behind. In there in the burned-up bits of Ma must still be some of Him, the black hairs lost all over and the balls of wet paper pushed into all the openings. Ma burned up with what Ma let in. Ma who maybe Marjorie should throw out with the trash, like Gram wanted. Ma who wanted to sit quiet and watch the fish. Ma who came home white-dusted and coconut-smelling. Ma who hurt Margie. Marjorie who remembers. Ma who did not know Marge. Ma who must have known. Ma who saved Lucy. Ma who carried Marjorie for so long warm and safe and growing inside her. Ma who started it all is finished, now, here in this plastic bag. The last of Ma, burned out, up, down to the smallest that People can be.

Marjorie is ready to let go of this pile of Ma.

Marjorie who might be feeling what it is to forgive.

The strong pull of the wave of wanting to move, of wanting to make the weight of what she is holding go away.

Is that forgive?

The giving in, to, away?

Marjorie stands up slow and tall and stretches her arms and legs. She picks up the bag of Ma and puts it down on the small table behind the box of Lucy. Things feel bigger, now, in the new lampshade light, bigger now that Marjorie has seen, now that these boxes have been opened and felt. Marjorie sits down on the bed and leans back, puts one hand on the purple box of Lucy.

Sorry, she says.

But I didn't know.

67. MARGE

You can't get away, Marge.

This is your home.

Your blood, Marge.

Where you're from.

You can't leave.

Nobody wants a big fat dyke like you.

Nobody but me.

And you bleed now, don't you, Marge?

I know.

I know you.

I know your smell.

You can't leave me, Marge.

I got all your secrets.

There's nowhere for you to go.

Where you going to go?

68. MARJORIE

Today Marjorie is taking her vacation.

A vacation day. Her first.

And it is sometime soon.

And Benjamin is coming.

Marjorie stands alone outside at the edge of the Store and waits for Benjamin. Not her usual place, not in front where she can see the parking lot stretching out and the People coming in, but around the side where it is quiet and only workers go. The warm of spring-evening sunset is falling yellow all around her, and Marjorie, held tight in her purple puffy coat, is starting to sweat, a little. Inside, Marjorie is not wearing her bra. Marjorie is taking her vacation today, is doing what she wants to do. What makes her feel free and good and let loose.

Marjorie holds one hand in her pocket and rubs the dust of Lucy soft and slow between her fingers. Lucy is easier to carry here, outside, in her pocket. Lucy is light is here is hers is a thing Marjorie can touch. In her other hand, she holds a plastic bag from the Store inside a bag from the Store inside a bag from the Store to make one strong plastic bag to carry the weight of the bag of Ma.

Marjorie, her vacation day taken.

Here, outside, in the yellow light, waiting.

Ready to do what she wants to do.

Marjorie walks slow beside the big stone side of the Store. She swings the bag of Ma as she walks, moves her wind easy in the warm air. Marjorie walks toward the front of the Store and looks out into the parking lot at the rows and rows and rows of cars shining red, gray, blue, green in the last yellow light of the day. All the People parking, passing by, looking for the needed things. And today, for today, Marjorie is not the one who will say Hello and help. Marjorie is deep into her vacation day, and today Marjorie is here to see Benjamin. To see what Benjamin wants her to see.

She picks one foot up, puts it down, picks her other foot up, puts it down. The hard of the ground, of parking lot, of shining Store floor, of sidewalk, gives Marjorie pains. The soft of the bed, too, gives Marjorie pains, though these are less now that the mattress is more the shape of Marjorie than Ma. Marjorie turns away from the People and the parking lot and walks slow in the other direction, more toward the parts of the Store where no one goes.

Benjamin said that he is coming to get her in a car.

It has been a long time since Marjorie last rode in a car.

Here, at the side of the Store, when Marjorie looks up and out, here, too, everywhere, always, there are the hills rolling out around her. She looks out at the smooth green sliding backs of the hills and holds on tight to Lucy, tight to the plastic bags holding Ma. Marjorie brings the bags up close to her nose and breathes deep breaths of the inside. The smell is plastic and chocolate and cin-namon and the almost-gone smell of cigarette smoke and the smell is the smell of the thick plastic bag of Ma. Marjorie moves her wind in low and long and in every breath she feels the last of Ma move up and in and and through her, feels the weight of Ma heavy in her hands.

Smell good in there, Marge?

The deep thin voice behind Marjorie is the voice of Steve. The big belly pressing against her arm is the belly of Steve. The wide forehead dripping sweat down the thick white neck, the smell of french fries and the standing too close all belong to Steve. Steve, here, touching her.

What's in the bag, Marge? You got some dinner? Some big fat ham?

No, Steve.

I thought you were taking a vacation day today, Margie. What are you doing here on your fancy vacation day? Is this your idea of vacation, Margie?

Marjorie, Marjorie says. My name is Marjorie, Steve. I've said before. Not Marge. Not Margie.

Marjorie, Marge, Margie. Marg-o-rine. Marj-monster. Marj-zilla. Sorry, Mar-jor-ie.

Marjorie steps away from Steve and holds her bags close. She does not like his small eyes, how they move and move and move and then stare and move again. Marjorie does not like the way Steve's big black-haired chin shakes when he talks and she cannot look at the bits of spit that come out from the sides of his lips. She does not like the smell of his sweat.

So what's so special about that bag, Mar-jor-ie?

Nothing special. Just bags.

What are you doing back here on your vacation day? Where are you going, Marge?

Somewhere, Steve.

Really? Because it seems like you're just here where you are every day. Margie and her precious store.

No. I am doing something different.

Steve moves his big belly closer to Marjorie and Steve puts his wet head down close to Marjorie's ear and Marjorie feels the pain of the sharp hairs above his lip and Marjorie feels the hot of Steve's wind and Steve puts his two hands on the two sides of Marjorie and he squeezes and pulls, tries to pull her self to him and him to her.

His voice is low and his wind is hot against her neck.

You waiting for your boyfriend back here, Marge?

No, Steve.

Marjorie tries to step away and Steve holds on harder. Steve moves his hand fast and puts his hands inside Marjorie's big purple coat. Puts his hands close to where she is free and let out braless. With his two hands he shakes Marjorie's sides, slow, up and down, coming close and closer to Marjorie's skin.

I know you're a slut, Marge. A secret slut, that's why you're hiding back here.

Marjorie swings the heavy bag of Ma hard as she can at Steve's head. She hits his cheek, his nose, and Steve right away lets go of Marjorie and holds his hands up around his face. Marjorie lets go of her bag of Ma and the dust of Lucy. With her two strong hands she pushes hard against the big of Steve. Ma falls to the ground between them and Marjorie steps quick steps away from Steve.

He bends his big body over and says, Fuck.

Fucking bitch.

Drops of dark red blood fall down from between Steve's fingers, down to the gray of the sidewalk at the edge of the Store. Little circles of red on gray glow gold in the light of the sun setting behind the hills.

Get away from me, Steve.

You bitch, Marge. You fucking bitch. You're going to get it.

Steve stands up straight as he can, his hands red-spotted, his nose dripping blood, and he reaches again for Marjorie. Holds his big arms out wide and steps toward her, tries to grab her arm, her side, her belly, her breasts. Steve's hand hits Marjorie's shoulder and he squeezes tight, tries to hold on.

Marjorie kicks and swings her arms and screams. Marjorie screams, loud, high, long, so that the People will hear, so that Ma, inside the thick plastic of the bags, will hear, so that Lucy, out there, will hear, so that Steve will stay away.

Stop.

Stop.

Stop.

Stop.

Marjorie screams as loud and long and hard as she can.

Stop.

Okay, okay, okay, Steve says. Okay.

Steve steps away from Marjorie, his hand covering his nose, blood dropped down onto his big blue t-shirt.

God, Marjorie. God. I'm just playing.

Can't take a joke, can you?

Go away, Steve.

Can't you take a joke?

No jokes, Steve. Get away.

What's your problem, Marjorie?

And then the sound. The low thunder of car stopped, door slammed, voice yelling.

What the fuck, Steve?

You fucking pig.

You asshole mother-fucking piece-of-shit scumbag.

The good, the yellow-hair-lit-up-in-gold-light beautiful of Benjamin. Benjamin, here, to help. Benjamin here, to see, to know. Benjamin here to take Marjorie to the good place he wants her to see.

You're so done, Steve. I see what you're trying to do.

I was just kidding around.

Fuck you.

Nobody around here has any sense of humor.

Marjorie closes her eyes and slows her wind. Listens to her heart beating hard inside, to the sound of her scream still rolling out in waves in the warm waters of her inside. But her departments are clear, her aisles open. Steve trying to hurt her and Marjorie taking care of her self. Benjamin come to see, Benjamin who knows.

Marjorie opens her eyes and steps toward Steve and leans down to pick up the bags that hold Ma. The plastic is dirty and ripped open in places but still holds, the three bags together strong enough to keep the big bag of Ma in.

Go away, Steve, Marjorie says.

She puts her hand back in her pocket where Lucy is and turns away from the big, bent, sweating, blood-drying body of Steve.

The car is long and brown. Benjamin opens the door for Marjorie and Marjorie sits down on the smooth seat. She holds the bags holding the bag of Ma heavy on her lap and sits back and waits. Benjamin shuts the door and Marjorie sits inside the quiet and watches Benjamin and Steve yell some more.

People and their angry.

Marjorie leans back and blows her wind through slow as she can. She feels her face feel less and less hot, feels her heart fall back where it belongs.

Marjorie and her angry.

Marjorie sits alone in the car and holds Ma with one hand and Lucy with one hand, watches Steve there leaning against the stone side of the Store, and Marjorie waits to feel bad.

Bad about hitting Steve with the bags of Ma.

Bad about his blood on the sidewalk.

Bad about her screaming.

Bad about her angry.

But Marjorie does not feel bad.

Marjorie feels good.

Benjamin opens the car door and gets in and sits with his hands held tight to the wheel. He breathes hard, his thin shoulders moving his t-shirt up and down with the waves of his angry. Benjamin's wind smells sweet and strong and that good sour like apples.

You okay, Marjorie?

Okay.

He's such an asshole. I saw what he did. I saw you fight back.

Steve is a bad man.

Fuck yeah he is. A fucking animal.

The car is making sounds beneath Marjorie. Low rumbles and loud coughs. Shaking, just a little, under her, around her.

Okay, Benjamin. Thank you.

You still feel like going, Marjorie? We can go another time if you want.

I feel like going, Benjamin. Today is a vacation day for me.

Okay, good. Let's get the fuck out of here.

Good.

Put your seatbelt on, to be safe. Got to be safe, don't want to take chances, you know? Up there. Yeah. That metal thing. Grab onto it and then pull it down around you and then click it in here.

Yeah. Like that.

Okay, good, got it?

Got it, Benjamin.

Benjamin starts driving the car and Marjorie sits back and feels the small shaking beneath her, the tight hold of the seatbelt around her. They pass by Steve still standing there against the stone side of the Store and Steve looks away and up and toward the hills.

Benjamin drives around the back of the Store and then back out and through the parking lot. They pass by People passing by and Marjorie smiles and feels good to be getting out, to be moving. She likes the sounds the car makes, sometimes loud and coughing, sometimes low and snoring. She likes sitting beside Benjamin as he moves his arms slowly this way and that way, as he moves his legs to make the car go and stop and slow.

A good feeling. Getting out, getting away. Dr. Goodwin will be happy to hear. Gram, too. Marjorie doing something for her self. Marjorie on her vacation day. Marjorie going somewhere that is not where Marjorie goes.

And Ma coming along.

Lucy, too.

Benjamin whistles while he drives. He taps his long thin fingers against the wheel and Marjorie watches his reflection in the glass in front of them. The sunlight is almost all gone now and the streetlights glow yellow-white above them, wave out into long lines of light as the car passes fast by them. Marjorie watches the blue and purple of the outside stretch and squish together. The houses, the People, the trees, the signs, all the shapes of the world making the same one line of moving outside the windows of the car. All the things becoming all the things in the last of the light. Passing by, passing by.

Inside the car Marjorie smells the sour apple of Benjamin and the left-behind smell of cigarettes. Marjorie moves her wind strong and slow, taking the car air in and giving some of her self out.

This isn't my car, Benjamin says. It's my buddy's. He lets me borrow it sometimes.

Good, Marjorie says. It's good to have friends.

Definitely. And especially friends with cars. Much faster than riding a bicycle.

Or walking, Marjorie says.

You got a lot of friends with cars, Marjorie?

No. My friends mostly walk.

Yeah, same here, Benjamin says. It's nicer, right? It's good to move slow sometimes so you can look around and see shit and smell the smells and all that.

But sometimes I like to go fast, you know? Sometimes I like to sit behind the wheel of this big machine and feel all this power and I say, Fuck you, to all the trees and I just smell the air and want to go fast. I get sick of being stuck inside me. I'm so slow, right? I just want to get where I'm going, you know?

I know, Marjorie says.

Benjamin goes back to his whistling and Marjorie goes back to her watching. They drive through the town and past the houses and up hills to where the trees are more and more. The big black shapes of the trees rise up high and shaking against the dark purple sky. Marjorie would like to take Gram out in a car, to show Gram how big the trees are out here past the houses, but Marjorie knows that Gram does not want to see. Gram wants to stay where she is in her room with her Stories, with whatever she talks about with the Lord. Gram is happy to sit quiet and watch and wait.

But Marjorie is different. Marjorie is out and moving. Sitting beside Benjamin in the wide of the car, in the big dark of the beginning of summer beginning of night. The car's lights are bright and strong and white out in front of them. The streetlights above become less, now, as they drive up into the hills. The little all-over lights of the stars show through and the moon, the bright white circle of the moon, rises up above the trees.

We're almost there, Benjamin says. This is the Glen, here, around us. The bottom of the mountain. And the place I want to show you is just up here a bit, just this big open place you have to see.

Good, Marjorie says. I want to see.

You'll love it, Marjorie. It's amazing, just fucking amazing.

The road is dark, now, lit only by the lights of the car. Benjamin drives slow, turning a lot. Benjamin, here, whistling, careful.

You know how on TV when there's a famous person or a really beautiful person or whatever, they always have all these photographers around them taking their picture?

Okay, Marjorie says.

Yeah, right, so, this place is like that. But better. More amazing. You'll see. You sit there and you feel like you've got all that attention on you. All those lights and everybody wanting to light you up. But the good thing is that it's better than that. Better than asshole people with cameras. It's just nature doing it. Wanting to show you something beautiful it can do.

In the dark of the car beside Benjamin, Marjorie nods.

Marjorie feels good.

She feels away. In her self and outside. Sitting back soft against the seat. The weight of Ma on her lap warm and waiting. Lucy at home safe in her purple box, Lucy here with Marjorie, in Marjorie, at rest. Marjorie, safe in her seatbelt, moving forward and up, feeling good.

Benjamin slows the car way down and turns far to the right and he drives up toward the trees. Off the road, onto the ground, the dirt. Marjorie hears the ground making sounds below them, rocks hitting the bottom of the car as Benjamin moves them slow and careful toward an open place in the circle of trees.

Okay, here it is, he says. Here we are.

Benjamin stops the car and turns it off. In the surprise of the quiet that comes after the car stops making sounds, Marjorie hears nothing but her wind and Benjamin's wind, blowing quietly through. And then the high, long singing of the bugs and the low sounds of frogs. Marjorie moves her breath quiet as she can through her and listens close to the night outside. She remembers the sounds of the night, of the outside, the sounds of the brook at the end of dead-end Summer Street, the warm dark air, the good of before.

It's so quiet out here, right?

Benjamin's voice is so soft Marjorie has to lean her ear close to hear him.

She does her best to make her self small, her voice small, to stay held inside the quiet of the night.

Yes. The quiet is loud out here.

I know, that's why I love it. I can really think, you know, like I told you.

Good, Marjorie says.

Now watch this. Look out there.

Benjamin points his finger in front of him, to where the lights of the car are making ghosts of the trees and the grass and the night around them. Marjorie looks at the glass, at Benjamin's finger pointing, at the soft light-outlined Benjamin she sees in the glass in front of them. She waits.

Benjamin turns off the lights of the car and for a minute Marjorie cannot see anything at all. Just bright, just the white of the car lights still burned into her eyes. She looks and looks and blinks and waits and when her eyes have forgotten the bright of the lights Marjorie looks out into the dark in front of her and Marjorie sees what Benjamin wants her to see.

Small lights blinking all around. A sea of lights waving on and off, holes of light breaking through the heavy dark of the night. The lights blink around Marjorie in colors something like yellow, like orange, like green, colors that

Marjorie cannot name and does not want to. Glowing lights. Soft wordless lights hanging on the air all around them, waves of light rolling up and down and out into the forever of the dark in front of them. Flying lights, tiny burning lights that together are just bright enough for Marjorie to see the dark shapes of the trees around them, circling them. Small lights on fire flying up toward the sky where the stars glow white and still, where the moon is a bright white circle that touches down soft and strong on the mountain that rises up in front, on the backs of the hills that roll out around.

The black of the night flashing and burning with the no-end beautiful lights.

Here, in front of Marjorie, is an exploding she has never seen.

A far-away let-out beautiful she is sure most People never see.

And here is Marjorie, out, away, seeing.

Fucking beautiful, Benjamin says.

Amazing, right?

Marjorie floats for a while in the dark quiet inside the car. Her big body gone, away, without weight. She watches the lights and does not feel her self, or Benjamin, or the car beneath. Marjorie looks out into the lit-up on-and-on of night surrounding her and Marjorie feels big, good big, feels skin and sky as the same. Marjorie would like to show this to all the People who are not here with her, to Gram and Mac and Suzanne and Dr. Goodwin. And maybe Norman, too. This is a sky that Norman might like to see.

Here is a place, a night, a huge beautiful thing Marjorie needs to show to Ma and Lucy.

Yes, she says.

Benjamin, Marjorie says.

She puts her two hands inside the plastic Store bags and soft as she can she lifts out the thick inside bag of Ma.

I have something to do.

You brought something with you, Marjorie? What do you need to do? What do you have?

Just something, Benjamin. Private. Sorry. Just a fast something I need to do.

Okay, sure, Marjorie. Whatever you want to do is good with me.

I just need the lights of the car. Just for a minute. Just so I can see my way out there.

Benjamin reaches up above Marjorie's head and turns on the light inside the car. In the bright white that comes, the dark outside is lost to Marjorie. She blinks, blinks, and sees only Benjamin and the brown inside of the car. Marjorie looks out to where the beautiful blinking was and sees only her self in window glass looking back. Turn the light on inside and that is all you will see, your self. Too much bright inside and the outside seems gone away.

Sorry, Benjamin, Marjorie says. I mean the outside lights. I need to see with the outside car lights.

Oh, okay, Benjamin says.

He reaches back up to the light and turns it off and soon as it is dark inside Marjorie can feel the quiet. Marjorie can see, again, the small endless lights out there.

Okay. I'll turn on the headlights and you go where you want to go.

And then make it dark.

You want to stand out there in the dark?

Just for a time. I just want to see all the light around.

All right, I got you. I understand. You just give the word, Marjorie. Just wave at me and I'll turn the lights off and then when you want to come back to the car you call out and I'll turn them back on for you.

Good. Thank you.

Take your time.

Benjamin turns on the car lights and in the bright white all the others go away again. But the floating lights are out there, and Marjorie will go to them. Marjorie holds the heavy bag of Ma close to her belly so that Benjamin will not see. This, Marjorie wants to do only with her self. She pushes down on the place where the seatbelt went in and frees her body from its tight hold. A time between Ma and Marjorie.

Marjorie opens the door of the car and steps out into the night.

Watch your step, Marjorie, Benjamin says. The ground is still soft. Be careful out there.

Marjorie nods and holds Ma close and shuts the door quiet as she can behind her. She steps careful steps away from the car, toward the place where the trees open up. Marjorie walks slow and straight to the edge of the car's bright light. She steps two more steps into where the shadows start and then turns. Holds on tight to Ma with one hand, waves to Benjamin with her other.

Marjorie is alone in the wide dark. She puts both arms around the bag of Ma and holds her self close. Marjorie's heart, beating there against Ma, there against the warm of her coat, there inside her where it is dark and quiet. Marjorie blinks and waits and waits and slowly, light by blinking light, the little flying fires appear again all around her.

Marjorie turns in a slow circle. One step by one step. To see how much she can see, to see what she cannot see. Marjorie turns in one whole circle and she cannot see Benjamin, or the car, or where she came from. She is alone with the glowing lights all around her. The shape of the mountain in the moonlight in front of her. Marjorie is alone with the dust of Ma pressed hard against her chest.

Okay, Gram, Marjorie says.

Marjorie is slow with her wind. She smells the smell of the grass, the trees, the wet of the ground, the dark of the night growing. Marjorie, slow, careful, with two hands holds the bag of Ma out and away from her.

Okay, Ma.

Goodbye now.

Marjorie pulls her fingers hard against the plastic, trying to find a way into the dust of Ma. The bag is thick and Marjorie must hold her self strong, her arms, strong, must scratch and pull and pull hard to open it up. The colored light beats quiet and steady inside the big body of the night. Marjorie makes a small hole in the plastic and pulls hard, makes the circle bigger, makes a place big enough for Ma to fall through, for what is left of Ma to get out.

Marjorie, in the dark, cannot see where Ma goes but she can feel her leaving. The slow losing, the lightening, the last of Ma let out and away and into the air. The lights surrounding Marjorie, circling Marjorie. Ma going, gone out to a good place, a place far from where Marjorie goes. Ma let loose to the soft wet of spring, to the deep of the dark.

And Lucy, too.

Marjorie lets go of the empty bag of Ma and puts her hand into her pocket and opens her pocket up inside-out to the air. Marjorie takes her coat off and shakes it out around her. She has more of Lucy at home with her safe in her purple box. This bit of Lucy, these tiny pieces of Lucy that Marjorie has been carrying with her, can go. Lucy would like it here, the wide open of the dark, the circling, surrounding of the living lights.

Marjorie, for a moment, for a while, for as long as she wants, stands, feels, floats. Takes her time. Inside the warm night light-blinking air and the always-here safe beating of her self. Marjorie, here, in the outside, feels uncontained and going on.

Marjorie feels good. Big. Wide. Light. Out. Let out.

Going. Let go.

Marjorie feels her self.

Here, she says.

Out. Loud. Louder.

Here, Marjorie says.

Marjorie gives her word, waves her arm high above her head.

Here.

The lights of the car rise up strong and bright. Marjorie closes her eyes and moves once more in her slow circle. To feel the warm of the outside let in, the light of the inside let go. Marjorie stays for a long moment in her self, with her self, down in the good deep of her self, and then she opens her eyes and turns back toward the lights of the car. Marjorie moves slow and strong, moves with the beat of her heart, her self. Marjorie is moving, is moving her wind like wings, up and down, inside and out, away and away and away.

<<<<>>>>

ACKNOWLEDGMENTS

So many Thank-Yous make up the world of this book:

To Deb Foss and Bill Goodman, for giving me life and allowing me to do what I will with it. To Grandma Mary and Grandma Edna, for your heart, your wit and your wisdom. To Joe Romanos, a best friend and the best reader I've ever had. To Rachel B. Glaser, for calling me to tell me she liked a story I wrote and for all the help she's given ever since. To the UMass Graduate School, for financial support in the form of a graduate school fellowship. To Noy Holland, for her empathy and support along the way. To Sam Michel, for saying that he wanted to read this book in a dark room. To Kate Johnson, whose patience and generosity can hardly be put into words. To Matthew Vollmer, for his enthusiasm and openness. To Yuchao, who will someday read this book, thank you for your kindness, your love, and all the ways you pull me up and out of my self. And to Bodhi, long awaited, newly here, and much, much loved.

BOOKS IN THE SERIES

21st Century Prose
Series editor: Matthew Vollmer, Virginia Tech

The 21st Century Prose series celebrates varieties of forms—of prose that breaks the rules, bends conventions, and reconfigures genre. The books in this series engage playfulness and experimentation without sacrificing accessibility and readability. The voices represented in the series come alive on the page through prose that is at once down-to-earth and also a reflection of an artist at home with his or her improvisations. Life-affirming but convention-defying, the language in these books strives to be both groundbreaking and readable. The 21st Century Prose series listens for and endorses voices that have been marginalized, reports from zones—physical and spiritual and emotional—from which we have yet to hear. Kind-hearted renegades. Things we can't describe but that leave us pleasantly puzzled, forcing us to say, "listen, just read it."

Books in the Series:

Full Metal Jhacket
Matthew Derby

A Heart Beating Hard
Lauren Foss Goodman

Settlers of Unassigned Lands
Charles McLeod

American Homes
Ryan Ridge

Printed and bound by CPI Group (UK) Ltd, Croydon, CR0 4YY

13/04/2025

14656538-0003